D1350969

C334130418

Also by Lynda Page

Evie
Annie
Josie
Peggie
And One For Luck
Just By Chance
At The Toss Of A Sixpence
Any Old Iron

Now Or Never

Lynda Page

HEADLINE

First published in 1999
by HEADLINE BOOK PUBLISHING

First published in paperback in 2000
by HEADLINE BOOK PUBLISHING

9 8 7 6 5 4 3 2 1

ISBN 0 7472 6122 9

Typeset by CBS, Martlesham Heath, Ipswich, Suffolk

Printed and bound by CPI Group (UK) Ltd,
Croydon, CR0 4YY

HEADLINE BOOK PUBLISHING
A division of the Hodder Headline Group
338 Euston Road
London NW1 3BH
www.headline.co.uk
www.hodderheadline.com

For Karen and Jim Green

This book is dedicated to you both with my deep gratitude.
Someone was indeed looking after me the day we met.
Without you both, I would never have got through
such a traumatic time. Thank you.

Many thanks to Frank Gutteridge for his invaluable information on the life of a funeral director, and for a good night spent in the pub!

Part One

Chapter One

'It's not true . . . it can't be. You wouldn't do that. Tell me it's not true? Mother, *please*?'

Piercing steel-grey eyes glared coldly into the terror-stricken ones staring wildly up at her. Prising away the hands gripping the front of her coat, Harriet Ashman swung back her arm and smacked her daughter hard across the face. The sharp slap resounded loudly around the tiny, sparsely furnished bedroom. 'Control yourself, Maude. What must Mrs Baldicott be thinking? Get dressed and put your things together, we have a long journey to make.'

But the journey, or rather what awaited her at the end of it, was of no importance to Maddie Ashman. All that dwelt in her mind was the devastating news her mother had just so matter-of-factly delivered. Spinning on her bare feet, thick calico nightdress billowing, she fled from the bedroom.

Downstairs in the inviting kitchen of the shabby but cosy village cottage, elderly Mrs Baldicott, the woman who had taken Maddie into her home and cared for her for the last seven months, was sitting at a well-scrubbed pine table, hands clasped tightly, looking grave instead of her usual kindly, rosy-cheeked self.

As her guest burst into the room, Nancy Baldicott's head jerked up. Maddie had only to witness that grim expression to have the truth of her mother's announcement confirmed.

'Maddie, I'm . . . I'm so sorry,' Nancy stammered, half rising. 'Believe me, I'd no idea what yer mother had planned.'

'You could have stopped her!' shrieked Maddie. 'She's

3

my baby. Mine. Not my mother's.' Picking up her nightdress, exposing bare legs, she dashed to the door, wrenched up the latch and ran down the ash path, screaming. 'Where is she? Where's my baby?'

Panting hard, Nancy caught up with Maddie at the gate, managing to stop the hysterical young woman from charging through by forcing her plump body in front of it. 'Come back inside,' she pleaded, grabbing hold of Maddie's arm. 'Yer'll catch yer death.'

'I don't care,' she cried, wrenching herself free. 'I want my baby. Where is she?' She grabbed hold of Nancy's shoulders, gripping hard. 'You must know. You must.'

The old lady's conscience stabbed her painfully but it was more than her reputation was worth to divulge what she knew. Vigorously she shook her head. 'I don't, me duck.' She hated telling the lie but had no choice. 'All I know is that yer mam took her out in the garden. Bit of fresh air, she said, while you got yerself ready for the journey home. When she came back alone all she said was: "A woman with money's taken her. She'll be looked after proper." That's all she told me.'

Maddie was devastated. Her whole body shook, face crumpling as a torrent of tears gushed down her cheeks. Releasing her hold on the elderly woman, she gripped herself tight around her stomach, swaying backwards and forwards in distress. 'How could my mother do this, Mrs Baldicott? How could she?'

Nancy gnawed her bottom lip anxiously, unable to find any words of comfort. 'Maybe . . . maybe she felt it were best, in the circumstances.' Her voice was kind. Forcing a smile, she tenderly placed one fleshy arm around the young woman's shoulders, drawing her close. 'Maybe it is, Maddie love. It's no picnic bringing up a . . . a . . .'

Maddie stiffened, lifting her head to look Mrs Baldicott straight in the eye. 'Bastard,' she erupted. 'Awful word, isn't it, for a baby without a father?'

'I was going ter say, it ain't easy bringing up a baby on yer own.'

'But that's just it – I wasn't going to be on my own. My baby has a father. It was the truth I told when I said Josh was thrilled about it. He knows all about my mother and how she is, and although he didn't feel it right, he said it would be best for us to run away and get married and face whatever we had to after. He said his mother would find room for us until we got a place of our own. But I couldn't do it Josh's way. I felt my mother didn't deserve that. I tried to break the news to her, I did really, but she challenged me before I could gather the courage.'

Maddie's face, already ashen, paled even more at the memory. 'It was awful, Mrs Baldicott. I thought she'd be angry. I thought she'd throw me out, want nothing more to do with me.' She shook her head in bewilderment. 'But not this. Never did I think she'd do anything like this. She got me here under false pretences, Mrs Baldicott. It never crossed my mind that her intention was to leave me here without a penny to my name until after the baby was born. I never had a chance to see Josh and explain in person. To do anything. I can't understand why he hasn't answered my letters.' She wrung her hands so tight her knuckles shone white. 'Oh, Mrs Baldicott, what's he going to say when he finds out what my mother's done? That she's given our baby away.'

From the corner of her eye Nancy spotted two village women approaching on their way to the shops. Wanting to avoid being drawn into conversation, she nodded a quick greeting then turned her back to them, steering Maddie down the path. 'I . . . Look, lovey, I know what you told me about Josh. He sounds a fine young man, but . . . well . . . I didn't want to speak me mind while you were expecting, didn't want to upset yer like. But I do think it's odd he's never bin in touch at all while yer've bin here.'

Maddie stared at her in confusion. Mrs Baldicott was

5

only voicing what she herself had agonised over for the last seven months while their baby had grown within her. She could excuse Josh's failure to visit, the journey being a long one and fares hard to find once dues from his wage had been paid out. Despite all the reasons she had come up with for his failure to appear, though, even *she* couldn't excuse him for not replying to her letters. But at the moment it was not her chief worry. Her missing child was.

'I can't think about that now. I need to find my baby, then I can worry about Josh.' Maddie eyed the older woman beseechingly. 'You must have seen something, Mrs Baldicott? Who she handed my baby to?'

The other woman shrugged helplessly. 'I didn't.' And she was telling the truth. 'I watched for a minute from the window as yer mother walked down the path . . .' Her voice trailed off. She wanted to say what a lovely sight she had witnessed, seeing grandmother and granddaughter becoming acquainted. But she couldn't. It had upset her greatly to see the way Harriet Ashman was holding her grandchild. If she hadn't known better she would have thought the woman was carrying a dead dog. Harriet had held the child stiffly away from her, her long thin nose in the air, as if there was a nasty smell wafting up it.

Mortified, Mrs Baldicott had turned away and busied herself mashing a pot of tea to fortify her guests before their journey home. 'She told me she was teking the baby for a breath of fresh air. I didn't suspect nothing amiss, Maddie, nor have a clue what she was up to. This state of affairs is as much a shock to me as it is to you. Usually I'm told beforehand what's gonna happen, so I can help prepare the likes of yerself whilst yer with me, soften the blow, but yer mam kept her own counsel. She never said a word. Maddie love, the job I'm paid ter do is to care for the mothers during their confinement. Even if I'd known yer mam's intentions, I'd have had no right to interfere.'

'And it seems I've no rights either, doesn't it?' sobbed

Maddie. Her face clouded angrily. 'But my mother's not going to get away with this,' she whispered fiercely. 'She's not, Mrs Baldicott. All my life I've had to go along with her wishes. But this time I'm not going to. This time she's gone too far. I want my baby back and I'm going to get her.'

Moments later, teeth gritted in determination, fists clenched, Maddie was back in her bedroom.

Blandly ignoring her precipitate dash from the room, Harriet clipped shut a faded tapestry carpet bag and said matter-of-factly, 'You should have had all your packing done, Maude. It's not as though you didn't know I was coming to collect you today.' After buttoning up her black coat, she repositioned the black felt hat over the tightly pinned iron-grey bun on the top of her head. 'Now get a move on. I'll not be happy if we miss that train. I want to be back before tea-time.'

Momentarily, Maddie froze, taken off guard by her mother's seemingly complete disregard for this dreadful situation, one she herself had masterminded and executed without any regard at all for her daughter's feelings. A vision of her baby gave Maddie the strength to resist. 'Stop it, Mother! Stop acting like there's nothing wrong. I want to know what you've done with my baby? I want her back and I'll not leave this room until you tell me where she is.'

Setting her jaw, Harriet glared at her stonily. 'I will not have you addressing me in that tone of voice. I will not tolerate it. Neither will I put up with hysterical behaviour.'

Maddie stared at her, eyes ablaze. 'Hysterical behaviour? Mother, you calmly announce that you've *given my baby away*. How do you expect me to react? Do you expect me to be grateful?'

Harriet seemed momentarily shocked. This was the first time her usually even-tempered, easily manipulated daughter had ever stood up to her. Her assumption that Maddie would accept this situation without a fuss had been very wrong and Harriet wasn't prepared for it.

7

Abruptly turning away, she walked to the window and stared blindly out, anger swelling within her. If she wasn't careful Maude's stupidity could jeopardise all she herself had worked hard for, and Harriet wasn't about to permit that. She hadn't worked hard all these years, clawing her way out of poverty, to have her hard-won position snatched away from her. Especially not by her daughter.

Her mind drifted back in time and she saw herself as a child of seven, just days after her father had been killed in an accident on the farm where he worked. Straight after the funeral came the humiliating eviction from the dilapidated tied cottage where she had lived all her short life. No remorse had been expressed, no sympathy shown, except for a few kind words from fellow workers as her mother had struggled with the borrowed handcart in which were piled their few worldly possessions. The dispirited mother and child trudged the mud-rutted lanes to the nearest town of Market Harborough, a thriving place twenty or so miles from the far larger city of Leicester, not having a clue what would happen to them there.

Sitting on a grassy hill overlooking the town, Harriet's grieving mother, Hilda Grimble, had stared down silently for what seemed like hours. Eventually she turned to Harriet, a steely glint in her eyes. 'We ain't gonna be beaten, 'arriet. You'll see we ain't. Me and you, we'll show 'em, so we will. I don't care how we earn our livin' but we ain't never gonna be chucked out of our 'ome again. Never, you 'ear? Now come on,' she'd said, rising. 'We've a lot to do before we sleep ternight.'

An excited Harriet had jumped up eagerly to help her mother push the cart towards town, visions of grandeur crowding through her mind. For as long as she could remember she had hated life on the farm. The conditions they had lived in there had been dire: the cottage damp and cold even in summer; the food they ate no better than pig swill; the clothes on their backs threadbare. She couldn't

8

even remember receiving a present at Christmas, except for a ragged doll salvaged by her mother from the farmer's dustbin, without his knowledge. It had had no hair and had lost one of its legs. For that Harriet had been expected to be grateful. Even at a tender age she'd inwardly questioned why she should be. The farmer's children had all they could ever want and she nothing, all because of who had parented them. It wasn't fair. Why couldn't she have been born to people who could provide better for her?

She'd shed no tears when her father died. Neither of her parents was the demonstrative kind. They hadn't had the time. All their efforts were channelled into keeping body and soul together, and from the moment she could walk Harriet was encouraged to do her bit. On her father's death she'd realised they would have to leave their home, but all that had meant to her was that life must surely now take a turn for the better. Hilda's declaration that morning on the hillside happily confirmed Harriet's belief and for the rest of the journey she indulged in wonderful fantasies.

Her mother would get a good job earning lots of money, and they would live in a nice house; Harriet would attend a good school wearing pretty clothes, with a special dress for Sundays. Just like the farmer's children.

But she was to be cruelly disappointed.

On reaching town, Hilda set about selling everything she possessed, including her thin gold wedding ring. Using a good portion of the money she paid a month's rent on a crumbling, filthy three-storey property up a side street, just off the town centre, on the poorest side of town. The day following, working all hours, Hilda and a by now sullen Harriet cleaned all the rooms, salvaging anything that could be of use, then distempered the walls.

The small front room was turned into a makeshift shop selling anything that would make a few pennies' profit. Nothing, whatever state it was in, was overlooked. A handleless chipped cup, a chair minus one leg, a book with pages missing . . . in Hilda's view anything might be of use to someone at a reasonable price. The two attic rooms, sparsely furnished, afforded a cheap night's lodging to a succession of rough working men.

Nothing was as Harriet had expected. Life now was worse than before, if that was possible. The shop was filled with stinking junk, the attics with stinking foul-mouthed drunks. Her mother was contented with the way she made her frugal living, for the first time in her life independent, not reliant on anyone else, and that was the way she intended to stay. So happy was Hilda that she remained oblivious to the bitter resentment seething within her daughter.

Harriet made no attempt to make friends with the neighbouring children, preferring her own company to playing childish games or becoming involved in petty squabbling. When she wasn't dragooned into helping her mother run the business, she took to filling her solitary hours by reading the piles of musty, dog-eared books that came through the shop. Reading opened up a new world to her and it did not take long for her quick mind to realise that in this way she could educate herself in more subjects than the basic 3 Rs she learned at school.

Over the years the mildewed pages taught her much and by the time she reached adulthood anyone who did not know Harriet's origins would never have guessed from her practised deportment, elocution, and carefully chosen good quality second-hand clothes, her lowly beginnings and humble home.

The bitterness of her life had hardened Harriet to such an extent that by the time her mother passed away from pneumonia at the age of forty-two, weakened by her years of toil and poor standard of living, she did not shed a tear, just stared around bitterly at her meagre legacy. Crumbling rented premises housing her own poor, sparsely furnished living accommodation; one room used as a shop which overflowed with what she felt amounted to no more than

10

rubbish; two small attic bedrooms offering a night's lodging hardly one step up from the workhouse to a bedraggled clientele barely able to afford the pittance charged.

Harriet was then seventeen years of age. Like her mother years before, she sat and contemplated her position. The conclusion she came to was that she could either shut the shop and carry on with her job, hoping that she might eventually acquire a husband and live the hand-to-mouth existence of her neighbours, or else put her years of self-education to good use and improve on what her mother had left her.

She chose the latter course, taking time to plan her future down to the smallest detail. At last she was satisfied it was a sound scheme, one formulated to ensure she never again tasted poverty. It would take skill, cunning and an iron will. She knew she possessed all three.

To finance her plan she kept on at her job for the time being. In her spare time, cutting her outgoings to the bone, she set about transforming the shop into a haberdasher's – haberdashery being as far removed as possible from what had been sold here previously. The attic rooms were cleared and given a fresh coat of paint, cheap but sturdy furniture installed, and the coarse workmen replaced with far more suitable lodgers for what she had in mind: travelling salesmen. To Harriet's delight, all this coincided with an upturn in the rundown area's fortunes and it became much more desirable.

The shop slowly began to pay its way and her two rooms were regularly occupied. Two years from the day Harriet had formulated her plan, all that remained for her to achieve was to find herself a suitable husband.

He came in the shape of twenty-three-year-old George Ashman, an insurance agent working from a large office in Leicester, who had been drafted to Market Harborough and had taken one of her rooms.

George was not at all good-looking, indeed had a severe limp caused by a club foot, but that did not matter as Harriet

11

knew her own lack of physical attributes meant she would never ensnare a handsome man. George with his own affliction, would more than likely be grateful someone was showing an interest in him. He was quiet, polite, and seemed eager to please his 'amenable' landlady. Insurance agents were respectable men with high principles and were, she guessed, reasonably paid in comparison to many other trades. He was an orphaned only child, so there would be no family interference. George was near perfect for what she was looking for. They were married four months later. Maude was to be their only child.

And nowadays Harriet was looked upon as a respectable widow, whose sadly deceased husband had held a good position in life. Looking back, she felt she could not have achieved more considering her poor beginnings.

But all that was in jeopardy. All she had striven to gain could yet be lost, and all because of the thoughtless, selfish actions of her own daughter. Harriet wasn't about to let that happen.

Her cold grey eyes narrowed. The man had been dealt with. The result of that sordid liaison also. Maude's sudden unexpected show of rebellion had momentarily taken Harriet off her guard but it was nothing she could not handle. Hadn't she handled everything else most satisfactorily? But one thing she felt she must do this time was to make sure Maddie never again jeopardised her mother's respectability.

Harriet took a deep breath and slowly turned to face her daughter who anxiously awaited her response. Head raised, back ramrod stiff, face stony, she spoke. 'I'll make allowances for your outburst this time, Maude. I suppose some sort of emotional display is to be expected in the circumstances. But never again. I will hear no more of your blatant lies or excuses for your own wanton behaviour which,' she hissed, 'I've taken great pains to cover up – something, I might add, that did not come cheap. No one has any idea about your shame. People think you've been nursing an old friend of mine through a difficult illness. And that's the way it's going to stay.'

She clasped her hands and pursed her thin lips. 'I don't suppose for one minute you stopped to consider what this would do to my reputation, or to your father's memory. I never thought you could be so selfish, Maude.'

She paused momentarily to draw breath. 'How could you?' she pressed on. 'How could you sink so low as to associate yourself with the likes of people living in such . . . such squalor! And to think that you seriously intended to marry him. Huh!' She shuddered and shook her head vigorously. 'Never, never would I have believed this could happen. I don't care what you say about the man. I don't care how wonderful you think him or what promises he's made you. I know without a shadow of a doubt that if I'd allowed you to marry, within months you'd have been reduced to his level.' Her eyes glinted maliciously. 'Is that what you want for yourself, Maude? A damp, infested hovel full of a horde of screaming offspring, and you forever wondering how you're going to feed them because that wonderful man of yours has drunk his wage at the pub?'

Maddie gazed at her, round-eyed. 'No, Mother, you have it all wrong!' she exclaimed. 'If only you'd listened to me, let me explain properly, agreed to meet Josh before you made me come here. He isn't like that, and neither is his family. Yes, they're poor but they're good people, Mother. They work hard like we do, they do their best. They . . .'

Harriet raised a hand in warning. 'Stop this nonsense! You've been blinded, Maude, blinded by what you thought was love.' Her face darkened. 'I did what any decent mother would do, and in time you will see that. When will you realise I've saved you, Maude? Saved you from a fate worse than death. I did the only thing I could, and that was to get you away from him and hope you would come to your senses.'

She thrust out her skinny chest. 'What you did was unforgivable. You committed the very worst sin and you're going to pay dearly for that. Your whole relationship with this man was built around deceit. You lied and connived your way through it. I thought I had raised you better than that. Raised you to respect yourself. I see now I was wrong.' Harriet snorted in disgust. 'You gave yourself to the first man who showed interest, never looking for the reason why. After all, Maude, you're approaching twenty-five, well past marriageable age, and hardly what would be classed as a beauty. No, far from it.'

Ignoring her daughter's gasp of horror, she continued, 'The man fooled you, Maude! He fooled you good and proper. I don't care what cock and bull tale you've told me about your plans for your future. If he'd been a decent type, he'd have called to introduce himself properly the very first time he courted you. Or at the very least, when you told him you were pregnant, he should have insisted you told me together instead of planning to sneak away like thieves in the night. Any decent man would never have thought of it. But then, he's not decent, is he? He did nothing to endear himself to me at all. Which was why I got you away. I thought if this man was as worthy as you declared him to be, then he'd come and show it. But did he? No, he did not!

'He's had plenty of time to prove his worth. I know you've written to him. Well, you have, haven't you?' she challenged. 'So knowing where you were, why didn't he board the first train heading this way? Or at the very least have the courtesy to reply to your letters. But you've heard nothing, have you? Not a peep. I know,' she said smugly, 'because I asked Mrs Baldicott. But I didn't need to ask, I knew it already. Made it my business to find out. He fled from Market Harborough only days after I brought you here.'

Face contorted in disbelief, Maddie cried. 'What? No, Mother! I don't believe you. Josh wouldn't do that to me. There's another reason why he's not contacted me, there has to be.'

Harriet's lips tightened indignantly. 'Don't brand me a

liar like you, Maude,' she hissed. 'He's gone, I tell you. Abandoned you without a by your leave. Now sit down,' she ordered, 'and if you interrupt again, you'll wish you hadn't.' She waited while her heartbroken daughter slumped into a chair. 'Admit it, Maude, you've been used. You can think what you like but I believe he saw you as his chance of bettering himself, getting out of that hell-hole he lived in and his lowly paid job. I expect his family thought the same and encouraged his relationship with you. After all, I have a business. It might not be much in some eyes, but it's a damned sight more than they have. Well, their plan backfired, didn't it?' She shook her head triumphantly. 'I *knew*. I saw it all the moment I forced you to tell me about your sordid affair. It was all as clear as daylight to me. And, as a matter of interest, if I hadn't have confronted you that night, when would you have told me?'

Maddie hung her head.

'Oh, Maude, how could you have allowed yourself to be taken in so easily? Were you that desperate for a man?' Harriet tutted in disdain. 'And I thought my daughter was a respectable woman. You do realise, don't you, that you've ruined any chance you ever had of getting married to anyone decent? Of course, with so many men losing their lives in the war, your chances were already severely reduced. The ones who are left have their pick, which doesn't leave much hope for you. The most you can hope for now is that some elderly widower will take you, but even that possibility seems remote now you've been soiled.'

Her nostrils flared. 'Now, I've said all that is ever going to be said on the matter. I won't hear that man's name mentioned again. And, before we leave this room, I want a solemn promise you'll go nowhere near his family enquiring after him – unless you want to be humiliated even more than you already have been. As for the child, it never happened. Is that clear? Maude, I asked you a question. I expect an answer.'

15

She raised her head slowly, face filled with horror. 'I can't, Mother. I can't just forget about my baby. Please don't expect me to do that. Just tell me where she is, please? I'll go away with her. I won't cause you any . . .'

'And how will you provide for yourself and the child?' Harriet erupted. 'You have no money to speak of, and don't expect any help from me. Within a matter of weeks you'd be facing the workhouse. Would that be fair to the child? Well, would it? Or to go through life branded a bastard? Think about *that*, Maude. She's been given to people who can care and provide for her. Be realistic. You cannot give your child what it needs. You were selfish enough to bring it into the world – don't selfishly deprive it of the right to a proper upbringing.'

Harriet paused momentarily to pick up her handbag. 'Anyway, none of this matters. The child is gone. You'll get over it.' She walked towards the door and pulled it open. 'Now I'm going to settle up with Mrs Baldicott. I expect you to be ready in ten minutes.'

Numb with shock, Maddie stared at the closed door for several seconds. Then the full realisation of her situation and its hopelessness struck her like a blow. So violent was the pain of it that she moaned in agony and slid to her knees. In her mind's eye she saw again the events leading up to this dreadful betrayal.

16

Chapter Two

She saw Josh: tall, handsome, a merry twinkle in his blue eyes, light brown hair cut tidily, shabby clothes covering his broad frame, but worn proudly. He had been the first person to awake within Maddie feelings she had not known existed. He had taught her to love.

For Maddie Ashman, before she met Joshua Jenks, life had been lonely. A naturally warm, bright and inquisitive child, from a very early age Maddie had learned not to expect emotional warmth from her cold, austere mother, and had received none. Of her father she had few memories; he had died when she was two years old. She knew little about him, practically nothing in fact, and had long ago stopped asking, knowing her questions would only receive a silent rebuff from her grieving mother.

She made few friends or close acquaintances as she grew up. At school the other girls – the ones who did not already ridicule and ostracise her for the way Harriet forced her to pronounce her vowels and be ladylike – stopped being friendly, fed up with the excuses constantly made to their well-meant overtures, despite knowing that Maddie's mother was behind them. Harriet made it blindingly obvious she thought nobody good enough to associate with her daughter. Maddie herself knew that to question or rebel against her mother's decisions was futile; the resulting punishment would be harsh and nothing would change her mother's bigoted point of view.

After school and at weekends, when her allotted chores

had been done, Maddie would sit and practise her sewing and knitting skills. These had not come easily but her mother had insisted on her acquiring them nevertheless.

At fourteen years of age, Maddie's stated wish to go out to work went unheeded. Her skills were to be put to the use her mother intended. A small windowless room under the shop stairs was cleared. A treadle Singer sewing machine, the one she'd over the years painstakingly practised on, was installed, along with a table, lamp, and drawers in which to hold her equipment and materials. There, from early morning until closing time, Maddie would sit carrying out alterations and repairs to customers' garments, emerging only for her lunch.

Occasionally, the pinning of a hem or tuck at the waist would bring her into contact with a customer. These intrusions into her solitary day were welcomed. For her work she received five shillings a week from which she was expected to purchase all her personal needs.

Outings were few. On Saturday afternoon she accompanied Harriet on their weekly shopping trip, on Sunday morning to church. Maddie's only luxury was her solitary walk on a Wednesday afternoon, and occasionally on a warm summer evening if all her work was finished.

So accustomed was she to this rigid routine and the years of having it instilled in her by Harriet that her chance of marriage was extremely limited, that Maddie had no expectations and, to save herself unwarranted pain, never allowed her thoughts to stray as far as sweethearts and marriage. She felt it was pointless. Her chance of ever meeting a member of the opposite sex in social circumstances was non-existent. Besides, suppose she should ever be fortunate enough to do so she would be terrified of making a fool of herself.

Having long ago accepted her lot in life, meeting a man she could love and having her feelings returned was totally unexpected.

One cold Wednesday afternoon in March, forgetting the lateness of the hour as she was enjoying her freedom, Maddie was wandering down her favourite stretch of the tow path beside the canal. Engrossed in watching a pair of elegant swans gliding silently by, she did not see an icy puddle, slipped and lost her balance. From the opposite direction, pedalling hard on a rusting bicycle, thinking only of his desire to get home after his long day as an apprentice machine mechanic in the local corset factory, twenty-year-old Joshua Jenks did not see the prostrate figure on the ground until he was almost upon it.

Shocked, he steered sharply away to avoid a collision. His front tyre met a protruding boulder and Josh tumbled over the handlebars to land in the canal. Screaming in shock, beside herself for having been the cause of the accident, instantly forgetting the pain of her own bruised backside and pride, Maddie jumped up and rushed to aid the sodden man emerging from the icy water.

'I'm so sorry,' she blurted, grabbing the dripping sleeve of his jacket to help him out. 'I slipped on some ice. I couldn't warn you, I didn't see you coming. I really am so dreadfully sorry.'

Standing on the canal bank, water draining from him, Josh shivered violently. 'If it's anyone's fault, it's mine. I was pedalling too fast and wasn't looking where I was going.' A twinkle of amusement lit his eyes. 'Anyway, there's no damage a good wash won't put right.' He glanced quickly at his bicycle. 'That's still in one piece thank God, 'cos it's me brother's and if 'ote 'appened to his precious bike he'd skin me alive.' He brought his eyes back to her. 'What about you?'

'Me? Oh, I'm fine,' Maddie insisted. 'It's you I'm concerned with. You're sure you're all right?'

'I'm sure.' He stared down at himself. 'But that won't be the story when I get home 'cos me mam's going to batter me senseless when she sees the state I'm in.'

Maddie's face clouded over in alarm. 'Oh, will she be terribly angry? Would you like me to call and explain . . .' Her voice trailed off when she saw the corners of his mouth twitch. 'You're having fun with me, aren't you?'

'My mother's always threatening to batter all of us senseless but she won't. I know her. She'll laugh when I tell her what happened then fuss all over me – but not before reminding me she always said that one day I'd fall hard for a pretty lady.' Josh quickly realised he had embarrassed the young woman before him and hurriedly added, 'I'd better get off before I freeze ter death.' He picked up his bicycle and sat astride it, making to set off, then he paused. 'Do you walk down here often?'

'Oh, er . . . yes, I do. Most Wednesday afternoons. Not usually quite so late as this, though.'

'Well, I'll just have to hope you're late again then, won't I? Tarra.'

She stared after him bemused as, still dripping water, he pedalled off. 'Tarra,' she said absently. 'Oh, I mean, goodbye.'

As Maddie made her way home she tried to work out just what these parting words had meant. It never entered her head that he was hoping to see her again.

During the following months, depending how she managed to time her Wednesday walks and when Josh finished work, they would occasionally encounter each other. Maddie found herself looking forward more and more to these weekly encounters which brightened her mundane life considerably, and becoming more and more disappointed when their paths did not cross.

As time passed their general polite chit-chat gradually progressed to including details about themselves, although it was Josh who did most of the talking as he had so many tales of his large, close-knit family to impart.

It took six months before he formally asked her out. They were walking along the tow path together, happily chatting, when suddenly he drew to a halt and stared at her nervously.

'Maddie . . .' he began, mindful of the red tide of embarrassment creeping up his neck '. . . I, er . . . thought I'd go for a walk in the park on Sunday. Thought I might listen to the band – I've heard they're not bad. Would, er . . . well, yer could if yer wanted?'

Perplexed, she frowned. 'Could what, Josh?'

'Come too. I could call for yer. Square it with yer mother. That's if yer'd like to, that is?'

Eyes wide, she stared at him dumbstruck. Was this handsome man really asking for her company? At twenty-one years old she suddenly felt unworldly, with not a clue how to respond to such an invitation, never having believed she would receive one. And she could not decide if he was asking to escort her or just asking if she was doing nothing better and wanted to tag along? To get it wrong would be so embarrassing for both of them.

A wave of acute self-consciousness flooded through her and she felt her cheeks glow. She knew how dowdy and old-fashioned she looked, the style chosen as always by her mother: unbecoming plain calf-length buttoned dress, hand-knitted cardigan, serviceable brown boots. Her long mane of chestnut hair was pulled severely back and tied by a piece of brown ribbon at the base of her neck.

In all the time she had been acquainted with Josh, despite being fully aware of her own growing attraction towards him, Maddie had never dared allow herself to hope he would be interested in anything more than friendship with her. A man as good-looking as Joshua Jenks could have his pick of the girls, of that she had no doubt. But now he was looking at her eagerly. Oh, it was all so confusing. Suddenly she realised he was speaking.

'Look, Maddie, I didn't mean to offend yer. I just thought you might like an afternoon out, 'cos from what I gather you don't get out much. Well, not at all, do yer?'

It's as I should have guessed, she thought, dispirited. Josh had only asked because he felt sorry for her. She raised her head, forcing a smile to her face. 'I don't go out much because I'm so busy, what with my work and helping my mother. I get hardly any free time. In fact, I was thinking I'd have to stop my Wednesday walks for a while,' she lied to save face. 'Thank you for your offer,' she added lightly, 'but I'll have to decline, I'm afraid.'

His unmistakable disappointment shocked her.

'Yer don't have to make excuses, Maddie,' he muttered, shuffling his feet. 'I shouldn't have asked yer. I'd no right. I'm sorry, really I am.'

Tilting her head, she frowned quizzically. 'Right? What do you mean by that, Josh?'

'Well, I ain't, have I? I mean, your mam owns a shop. Me and my family . . . well, we work in factories. Me dad takes whatever he can get but he's outta work more often than he's in. That's what I mean. I ain't in your class, Maddie, and I shouldn't have embarrassed yer.'

Anger welled within her and before she could check herself she blurted out, 'How people earn their living is of no consequence to me, Josh, and I'm surprised to hear it is to you. May I remind you that it is my mother that owns the shop, not me, and as such I work for someone to earn my living, the same as you.' Although, she thought, my mother certainly wouldn't voice the same opinion.

He grimaced. 'Well, that's told me, ain't it? I'm sorry I offended yer.' His face fell. 'It doesn't matter to me neither, honest it doesn't. I like yer, Maddie. I don't care what yer mother's got. I just thought she might object to me, that's all. Look, I'd really like to take yer for a walk. I'd be honoured. I've been trying to summon up the courage to ask yer for ages.'

She gasped in surprise. 'You have?'

He nodded solemnly.

Her face lit up, her delight obvious. 'Then I'd like that very much too.'

His grin was eager. 'Sunday then? I'll call for yer, will I?'

'Call for me? Oh!'

He frowned. 'What is it?'

Her thoughts whirled, knowing instinctively from past experience that should she tell her mother about her outing Harriet would want to know all the details and when she did her disapproval would be voiced and the outing stopped. Maddie couldn't bear to risk that. She wanted so much to accompany this man. Besides, she doubted there'd be another invitation after Sunday so what was the point of causing unnecessary affront? Her decision, rightly or wrongly, was made quickly. 'My mother doesn't like to be disturbed on a Sunday afternoon so it might be best if I met you somewhere.'

Josh nodded in understanding. 'My folks like to take a nap after dinner. With all us lot in the house, they reckon it's the only time they get any peace to . . . to . . .' He cleared his throat in embarrassment. 'Well, if yer sure yer mam won't mind me not introducing meself, I'll meet you at the park gates. Will two suit yer?'

She smiled and nodded.

Over the three days that followed, Maddie fought to keep check of her excitement, wishing with all her heart she had someone in whom to confide. It took all her strength to keep her emotions in check so as not to arouse any suspicions within her mother. But as nervous anticipation mounted she wished wholeheartedly she had refused the invitation; the build up to it was making her feel ill.

To her relief Sunday finally dawned.

The morning dragged slowly. All the usual routine tasks seemed to take longer than normal. Finally she managed to escape to her room to tidy herself and hopefully calm her nerves.

Taking a last look in the mirror, she smiled, pleased with her reflection. Her hair was tied in its usual style but several tendrils had been freed to frame the sides of her face. She felt that the slight alteration softened her features.

23

On her plain Sunday blue dress she pinned a brooch, the first piece of jewellery she had ever owned. It was only costume jewellery, costing one shilling and sixpence, and in order to fund it she had gone without purchasing several weekly necessities, deciding she could make do until the following payday. She felt her decision had been right as the brooch's presence helped to alleviate the plainness of her attire. She would have liked to wear some lipstick but makeup of any description was forbidden by her mother and besides she did not own any, so Maddie pinched her cheeks and rubbed her lips until both glowed pink. Finally, taking a deep breath, she slipped her coat over her arm and made her way down the stairs.

Standing in the backroom doorway, heart beating painfully, she addressed her mother, praying that nothing would happen to put a stop to her outing. 'It's . . . it's such a lovely afternoon, I thought I'd go for a walk. Leave you in peace to have your nap.'

Her mother's beady eyes missed nothing and as she eyed her daughter shrewdly, Maddie was suddenly afraid that somehow Harriet had guessed what she was up to. Her heart beat so loudly she was terrified it would be audible. 'I've nothing else to do, Mother. I've no sewing outstanding. The tea things are ready. I forgot to renew my books at the library so I've nothing to read. I thought I might go to the park and listen to the band.'

Harriet looked at her for several long moments before sniffing dismissively. 'Well, go if you're going. And don't be late. Tea's at five, not a minute after.' She glared at Maddie. 'And no talking to strange men, you heed?'

She nodded.

She made to depart but her mother's voice stopped her. 'What have you done to your hair? It looks stupid. Go back upstairs and do it properly. And what's that on your dress?'

Maddie's hand flew to the brooch. 'Just something I bought. I . . . I thought it was nice.'

'Nice!' Harriet snorted in disgust. 'It's trash. Take it off.'

'But, Mother, I . . .'

'I said, take it off and throw it away. No daughter of mine is cheapening herself by wearing gaudy trinkets like that. And another thing, my girl. If you can afford to waste good money on such things then I'm paying you too much.'

Resigned, Maddie did as was told, realising she should have known better. She threw the offending article in the waste basket by the fireplace then returned to her bedroom to redo her hair.

Back in the doorway she addressed her mother again. 'Can I go now, Mother?'

A dozing Harriet opened her eyes and studied her daughter hard. Her mean mouth tight, she nodded grudgingly.

Maddie did not dare allow herself a sigh of relief until she had closed the front door securely behind her and was halfway down the street.

The outing went much better than she had dared to expect. Despite her nervousness, within minutes of meeting Josh she began to relax. Her escort was attentive, entertaining, a pleasure to be with, but what came as the greatest surprise to Maddie was that he made no effort to hide his own obvious delight to be in her company and took great pains to ensure she was enjoying herself. He need not have worried.

Never in her life had Maddie been so happy. Mingling amongst the crowds, they licked ice cream from cones bought from the vendor, drank tea from the pavilion, strolled around the ornamental lake and listened to the band. The afternoon passed far too quickly for both. Reluctantly they parted but not before arranging to meet again.

On her way home, Maddie's thoughts returned over and over again to every minute detail of her lovely afternoon and she wondered how she was going to get through the days that followed until she saw Josh again. Suddenly she stopped walking as worry began to fill her. She stood deep in thought for several long moments, mulling over her dilemma, then smiled in relief. No, she hadn't lied to her mother. She *had* gone for a walk in the park and she hadn't spoken to any strange men. Josh wasn't a stranger at all. She'd known him for months. Her only crime, should her mother choose to see it that way, was that she had been economical with the truth. But the truth was still the truth.

Over the months that followed they would meet whenever possible. The winter months proved the most difficult. Making excuses to her mother for wanting to take walks in the bitter cold was hard and sometimes two or three weeks would pass when Maddie did not see Josh at all. These times proved purgatory for her as she missed his company dreadfully. She knew that he had trouble understanding the problems she faced over meeting him openly but gradually, as they got to know each other better and the truth of her closeted life slowly emerged, he began to appreciate her difficulties.

Getting out to meet him was not her only problem.

Forming a close relationship with Josh did not come without its setbacks for Maddie. As their feelings grew more serious she spent many a sleepless night worrying if she was handling matters right, feeling so unprepared and, worse, having no one to turn to for advice on these alien emotions. But she need not have worried. Josh, she was to learn, was a gentle and patient man with no intention of forcing her into anything with which she did not feel comfortable.

As their feelings intensified and Maddie began to understand and appreciate how it felt to be loved and needed, the truth of how starved of affection she had always been, of how truly cold and unemotional her mother was, became glaringly obvious. She began to pity Harriet, and to pity herself for what her mother and she could have shared had things between them been different. But Maddie knew it was no good wishing for any change in Harriet. Despite her great sadness for what might have been, she was happy in her love for Josh.

He was a man who was proud of his family and never tired of telling Maddie about them. She in turn never tired of listening to his tales of this close-knit family, and as time passed felt that through him she had come to know all the Jenkses. As her picture of them built, the one thing above all that became clear to her was that what they might lack in material wealth was more than compensated for by the love and respect they felt for each other. She could not help feeling a certain envy and sadness for what she herself had never had.

Their first embrace was a clumsy attempt brought about by Maddie stumbling as she slipped on a grassy incline. Josh automatically jumped to her aid. Despite springing from him in alarm, unused to being held in such an intimate manner by another human being, never would she forget first feeling his arms around her: the warmth, the comfort, the surge of excitement shooting through her, flaming through her whole being. Neither could she forget his first kiss, as he, unable to resist her anymore, momentarily forgot himself and clasped her in his arms, planting a quick, stolen, peck on her lips then immediately begging her forgiveness.

He did not need it. Maddie had liked the feel of his tender lips on hers and in truth wanted more.

It was a lovely summer's evening when Josh asked her to marry him. They had been seeing each other for nearly three years. Three years of secret meetings.

Sitting in a deserted field under a hedge, content in each other's company, they had watched in silence as the sun began to set, marvelling at the spectacle created by its wide golden rays spreading right across the darkening sky. She had been conscious of the time, that she really ought to be getting home, but her desire not to leave the man she had fallen deeply in love with proved too great and she prayed just a few minutes longer with him would cause no harm.

Turning to look at her, Josh took a deep breath, praying his nerve would not leave him, desperate to ask something he had wanted to for such a long time. This place would make the perfect setting. Conscious that he was staring at her, Maddie turned to smile at him. As she did so he cupped her chin gently in his large hand, looking deep into her lovely eyes.

'Maddie?'

'Mmmm?' she whispered.

Steeling himself, he took a deep breath. 'Marry me, Maddie? I've had enough of sneaking around and I know you have too. I know yer mam won't think I'm good enough, but I am. I work hard and I'm clean-living. I love yer, and I'll make yer happy. She won't be sorry she's got me as a son-in-law. I think she could do a lot worse in fact. When I get to meet her I'll do me best to get on with her, I promise.' His eyes clouded in anxiety. 'What d'yer say, Maddie?'

His proposal, something she had longed for but never thought to hear, came as a complete shock and she stared at him for several long moments before finally uttering, 'Oh, Josh, I love you too. Are you sure? Are you really sure it's me you want to marry?'

'Sure?' He laughed. 'Maddie darlin', Maddie, I wouldn't have asked yer if I weren't.' He eyed her gravely. 'Yer not still believing that nonsense about being ugly, are yer? 'Cos yer not, Maddie. How many times do I have to tell yer? Anyway, ugly or beautiful, it ain't yer looks I want to marry yer for, it's you.' Then he added, with a twinkle in his eye, 'But it does help that you're as pretty as a picture and I wish you'd believe me when I tell yer that.'

She gave a tight smile. She wanted to believe him, she had no reason not to believe anything he said, but after years of having her mother – the one person who was supposed to have her best interests at heart – instil in her that she was plain, despite what the mirror told her, that belief was deeply rooted within her.

For reassurance she looked deep into his eyes and would have had to be blind not to see the devotion there. However he judged her beauty, he did love her, there was no doubt of that in her mind.

'I want to marry you too, Josh,' she responded softly. 'I want that so much and feel so honoured you've asked me, but . . .'

'But what, Maddie?' he erupted anxiously. 'Yer not going ter turn me down? Please say yer not?'

She shook her head. 'No, I'm not. It's my mother who will.' She wrung her hands despairingly. 'I've not exaggerated what she's like – if anything I've played it down a little. She's never allowed me to have friends in any shape or form. We'll have a fight on our hands and I'm not relishing the prospect.'

He sighed in exasperation. 'Me mam says she's always been strange.' The words slipped out before he had had a chance to check himself.

Her eyes flashed a question. 'Pardon? Your mother? You've told your family about me?'

Frowning quizzically, he nodded. ''Course I have. We don't have secrets in our house, I've told yer that often enough. The only reason I ain't took yer round to meet 'em is that I didn't want to scare you off. They can be a rowdy lot. Me mother's chuffed about us because she knows how much you mean to me. She knows you're special. But it's no good me lying: she doesn't think much of yer mam. Said she can't for the life of her understand how she managed to get herself married in the first place.

'My mother and yorn were at school together. Me mother remembers Harriet well. Says she was different from all the other kids. Never had any friends and never made any effort to make any. Me mam's family was poor, Maddie, same as all the folks roundabout our streets. Your mam was dressed no better than the rest. Sometimes she never had no shoes on her feet nor arse in her britches.

'Me mam remembers the shop before it was altered. Said

29

all but rubbish was sold there and pennies were snatched at 'cos yer mam and grandma bloody well needed 'em. They were making a living, there ain't n'ote wrong in that. But yer mam's no right to feel she's above the likes of my family just 'cos she had the good fortune to make life a bit better for herself.' His face fell as he noticed the astonished expression on Maddie's. 'Didn't you know about that?'

She shook her head. 'No, I didn't. I thought we'd always had the haberdasher's. My mother's very sparing in what she tells me about the past.'

He grimaced remorsefully. 'I'm sorry, Maddie. Me and me big mouth.'

'It's all right,' she whispered, suddenly struck by how little she knew about her own family, something she had never dwelt on before because she hadn't thought there was anything to know. But now she wondered. 'You've a right to your own opinions,' she said distractedly.

'I've not met yer mam, so they ain't my opinions, Maddie, they're me mam's and she never hides what she thinks.' He paused, just stopping himself from telling Maddie that when he had first informed his mother about his sweetheart, she had asked him if it was wise to associate himself with the daughter of Harriet Ashman and had advised him to be careful. Advice he had chosen to ignore, thank goodness. 'Regardless of her mouth, you'll like me mam, Maddie,' Josh said with conviction. 'She's a good woman and her heart's in the right place. You'll like all me family. And they'll love you.'

She sighed. 'I do hope so. And if your family are anything like you, I shall have no trouble in liking them. But I can appreciate how your mother feels about mine. She's . . . well . . . she can be very difficult to get along with. But, regardless, she's my mother, Josh, and there's a part of me that admires the way she must have worked to improve her life after what you've told me.' Her face grew troubled. 'She won't give her consent to our marriage, you know.'

'You don't need her consent, Maddie, you're over twenty-one.'

'I know, but I can't get married without it. I wouldn't feel it was right. And there's the fact that I've been seeing you for such a long time without her knowledge. They'll be hell to pay when that comes out. Oh, Josh . . .'

He grabbed her in his arms, holding her protectively. 'Stop worrying over problems that ain't happened yet,' he soothed. 'We'll tackle her together. Once she sees how much we care about each other and how determined we are, I'm sure she'll be glad for us.'

Looking up into his eyes, Maddie smiled wanly, praying he was right but knowing deep down he wasn't.

'You'll arrange for me to come around to meet her soon then?'

'Er . . .' Maddie frowned. 'Give me a little time first, please. I'll . . . I'll try and break it gradually then it won't come as so much of a shock to her.'

He sighed. 'All right, but not too gradually, Maddie. I don't want to wait forever. I want to make yer me wife as soon as possible. Me wage ain't that great but I keep me head down in the hope I'll get promoted. I've worked things out and I can afford to rent us something small to start with, but me mam said in the meantime she'd find room for us. We'd be cramped but we'd be together, Maddie.' His grip tightened. 'Oh, Maddie, I love you so much. You were well worth landing up in the canal for. I know facing your mother ain't going to be easy but I'll be there with yer all the way.'

He released her, bent his head and kissed her with deep longing. She responded willingly and before they both realised what was happening all their pent-up emotions were released and in a deserted field, sheltered by a dense hawthorn hedge, they sealed their love.

When it was over Josh stared at her in utter remorse. 'Oh, Maddie, Maddie, I'm so sorry! I didn't mean that to

31

happen. I just got carried away. I've wanted to love you like that, to feel you, be near you, for such a long time. Please forgive me?' he begged.

She reached up, running one hand tenderly down the side of his face. 'Hush,' she soothed. 'I should feel it was wrong but I don't, Josh. Loving you is right, I know it is. I'm as much to blame as you are. I wanted you too. But we mustn't do it again. Not until we're married.'

He nodded vigorously. 'The sooner you tell your mother, Maddie, the sooner we can stop this sneaking around.'

Maddie dreaded the confrontation and it was all she could think of. It filled her every waking moment and troubled her sleep. How did you approach your unapproachable mother and inform her you were going to marry a man she had never met, had never actually known existed? Hardly casually over a cup of tea.

Fully aware of Josh's growing impatience and of her own need finally to unburden herself, at the very last minute her nerve would always desert her. Over two months later Maddie was no further forward. But over that two months another, more serious reason for tackling her mother began to manifest itself and now she was sure. Since making love to Josh she hadn't had her monthly curse and that could mean only one thing. She was carrying his baby.

Any worries she'd had over Josh's reaction to her condition were quickly swept away. Grabbing her up in his arms, he swung her around, yelling out in delight. 'You'll have to tell her now! We'll get married straight away. If yer that scared, we'll run away. I mean to marry yer, Maddie, one way or another, and with the baby coming I'm even more determined. Me parents will be all right about it. They understand these things happen.' He pulled her tightly to him, crushing her protectively, trying in his rough way to alleviate her fears. 'Let me come with yer now? Let's go and tell her together. Let's go and get it over with.'

'No, no, Josh!' she cried, alarmed. 'It was bad enough thinking about facing her before. But to tell her I'm expecting ...' She paused momentarily, the enormity of the task filling her with dread. Her voice faltered. 'I ... I have to do this myself. To prepare her before she meets you, Josh. At the weekend. Sunday after church,' she assured him. 'I'll do it then, I promise.'

It was a Wednesday evening. She had three days to build up her courage. She had to do it now. She had no choice.

But she had bargained without her mother.

That night, as she was getting ready for bed, Harriet appeared unexpectedly in the doorway. Maddie knew instinctively by her whole manner that something was terribly wrong. In her mother's hand were several strips of padded linen which she was brandishing.

'Is there something you have to tell me, Maude?'

Her voice was hard and cold. Maddie flinched. Her eyes flew to the articles in her mother's hand and the horrifying truth dawned. In her worried state she had forgotten that someone else would notice she had not used them recently. Her mother knew she was pregnant.

Face draining of colour, she fought to stop her body from quaking. 'Mother,' she murmured, 'I ... please let me explain. I've met a man. Josh ... his name is Josh. I've known him nearly three years. We love each other, Mother, and we're going to be married. I've tried to tell you, I have really. He wants to meet you. You'll like him. I ...'

'So you won't be needing these then?' Harriet cut in icily, flapping the strips of linen in a sarcastic gesture.

Maddie's whole body sagged. 'Oh, Mother, I'm so sorry. I didn't mean to hurt you. Please believe me, I didn't.'

'When's it due?' Harriet asked stonily.

'Due? Oh, I ... I ... haven't worked it out. March ... no, sometime in April next year.'

Without another word or displaying any emotion, Harriet turned and left the room.

Maddie slept not a wink that night and rose the next morning, gritty-eyed and drained of energy, worried witless as to exactly how her mother was going to react. Several possibilities raced through her mind, none of which she relished. She had heard her mother's scathing opinions of fallen women before. At the least she would be disowned and thrown out on the streets, Maddie thought.

The response she did get totally confused her.

She arrived in the kitchen to find her mother donning her coat.

'I'll need you to manage the shop today. I've an errand to do,' Harriet announced matter-of-factly as she picked up her hat and pulled it on. 'Mrs Day is coming in to collect the dress you altered. Charge her a shilling.' Picking up her handbag, she headed for the door. 'I'm not sure what time I'll be back so keep me some dinner hot. Use the remains of the meat pie from yesterday.'

Maddie's thoughts raced. It was most unusual for her mother to be going out at such an early hour, and where on earth was she going? But she knew better than to ask. She was worried, though. Harriet had never allowed her behind the counter before. The shop was solely her domain. But Maddie supposed she could manage. Far more disconcerting was her mother's calm demeanour. It was as though the dreadful revelation of yesterday evening hadn't happened.

'You did hear what I said, Maude?'

Maddie jumped, startled. 'Pardon? Oh, yes, I did. But, Mother, I've never worked in the shop before. I don't know what to do.'

Passing by her as she headed for the door, Harriet eyed her blankly. 'I'm sure you'll manage,' she said tonelessly as she departed.

By the time she returned it was well after eight and Maddie's nerves were frayed.

As she heard the back door open and shut, she shot out of her chair, the sewing she had been trying to concentrate

34

on falling in a heap on the linoleum. 'Oh, Mother,' she exclaimed when Harriet appeared. 'I was worried about you being as it's so late. I . . .'

'No need to be,' she cut in sharply, taking off her outdoor clothes and hanging them up. 'My dinner in the oven, is it?'

'Er . . . yes. I'll get it for you and make a fresh pot of tea.'

Maddie rushed off to the kitchen and when she returned Harriet was seated at the table. Maddie put the plate in front of her. 'Be careful,' she warned. 'It's scalding.'

'One thing I am not, Maude, and that is stupid. Isn't it obvious that a plate taken out of the oven is bound to be hot?'

Maddie gulped. 'Yes, Mother,' she said quietly.

'How did you get on in the shop?'

'Very well, I think. The customers . . .' She paused, about to say that they had seemed happy with her service. Several had remarked that they hoped to be served by her again, but she thought better of repeating this. 'Asked after you, Mother. Mrs Day came in for her dress and I charged her a shilling as you instructed. Mrs Hardy asked if we could get her some special braiding for some cushions she's making. I told her I was sure you would try the next time the representative came in. The takings are in the bag on the sideboard along with the receipts for you to check. Did I do right, Mother?' she asked tentatively.

'Did you quote Mrs Hardy a price?'

'No. I couldn't, could I, as I have no idea of costings.'

A disgusted look on her face, Harriet pushed the plate away from her. 'I can't eat that, it's all dried up,' she said, rising. 'I'm going to bed, I've had a tiring day. Make sure you lock up properly before you come up.'

After Harriet had left, Maddie stood staring at the nearly full plate, her fraught nerves jangling. Apart from the fact that her mother's complaint about the food was totally unwarranted, the fact that she still had not mentioned a word about her intentions regarding Maddie's condition was worrying in the extreme.

It was still two days before she could see Josh and they suddenly seemed endless.

By Saturday evening Harriet still had not commented on the subject and Maddie was reaching breaking point.

'That food cost good money, Maude, stop pushing it around your plate and eat it before it gets cold.'

'I'm not hungry, Mother,' she replied, laying down her knife and fork. 'I have a headache. If you don't mind, I'll clear the kitchen and go to bed.'

'I *do* mind. As you are fully aware, Maude, I abhor waste of any description but especially that of food. Now I'm sure your headache will not hinder you from eating what is on your plate.'

Maddie stared down at the two boiled potatoes, spoonful of Savoy cabbage and small helping of mutton stew growing cold on her plate. The sight of it made her feel sick, let alone the thought of forcing it down her throat. But she knew she must. Harriet would not allow her to leave the table until she had.

Not waiting for any response her mother snapped, 'Eat up, Maude.'

Maddie took a deep breath before replying quietly, 'Yes, Mother.'

It was nearly two hours later before she felt it safe to announce she was going to bed. Harriet was sitting stiffly in a worn leather armchair by the sparse fire, reading a book.

'Goodnight, Mother,' Maddie ventured tentatively.

Harriet's reply was curt. 'Goodnight.'

That night was much like all the others recently: restless, with sleep a long time coming. Maddie awoke the next morning feeling totally unrested, eyes gritty, wishing wholeheartedly she could stay in bed until it was time to ready herself for her meeting with Josh.

Arriving in the kitchen she was surprised to see her

mother had already prepared breakfast, something that was usually Maddie's task.

Without a word of greeting Harriet announced, 'We're not going to church today, Maude. You're to accompany me on a visit to an old friend of mine. She's not well. We need to set off shortly as it's quite a journey.'

As she stood rooted to the spot Maddie could not decide what had shocked her the most. The fact that for the first time in living memory they would not be attending Sunday service or the fact that her Mother had a friend, someone she had never mentioned before. And not only that but Harriet was concerned enough about her to pay a visit because she was sick. Maddie knew better than to ask any questions. Then, suddenly, another thought struck her and a sickening fear rose up inside her.

'What ... er ... what time d you expect we'll arrive back, Mother?'

Saucepan of porridge in hand, Harriet spun around. 'Late, I would have thought. Why?'

Maddie eyed her anxiously. She had arranged to see Josh at two-thirty down by the canal. He was expecting to hear what reception she had received on divulging her news and to make plans for their wedding. He would be worried if she did not show up and the thought of not seeing him filled her with dread. What could she do? Her mind raced frantically. 'I . . . I have some sewing to finish,' she lied, hoping she could find some.

'It can wait,' Harriet snapped dismissively, slapping a spoonful of porridge in a dish which she placed before Maddie. 'Eat up,' she ordered. 'I'm just off upstairs to collect a few things to take to my friend. A few clothes that are of no use to me anymore that I know she can make use of.'

Maddie was too distressed to listen to her mother. All she could think of was Josh and what he would be feeling and thinking should she not arrive back in time to meet him. How could she get a message to him?

The journey was a long and confusing one for Maddie, consisting of a three-hour rail journey, the train stopping at every station en route, then an age on an omnibus. They had been unceremoniously bumped up and down on the uncomfortable wooden seat for several miles down uneven narrow country lanes before Maddie dared venture to ask her mother where they were heading.

'Not far now,' she replied in a tone that warned Maddie against probing any further.

They alighted from the omnibus in the middle of a busy village which Maddie just caught the name of as the vehicle entered its boundaries: Ibstock. She had never heard of it.

Hurrying ahead of her, Harriet finally stopped by a garden gate, leading to an old miner's cottage in the middle of a row of eight identical houses. All the gardens were neat and the cinder paths running down to the front doors evenly edged by bricks.

Harriet faced her daughter. 'Take this bag,' she ordered, handing Maddie the heavy carpet bag of clothes she had insisted on carrying. As Maddie did as she was bade, Harriet snatched her handbag from her. 'You won't be needing this.'

Maddie eyed her in confusion but before she had time to query it, from the pocket of her coat Harriet produced an envelope which she thrust at Maddie. 'Give this to Mrs Baldicott. She's expecting you.'

Maddie eyed the envelope, bewildered. 'Mother, I don't understand. What's going on?'

'I'm sure it'll all become clear, Maude. I haven't time to explain, I have a bus to catch.'

'You're not staying to see your friend? What . . .'

Harriet grimaced. 'I said, Mrs Baldicott will explain.'

Open-mouthed, Maddie stared in mystification as her mother abruptly turned away and hurried off in the direction they had just come from. Her mind raced wildly, trying to fathom a reason for this bewildering behaviour, but nothing tangible emerged. And just how did her mother, she thought, expect her to get home without any money? Had she not realised what she was doing when she had taken her handbag from Maddie. Why had she done that?

Gnawing her bottom lip, extremely troubled as she wondered what best to do, she turned and stared at the cottage and as she did so the door opened and a small, tubby woman appeared, kindly face smiling, one outstretched arm beckoning her forward. She looked the picture of health, nothing like what Maddie had been expecting from the picture her mother had conjured up of her desperately ill friend. Despite her confusion Maddie had no alternative but to go and greet the old lady, but what excuse she could make for her mother's sudden departure was beyond her.

'You must be Maude, dear, come on through,' she said as Maddie reached her. 'I'm Mrs Baldicott. I thought yer mother would've stopped at least for a cuppa before she made her way back. Still, never mind, you're here now so let's get you settled. But tea first, I think, eh? It's a fair journey from Harborough. I've never been further than Coalville meself which is our nearest town. Put yer bag down, dear, I'll show you up later and then you can unpack,' she said, busying herself making the tea.

'Unpack?'

Nancy Baldicott stopped what she was doing and looked across at the bewildered young woman standing just inside the door. 'Well, yes, you'll want to put yer clothes away, won't yer? They'll be all creased in that bag. There's plenty of drawer space in the tallboy and I've lined the drawers 'specially for yer with fresh brown paper. There's a vase of wild flowers I collected this morning on the window sill. Wanted to make yer feel welcome 'cos ...' she sighed heavily '... 't'int really nice circumstances that brings yer to stay with me, now is it? Still, we won't talk about that just now. But just to put yer mind at rest, I'll try and make yer stay as pleasant as possible and when the time comes Mrs Sims –

she's the woman that sees to all the deliveries in this village – will be on hand for yer.' The look of steadily growing horror on the young woman's face suddenly registered and she asked, 'You did know why yer were coming here, didn't yer? Yer mother has explained our arrangement?'

A sickening fear was rising within Maddie as slowly the kindly words struck home and the dreadful truth of her situation flooded through her. Her eyes flew to the bulky envelope she was still clutching in her hand and suddenly she knew what was in it. It wasn't a letter, it was money. Payment for her keep.

Her mother had lied to get her here and left her a virtual prisoner to hide her shame. And, equally as important, get her away from Josh.

And here she had been for the past seven months, fussed over by Nancy Baldicott. And if truth be told, if the situation had been different, Maddie would have been very happy. Nancy Baldicott was everything her mother was not and had been kindness itself during the whole of Maddie's confinement. But not once during that time, not while helping around the house, or going for walks, or when Mrs Baldicott had been allaying her fears and educating her on the life growing within her – nor even when she had been becoming increasingly anxious over the lack of any communication from Josh – did Maddie ever have a suspicion that her mother would plan something so terrible as taking her baby from her without a word of warning.

Suddenly a vision of her baby returned to haunt her. She had been beautiful, a fine coating of dark hair on a perfectly shaped head, violet-blue eyes staring knowingly from her tiny round face. Maddie had fallen instantly in love with her as soon as the elderly midwife had placed her in her arms. A great surge of love, joy and protectiveness had filled her very being, a feeling that was utterly indescribable. If only Josh could have been there to share these precious moments, her happiness would have been complete.

But Josh was not for whatever reason and the little being responsible for her momentary happiness had been taken from her. Her arms and heart were empty, aching excruciatingly. The loss of Josh she could possibly accept in the end, but not the loss of her child. That Maddie knew she could never do.

Her eyes alighted on a scrap of white linen that had fallen to the floor, a minute nightgown sewn with so much love and care that she had removed from her baby's tiny body only an hour or so ago after tenderly bathing her, ready, as she had innocently thought, for the journey home. With a choking sob, Maddie leaned over to scoop it up, burying her face in the softness of the fabric. She could smell the sweet odour of her child still lingering.

Her thoughts flashed to the woman who was holding her now. What was she like? Was she kind? Caring? Would she love and protect her baby to the exclusion of all else, as Maddie herself would have done?

A surge of great anger against her mother welled up in her. How could Harriet have done this? How could she have acted so cruelly and insensitively?

But despite the lust for revenge that swirled through her, Maddie knew that retaliation against her mother of any sort was futile. She could rant and rave and issue threats until she was blue in the face – Harriet would remain unyielding, of that Maddie had no doubt. Since she'd been a very young child she had known of her mother's inability to show any form of emotion, but not until now had she realised how cold and calculating Harriet truly was. The fact frightened her.

She raised her chin, eyes narrowed determinedly. Her mother might rule her life but one thing she could not do and that was crush her hopes. Maddie knew she would never be able to forgive her for what she had done. Returning home with her and carrying on with her old way of life as though nothing had happened was a challenge she did not

41

know if she could rise to, but as matters stood now she had no choice. She had no money and nowhere to go, no relatives that she knew of, no friends to offer safe harbour while she got herself sorted. But, she silently vowed, one day, she didn't know when or how, she would be reunited with her child. That faint hope would have to be enough to keep her going. Give her a reason to carry on. Because as things stood now, she had nothing else. Her mother had made sure of that.

Rising awkwardly, she took a deep, ragged breath and began her packing.

'Young Maddie gone then? Pity I missed her, I wanted to say cheerio. Nice gel, Maddie. About the best one yer've had, Nancy. I will have a cuppa, thanks for asking. Oi, Nancy, you ain't heard a word I've said, 'ave yer? In fact, I don't think you even noticed I'd come in.' A disgruntled Betty Rumkin plonked her heavy body down on a chair opposite her neighbour at the table and eyed her in concern. Although unrelated, the two widow women, who had been neighbours for more years than either cared to admit, were like two peas in a pod and were often mistaken by strangers for sisters, much to their amusement.

But Betty could see Nancy was far from amused at the moment. By the look on her face, her neighbour was deeply troubled about something. 'Come on, old gel, what's ailing yer?' Betty asked helping herself to a cup of tea. She looked in disgust at the liquid as it spilled from the spout of the brown teapot. 'By God, Nancy, I like me tea brewed but this'd kill weeds! How many spoons did you put in the pot and how long has it been stewing?' She took a tentative sup and shuddered. 'Well?' she demanded. 'Sprouts gone watery? Forgotten to peel the spuds? I ain't leaving 'til yer tell me. And yer'd better hurry unless yer want me burnt dinner on yer conscience.'

Nancy sighed heavily. 'Oh, yer n'ote but a nosy busybody, Betty Rumkin,' she said good-naturedly. 'Well, if yer must know, I'm worried about Maddie. No matter which way I look at it, it i'nt right.'

'What ain't?'

'What the mother done, that's what.'

Betty pursed her lips. 'That thin, stuck-up-looking creature I saw coming up your path this morning?'

'That's 'er.'

'Come to collect Maddie, din't she? You did tell me it was today she was going home, din't yer? So didn't her ma take her then?'

'Oh, she took her all right. It's what she done with the baby and how she done it that's bothering me.'

'For God's sake, Nancy, will yer stop going round the 'ouses and tell me?' Betty erupted impatiently.

Nancy wrung her hands angrily. 'Got the little mite adopted without a word to young Maddie, not a peep, *that's* what she done. Maddie was beside herself. Before yer say it, I know that having the baby farmed out was probably best all round in the circumstances, but she could have discussed it with the girl first, prepared her like, or even told me so I could do it. But that's not the only reason I'm so het up.'

'It ain't?' Cradling her cup, Betty's eyes narrowed in interest.

'No, it ain't. Yer know yerself how thin these walls are, don't yer, Betty?'

'I do. Often I've heard the bones creak on yer corsets, Nancy, as yer've struggled to get 'em on.'

She was too upset to comment on her neighbour's flippancy. 'Well, Madam obviously didn't realise and I heard all she said to that poor gel.'

'And just what did she say?'

'Said Maddie was plain. *Plain!* Can yer credit it? And that young gel as pretty as a picture, and with a lovely nature too. Goodness me, most mothers'd be beside 'emselves to have a daughter like Maddie and want the best for her like we did for ours. But obviously not her. And that's not all.

43

She told Maddie she'd no chance of ever getting a husband now she was soiled. And what she said about that young man of Maddie's defies belief . . .' Nancy reeled off to Betty most of what she had overheard.

'Maddie really loved that young man. There was no need for it, Betty. No need for her to be . . . be . . . well, so nasty about it all, especially considering what she'd done with the baby. Maddie was upset enough about that without the rest on top.'

'This is Maddie's *mother* yer talking about? Her own mother?'

Nancy nodded. 'The very one who abandoned that poor gel with not a penny to her name and only condescended to visit her once in all the time she was here. Brought a woman with her then. Said she was a friend of 'ers. Said her name was . . . oh, I can't recall it now, but I'd know it again 'cos it was so posh-sounding. Hardly said a word the whole time she wa' here, but nice woman she wa'. I must say, I took to 'er. Lovely clothes she had on. I remember it crossing me mind that it were odd that a nice woman like that would be friendly with the likes of Harriet Ashman. Still . . . Oh!' Nancy suddenly exclaimed. 'So that's who she wa'. Well, I'll be blowed.'

'What is it, Nancy?' asked Betty, confused.

'It's obvious, ain't it? That woman were no friend, she wa' the woman who took the baby. Mrs Ashman had brought her along to give Maddie a look over, see what she was like before she made the final commitment. Fancy me not realising at the time. Too blooming trusting, that's what I am.' Her eyes blazed angrily. 'D'yer know summat, Betty? In all the time young Maddie was with me, not once did she ever say a word against her mother. Not once.' She paused for breath. 'We're both mothers, Betty. How can a real mother be like that, eh? You know I've come across some in my time doing this kinda work, and some of the things that have happened have made me weep. How many times have you comforted me, Betty? And I've vowed never to do it again, no matter how much I needed the money. But then I have, mainly because I feel in my way I'm helping these poor young gels. But this . . . this has to be the most terrible situation and she has to be the worst mother I've ever come across.' She sighed distractedly. 'It just seemed to me . . .'

'What? Seemed what ter yer, Nancy?'

'Maybe I'm imagining things, Betty, but I feel that Mrs Ashman wanted to . . .' She tutted. 'I don't know the right word for it . . . make young Maddie believe she was worthless, I suppose. That's what it seemed like to me. She just went on and on at her, never letting up. Oh, Betty, 't'aint right what that lovely young gel's got to put up with,' she muttered in distress.

'Eh, now, come on, gel,' Betty soothed, placing a comforting hand on top of her friend's. 'There's n'ote yer can do. There ain't no point in upsetting yerself needlessly.'

Nancy sniffed. 'I know. I'd give anything to have talked to Maddie before she left, tried to comfort her somehow, but I never got the chance. Oh, it grieves me, so it does.'

'I got to like Maddie very much meself but you were really fond of her, weren't yer, Nancy?' Betty said softly.

'Yes, and I still am.' She shrugged her shoulders helplessly. 'But yer right. What can I do, eh? I was paid to do a job. I ain't supposed to get involved. Anyway, what's done is done. Maddie's gone home and I don't expect I'll ever hear from her again. But I'll tell yer this, Betty,' she said, struggling to raise her weary body from off the chair, 'if ever I clap eyes on that woman again, I'll give her a piece of my mind!' She made a grab for the teapot. 'But then, d'yer know summat, Betty? I don't think whatever I said would make an 'aporth of difference to her.'

Her neighbour grinned, trying to lighten the situation. 'I dunno, Nancy, it might. You do have a way with words when yer dander's up.'

Her friend shook her head vigorously. 'No, Betty, not a

45

chance. Even with my tongue. That woman is selfish, and it's my opinion that what she done with that baby, and what she said to Maddie, and the way she treats her, is all done for her own ends and nothing more. Well, it's obvious, ain't it? She don't want her daughter to have a life, does she? And the worry is I don't think young Maddie knows what her mother's up to. Selfish bitch that she is.'

'Oh, Nancy, them's strong words for you.'

'The way I'm feeling at this moment, Betty, I could easily use stronger but . . .' A glimmer of amusement kindled in her eyes. 'I won't 'cos I don't want to make you blush. Now I'm gonna put the kettle on and try and put all this to the back of me mind.'

Nancy Baldicott knew they were brave words. Never in all her years remaining would she forget this day. All her thoughts were for the devastated young girl who had just left and the fear she felt for Maddie's future. Indeed, if there *was* much of a future for her with that woman as her mother.

46

Chapter Three

'Ouch! Goodness me, watch what you're doing. You're supposed to be putting those pins in the hem of my skirt, not sticking them in me.' Mrs Green turned on Maddie in annoyance, then her face softened. 'You've been doing alterations for me for how long now? Must be getting on for ten years, and I've never known you to be so careless, Maddie. And you've hardly said a word since I arrived. Is something the matter?'

From her kneeling position on the floor, slowly removing dressmaking pins from her mouth, Maddie stared up at her client. Yes, something was the matter, she wanted to scream. It was her daughter's birthday today. Her first birthday. A day that should have been filled with celebration. A day for happiness. Instead she felt so wretched she was having trouble even thinking straight.

It was a year since that devastating day at Mrs Baldicott's, a year of pure living hell for Maddie as she'd fought to appear outwardly normal while inwardly fighting terrible emotions.

Josh's desertion of her she still could not fathom. Although it had been extremely difficult, out of respect for her mother she had kept her promise and stayed well away from anywhere she might bump into him. In fact she had hardly left the house at all except to accompany her mother to church and to help with the shopping. Secretly she had hoped that one day Josh would miraculously appear, his excuse for his disappearance something she couldn't imagine, but nevertheless something valid and believable. But as weeks then months passed she knew her hopes were futile and painfully began to accept her mother's interpretation of events as the truth despite her own terrible regret for feelings which would not die, no matter how hard she tried.

The loss of her child was another matter and no matter how hard she fought it was something she could not overcome. The ache in her heart, the emptiness of her arms, were still as acute as ever and she continually battled with frenzied worries as to how her baby was faring and terrible longings to gather the child to her and never let her go.

But how could she explain any of this to Mrs Green, when she, like all the others who knew her, had no idea of the true reason why Maddie had spent seven months away in the country?

'Let me fetch your mother,' she heard Mrs Green suggest.

'Oh, no, no,' Maddie interrupted, awkwardly rising. 'I'm all right, really I am. Just a bit of a headache, that's all.'

'Looks more than that to me. You're as white as a sheet.' The customer frowned, eyes narrowing thoughtfully. 'In fact, you haven't been the same since you came back from looking after your mother's sick friend. What illness was she suffering from? I know it's about a year ago but was it anything you could have picked up, do you think?'

Mrs Green placed a kindly hand on Maddie's arm and this small act shattered all the girl's self-control. She burst into tears.

'I'm so sorry,' she sobbed. 'Please forgive me,' she gasped, rushing from the room. She flew up the stairs and into her bedroom where she collapsed on her bed, sobbing hysterically.

Moments later her mother strode into the room, to loom over her. 'What on earth is going on?' she demanded impatiently.

She was the last person Maddie wanted to speak to at

this moment, the reason for all her misery. 'Please leave me alone, Mother.'

'I beg your pardon?' Harriet hissed indignantly. 'Just who do you think you are, addressing me in that tone of voice? I'm your mother. Now stop this nonsense and get up. You have a client waiting.'

Between choking sobs, Maddie struggled for breath. 'I . . . I can't.'

'Can't! You will. I haven't time for this. I've left the shop unattended. Now compose yourself, rinse your face and get back to Mrs Green.' Harriet leaned over, grabbed Maddie's arm and yanked her upright. '*Now*, I said.'

'I can't,' she wailed, chin buried in her chest. 'I can't face anyone. You know, don't you? You know what day . . .'

'Don't you dare!' Harriet warned. 'I told you a year ago that what happened was over and you were never to mention it again. I meant what I said, Maude. All that happened you brought on yourself.' Folding her skinny arms under her flat chest, she reared back her head. 'I told you you were going to suffer and you have, haven't you? Well, it's my opinion you're getting your just deserts, and wallowing in self-pity is only making matters worse for you. You've had more than enough time to put all this behind you.' Pulling a large handkerchief from the pocket of her black shop dress, she blew her nose noisily. 'If anyone deserves pity it's me, what with this dratted cold I can't shift. Now pull yourself together and get back to attending Mrs Green before we lose her custom.'

Her tone was hard and cold. Maddie flinched. Slowly she raised her head and looked straight at her mother. What she saw shocked and frightened her. The harsh lines of cruelty etched around those thin lips, the smug gleam in the hard grey eyes. But most alarming for Maddie was the gnawing suspicion that her mother appeared to be enjoying her misery and was deliberately adding to it by a refusal to show any sympathy towards her, even a show of compassion.

She shuddered, desperate to rid herself of these dreadful feelings. Dear God, she thought, please tell me I'm wrong. Her mother had told her that what she had done had been carried out in her own and the baby's best interests. She *had* to believe that. The alternative was just too terrible to contemplate.

'I'll tell Mrs Green you'll be down in a moment,' Harriet announced stonily as she turned and made her way out of the room.

Chapter Four

'What about cottons, tapes and elastics? Need any of that stock replenishing this time round?'

'Oh, er . . .' Maddie frowned, feeling mortally inadequate, still taken aback by this salesman's unexpected appearance. Her mother had not informed her that the Coates Cottons and Haberdashery representative was due to call and she knew nothing of their stock levels. It was remiss of her, Maddie thought, to leave her so unprepared. But then, she supposed, Mother was ill, bad enough to have taken to her bed for the last three days, something that had never happened in living memory before, which left Maddie to cope with the care of her, the house, run the shop and keep the customers' alterations and repairs up to date. Regardless of how ill she might be, Harriet still wanted a blow by blow account of the events of the day and no matter how well Maddie felt she had done, her mother would always find something to grumble about.

For Maddie, although she did not like to see her mother suffer, this illness had afforded her some measure of freedom which she was enjoying immensely. Despite her mother's carping she felt she was handling it all very well, especially the shop, considering she had only once before been allowed behind the counter and that only for a day.

She decided it was best not to guess what stock to take and risk the inevitable reprimands but, rightly or wrongly, to trust the salesman. 'Well, actually, I've no idea how much stock Mrs Ashman usually holds. I presume you're more knowledgeable on that than me?'

As the words left her lips a rush of excitement raced through Gilbert Frisby, a tall, swarthy man, his dark hair plastered down with brilliantine. He flashed Maddie a brief winning smile as he set his trilby hat aside and turned around his large brown stock case, filling the counter, giving her a better view of the range he was carrying.

The owner of Ashman's was his least favourite on the list he'd inherited when he had taken over from old Harry Dolby on his retirement six months ago. As usual this visit to Ashman's was first on his daily agenda in order to get it over with. Harry Dolby, when handing over, had not had a good word to say about Harriet Ashman and Gilbert's own opinion seconded that. He too found her a humourless, austere woman, any salesman's skills wasted upon her, and never in all of Harry's or his fortnightly visits had she offered any kind of refreshment, unlike most of his other small outlet customers who enjoyed perusing his new lines and listening to his advice, whether good or not. Sales were always paramount in Gilbert Frisby's mind, no matter how they were acquired. Selling was his job and what paid his wage.

It had been a pleasurable surprise to breeze into the shop this morning, steeled to deal with Mrs Ashman, and then find this diffident assistant behind the counter. Visions of persuading her to place a large order tantalised Gilbert.

'I suppose that's understandable, you've obviously not worked here long,' he replied jauntily, concentrating on unearthing from his case several samples of new lines with which he hoped to tempt Mrs Ashman's new assistant. 'I carry all the basics so why don't you look over these samples while I check the drawers of stock and fill up? Then we can discuss what quantities of new lines you want and I'll take your order. The new braidings are particularly worth a look. Going down ever so well with my other customers they are. And we've extended the colour range of the mother-of-pearl sequins.'

Maddie accepted the sample pieces and glanced over them. The salesman was right, they were very attractive and of good quality and would enhance the plainest of outfits. But her mother did not stock anything like this for her regular customers. The most frivolous items in the shop were embroidered white handkerchiefs with a choice of a butterfly or flower in the corner or ones edged in white Nottingham lace.

'Yes, I think they're very nice,' said Maddie, putting the samples down next to his case, 'but we don't have any call for items like this.'

'If you don't mind my saying so that's the mistake your employer makes.' Gilbert lowered his voice confidentially. 'Of course, I've no idea how well this shop does but judging by the stock levels it can't do *that* well.'

A natural instinct to defend her mother rose up in Maddie. 'It's Mrs Ashman's shop and whether it does well or not is her business.'

'Yes, but . . .' Gilbert looked at her more closely, intending to inform this woman that what was sold paid her wages and so it was in her own interests to try and persuade Mrs Ashman to buck up her ideas. Instead, as his eyes met hers, he openly stared, realising with a sense of shock that his first impression of this woman had been very misleading. Admittedly the severe scraped back hairstyle did nothing at all for her but it still could not disguise a very attractive face. And those eyes! Arresting big violet-blue ones . . . he was finding it difficult to drag his own gaze away from them. And if he was not mistaken, beneath her unbecoming plain beige dress was a very shapely figure. With the right clothes and a change of hairstyle, she would be stunning. No woman would deliberately make themselves unattractive, so maybe it was a condition of her job she should dress like this for work. That would be typical of Mrs Ashman.

With growing unease Maddie wondered why he was staring at her so intently. 'Is anything the matter?' she asked, wondering if she had grown an extra head or worse.

Gilbert jumped. 'Eh? Oh . . . I was . . .' He suddenly realised he had completely forgotten what they had been talking about.

'You were about to tell me how Mrs Ashman should run her business?'

'I was?' He grinned suddenly and shrugged his shoulders. 'I was just trying to help, that's all. It's in my interest as well as yours if our goods sell well. But, to be honest, I know I'm wasting my time so far as Mrs Ashman's concerned. She's not the approachable type. I'll check your basics, will I?' And he added, as the bell on the door clanged, 'While you see to your customer. Er . . . what did you say your name was?'

'I didn't – but it's Maddie.'

She had to send the customer away empty-handed as she could not supply the style of replacement black suspenders wanted for her fashionable corselette and suddenly realised, with some concern, exactly what the salesman had been getting at.

Her mother's kind of shop was slowly dying out. Now the Great War was over, fashions were changing. 1926 saw the modern woman wearing shorter skirts and dresses which were made from much softer materials and in a wider variety of colours. Undergarments and accessories had not escaped the dictators of style either, and customers demanded the right to purchase the latest designs. Subsequently competition among retailers was fierce. Maddie had noticed as she had passed it on her way to church a display in the shop window of a close competitor a couple of streets away. Judging by the carefully thought out window, the owner stocked a wide range of lingerie for the younger woman, together with various accessories such as belts and scarves, while still catering for regular older customers. If Maddie had not been with her mother she would have liked to have stopped and looked more closely at a delicate ivory slip edged with lace that had caught her eye.

Worried by the recollection, she tightened her lips. The salesman's warning was timely. Her mother's business would gradually grind to a halt as her loyal customers died off if she didn't modernise her ideas and bring in a new clientele. The trouble with Mother, Maddie thought, was that she was so set in her ways and unwilling to change, or even listen to informed suggestions, that she could not see she was heading for her own downfall.

'So I can't tempt you to try any of the new lines?' Gilbert said as, business concluded, he shut his case and handed Maddie an invoice for the replacement stock.

Settling up, she smiled. 'Not this time around. But I will speak to Mrs Ashman,' she tentatively volunteered. She felt she must at least try. It was against her nature to do otherwise.

'You will?' He laughed. 'Rather you than me!'

Slapping on his trilby, he picked up his case and headed for the door. 'Tarra, then. See you in a fortnight.' Pulling the door open, he hesitated before turning back to face her. 'I've been given complimentary tickets for the music hall next Wednesday evening. I deal with the wardrobe department there and sometimes they give me spares.' He pulled a wry face. 'Well, it's no fun going on your own, is it?'

'No, I suppose not,' she responded a mite uncomfortably, wondering where this conversation was heading.

Shutting the door again, he put down his case and returned to the counter. 'To tell you the truth, I don't half get lonely when I'm travelling. While I'm in Harborough I lodge with Ma Griffin on Wartnaby Street. It's cheap and cheerful and she's a nice old dear but not much company and the evenings drag.' He smiled at her encouragingly. 'Anyway,' he said, scanning her up and down, 'you look to me like you could do with a good night out. I don't expect you have much fun working here.' He frowned suddenly. 'You haven't already got a fella, have you?'

Maddie reddened. 'No, I haven't.'

The relief on his face was apparent. 'Well then, what do you say? I happen to know there's some good acts on.'

An array of thoughts raced frantically through her mind. Was this man really asking for her company? And would her mother let her go? Holding her breath, Maddie pressed her lips together. Although she was not particularly struck by Gilbert Frisby, he seemed a decent enough man and surely her mother couldn't object to her accompanying him to the music hall for one night. The thought of an evening out was appealing. Although she had always longed to, she had never been to the theatre. And he was right, she could do with a night out, and in return could give him the company he sought. Mother should be well on the mend by next Wednesday and it was half-day closing so Maddie had plenty of time to finish her chores and ready herself. She would just have to be very careful about when she chose to tell her mother.

'Yes, I would like to go. Thank you for asking me.'

'Right then,' said Gilbert, pleased. 'I'll call for you, shall I, about seven?'

Maddie smiled. 'Seven will be fine.'

'What's your address?'

'Pardon? Oh, here. Call for me here.'

'Here? You live in then, do you?'

She nodded. 'I do. Mrs Ashman's my mother only she's ill at the moment – that's why I'm in the shop. Usually I'm in the room at the back taking care of the alterations.'

The shock in his eyes was unmistakable and she knew it wasn't all down to the fact that Harriet Ashman was her mother; it was remorse for his plain speaking about her. 'I'll understand if you want to change your mind,' Maddie offered politely, as a get-out for him.

Common sense told Gilbert that he really should not get himself tangled up with anything to do with Harriet Ashman but he couldn't very well retract the invitation now. Anyway, it was only one night. He didn't need to ask her out again. Pity. From what little he'd seen of her, he felt he would have liked to have got to know Maddie Ashman better. 'No, I don't. I'll call for you at seven on Wednesday then.'

It wasn't until several minutes after he had left that Maddie discovered he'd left behind a box of three dozen cotton reels. She put them aside to give to him when he returned after discovering his loss.

Two days later Harriet had felt well enough to get out of her sick bed and was issuing orders from a chair by the fire. 'There's dust in here, Maude. You know very well I abhor filth. And what about Mrs Cotting's cushion repair? A ten-minute job. Why haven't you done it?'

'I hadn't the time,' she replied evenly as she placed cutlery on the table. 'I didn't finish until after eleven last night and by the time I'd prepared today's meal and tidied up, I didn't get to bed until well after twelve. Mrs Cotting did say she wasn't in a rush.'

'Mrs Cotting is a customer of long standing. No matter what she said you should still have got it done. It's obvious you can't cope, Maude.' Ignoring the hurt expression in her daughter's eyes she continued, 'I'll have to come back to work tomorrow, whether I'm well enough or not.' Harriet sniffed and blew noisily into her handkerchief. 'What have you prepared for lunch? Did you fetch that piece of haddock like I asked, and have you remembered to cook it slowly? My stomach is still very delicate.'

'I'm sorry, Mother, again I didn't have the time. The customers this morning seemed to take ages choosing what they wanted, and there were repair jobs coming into the shop too which I had to deal with. I didn't feel it right to shut up while I went out on an errand, I didn't want to lose the custom.'

Harriet grimaced, nostrils flaring. 'Oh, you didn't? The fishmonger is only a few doors down. You'd have been five minutes if that. The customers would have waited.' She exhaled sharply. 'Through no fault of my own I leave the running of the business to you for four days and that makes you an expert, does it?'

Maddie took a deep breath. 'No, Mother, of course it doesn't. I was just trying to do my best for you, that's all.' As she was speaking she thought how contradictory her mother was. First she was being reprimanded for being inconsiderate and not completing Mrs Cotting's work, despite the customer's saying she wasn't in a hurry: now she was being scolded for considering the customers by not shutting up shop while she went out on an errand. Whatever she did she could not win. Regardless, Maddie fixed a smile on her face. 'I've done you a nice piece of ox liver that I'd already arranged for the butcher's boy to deliver. I've stewed it slowly with vegetables. But I could do you a lightly boiled egg if you'd prefer?'

Harriet sniffed disdainfully. 'The liver will have to do, being's you've already done it,' she said grudgingly. Through narrowed eyes, she watched her daughter turn back to the kitchen and her mouth clamped tight as her thoughts returned to their previous conversation. Her daughter was right. Business had never been great and to lose even one customer could damage their meagre profits. Harriet cared very deeply about money but to achieve greater profits would be far too costly in other ways. Things were working out just the way she had planned many years before. To change the plan now could bring outside influences to bear and then she could lose control of everything she held dear. Harriet wasn't prepared to risk that. She realised Maddie was hovering by the door, eyeing her uncertainly.

'What?' she snapped.

Clasping her hands, her daughter stepped several paces forward. 'Well,' she began slowly, choosing her words carefully, trying to keep her enthusiasm from showing. 'When Mrs Green came in to collect her skirt she informed me she had recommended me to a Mrs Wilcox who's just moved to town with her husband from somewhere up north. I don't know how Mrs Green came across her but apparently Mr Wilcox is a solicitor and is going to be opening an office here. He has just bought a big house on the Kilby Road. Mrs Wilcox needs someone to make all her curtains and matching cushions. Wasn't it good of Mrs Green to suggest me? She said Mrs Wilcox would be in touch.'

'I can't spare you. You'll have to tell her to find someone else,' Harriet declared resolutely.

Taken aback, Maddie stared at her, wanting to question her reason for turning down such a lucrative offer, not to mention the further work it could generate. It didn't make sense. Why deliberately turn down work without even attempting to see if they could handle it? Maddie knew she could do it, but more importantly she would really have liked to have done it. Being inside that lovely big house, advising Mrs Wilcox on fabrics and designs . . . For a moment she pondered taking the job without her mother's knowledge. But she knew the thought to be an idle fantasy. Her mother felt it was her right to know exactly how Maddie's time was spent every minute of the day.

'Are you going to get my dinner or stand there gawping like an idiot while I starve? It'll soon be time to open the shop again.'

'What? Oh, yes, Mother, of course.'

A preoccupied Maddie made her way back to the kitchen. In view of Harriet's response she thought it best not to mention her conversation with Gilbert Frisby on considering new lines, nor did she relish the prospect of telling her of her trip to the theatre.

It was Wednesday by the time Maddie did pluck up the courage and then only because she dare not leave it any longer. She waited until her mother had laid down her knife and fork after their midday meal. Taking a deep breath, she opened her mouth to speak but Harriet beat her to it.

'That piece of chin beef was tough,' she complained. 'Or maybe it was your cooking, Maude. Did you sear it first in hot fat to seal in the juices, like I've instructed you?'

Maddie inwardly flinched. Why did her mother always have to address her as though she was a child? 'Yes,' she replied evenly. 'And I cooked it slowly in the oven.'

'Well, obviously not slowly enough. Why can't you do as you're told, Maude? I really can't be expected to run the shop as well as cook the midday meal, but I suppose I'll have to. I can't risk my teeth on tough meat again.' She eyed Maddie sharply. 'Have you something you want to tell me? You're acting like a scared rabbit.'

She gulped. 'Oh, well . . . yes, I do. I'm . . . well, I'm . . .'

'For goodness' sake, girl, out with it. I haven't all day!'

Maddie blurted out, 'I'm going to the music hall tonight.'

Harriet pursed her lips. 'Really?' she said matter-of-factly, rising to gather the dirty crockery. 'Well, if that's your idea of entertainment, I hope you enjoy yourself.' Maddie stared at her astonished, this response the very last she had expected. She took a deep breath. 'With Gilbert Frisby, the Coates Cottons salesman,' she added, hesitantly.

Still continuing her task, Harriet sniffed. 'As I said, enjoy yourself. Just make sure you're home before ten. You still have to get up for work in the morning.'

Shocked, Maddie muttered, 'I will. Thank you, Mother.'

Frowning, Maddie glanced at the clock above the jeweller's across the road, then up and down the street. It was a warm, pleasant June evening and plenty of people were about, either coming or going or just milling around talking with friends. Although she wasn't, she felt conspicuous standing outside the shop and the longer she waited the worse the feeling grew.

It was ten minutes past seven and there was no sign of Gilbert. For a moment she wondered whether she had mistaken their arrangement but she knew that she hadn't.

Seven o'clock, he had said. Well, it was now nearly a quarter past and if he didn't hurry they would be late. Maddie understood the show started at seven-thirty.

At a quarter to eight all her hopes had faded, there were no excuses left. Resigned, she made her way back inside.

Her mother looked up from her book as Maddie entered the sitting room. 'You're back early.'

She swallowed hard. 'Mr Frisby didn't come,' she said softly. 'Something must have happened and he couldn't let me know.'

'Or just didn't bother.'

'Pardon?'

Harriet snorted, glancing her daughter up and down. 'Well let's face it, Maude, the man felt sorry for you, that's why he asked you out in the first place. It's my opinion that as soon as he left he regretted his action. When will you learn? Men like him don't take out plain women like you unless there's good reason to.' She ignored the look of devastation on her daughter's face. 'Best advice I can give you, my girl, is not to accept any invitations in future, no matter how genuine you think they are. It'll save you the humiliation. Now why don't you get yourself a glass of warm milk and go to bed? A good night's sleep and you'll forget all about it come morning.'

Maddie was too dispirited to respond with any more than, 'Yes, Mother.'

Upstairs in her cold, sparsely furnished bedroom, a dejected Maddie caught sight of herself in the mirror just as she was about to get undressed. She stared at herself. She had made such an effort to look nice even if her skirt was not made of fancy material, her high-buttoned blouse just a sprig cotton print, and her hair tied back in a plain bow. If she'd done otherwise Harriet would have given her no choice but to revert to her original style. But she did look clean and neat.

She sighed. Men preferred good-looking, fashionably

dressed women on their arm. Her mother was right. Neat, clean and plain-faced only got a look in if nothing else was available. Maybe Gilbert had had a better offer but she herself preferred to think that as the busy man he was, work had waylaid him and he just had not found the time to let her know.

Slipping off her clothes, she folded them neatly, thinking this was another hard lesson she had learned. How many more must she be cruelly taught before her days ended?

But Gilbert's thoughtlessness was not the only matter that was troubling her – something far more worrying was.

Crossing to the window, she pulled aside the net curtain and peered out. The pleasant early-summer evening was drawing to a close. Voices and sounds drifted on the warm air. Mothers herded their offspring inside; men's boots clattered on the cobbles as they made their way home from work or off to the pub to wash the day's grime from their throats; groups gathered on corners. There was the clip-clop of horses' hooves pulling late delivery carts; a distant factory hooter sounding the beginning of the evening shift. Maddie heard little or none of this. All her thoughts were centred on her mother.

Lifting her eyes she focused them blankly on the bright crescent moon hanging low in the darkening sky, wispy clouds drifting across it. She frowned. Just why was Mother so caustic towards her? Why was it she appeared to go out of her way to add further pain or humiliation to any Maddie was already suffering? Were not mothers supposed to nurture their children, encourage them to do well, share in their happiness, be a comfort in physical or emotional pain? Why did hers show none of these traits? In fact, just the opposite.

Sighing, she tilted her head, eyes narrowing questioningly. But more importantly, why did she herself, no child any more but a grown woman of twenty-six, allow herself to be intimidated so blatantly, so much so that she was frightened to be herself or voice any opinion? She allowed her mother to rule her, going along with her wishes in order to live a peaceful life. Why couldn't she stand up for herself, put her own point across? What was it about Harriet that made her feel unable to do this? Or was it that she herself had acted this way for so long she didn't know how to do otherwise?

Her thoughts, as they had done many times in the past, strayed to the man who had fathered her and suddenly she wished her mother would unyield and talk to her about him, then maybe she would understand herself a little better. Maddie tried to picture her father but couldn't. She didn't know if he was tall or small, fat or thin, and of his features she had no idea. Did she take after him in any way at all? She sighed. Was his death the reason behind her mother's bitterness, her coldness, her unwillingness to administer any kind of warmth? Had his death affected her so much she had closed down her feelings by way of shielding herself from further hurt? If that was true then she must have loved him very much.

Maddie tried to picture her mother happy, the several brothers and sisters Maddie might have had clinging to her skirts. Tried to feel the family unity that could have reigned, had her father lived. She couldn't. She had never seen her mother smile, never witnessed her happy, and even visualising Harriet in different circumstances was impossible. She knew she was wasting her time trying.

People suffered greatly through their lives and dealt with grief in varying ways but their basic natures did not alter. If she was honest with herself Maddie knew her father must have been a man very much of her mother's nature or else there would have been nothing to have brought about a marriage between them in the first place. Maddie shuddered violently and suddenly felt a great need to get out of this house, away from the walls that had been her sanctuary for over a year while she had striven to heal herself. For a while she needed to be away from her mother's prying eyes and critical tongue, to be alone with her thoughts. She had once enjoyed solitary walks. Maybe she could do again. She would have to do something unless she wanted to become a total recluse.

Tomorrow night, she decided, she would go for a walk after all her chores were done. The fresh air might clear her head and help her to think straight, stiffen her resolve to face things as they were. She must get on with things. If she was honest with herself, her life could be much worse. She only had to poke her head out of the door to see the poverty that reigned locally, worry and deprivation etched on people's faces. In that respect at least she could consider herself lucky.

Chapter Five

'I shan't be long, Mother.'

'Where are you going?'

Maddie shrugged her shoulders as she made to pick up her handbag then decided she wouldn't need it. 'Nowhere in particular – just for a walk.'

'It's too late to go walking by yourself. You are going to be by yourself, I trust? Nothing you're keeping back from me, is there?'

'No, Mother,' she replied evenly, trying to keep her irritation from showing. 'I'm going completely by myself. And it's only just gone eight, still plenty of light left.'

'Huh! Well, if you must. Just show some consideration and don't be long. I don't intend sitting here until all hours worrying on your behalf.'

Maddie looked across at her. Was Harriet showing genuine concern for her welfare or giving way to displeasure that her daughter was doing something that brought her into contact with the outside world, something Harriet couldn't control without insisting she accompany her? And Maddie knew she wouldn't relish that prospect, not after she had settled herself for the night. If she herself was honest, wasn't that why she had left it this late, to avoid the prospect of Mother insisting she came too?

'Well?'

'Pardon?'

'I thought you were going for a walk?' Harriet snapped.

'I am. I . . . I was just contemplating whether I would

65

need a cardigan. I don't think I'll take one.'

Harriet tutted. 'Well, at least you've made one decision. Just fill the kettle and swing it across the fire first. I'll have to make my own cocoa.' It was not a statement but an accusation.

'Oh!' Maddie's face filled with remorse. It fell to her to make the last drinks of the evening and in her haste to get out she had forgotten that task. 'I'll do it before I go.'

Harriet flapped her hand in irritation. 'No need. I'm sure I can do it myself . . . for one evening,' she emphasised.

Standing outside on the pavement, Maddie looked up and down the street, undecided as to what route to take. Left took her towards the canal, an area she hadn't been near for well over a year in order to avoid reviving memories she was trying hard to forget. Right took her to the town centre just past which was the park. In her frame of mind the park would be the ideal place for a stroll at this time of night; plenty of people would still be about on this warm summer evening, enough to stop her feeling any more conspicuous than normal.

She had just turned into the main high street when she noticed a figure approaching, head bowed, hands dug deep in his jacket pockets. Her heart thumped and her footsteps slowed. It was Gilbert Frisby. He was only a few feet away from her and a meeting was unavoidable. Maddie's thoughts raced frantically. She wasn't sure what to do. Despite the fact that he'd let her down, it wasn't in her nature blatantly to ignore him, though in the circumstances neither did she feel she could casually pass the time of day either.

Suddenly she frowned. There was something about him that wasn't right . . . then it dawned on her that his whole persona radiated unhappiness. Her immediate thought was that someone close to him had died. Her own concern as to how to handle this awkward situation was forgotten as her caring nature took over.

As he passed her, she waylaid him. 'Mr Frisby, are you

all right? Mr Frisby?' she repeated.

He stopped abruptly and eyed her, confused. 'What?' Then his eyes flashed recognition and his already frowning face filled with fury. 'You!' he spat. 'You've some brass neck, talking to me.'

Maddie gasped, shocked. She had been wrong. Gilbert Frisby was not upset – he was furious about something and all her instincts were screaming a warning that it was something to do with her. Though how was beyond her, she barely knew the man. 'I beg your pardon?'

'You can beg as much as you like but you'll get no pardon from me. Proud, are you?'

'Pardon?' gasped Maddie.

'Pardon,' he mimicked. 'Is that the only word you know? You heard me. I said, proud.' He pushed his face so close to hers she could smell his breath. He'd been drinking. 'How does it feel, eh, to lose a man his job? Makes you feel good, does it?'

Maddie recoiled in shock. 'I . . . I don't understand?'

He looked at her in disgust. 'Don't play the innocent with me. She told my boss I was hounding you. Wouldn't leave you alone. Is that what you told her? For God's sake, I only asked you out for the evening. You call that harassment, do you? You're mental, you are. You want locking up.' He pushed Maddie so hard she stumbled backwards. 'Get out of my way,' he spat, and strode off.

Recovering her senses after his attack, her mind raced, trying to fathom a reason for his behaviour. But she couldn't. Neither could she work out who this 'she' he referred to was. Regardless, she was innocent of his accusation and couldn't let him go without making him believe her. 'Mr Frisby, wait!' cried Maddie, running after him and grabbing his arm. 'Believe me, I don't know what you're talking about. Honestly,' she stressed. 'Will you please stop and listen to me? Please, Mr Frisby.'

The tone of her voice halted him and he studied her hard

for several long moments. 'You don't, do you?' he said finally, his harsh expression softening slightly. 'You haven't a clue what I'm talking about, have you?'

Maddie shook her head. 'No, I haven't.' She raised her hands in a helpless gesture. 'The only thing I do know is that we had an arrangement for Wednesday evening at seven. I waited for you but you never came. I thought . . . thought you were too busy to let me know. So I went home.'

He frowned, confused. 'Eh? And you didn't send her to see me?'

'No.' She eyed him, frowning in bewilderment. 'Just who is this person . . .' Her voice trailed off as slowly the truth dawned. 'Oh! You mean . . . my mother? That's who you're referring to?'

Flaring his nostrils, he nodded. 'She came to my digs. Demanded to see me. Told me how upset you were that I'd dared to proposition you in that way. That you had no intention of being seen out with the likes of me and I wasn't to humiliate you by asking you out again. In front of my landlady as well.'

'What?' Gasped Maddie, mortified. 'I can assure you, Mr Frisby, I never said any such thing.'

'You didn't?'

'No, I didn't.' Her confusion mounted. 'When was this? When did my mother come to see you exactly?'

'Tuesday evening.'

'Tuesday evening? Then it couldn't have been her. I didn't tell her I was going to the music hall with you until about an hour before we were to meet. You must be mistaken.'

His face darkened. 'Listen, it was Mrs Ashman, I tell you. I'd know that woman if it were pitch black. The sound of her voice is enough to set anyone's teeth on edge! She may be your mother, but she's been the bane of my life since I took over Harry Dolby's round. I can't pretend I'm fond of her and there's no way I'd ever mistake anyone else for her. There is no one else like her. So when I say she came on

Tuesday, she came on Tuesday.'

He was so adamant Maddie had to believe him. And thinking about it, her mother had popped out that night without saying where she was going. But all the same . . . 'It doesn't make sense. As I've already said, I didn't mention a word of our arrangement to her until an hour before. So it couldn't have been her who came to see you, could it?'

'Oh, but she did know.'

'She did? How?'

'I told her.'

'You?'

'Yes, I mentioned it when I dropped in for the box of cottons. I'd had a run on white cotton and it was my last box. I hadn't realised I'd left it behind at your shop until I needed them. Monday morning it was. I wouldn't normally have bothered, it was miles out of my way, but one of my customers was desperate and couldn't wait until my next visit. As I was leaving I just asked her to tell you I was looking forward to our night out and not to be late as the show started promptly. She asked where I was taking you. Seemed really interested. I told her and she said she hoped we had a nice time. Quite pleasant she was. Not like her normal self at all,' he snarled. 'So, you see, she did know.'

Maddie listened, stunned. This situation was dreadful. How could her mother do this to her? She felt so humiliated she wanted the ground to open and swallow her up. To die on the spot would be better. What must this man think of her. With an effort she raised her eyes to meet his. 'Look, I . . .'

'Don't bother,' Gilbert told her. 'Nothing you can say will put any of this right. I have nothing but pity for you. You can't have any life living with her.' A nasty smirk curled the corners of his mouth. 'But then, maybe you deserve each other. But one thing I'll never understand – why did she have to write to my boss and get me the sack? Why did she have to do that, eh? The evil bitch.'

69

Maddie gasped. 'She did what?'

'You heard. Sent the letter special delivery. Wrote that she was disgusted the company employed people like me and consequently didn't want any more to do with Coates Cottons. She hoped my conduct would be suitably addressed. *Suitably addressed,*' he hissed. 'Oh, they did that all right, didn't they? My boss came personally to do the deed. Wouldn't listen to my side of things but finished me on the spot. And without a good reference, I'll be lucky to get another job. I was so shocked by it all I had to have a few pints.' He glared at her. 'Yeah, I'm drunk, and who can blame me, eh?'

Totally horrified, Maddie clasped her hand to her mouth. 'Mr Frisby, I'm so sorry. I don't know what to say . . .'

'Then don't say anything,' he exclaimed, expression murderous. He jabbed her hard in the shoulder with his finger. 'Your family has done enough. I wish I'd never clapped eyes on either of you, especially her. I just hope she can sleep at night. Now I think I'd better collect my belongings from my digs before I do something I regret.' He raised his hat and said sarcastically, 'Good evening, Miss Ashman. What a pleasure it's been.'

Spinning on his heel, he clapped his hat back on his head and marched off down the street.

Maddie stared after him, unaware of passers-by taking an interest in her, wondering why she was standing in the middle of the pavement, her face white with astonishment.

It took someone accidentally bumping into her to get Maddie moving. Although it was not her fault, she apologised profusely then stepped back until she came up against a wall which she slumped against, mind fully occupied with her conversation with Gilbert Frisby. He just had to be lying, he had to be. It was too terrible to think that her mother would go to such lengths in order to deny her a night of pleasure. But why would he lie? What reason would Gilbert Frisby have for concocting such an elaborate tale?

Her jumbled thoughts whirled madly. It seemed they didn't quite fit together, but she knew they would if she allowed them to. It was only fear that held her back. Fear to face the truth about her mother.

Maddie's heart beat painfully. If her mother had done this terrible thing then an innocent man had lost his job and that wasn't right. Maybe it was too late to do anything about that dreadful situation, but regardless, she had to know the truth. The only way to get it was to do something she had never done before and that was to tackle Harriet. The thought petrified her.

Face ashen, a deeply burdened Maddie slowly made her way home. She stood for several minutes at the back door, summoning all her courage, before she took several deep breaths and let herself in.

Harriet was in the kitchen, bending over the sink washing the cup and saucer she had used for her nightcap. Without raising her head, she said, 'You didn't stay out long.'

Maddie's hands felt clammy and beads of sweat began to form on her brow but she was determined not to let her courage fail her. 'I . . .' she began faltering.

'For goodness' sake, Maude, stop stammering and say what you've got to say. I haven't all night.'

Her mother's sharp retort sent a wave of panic through her and Maddie felt her courage begin to ebb. But she knew that she must not let it. If she did not get to the bottom of her problem she knew she would never rest easy. Steeling herself, she took a deep breath. 'I only got as far as the main street when I met Gilbert Frisby. You know, Mother, the Coates Cottons salesman.'

Maddie watched her mother closely for any tell-tale signs but not a muscle on Harriet's face twitched as she reached over for a drying cloth and turned to face her daughter. 'I do know who Gilbert Frisby is,' she said tersely. 'Is there a point to this story, Maude?'

'Yes, there is.' She clasped her damp hands together

tightly. 'I . . . thought you'd be interested to know he's been sacked.'

Harriet sniffed disdainfully. 'Really? And what makes you think I'd be interested in that? He's nothing to me. Now I'm tired and I'm going to bed. The kettle is just off the boil if you want a cup of cocoa. Make sure you lock up properly before you come up.'

With that she headed out of the room, leaving Maddie none the wiser, listening to her footfall as she climbed the stairs.

Early the next evening Maddie stopped suddenly at the bend in the tow path and surveyed in delighted surprise the busy scene before her. She had had the most dreadful day, unanswered questions still whirling in her mind as she'd fought to carry out her daily duties as though nothing was amiss.

Sitting opposite her mother during mealtimes had been the hardest thing to do. She had found it difficult to look her in the eye without wondering if Harriet could possibly be the terrible person Maddie now strongly suspected she was.

Her announcing that she was going for another walk that evening had not pleased Harriet at all and several obstacles had been put in her way. But, much to her own surprise, Maddie had stood her ground, her need to get out of the house far outweighing the backlash for blatantly disobeying her mother's wishes.

So distracted was she, she hadn't realised her route had taken her down the canal tow path, let alone a mile or two along it, until the noises of the barge people going about their business only yards away suddenly broke in on her. For a moment her worries flew from her. Foxton Locks! She could not remember the last time she had come here and it was like seeing it for the very first time.

A series of canal locks, seven in number, had been cut

into a hillside, affording a never-ending succession of canal traffic passage on its journey to and from the Grand Canal that shipped goods from the Liverpool and Manchester docks right across the Midlands and beyond. It was an extremely pretty countryside setting between Market Harborough and Leicester, quite near the borders of Northamptonshire, and local people would come to spend their leisure time watching the antics of the canal folk as they went about their business.

Not far away from where Maddie stood a wide basin off the main artery of the canal afforded barges moorings for the night and in early evening it was a hive of activity.

As she wandered forward, Maddie could see several barges queuing to journey through the locks to the top of the hill. At the top other barges were lined up to make the journey down. She smiled to herself. The locks reminded her of steps, only these were water steps. How clever of the engineer who had managed to solve this problem when confronted with the hill during the construction of the canal.

Some of the barges were great rusting monsters, their long narrow cargo holds filled with coal and steel, the men in charge dirty rough-looking types, the horses pulling them, although looking reasonably well-fed, pitifully tired. Other barges were obviously used as dwellings and were brightly painted with intricate designs peculiar to the canal people. Tattered washing flapped from raised lines running the length of the barge roofs and chimneys smoked from ovens burning down below.

Bare-footed, grimy children skittered up and down the tow path, some doing their best to hinder the harassed lock master and his helper as they strove to open and close the huge wooden gates in order for water to fill or empty from the locks. Until all the barges had received safe passage there would be no rest for them.

On a barge nearby, sitting on a stool by the tiller, legs spread wide, sat an elderly woman, her skin weathered to a very dark brown and creased to such an extent it reminded Maddie of a piece of crumpled linen. She was contentedly smoking a clay pipe, eyes fixed on several small children whom Maddie assumed to be in her charge. She was probably their grandmother or maybe even their great-grandmother, her age being indeterminate.

Immersed in the activity around her, for once free from painful thoughts, Maddie did not at first see the child before her until the younger one that was perched on her hip made a sound. Maddie was startled at first, then smiled warmly at the owners of two pairs of large brown eyes set in two grubby faces, feeling sadness rise in her at their dirty, unkempt appearance.

'Hello,' she said softly.

Still staring, the child she guessed to be about five shifted the baby higher on to her hip. As she did so Maddie's attention was drawn and a great surge of sorrow washed through her. The baby was around the age her own child would be now and it took all her strength to fight a desire to grab it to her and wrap it in her arms, just for a minute.

Faced with a total stranger gazing so intently, the baby's face puckered and it let out a shrill wail.

Before Maddie knew what was happening several people were upon her and a bedraggled woman roughly caught her arm, pulling her back, while another grabbed up the baby in one hand and snatched the young girl's hand in the other.

A shabby man raced up. 'What's 'app'nin', Rosa?' he demanded, whipping off a stained red-spotted neckerchief to wipe his brow. He shot an accusing glance at Maddie.

'Gon' pinch baby, she wa',' the woman holding the children spat accusingly.

Astounded, Maddie struggled free from the other woman's grip. 'I was not!' she proclaimed. 'I was only . . .'

'Ged out of it,' Rosa hissed, clutching the baby protectively to her. 'Gon' pinch my baby you wa'. I saw the way you were lookin' at 'er.'

'Rosa!' a deep voice bellowed. 'Leave the woman alone. Wan't doin' no harm. Get children inside and be about yer business. And you too, Harry and Mary.'

All eyes turned to stare across at the old lady on the barge.

'But Gramma . . .' Rosa protested.

She wagged her pipe warningly.

Rosa's lips tightened and with a jerk of her head towards Harry and Mary, she turned and marched back down the tow path, the others following.

'You,' the old lady addressed Maddie. 'Come,' she beckoned. 'Come here.'

The terrible misunderstanding still fresh in her mind, Maddie hesitated.

The old lady beckoned again. 'Come, chile.' She smiled, her lined face creasing into folds, mouth revealing two rows of tobacco-blackened gums.

Maddie stared at her. A great desire to turn and flee from this situation filled her but there was something about this old lady, something that was drawing Maddie towards her. Not knowing why, she suddenly found herself negotiating the short narrow plank from the path on to the barge.

On board the old lady indicated a rickety wooden stool set to one side of her. 'Sit,' she ordered.

Maddie eyed the stool, then looked uncertainly at the old woman. 'Please believe me, I wasn't going to take the baby. I was only . . .'

The woman raised her hand to silence Maddie. 'Sit,' she ordered again.

Maddie obeyed.

Laying down her pipe on an upturned rusting pail nearby, the old lady took Maddie's hands in hers and as she did so shut her eyes, emitting low inaudible murmurs.

At the touch of her fingers a shiver shot down Maddie's spine, then she felt warmth spread right through her and sat transfixed.

Several long moments passed before the ancient woman's hooded eyes opened and she released Maddie's hands. She nodded several times.

'You've known deep pain, chile, but have faith,' she muttered in a deep throaty drawl. Rheumy eyes fixed on Maddie's, boring deep. 'What is lost can be found, you 'ear me? But you, chile, open your eyes. See what is there. Face it. Nothing'll begin for you 'til you do. Be strong. You're kind,' she said, one fist thumping her own chest. 'In 'ere where it matters. A good chile, you are.' She reached over and ran a gnarled hand down the side of Maddie's face. 'Pretty lady, you must believe that.' She took a deep breath and picked up her pipe which she placed in her mouth. 'Now go, and think on.'

The next thing Maddie knew she was on the tow path yards away from the barge, not able to remember how she had got there. For several moments she stood bewildered, staring around her. The barge people were going about their business just as they had been when she had first turned the corner minutes earlier, the children either playing or annoying the lock master. She looked across at the old lady on the barge who appeared to be asleep.

Maddie frowned. It was as though the whole episode had never happened, as though she'd imagined it somehow. But she knew she hadn't.

Deeply disturbed, she turned slowly and made her way back down the path, mind going over and over the words spoken by the old lady.

Presently she came to a small recess in the thick hedge and absently squatted down on a flattish boulder embedded in the ground, heedless of the scruffy young boy several yards downwater, fishing with a home-made rod, anxious to catch his family their supper.

What had the woman been trying to tell her? 'What was lost could be found . . .' What had Maddie lost? And what else had been said? 'Open your eyes.' What did that mean

76

exactly? She pondered deeply but couldn't make sense of it.

Elbows on knees, she rested her chin in her hands, fixing her gaze on the ripples of the canal, and as she did so a vision of Josh appeared and her heart began pounding painfully. She saw him climbing out of the canal after the accident on their very first meeting and although he hadn't at the time, now he was smiling that special smile that was for her alone, eyes filled with love. Other scenes from the past followed swiftly.

Their first outing to the park, the first time he'd ventured to hold her hand, their very first clumsy kiss, then the memorable night they had celebrated their love under the stars. Despite her determination to lock away these memories, so strong were they still, so fresh, that she could feel the pressure of his arms around her.

Then her thoughts fixed on the man himself. The Josh she knew. The man who had taken the time to get to know her, showing patience, consideration and understanding towards her problems when she knew deep down they must have frustrated and annoyed him. He'd told her he loved her and wanted to marry her. And how willing he had been to confront her mother, despite knowing the reception he'd receive when Maddie had told him of her worrying condition.

She took a deep breath. Now she had allowed herself to reflect she knew without a doubt Josh had not set out to entrap her just to better his own position, and nor was he a man to abandon her without good reason. Her mother had been wrong. And, anyway, Harriet was in no position to judge him when she had never met him and taken the trouble to get to know him.

Suddenly the vision of Josh vanished and a picture of Gilbert Frisby appeared. An angry Gilbert Frisby, one who had just lost his job through . . .

Maddie gave a startled gasp, hand clamped against her

mouth, nails digging into the flesh. 'My God!' she groaned as it all suddenly became clear and she realised just what the old woman had been trying to tell her. See! Look! Not at everyday sights but at what was actually going on right under her nose. Important things, terrible things she did not want to acknowledge. But suddenly she was forced to because of an old woman's ramblings.

She knew she was being told to acknowledge that if her mother had gone to such trouble over a night out with Gilbert Frisby, what else had she been capable of? What else had she done to stop Maddie from straying? Was that why Josh had not replied to her letters, had seemed to desert her? Had her mother warned him off too?

Clasping her hands to the sides of her head, Maddie doubled over and rocked with agony. Every fibre of her being begged for these thoughts not to be true, while every ounce of her intelligence struggled to force her to acknowledge that they were.

She raised her head and stared blindly around. She needed answers. She could not go on any longer fighting her emotions, day in, day out, living with a woman she did not know if she could trust, mother or not.

Maddie knew what she had to do. The only thing she could do to have her suspicions allayed or confirmed. Something she should have done well over a year ago but which she had shied away from for fear of what she would find out.

She would have to go and see Mrs Jenks, Josh's mother. She would have to go now, it could not wait. The thought made her shudder violently and she bit her lip so hard she drew blood and wiped it away with the back of her hand.

She rose resolutely and almost ran back down the path, conscious that if she did not hurry, her courage might fail her.

She knew where Josh lived, he had never hidden the fact from her, and as she turned the corner of a street in a miserable over-populated area of dilapidated terraces on the west side of town, a fleeting worry that he might have returned and she would encounter him raised itself and was hurriedly rejected. Whether Josh was back in Market Harborough was not important at this moment. Getting to the truth was.

What she would do when armed with the information hadn't crossed Maddie's mind.

The door she arrived at, although badly in need of a coat of paint, was clean, as were the windows and old nets hanging inside. The step, although not Cardinal polished, had been recently swept and mopped. The same could not be said of the other houses she had rushed by. Maddie stood for a moment and stared at the tarnished iron numbers nailed to the door: 81. The number, Josh had once laughingly told her, reminded him of his parents. Eight for his mother as she was small and fat, and one for his father who was tall and thin.

As she raised her hand to knock, Maddie hesitated for a moment. But before she could think or do anything further the door suddenly shot open and a woman not far from her own age stood there. Maddie knew then she had come to the right house as this person was the image of Josh, only the features were finer and she was not so tall. She was dressed in a plum-coloured dress with a Peter Pan collar, obviously on her way out.

They both stared, startled to see each other.

'Oh!' the woman exclaimed, a smile on her pretty face. 'Yer gave me a shock. Who did yer want? Silly me. Me mother, in't it?'

There was no going back now and Maddie gulped. 'Yes, please, if she's in?'

'Mam!' the woman turned and called down the passage. 'Miss Bundy's 'ere to see yer about our Jeffrey.' She turned back to face Maddie. 'She's in a flap is me mam 'cos you're coming. But we've all said to 'er that if our Jeff is brainy enough to go to the grammar, then it's up to us to see that 'e does.' She cocked her head proudly. 'Right bright spark is our Jeffrey – but then, you know that, don't yer, Miss Bundy? You being his teacher. And it wouldn't be right to deny me brother this chance, now would it? Fancy our Jeff, eh? The first of the Jenkses to get the chance not to land up in the corset factory. Mam!' she called again as she stepped on to the cobbled pavement. 'Yer'll have to excuse me, Miss Bundy, I'm late. Always late I am. Still, never mind, if 'e doesn't wait for me then 'e ain't worth it, is 'e? Tarra,' she called, heading off down the street.

A small woman came bustling down the dark passage. She was wiping her hands on a stained floral wraparound apron. 'Oh, I am sorry, Miss Bundy,' she murmured apologetically as she arrived on the doorstep. 'I din't expect yer 'til about nine. Yer note did say you couldn't mek it before 'cos yer'd school things ter see to. Oh!' she said, taken aback. 'You ain't Miss Bundy.'

Maddie nervously cleared her throat. 'No, I'm not. I'm . . . Mrs Jenks, my name is Maddie Ashman. I've come to see you . . . come to ask you . . .'

As she was speaking Sadie Jenks's face turned white then red as her caller's identity registered. 'You!' she spat. 'You ain't got n'ote to ask of me. How dare yer? How dare yer stand like a brazen hussy on my doorstep after all you've done? Clear off, yer 'ear me? Clear off. And I ain't a violent woman but if you ever show yer face round 'ere again there'll be n'ote left of it, time I've finished.' She stepped back and grabbed the door, aiming to slam it.

'Please, Mrs Jenks, please listen to me,' Maddie pleaded, placing one hand on the door to stop it from shutting. 'It's not what you think.'

The door was pushed open again, hitting the passage wall. 'Not what I think? I don't 'ave ter think – I *know*. You ruined my son's life you did, wi' what you done. Scarpered, din't yer, without a word, wi' 'is child in yer belly? But yer

80

couldn't tell 'im yerself. Oh, no. Sent 'er down. She stood on my doorstep just like you are now. Told me 'ow you wanted n'ote more to do wi' my Josh after 'im forcing 'imself on yer like that and that the baby wa' gonna be adopted. That baby wa' our first grandchild, our own flesh and blood. But never a thought wa' given to our feelings, wa' there? My son,' she cried furiously, stabbing herself in her ample chest, 'wouldn't force 'imself on anybody, let alone the likes of you.

'I told 'er to fetch the coppers and we'd sort it out proper. Oh, she backed off then, din't she? 'Cos she wa' bloody lying about that and she knew I knew she wa'. I sent her scarpering then, I can tell yer. I weren't 'aving the likes of 'er standing on my doorstep telling me a pack of lies. I remember 'er when she had no shoes on 'er feet and 'oles in her knickers. I've better in my 'ouse than what 'er own mother sold in that shop and that's saying summat. She ain't got no right to try and mek me feel my son ain't good enough for 'er daughter. She should remember where she came from, she should.'

Without pausing for breath she continued, 'It broke my Josh's heart when I told 'im. Cried like I've never seen a man cry. Before I could stop 'im 'e rushed round to see yer mam, plead wi' 'er to tell 'im where you were so 'e could 'ear the truth of it from yer own lips. But would she? Would she 'ell tell 'im? She said to 'im you were frightened of 'im and had had to go away. And then she had the nerve ter say that 'e only struck up wi' you ter better 'imself. Who the 'ell does she think she is? My son wouldn't take up wi' bloody royalty itsel' just to do that. We Jenkses might not 'ave much but we do 'ave our pride.

Sadie's eyes blazed furiously. 'Anyway, missy, 'ow come if 'e forced 'imself on yer, he was thinking yer were getting married? Asked me and 'is dad if yer could both live 'ere for a while 'til yer got a place of yer own, 'e did. Answer me that, eh?' Without waiting for a reply she stabbed Maddie angrily in the chest with her finger. 'No, yer can't, can yer? Because yer *ad* promised ter marry 'im. My Josh is not a liar. Not like you. Told yer mam that cock and bull when yer found you were expecting, did yer, to cover up what you'd done? Well, madam, yer needn't think yer can come round 'ere now for whatever it is yer want. I won't 'ave it. Yer've caused enough trouble in my 'ouse, you'll cause no more.

'My Josh is 'appy where 'e is. It took 'im long enough to get over you. I ain't 'aving it raked up again just for you to upset 'im.' Sadie puffed up her chest. 'For your information 'e don't live round 'ere no more and 'e's happily married wi' a kiddy on the way. And yer needn't think of writing any more letters 'cos they'll go the same way the others did. Unopened on the fire. It's my opinion he had a lucky escape, just like your father. I don't hold wi' men who walk out on their families but in yer dad's case I wanted to pat him on the back when I heard and congratulate him fer having the courage.

Maddie was gazing at her, stupefied. 'What do you mean?' she gasped. 'My father's dead. He didn't leave my mother.'

Sadie Jenks gave a loud bellow. 'Is that what she told yer? Dead indeed! He's no more dead than my old man and your mam's no more a widow than I am. The last I heard of yer dad he was very much alive and living in Leicester, still working for Amicable Refuge Insurance. Now, I've said all I'm gonna say to you and that were far more than I ever intended should I clap eyes on yer. So clear off.'

'What's goin' on, Sadie? What's all the shouting about?' a male voice called from inside.

'N'ote, Albert. Just a woman got the wrong 'ouse.' She glared at Maddie warningly. 'But I've put her straight. Told 'er where to go.' She leaned forward and pushed an open-mouthed Maddie hard in the chest again. 'Now, I said, clear off.'

With that she stepped back inside and slammed the door.

Maddie stood rooted to the spot, eyes wild, mouth still

open and mind running riot. Of all that she had expected to hear, this was the very last thing. She shut her eyes tightly. She had what she'd come for, hadn't she? She had heard the truth, no matter how shocking. But above all the words 'he's happily married with a kiddy on the way.'

Her Josh, the man she still loved more than life itself, now loved someone else and that someone was having his baby. It should have been Maddie having her second by now if her mother had not interfered. And then to learn that her father was not dead but very much alive and living in Leicester . . .

The pain building within her had only just begun to manifest itself but already it was unbearable.

It was then that Maddie knew she hated her mother. All these years she had suffered Harriet's harsh, unfeeling ways, her own continual fight to appease her, and then to find that Harriet had done all this to her for reasons she could not begin to fathom.

'No more, Mother,' Maddie uttered with conviction. 'No more.'

Filled with a rage so intense that she shook, she made for home.

There was no hesitating outside the door to gather her courage this time. On arriving, she almost wrenched the handle off in her haste to get inside.

Harriet was making herself a drink when the door burst open and Maddie charged in. The unexpected commotion made her drop the cup she was holding and she spun round to see what was happening.

'What the . . .' she cried.

Spotting her, Maddie stopped abruptly, eyes blazing, fists clenched. 'Why, Mother?' she erupted. 'Why?' Unable to control her fury she leaped at Harriet, grabbing her shoulders and shaking her hard, far too incensed to be shocked by her own uncharacteristic violence. 'Why? Tell me why?'

Placing both hands on Maddie's shoulders, with all her

strength Harriet pushed her away, glaring at her in a mixture of outrage and bewilderment. Maddie stumbled against the stone sink.

'What on earth has got into you?' Harriet demanded, straightening her rumpled blouse. 'How dare you manhandle me in such a way? Have you been drinking?'

'No, I have not,' Maddie cried, righting herself. 'You didn't think I'd find out, did you? But I have. I know it all now. Every last despicable detail. What have I ever done to you for you to treat me this way? Answer me! Tell me. Try and make me understand.'

Harriet's mouth was opening and closing as a terrible fear began to dawn on her. 'I don't know what you're talking about.'

'Yes, you do. My father! He's not dead, is he? Why did you lie to me?'

'He *is* dead,' Harriet snarled. 'To me he died the day he walked out on us.'

'But I had a right to know he was still alive. I . . .'

'Right?' her mother hissed. 'That man fathered you and nothing more. Where he's concerned you have no rights. I'm the one who raised you, your loyalties lie with me. So far as I'm concerned he's dead and I'll have no further mention of him, is that understood? Now go to your room.'

'No, I haven't finished yet, Mother. You sent Josh away. You did, didn't you? Admit it. You told the most terrible lies to him and his mother. You . . .'

'Against my orders you've been to see that man's mother?' Harriet erupted.

'Yes.'

Face purple with rage she slapped Maddie hard across the face. 'How dare you disobey me? Go to your room,' Harriet repeated.

Gasping for breath, Maddie clasped one hand to her smarting cheek. For several seconds, while she fought to regain her senses, the silence that engulfed the room was deafening. Then Maddie said firmly, 'I will not go to my room. I'm not a child, Mother. I'm an adult with a mind of my own and I wish to be treated as such. I'm not going anywhere until you give me some answers. I want to know why you've gone to such lengths to keep me tied to this house. You've done everything you can to stop me from having an outside life. You took my baby from me, got rid of the man I loved and who loved me back. You even got Gilbert Frisby the sack for daring to ask me out to the music hall. I want to know why. It's not as if you love me, Mother, is it? You've never said a kind word to me. In fact, I don't think you can stand the sight of me. So why have you gone to such trouble to keep me here?'

Open-mouthed, Harriet stared at her for a moment then her whole face contorted darkly. 'I have nothing to answer for.'

Maddie stared back, dumbfounded. 'Nothing, Mother? Nothing at all?'

'Nothing.'

Maddie stared at her for several long moments. 'Then I have my answer,' she said softly.

Calmly she turned and headed out of the room.

Upstairs in her bedroom she unearthed the canvas bag, the same one that had held her clothes for the journey to and from Mrs Baldicott's the year before, and pulling open the drawers of her tallboy, filled the bag with her clothes and personal belongings. Then she opened the tin containing her meagre savings, tipping the contents into her purse. Putting on her coat, she closed the bag, picked it up, and without a backward glance headed down the stairs.

Harriet, having swept up the smashed cup, was filling the kettle. She was shocked to see Maddie dressed for outdoors, eyed the bag then lifted her brows questioningly. 'Where do you think you're going?'

Hand on the back doorknob, Maddie turned to look at her. She paused, suddenly realising she hadn't given that a thought, just knowing she could not stay in this house with her mother a moment longer.

As Maddie looked back at her for the last time she realised that even hatred for her had gone. She felt nothing for the woman before her. But then, how could she be expected to? Harriet obviously didn't consider her worthy of so much as an explanation for her own dreadful misdeeds.

Maddie took a deep breath. 'I've no idea,' she said matter-of-factly. 'But I've nothing to stay for here so wherever I end up it has to be better.'

'Where you end up! You're leaving?' Harriet said incredulously.

'Yes, Mother, I am.' Maddie could hardly believe her own calmness.

Harriet smirked. 'You'll be back. You're incapable of fending for yourself. You'll soon realise what I did was just to protect you.'

'Protect me? From what, Mother?'

'Yourself,' came the harsh reply.

Maddie's face hardened. 'Oh, yes, Mother. Because I'm plain and easy prey for all those men out there who see me as a way to better themselves. Well, maybe I am plain, I have no choice but to believe that because you've constantly told me so, but you've never done me the courtesy of letting me make my own mistakes either. Allowed me to trust in my own judgement.' Her eyes narrowed and she stared at Harriet hard. 'I don't believe you've done all this just to protect me. This is to do with you, Mother. I don't know why, though, and as you're obviously not going to tell me then I'll never know, will I?'

The second brutal slap that Maddie received on her cheek sent her reeling back to slam against the wall. Hand on cheek, she froze momentarily. She had never before seen her mother in such a temper, such bitterness emanating from those icy grey eyes. She shuddered as old fears rose within her and for a fleeting moment an automatic instinct to appease her mother began to take hold. Then the words the old barge lady had spoken echoed in her mind. 'Face things. Nothing will begin for you until you do.' And she had faced up to things, had got to the hurtful truth. If she backed down now, even long enough to formulate some plans, she ran a grave risk of allowing her mother to regain control and then she would never get away. To run her own life, she had to strike out on her own. That would never happen while she stayed under this roof. It was now or never.

Righting herself, and with all the force she could muster, she retrieved the bag from Harriet's grasp, spun around and walked out of the door.

She had reached the park, put the heavy bag to one side of a bench and sat down before she dared allow her thoughts to dwell on just what she had done.

Maddie stared around her. It was growing dark and apart from a few people out walking their dogs, the park was deserted. Soon the gates would be shutting. She couldn't stay here.

She suddenly felt so alone. She had no idea where to go, no one she knew well enough from whom to seek sanctuary. Tears pricked her eyes as the enormity of her situation filled her. 'Oh, God,' she uttered. 'What am I going to do?'

She jumped as she felt a hand touch her shoulder. 'You all right, miss?'

Her head jerked up. 'Oh, yes,' she gulped to the park attendant who despite his kindly question appeared to Maddie to loom menacingly over her.

'Only I'm about to lock the gates.'

'Oh, yes, of course.' She rose hurriedly and retrieved her bag.

By the iron railings outside the park gate, she put down her bag again and stared around. She needed somewhere to rest for the night, somewhere she could gather her thoughts and make some sort of plan. Despite the lateness of the evening she supposed she could try and get a room in a lodging house. But its being such a small town, it was all so close to home and the thought of bumping into her mother, whom she couldn't be sure hadn't come out in search of her, terrified Maddie witless.

That question again. Where would she go?

She stood for several moments, deep in thought. Then the answer was revealed. She wasn't quite on her own, was she? There was one person she could turn to now, despite believing for the past twenty or so years that he was dead. In her hour of desperate need she had no alternative but to seek out her father.

Chapter Six

Maddie woke with a start as, brakes applied, the early-morning train hissed and chugged on its approach to Leicester station, clouds of steam and white smoke billowing. She stifled a yawn, put her hands on her hips and stretched her aching back. She had just spent a most uncomfortable night on a hard wooden bench in a dark corner of the deserted, chilly waiting room of Market Harborough railway station. It had been somewhere to hide from her mother and, her finances being as they were, she'd felt it unwise to spend money on lodgings for the night.

Her racing thoughts had not allowed her to sleep until an hour before dawn, then she had slept so deeply that not even the comings and goings of the milk then mail trains, the loading and offloading of freight which had included cages of squealing piglets and squawking fowl off to various markets around the shires, had woken her.

The Station Master had, though, and Maddie had been mortally embarrassed. Now she was embarrassed again, having fallen asleep on the hard seat, the side of her head bumping rhythmically against the window of a third-class carriage. Her confusion this time was caused by a shabby young man sitting opposite, staring at her. Ignoring him, she turned her head to look out of the window.

They had just travelled under a soot-blackened iron bridge, then a canal. Now the view consisted of the backs of grimy rundown red brick terraces, well-worn washing on lines, barefoot grubby children sitting on crumbling back walls, waving at the train as it passed. The young man opposite waved back, which Maddie thought to be a kind gesture. They passed several factories, tall chimneys oozing black smoke, then a coal yard. On the embankment bordering the yard, Maddie caught sight of several women and children armed with sacks scouring the bank for lumps of coal that had tumbled from the heaps above, constantly on the lookout in case they should be spotted.

'Poor sods, I 'ope they don't get caught like I did once,' the young man said absently.

Maddie turned her attention to him. 'I beg your pardon?'

He pointed out of the window. 'I thought that kinda thing only 'appened in Ket'rin'. Thought the folks that lived 'ere 'ud be able to afford the coal man callin'.'

'Is that where you come from?' Maddie asked politely.

'Kettering. That's a few miles from Market Harborough where I li— used to live.'

He eyed her keenly. 'They're all rich there too, ain't they, in 'Arborough?' He ran his eyes over her. 'But you don't look rich,' he said bluntly. He didn't wait for a reply but continued, 'I'm gonna be rich one day. I've finished me 'prenticeship. Me mam worked her backside off to get me a trade but they didn't keep me on, the bastards! So I'm off to Leicester. Loads more factories in Leicester. I spent nearly all I've got on me train ticket so I 'ope I get set on quick. I'm gonna 'ave ter find cheap lodgings 'til me money starts rolling in but that should be easy enough 'cos I ain't gonna be fussy, then I'll get a place of me own and send for me mam and brothers. I'll keep 'em all, I will. Then me mam won't 'ave ter scrub floors no more or take in washing. She can rest, purra feet up while I tek care of 'er.'

As the young man relayed visions of his prosperous future, pity for him rose within Maddie. She had a terrible suspicion that very shortly he was going to have his dreams cruelly dashed but could not bring herself to comment. Far better he found out in his own way than from a stranger on a train.

She smiled at him. 'I bet your mother's very proud of you?'

'Oh, she is. Since me dad scarpered wi' that trollop from the factory I've bin 'ead of the 'ouse. Wouldn't 'ave managed wi'out me, wouldn't me mam. She cried buckets when I left. But I told 'er, she won't be crying when she sees the 'ouse I'm gonna get 'er or the balance in me bank book. A year, maybe two, I reckon it'll tek me. 'Cause in the meantime I'm gonna send 'er money each week.'

What plans this young man had, which Maddie did sincerely hope would come to fruition, but it was her guess that inside six months he'd be heading back on the train, wiser but no richer. But she hoped he was right about his job prospects because she needed to get a job herself and as quickly as he did. The only difference between them being that she only expected to earn a basic living. Becoming rich, if you were not born it, happened only to a chosen few.

''Ere we are,' he cried, jumping up. 'Wanna 'and wi' yer bag to the platform?'

'Yes, please,' Maddie replied gratefully.

After he had deposited her bag, she held out her hand to shake his. 'Thank you,' she said. 'And I wish you all the best.'

'Ta very much, but I won't need it.'

He touched his threadbare cloth cap and headed off.

Heaving her bag along, Maddie followed with the rest of the throng.

The tea was weak, leaves floating in it, and was only lukewarm; the bread, which could not be classed as the toast she'd asked for as it had hardly seen the inside of the grill, was dry whatever it was spread with – she had asked for butter, which this definitely was not. But Maddie was ravenous and at least what she had eaten had gone some way to stop her stomach from rumbling. She dare not order anything else on offer, mindful she had no idea how far her savings had to stretch.

As she had emerged from the station the hustle and bustle of the city hit her full force and immediately a dreadful fear of the unknown filled her. She suddenly felt so lost and alone. Market Harborough had been the town of her birth, the sights, sounds and smells of it familiar, and although her mother had seen to it she had no friends there, she had at least known people to pass the time of day with. She had no such luxury here.

Maddie had spotted the café just after leaving the station, its shabby exterior and what lay within not registering, and had hurried towards it, feeling an overwhelming need to sit for a while and gather her thoughts.

Staring down into her empty tea cup, frightening thoughts had flooded in. What if she couldn't find her father? And if she did, what if he demanded to know what had caused her to leave Market Harborough to seek him out? How could she explain to a man whom she had thought dead until hours ago all that had transpired, expect him to understand and show sympathy towards her? What if he turned her away in disgust? If only she knew what his character was and the reasons for his abandonment of herself and Harriet. Being armed with just a little knowledge would have helped her prepare her approach to him. But she had none and couldn't envisage what was going to happen.

Her worries mounted at the thought of being unable to secure work or anywhere to live. What would she do if she found she had no choice but to return to her mother? Oh, God, her mind screamed. That was one thing she *couldn't* do. After all that had transpired, whatever happened to her, whatever she was reduced to, that was one thing she couldn't do. Determination filled her then. She had come this far, there was no going back. She would have to face her father, then, whatever the consequences.

The lanky young waitress hovering nearby approached

her as she pushed away her empty plate. 'Can I get yer 'ote else, Madam?'

Distracted, Maddie raised her head. 'Pardon? Oh, just the bill, please. Oh, and maybe you can help me. Can you point me in the direction of the Amicable Refuge Insurance Company offices, please?'

The waitress stared vacantly. 'The what?' Grimacing she shook her head. 'Never heard of 'em,' she muttered as she wrote out Maddie's bill on a pad hanging by a chain from the belt around her waist. 'Me mam uses the Widows and Orphans for her funeral. Tenpence a week she pays to Reg Nunn who calls.' She tore off a copy of the bill and handed it to Maddie. ''Ope everythin' was all right for yer, madam.' The practised phrase was spoken insincerely. Without waiting for a reply she turned and was immediately summoned by the customers on the next table.

Reaching inside her handbag for her purse, Maddie glanced at the total due on the bill and her eyes widened in shock. A shilling for a cup of insipid tea and slice of thin dry toast! It was daylight robbery. Not that it had been a regular occurrence for her to visit a café but she did know that the bill was twice as much as it would have been in Market Harborough. She hoped everything else in Leicester wasn't as expensive. She remembered the young man on the train. Maybe her prophecy of six months' survival in this city should be cut to three.

She hurriedly slipped out of the café without leaving a tip. In her precarious financial state she felt she could not afford to be that generous.

Back on the main street, the bag containing her worldly belongings seeming to get heavier with each step she took, she headed off again in the direction of the town centre, feeling that was the best place to begin her search.

Under any other circumstances Maddie, whose solitary walks along the canal tow path had been the furthest she had ventured out of the small market town of her birth, would have taken the time to stroll along and savour the sights of this new and exciting place. She would have stopped to admire the fine Victorian redbrick buildings housing banks, hotels and the numerous businesses operating in this thriving city, and then, as she drew nearer the town centre, weaving her way through the crowds, taken time for a leisurely look in the windows of the shops selling everything the residents of the city and surrounding villages could ever want to buy. Even the amount of traffic, the trams and buses, horse-drawn drays and cabs and motor-powered trucks and automobiles congesting the road she was walking down, would have had her gazing in awe.

But she had no time for any of that at the moment.

On her way she stopped several people to ask for directions but their responses were all the same: a shrug of the shoulders and a shake of the head before hurrying on their way. Maddie began to wonder if the natives did not take kindly to strangers, even those from only twenty miles away.

She was at a crossroads now, where Granby Street ended and Gallowtree Gate began. The shops were dense hereabouts and she guessed this was about the centre of town. Spanning one corner of the crossroads was a large branch of Woolworth's, and across the road, through a wide gap between the buildings, she saw the entrance to the market place. It looked to be a large market from the part she could see, far bigger than the small Wednesday and Friday one held in Market Harborough where local farmers sold their produce. Opposite was a bank and across from that a building society. She glanced down Gallowtree Gate and looming in the distance could see the Clock Tower, the famous Leicester landmark. The hands on one of the four faces read twenty minutes past twelve. Time was marching on and she had nowhere to sleep tonight. Surely her father's place of business must be in the vicinity somewhere? Someone must be acquainted with it. She rubbed her cheek worriedly.

'Excuse me?'

Maddie jumped, spinning around to find a man of about her own age emerging from the gents' outfitters behind her.

'I've been watching you. You seem to be lost. Can I help at all?'

Her previous fear that the people of this city did not take kindly to newcomers was dispelled. 'Oh, I do hope you can,' said Maddie hopefully. She told him the name of the place her father worked. 'I haven't a clue where to begin to look so I'd be grateful for any help you can give me.'

'I can tell you exactly where that is. I used to work for a company next door until I got fed up with office work and decided to try my hand at selling. It's a few streets away but if you follow my directions you should find it easily enough.' He proceeded to explain to her. 'Now have you got that? Go back up this road, and turn left into Rutland Street. When you cross Charles Street you'll see the police station opposite. Go down it until you come to Queens Street. The Amicable is halfway down. You can't miss it.' He smiled. 'Leicester might not be the size of some cities in England but unless you're born and bred here, like me, it can be confusing to a visitor.'

'Yes, I'm beginning to realise that. Thank you so much for your help.'

Before responding he admired for a moment the tired-looking, plainly dressed but very pretty young woman before him. 'It was my pleasure, and if ever you get lost again, don't hesitate to come here and ask me for directions. I'd be only too happy to oblige.'

The suggestive tone of his voice made Maddie blush. 'I will,' she said, hurriedly making her departure.

His directions were very precise and ten minutes later she turned into Queens Street. The long street, other roads intermittently branching off it, contained an assortment of buildings, some, she deduced by their crumbling appearance, dating back maybe two hundred years. The one she was seeking was halfway down, of newer construction than the others. It was a narrow four-storey building which seemed to have been squashed in as an afterthought between two others housing coal and wine merchants. She checked the brass plate on the front of the building. AMICABLE REFUGE INSURANCE COMPANY, Established 1827. The company her father worked for was ninety-nine years old.

Heart pounding painfully, she took a very deep breath, steeling herself for what faced her, climbed the worn stone steps leading up to the imposing door and entered,

The narrow reception hall was panelled in dark oak the floor stone-flagged. Several doors off it, which were shut, led she presumed into offices. Halfway down the passage rose a steep narrow staircase. What lay beyond it was impossible to make out. From somewhere inside the building she could hear the muted rhythmical clacking of a typewriter. Apart from that indication of a human presence the place seemed deserted. She stared around, unsure what to do. Then she saw a door marked WAITING ROOM and thought this must be where visitors were supposed to go until someone came to attend to them. She made her way towards it.

The room, like the entrance hall, was dimly lit, the same oak panelling lining its walls, the only furniture five straight-backed chairs placed in a row, nothing covering the heavily varnished wooden floor. A huge round clock ticked loudly on one wall. It was a minute to one. Placing her cumbersome bag to the side of the chair at the end of the row, Maddie sat down and waited. And waited. The clock ticked slowly on. It now read ten minutes to two. Fifty minutes had passed and seemed to Maddie like so many hours.

Outside, Maddie heard people coming and going. A man entered the room and sat down. He didn't appear to notice her presence, but instead was preoccupied with a letter in his hand. A male face poked around the door and a pair of squinting eyes focused on the seated man who rose and left the room. Maddie frowned, it should have been her turn to be fetched as she had arrived first.

Then, too maiden-looking ladies came in and, moments later, the same male head poked around the door. 'Misses Jones, this way, please.' The women rose and departed.

'Just a minute,' called Maddie, but she was too late. The man had gone. Next time he appears I'll make sure I catch his attention, Maddie inwardly fumed, angry that she was being so blatantly ignored.

The room was stuffy and she found it increasingly difficult to stop her eyelids from closing.

The next thing she knew someone was shaking her arm.

'Oi, come on, wake up! Yer can't sleep 'ere.'

She woke with a start, staring straight into a grotesque face just inches from her own. Maddie yelled in shock. 'Where am I?'

The face receded as the body it belonged to straightened up. 'Why, yer 'ere, that's where yer are.'

'Here? Where . . . Oh!' she exclaimed as it all came back. Her eyes flew to the clock which now read twenty minutes past six then back to the shabby woman standing before her. She was old, very old, judging by the deeply lined skin covering her face which was heavily pitted with blackheads, especially on her nose. Her sparse, snow white hair was scraped up into a thin knot on the top of her head. She stooped due to a hump on her back. In one hand she was holding a scrubbing brush.

Another woman, equally as old, shuffled through the door. 'What's goin' on, Myrtle?'

'We've a trespasser,' she cackled gleefully. 'Better get the bobbies.'

Maddie jumped up, all traces of sleep flying from her. 'No, I'm no trespasser. I was waiting to see Mr Ashman. Only . . . well, I waited in here and no one came. I must have fallen asleep.

97

'Did yer report to the office?' Ethel asked.

Maddie shook her head. 'No. I didn't know I had to.'

Myrtle eyed her scornfully. 'If yer didn't announce yer presence, 'ow d'yer expect anyone ter fetch yer?' She gave a gleeful cackle. 'Mr Dibble, the Clerk, wouldn't 'ave spotted yer huddled in the corner, 'im being so short sighted. I've heard it said he won't wear spectacles 'cos he's afraid the young ladies won't take a fancy to him. Vain bugger, he is. I wouldn't mind, but he's as ugly as sin, so specs or not he's no chance wi' the ladies.' She chuckled again and so did Ethel.

Myrtle eventually composed herself and eyed Maddie sternly. 'Mr Ashman's gone 'ome. Said goodnight ter me a few minutes ago. They've all gone 'ome,' she announced. 'Yer'll 'ave ter come back termorra. We're ter lock up, see, once we've finished the cleaning. It's our responsibility, ain't it, Effel?'

'It is,' she agreed proudly. 'Responsible we are.'

Maddie's mind raced frantically. She had to see her father tonight. She had nowhere to sleep. 'But I need to see Mr Ashman tonight! It's really important. I need to find out where he lives. Do you know by any chance?'

'Can't tell private things like that to strangers. Anyway we don't know.'

'I do,' piped up Ethel.

Myrtle turned on her. 'Yer do? 'Ow?'

She just shrugged her shoulders. 'Yer don't work somewhere fer thirty years and not find out things.'

'Oh, pokin' around, was yer? You'll get shot one of these days, wi' yer pokin' and pryin'. By the way, did yer ever find out . . . Oh, never mind that now.' Myrtle turned back to address Maddie. 'You could be anyone. Yer'll 'ave ter wait 'til termorra.'

'But I can't!' Maddie's shoulders sagged despondently at the thought of trying to find lodgings for the night in this alien city then beginning this process all over again. Her whole sorry situation crowded in on her and before she could stop herself she burst into tears.

Both women stared at her.

Chores forgotten, Myrtle took charge. "'Ere, come on, me duck, sit yerself down,' she ordered, grabbing Maddie's arm. 'N'ote's that bad it's worth bawlin' over. Effel, go and mek the gel a cuppa. And mek sure yer tidy away just as yer found things. Don't want them knowin' we mash up. Be 'ell to pay. Oh, and Mr Partridge keeps 'alf a bottle of whisky behind the black box on the third shelf of 'is bookcase. Put a tot in the tea.' She addressed Maddie. 'Medicinal, me duck.'

"'Ow d'yer know about the whisky?' asked Ethel.

'Same as you know where Mr Ashman lives. Now 'urry up afore this gel keels over.'

Ethel scuttled away.

'Now what's so important yer need ter see Mr Ashman ternight?' Myrtle asked, settling her aged bones on the chair next to Maddie, beady eyes glinting keenly.

Maddie reached inside the pocket of her coat and pulled out a handkerchief. She dabbed her eyes then blew her nose noisily. 'He's my father. I've travelled from Market Harborough to see him. Surprise him,' she added, feeling some sort of explanation was needed but not wanting to go into further details at present. 'Only I've mislaid his address.'

'Oh, well, why didn't yer say yer wa' 'is daughter? Oh, lovely man is Mr Ashman. Always teks the trouble to speak ter me an' Effel. Not like the rest. Stuck up they are. Ah 'ere's Effel now wi' the tea. Did yer find the bottle?'

'I did,' she replied, carrying the china cup carefully as she shuffled in, the large holey slippers on her feet flapping. One of her knitted stockings had slipped down and was bunched around her ankles, just visible beneath her threadbare black twill skirt. 'I put a good dollop in.' And had herself another good dollop while she was at it, probably would again in the future now she knew where the bottle was hidden. But she wasn't about to divulge that. 'Drink this while it's 'ot,' she ordered, handing the cup to Maddie.

She accepted gratefully. The tea had grown tepid during the time it had taken Ethel to journey from the kitchen to the waiting room and Maddie gulped it down, shuddering as the sharpness of the alcohol hit the back of her throat. Regardless, she instantly felt better as its effects began to seep into her blood. She handed the cup back to Ethel. 'That was much appreciated, thank you.'

Ethel gave a toothless beam. 'My pleasure, me duck. Famous for me tea I am.'

'This is Mr Ashman's daughter,' announced Myrtle. 'She's 'ere on a surprise visit all the way from Markit 'arbor and can't remember the address.'

Ethel scowled thoughtfully. 'Daughter, eh?' She scratched her neck worriedly. 'Yer did say daughter?'

'Fer God's sake, Effel, yer deaf or summat? Just give the gel the address. She needs to get on 'er way and we need to finish what we're paid fer.' Myrtle turned to Maddie, looking worried. 'Yer won't tell no one where yer got the address from, will yer, me duck? Only we'd get the sack.'

Maddie patted her arm reassuringly. 'Don't worry, I won't.'

Standing at the front door the two aged women watched Maddie, armed with directions, make her way down the street.

'Summat fishy goin' on,' muttered Ethel as they made their way back inside.

'Wadda yer mean?'

Ethel grimaced as she grasped hold of the broom she had propped against the door earlier and began to sweep the floor. 'She ain't 'is daughter. I've seen Mr Ashman wi' 'is daughter and that ain't 'er. 'Is daughter's younger for a start and 'er hair's fairish. That woman's much darker. I saw 'em, see, shopping in the market just before last Christmas.'

Down on her knees now, Myrtle dipped a scrubbing brush into a pail of water and began scrubbing the floor. 'Well, yer must be mistaken. Yer know what yer eyesight's like. I keep telling yer to get down to the Sally Army and get yerself some specs.'

'N'ote wrong wi me 'earing, though. The gel that was wi' 'im called 'im Dad. Anyway, when he saw me he said 'ello, introduced me to 'er. Said, "Ruth, this is Mrs Crump what does for us at the office." Now who but Mr Ashman would acknowledge the likes of us, eh?'

Myrtle paused thoughtfully for a moment, then looked up at Ethel knowingly. 'Well, yer daft 'a'porth, maybe 'e's *two* daughters. Never thought of that, did yer, eh?'

Ethel pursed her lips. 'Maybe 'e has. One living in Collins Court and the other in Markit 'arbor. Fishy, don't yer reckon?'

'Oh! Mmmm. Well . . . if she ain't his daughter, who d'yer reckon she wa' then?' Myrtle muttered worriedly. 'Fancy piece, d'yer reckon? And she seemed such a decent type.' Her lips tightened, eyes narrowed. 'Mind you, yer can't tell these days. No, yer can't. Teks all sorts, dunnit? Oh, I'm all intrigued now and we'll never find out 'cos it's not like we can ask Mr Ashman if she's 'is fancy piece, now can we?'

Ethel laughed, a dry cackling sound. 'Not likely!'

Myrtle grimaced as a worrying thought suddenly struck her. 'Listen, Effel. A' yer listenin'?'

'I said, there's n'ote wrong wi' me 'earin'.'

'Good, 'cos if 'ote should come of this, best say we've never seen that woman before, all right?'

'Whatever yer say, Myrtle. You seem ter think you're the boss.'

She frowned crossly. 'What were that?'

Ethel started brushing vigorously. 'N'ote, Myrtle, it were n'ote.'

Chapter Seven

The small shabby courtyard had been hard to find and surprising to come across, seeming oddly out of place amongst the maze of back-to-back streets surrounding it. Maddie had got off the tram halfway down the Uppingham Road as the two old ladies had directed, then walked down several terraced streets, the last one up and down several times before she had found the narrow cobbled jitty that led to Collins Court. It was growing dark, the gas lamps yet to be lit, and although children were evident in the main streets, the courtyard was deserted.

The paintwork of all the surrounding houses was an identical dull brown, peeling in places, and the guttering on several roofs was loose in parts, but regardless Maddie could tell by the white nets at the windows and the clean steps that the residents of these houses looked after their homes as best they could.

Her father lodged in number 10, so Ethel had told her, and Maddie hoped the old lady's poking and prying had elicited the correct information.

She stood before number 10 and stared at it. What had happened in the last twenty-four hours and brought Maddie to this door had left her exhausted, mentally and physically. Should this address be wrong, or should she not be welcome here, offered help to begin her new life . . .

Shutting her eyes, she said a silent prayer then raised the metal knocker, letting it fall with a thud against the door.

After what seemed an eternity she heard the soft sound

of approaching footsteps and the door opened to reveal a pleasant-faced, middle-aged woman of medium height, her light brown hair parted down the middle and arranged in coils around her ears. Her clothes, a plain wraparound apron covering a dark skirt and white high-necked blouse, although far from new were clean and pressed. She radiated warmth and Maddie immediately took to her.

'Hello.' The woman's tone of voice was not refined but neither was it coarse. 'Can I help you?'

From inside the house Maddie could hear the sounds of people talking, laughing, the clattering of cutlery and china. Instantly she knew this to be a happy home and her hopes of being made welcome here soared.

'I do apologise for calling at this time,' she began. 'You're obviously in the middle of your meal . . .'

'That's all right, my dear, this door is always being knocked on for one thing or another,' the woman interrupted, smiling to put Maddie at ease.

Sarah scanned her eyes quickly over the woman on her doorstep. She looked worn out, ready to drop, the weight of the world pressing down on her slim shoulders. She was too old to be a friend of Sarah's daughter, though. She wondered what was in the large bulky bag by the caller's feet and frowned as a strange sensation washed over her. It was most peculiar but the young woman seemed familiar somehow though Sarah couldn't place what it was that would give her that feeling. She mentally shook herself. She was tired, had had a long day and the light must be playing tricks.

'What can I do for you?' she asked.

Maddie's reply made Sarah's blood run cold.

'I'm looking for my father, Mr Ashman. I've been told he lodges here.' Maddie watched with rapidly growing horror as the woman's face drained of colour. She had clasped her hands and was wringing them. Maddie frowned, bewildered. What on earth had she said to cause such a reaction? All she'd done was enquire after her father.

'Does he live here?' she asked tentatively.

Sarah stared at her blankly and Maddie repeated her question.

'Oh . . .' she gulped. 'Er . . . yes, yes. Mr Ashman lives here.'

Maddie sighed, relieved. 'Oh, I thought for a moment I'd got the wrong address. If it's not convenient I could call back?' It was the last thing she felt like doing, having to wile away an hour or so in strange streets, but she felt she must at least offer, having called, at such an inconvenient time.

Sarah's thoughts were racing frantically. Never had she envisaged this dreadful situation. Not given it the least consideration or prepared herself for it. What on earth was she to do now?

'Mam,' a voice called. 'Dad sez hurry up, your dinner's getting cold.'

Sarah turned her head. 'I'm . . . I'm just coming.' She looked back at Maddie. There was nothing she could do, this situation was beyond her control and had to be faced. There was no time for warnings. Taking a deep breath, she stood aside. 'Please, Maddie, come in.'

Leaving her heavy bag just inside the doorway, she followed her father's landlady down the dimly lit passageway. Despite her rapidly increasing apprehension of what lay in store, it did strike Maddie that the woman had addressed her by name, and the name she preferred at that. Her father had obviously spoken of her to his landlady which must be a good sign. But the question of how he had known her name, considering he had left when she was not much more than a toddler and hadn't started to call herself it then, also occurred to her.

Before she could think about it further they had arrived.

As they entered the room Maddie was instantly enveloped by a highly charged atmosphere of warmth and family unity. A well-stacked fire was burning in the grate of the black leaded range which practically filled the wall opposite and the dark oak furniture was lovingly cared for. Embroidered cloths on the back of the two worn but comfortable-looking fireside chairs to either side of the range, several cheerful prints and fluted glass bowls, plus various articles and personal bits and pieces left lying around by the room's occupants, enhanced its air of homeliness.

Maddie became aware of three people sitting around a table in the centre of the room: a good-looking young man of about eighteen, a very pretty girl a year or so older, and a middle-aged man at the head, all chattering as they ate their meal. The man was of medium height, thick-set, the strip of greying hair framing his balding pate trimmed neatly, features pleasant. He wore a pair of metal-framed glasses on his short nose. From Maddie's instant appraisal he looked a kindly sort. This was obviously the woman's family. Her own father must be in his room, thought Maddie.

'George,' Sarah addressed the man, and there was a tone in her voice that made his head jerk up. 'George dear, you have someone to see you.'

Maddie fixed her eyes on the man, thinking it a coincidence that her father also was called George.

Mouth curving in an automatic smile of welcome, he turned his attention to the visitor and as he did so the smile faded, the clatter of his knife and fork hitting his plate resounding loudly in the still room. Maddie frowned at him, bewildered, wondering why her presence had had such an effect but before she had time to think further the pretty young woman blurted out worriedly, 'What's the matter, Dad?'

'George,' Sarah urged. 'Why don't you take Maddie into the parlour? You need privacy to talk.'

Maddie flashed a bewildered glance at Sarah. There was something going on that she didn't quite understand.

'Yes, my dear, you're right,' he replied, rising.

As he came towards Maddie foreboding rose within her

and she wanted to pick up her bag and flee, but was unable to.

He was at her side now, smiling reassuringly, but his eyes were those of a deeply troubled man.

'Come, Maddie,' he urged, cupping her elbow.

Totally dumbfounded, she allowed him to guide her out of the room.

In the corridor she stopped and turned to him. 'Has something dreadful happened to my father? Is he dead? Is that what you have to tell me?' she whispered.

He shook his head, eyes filling with tenderness. 'Your father is very much alive, my dear,' he replied, voice thick with emotion. 'You're looking at him, in fact. I'm your father.'

Her shock was immediately apparent and George tightened his hold on her arm. 'Come through to the parlour, Maddie dear, we need to talk.'

Those left behind in the back room sat in silence for several long moments after George and Maddie had departed. It was the young man who spoke first. 'Mam, who was that woman?'

'Yeah, Mam,' echoed the girl. 'Who . . . ?' Then a possibility struck her and her hazel eyes widened excitedly. 'Mam, is that . . . is she . . . ?'

Sarah raised her hand. 'Not now, Ruth. Not now.' Sighing deeply, she shut her eyes, acutely aware that her own children needed to be spoken to as well. But at this moment all her thoughts and feelings were with the two people who had just left the room.

Standing with his back to the empty fireplace, George Ashman shifted nervously from foot to foot, acutely aware of Maddie's unblinking eyes fixed upon him. She was standing against the horsehair sofa, both hands clutching one arm for support, waiting for him to begin his explanations. But he didn't know how to. 'I'm . . . er . . . afraid it's a bit chilly in here,' he babbled uncomfortably.

'We don't use this room much. Hardly at all really.' His voice trailed off as he became conscious he was using unnecessary small talk as a stalling tactic.

A feeling of helplessness washed through him. Standing so near was the person whose very existence was the reason for this whole dreadful mess, a person he'd striven hard to protect, to the detriment of others yet no blame could be attached to her for their suffering. You couldn't blame anyone for the fact they'd been born.

At this moment she looked so lost, so vulnerable, far younger than her twenty-six years. A sudden great rush of deep love for her filled him. He fought a compulsion to rush across to her, crush her to him and beg her forgiveness for the pain he knew he was about to cause her. But he couldn't do that, he had no idea how she would react.

There were many questions he wanted to ask Maddie too, but all that would have to wait until a story had been told.

He realised she was speaking, her voice so low it was barely audible. 'Pardon?' he said.

She cleared her throat. 'They . . . they called you Father. Are you their father?'

He gnawed his bottom lip anxiously for what seemed an age. 'Yes, Maddie,' he answered finally, face grave, his low voice filled with emotion. 'Yes, I am. Please, sit down and let me explain. It's a long story. I knew one day it would have to be told, but not in these circumstances.'

He watched in concern as she sank down on the sofa, clutching the front of her coat as if for comfort.

'Are you cold, Maddie? I'll light the fire.'

'No, no,' she uttered. 'I'm just . . . just . . .'

'I know, my dear,' he interrupted. 'You must be very confused.'

She looked at him for a moment and suddenly her bottom lip started to quiver as tears pricked her eyes. 'You said I'm your daughter?'

'And you are. You're as much a part of me as Ruth and Roy.'

'So you divorced my mother? She just said she was a widow to cover that up?'

He looked astounded. 'Widow!' he exclaimed. 'Your mother told people that?' His eyes filled with horror as a terrible thought dawned on him. 'Maddie, did she tell you I was dead?'

She nodded. 'I thought so until I found out by accident yesterday that you weren't.'

'Oh, my God,' he groaned. 'How could she?' His eyes filled with tears. 'Maddie, have you never received the gifts I've sent you each birthday and at Christmas? Or any of my letters?'

She shook her head. 'I've received nothing. As I said, I thought you were dead.'

'Has Harriet told you anything about me at all?'

'No,' she uttered. 'She wouldn't speak of you.'

He sighed long and loud. 'Now I know why you've never contacted me. I always wondered . . .' His voice trailed off and he eyed her searchingly. 'I've watched you grow, Maddie. Several times a year I've travelled to Market Harborough and hidden, waiting until I could catch a glimpse of you. Sometimes it was for hours but as long as I saw you I didn't mind. As you grew older it became harder to see you but I made discreet enquiries to find out if you were faring all right. Times – oh, so many times,' he whispered sadly, 'I've wanted to approach you but knew it best not to. I knew, you see, that should your mother find out we'd had any contact, you'd incur her displeasure.'

Maddie was staring at him dumbstruck, these revelations the last she'd been expecting to hear. 'I wish you had though, Father,' she whispered.

He smiled sadly. 'So do I.'

She frowned at him, bewildered. 'If my mother is still your wife then that woman . . . Sarah . . .'

He squeezed her hands tightly. 'Maddie, please let me explain it all to you. Allow me to do that first, then you can ask anything you like and I'll answer as best I can. I have to warn you, though, it's not a pleasant story. It will be painful for both of us.'

A tap sounded on the door and Sarah entered carrying a tea tray which she put down on an occasional table to one side of George. She smiled hesitantly at Maddie. 'I've made you a sandwich for now. I hope cheese is all right for you?'

The last thing Maddie felt like was eating but she managed to say thank you.

Sarah glanced worriedly at George. 'If you need me . . .'

He smiled wanly. 'Thank you, my dear, I'll call if I do.'

She hovered uncertainly. 'Right, I'll leave you to it then,' she said, walking out of the door which she shut behind her.

Several moments of tense silence passed while George poured the tea and handed a cup and the plate of sandwiches to Maddie. He eased himself back on the sofa. The time had come, he could stall no more. He smiled weakly at his daughter before taking a deep breath and forcing his thoughts back over the years to when he was a young man of twenty-two and the fateful day it all began.

110

Chapter Eight

'The first time I met your mother was one bitterly cold night when I was desperate for lodgings. It was my first visit to Market Harborough and I didn't know the town. I'd just been promoted and given my own area, covering the south of Leicestershire. Other agents in the firm weren't happy, felt I was too young and inexperienced for such responsibility, wouldn't have been sorry to see me fall flat on my face. In truth, they wanted the round for themselves.'

He paused thoughtfully for a moment. 'I've started at the wrong place, Maddie. I should tell you about myself first. Maybe then you'll understand things . . .' he sighed '. . . a little better. I was raised by an elderly great-aunt and uncle who welcomed me to their home after my parents died of cholera after it swept through the village of my birth, killing half the population. That was 1878. A terrible year. Many children were orphaned and parents left childless. I don't remember it. I was only two. They were a grand couple, Robert and Laura Hubble, with no children of their own. This . . .' he tapped the side of his foot, '. . . I was born with. A club foot. It stopped me doing many things. I couldn't play football or run very well. My biggest regret was that I couldn't fight in the war.' He shook his head sadly. 'All I could do was help the police as a voluntary night patrol man and a fire helper. Anyway not many people would have taken in a child with my deformity, family or not, but they did, bless them, and never made me feel any different from anyone else. Aunt Laura said it made me special.

'My aunt and uncle didn't have much themselves, actually they were quite poor, but they gave me a lot of love, Maddie.' He exhaled slowly. 'I wish you could have known them. You would have liked them and they would have loved you. I still miss them very much.' He looked at her, smiling distantly. 'I've always thought you have a look of your Great-great-aunt Laura about you. I have a photograph of both of them somewhere. I'll look it out and you can judge for yourself.

'I was quite a shy boy, liked to read and fish – the usual boy stuff. I had a friend named Nobby Clarke and we were usually to be found together.' He grinned. 'The tales I could tell you about some of the things we got up to! Just boyish fun, you understand, Maddie, nothing more than that. I helped Aunt Laura as much as I could around the house or by running errands for her.

'Uncle Robert worked for the Amicable Refuge, spent his entire life selling and collecting weekly payments for penny policies, winter and summer, whatever the weather. The old widow ladies loved him. Nine times out of ten he'd end up fetching their shopping or helping to get the washing in. In the school holidays I used to accompany him on his rounds and some evenings if I'd done my chores. That helped with my shyness. Those customers of his, especially the old ladies, didn't hold with shyness. If they asked a question they expected an answer.' He smiled. 'It did me good, helped bring me out of myself.

'That's the reason I grew up wanting to be an insurance man. I couldn't see myself doing anything else. By the time I left school at fourteen, Uncle Robert had retired, he was over seventy and his health not so good, but out of respect for him his old firm took me on as a clerk. Glorified tea boy was more like it to start with but I loved the work. I listened and learned and when I was eighteen I was put with a master of his trade.' George smiled at the memory. 'Archie Crabtree. What a character he was! Wouldn't have anything to do with

112

penny policies, was into larger deals for companies and the well-to-do, and what he didn't know about the business wasn't worth knowing. He taught me well.

'I knew Archie was the main instigator of my promotion. Really stuck his neck out to persuade the bosses to give me the chance. I couldn't let him down. Didn't want to let myself down either. Chances like that didn't come along very often and certainly not at the age I was. I was determined to do well. That's what took me to Market Harborough late that night. Armed with no more than a list of old established customers and some possibles to try, I thought it best to start as I meant to go on. So instead of catching the train in the early morning to begin my round, I caught the last one the night before to get an early start.

'It was pitch dark when I arrived, it had just begun to snow and the town was deserted – not the best time to be looking for a place to stay. I nearly missed the Vacancy sign when I passed by the haberdasher's shop. It wasn't the usual kind of establishment offering a bed for the night. I can't honestly say I took a fancy to the place but I was relieved when I was told a room was available.'

George paused for a moment, realising that the story he was relating was going to be painful enough for Maddie to absorb and very aware it concerned her mother, therefore some details, although pertinent to himself, he felt it best to miss out. So he did not mention that on stepping into the house he was immediately transported to a place straight from Dickens. The rooms had the minimum of furniture and the whole place was icy cold, the small fire burning in the grate of the main room doing nothing to raise the temperature. No fuel lamps evident, just tallow candles, although when he did agree to take the room a lamp was produced with only enough oil for an hour or so's use.

Harriet's welcome to him, a paying customer, was sparingly given, as if she was doing him a great service by just letting him into her house, which wasn't done without

113

searching questions being asked or until satisfactory credentials had been produced.

He also felt it best not to tell Maddie that his first impression of Harriet Grimble had not been favourable either. He had found not one endearing quality about her at all, from the severe style of dress covering her thin shapeless frame to her abrupt, cold manner.

'In the morning as I was leaving,' he continued, 'Harriet offered me a cheaper rate should I take the room for the rest of my stay. I accepted.' He missed out the fact that he had deliberated deeply before agreeing, finding the lure of a more comfortable abode and cheery landlady difficult to fight against. 'It seemed sensible at the time as every penny counted.' Those saved pennies, he thought, had cost him dearly in more ways than one.

'I left the Friday morning and to be truthful never expected to see Harriet again as I'd been told of another place I could stay when I was next in the town which . . .' he chose his words carefully '. . . sounded like it would suit me better.'

He stopped his narrative for a moment and eyed Maddie in concern. 'You're shivering. It'll only take me a moment to light the fire,' he said, attempting to rise.

'No, I'm fine, really I am,' she insisted, the chilliness of the room the last thing on her mind. 'Please, go on.'

George settled back again to take up the story.

'As I was saying, I never expected to see Harriet again and it came as a surprise to be told a few weeks later that she had written to the office and had asked for me to call personally on her and discuss her insurance needs. I never thought of anything other than possible new business.

'I wrote and arranged to call on her the following week when next I was in Harborough. A Wednesday night.' His lips tightened. 'I remember that night well,' he said coldly. How could he ever forget the night that had led to the sealing of his fate. 'I was quite taken aback when she opened the door. The change in her was marked. For a moment I thought I had the wrong house. Her hair had been styled, she wore a very nice blue velvet dress, old-fashioned but it suited her, and rouge.' And as he had done so many times in the past, he wondered how he could have been so naïve as not to have suspected what was in Harriet's mind.

'There was a large fire burning in the grate and a bottle of sherry and glasses on a small table by her chair. I've never been a drinker but felt obliged to have a glass. Being on the road can be lonely and it was nice to pass an hour or so in company, albeit on business too.' He leaned forward and clasped his hands. 'Harriet was talkative and very attentive and I have to admit the time passed very pleasantly. I was surprised to find that several hours had gone by when I came to take my leave. I arranged to call again as soon as I had the information she had asked for.

'It took several calls over a period of weeks before she instructed me to go ahead and have the documentation prepared.' He omitted to tell Maddie that it did strike him at the time that although her queries were very plausible, Harriet purposely delayed matters to keep him having to call. Despite her obvious efforts, Harriet held no appeal for him in any form but that of client and her attempts to charm, including the girlish giggle that constantly shrilled out, did nothing but grate on him. Nevertheless, to be truthful, he couldn't deny that although he gave her absolutely no encouragement, her blatant attentions towards him did much to bolster his ego.

'Each visit I was made comfortable before the fire with a glass of sherry, Harriet listening attentively to everything I had to say. When I arrived with the policies for her to sign I was taken aback to find she had a meal waiting, and whisky instead of sherry. She said it was the least she could do considering all the trouble she had put me to in organising her affairs. I had already eaten, but I couldn't hurt her feelings. The meal was very palatable and I found I had a taste for whisky . . .' His voice trailed off and he lowered his head. 'I realised how much when I woke the next morning.'

Her father was just staring at her and Maddie frowned back, confused, then the truth hit her. 'Oh!' she exclaimed, reddening. 'I see,' she muttered, averting her eyes in embarrassment.

No, you don't, Maddie, George thought ruefully. You automatically think that, plied with drink, I seduced Harriet that night. But that was not how it was at all. His mouth set in a grim line as he remembered just what had taken place.

It was still dark, he guessed it to be the early hours of the morning, when he had woken totally befuddled, to find Harriet slipping between the sheets beside him. She was naked.

The closest he had ever come to a naked woman before was a hurried glance at the black and white postcards of nudes the men at work slyly passed around. To be in such close proximity to one obviously very willing, and himself unaccustomedly mellowed with whisky, was too much for will power or common sense.

He cleared his throat uncomfortably before continuing. 'I make no excuses, Maddie. What happened, shouldn't have. I left before Harriet woke the next morning. I suppose I was too ashamed to face her.' He paused for a moment while he took a drink of tea. 'About two months later I got a summons to call upon her. I automatically assumed it was a matter of business.' He kept to himself that he would have done anything not to have made that visit, not particularly wanting to see Harriet again. But as he was the sole representative for Amicable Refuge in that area he had no choice.

'She welcomed me in, sat me down and we chatted for several minutes about . . .' he shrugged his shoulders '. . . the weather, this and that.' He paused, lips tightening grimly. 'Then she told me the real reason she had requested I call. It had nothing to do with insurance.'

116

He stopped abruptly and, shoulders slumping, ran a hand over his chin. What he had to tell Maddie next could not be prettied up to save her feelings. He hoped he had managed successfully to withhold the full extent of Harriet's guilt, letting Maddie assume the blame lay with him. But regardless of where blame lay, just how did you tell your daughter that a good measure of whisky was solely responsible for her existence?

Lowering his head, he took a deep breath but before he could say a word Maddie whispered. 'Mother was pregnant, wasn't she? With me.'

He stared at her for several long moments, then nodded. 'Yes.'

Maddie's whole being felt numb as she fought to comprehend just what her father was telling her. As realisation took hold her heart began to thump, its beat growing faster until it battered so painfully she thought it to be trying to break out of her chest.

No, she wanted to scream, please tell me this isn't true! After all she had learned in the last twenty-four hours, some of which she was still having difficulty trying to understand, let alone come to terms with, this news was just too terrible to take on board.

So that was why her mother had been so cold towards her! Her birth had been a dreadful mistake. A great burden of responsibility weighed her down. There were so many questions still unanswered, so much explaining still left undone, but at this moment Maddie was too distressed even to think further than the pain she had been the cause of. An overwhelming urge to get as far away as she could from the man who had accidentally fathered her filled her.

She leaped up from her seat. 'I'm so sorry,' she blurted out. 'Truly I am. However can you ever forgive me?'

The compulsion to leave grew and, spinning on her heel, Maddie fled from the house.

Hearing the commotion of doors opening and banging,

Sarah appeared in the parlour doorway. The haunted look on George's face sent fear racing through her. She rushed over to him and laid a hand on his arm. 'George dear, what's happened? Where's Maddie gone?'

'I couldn't stop her, Sarah. It's all gone wrong. She . . . Oh, God, from what she said . . .'

'What did she say?'

'She apologised. Asked my forgiveness. Oh, Sarah, I never got a chance to finish what I had to tell her. I only got as far as Harriet's summons to me on finding herself expecting. Maddie has got it into her head that it's all her fault.'

Sarah sighed heavily. 'That poor girl, she must be in a terrible state. And we still don't know what brought her to us in the first place, do we? Come on, we must find her. She can't have got far. Ruth and Roy will help.'

Chapter Nine

Maddie had not known which way to turn when she bolted from the house. Not that the direction mattered to her. Getting away from somewhere she was obviously not wanted had. Her lungs were at bursting point, legs like lead, when the road she had run down ended at an iron gate. She had arrived at the side entrance to a small park. Panting heavily, she stared through the railings into the green area beyond. The tranquil scene spread before her, beckoning her in along with the empty wooden bench she could see beneath the branches of a huge oak. It offered sanctuary while she gathered her scattered thoughts. Maddie pushed open the gate and hurried through.

Sometime later night was rapidly falling, a half moon now visible and several stars twinkling in a cloudless sky. A chilly wind was rising, rustling eerily in the leaf-laden branches above. Maddie shivered, hugging her coat closer around her. A woman, fur collar turned up on her smart coat, heels clicking on the asphalt path, arrived abreast of her, a brown and tan cocker spaniel pulling on its lead. The dog stopped and sniffed at Maddie's leg. Stiffening, she watched it warily.

Seeming not to notice how uncomfortable her dog's actions were making Maddie, the woman smiled brightly. 'Good evening,' she said.

Maddie stared vacantly at her, finding it hard to give a reply. To her, there was nothing good about this evening whatsoever.

Indignant at receiving no reply, the woman give the lead a tug. 'Come along, Mimi, there's a good doggie.' Dragging the spaniel behind her, she went on her way.

To her cosy home, Maddie assumed. The dog to its warm basket.

At the vision she had created, she groped for her handbag. The small amount of money it contained was all that stood between her and the workhouse. She suddenly realised she had left behind the bag and all her worldly possessions. She couldn't go back for it. Knowing now what she did, she couldn't face her father again.

With that thought, the misery she was struggling to contain suddenly became too much for her. Tears danced precariously on her bottom lids and fell. She succumbed then as her whole sorry situation crowded in on her. Burying her face in her hands, rocking backwards and forwards, Maddie wept.

It was Sarah who eventually found her.

It was almost dark, too dark to be out aimlessly searching, but none of them would give up, the thought of Maddie in a distressed state and unfamiliar territory urging them on. George was beside himself and Sarah knew he would not rest until he had found his daughter and she was safe.

Reluctantly she was making her way home, having covered every conceivable nook and cranny she could think of. She'd almost dismissed the park as she had passed by the gates; it was delightful in the daytime but dark and eerie at this time of night and the thought of venturing inside on her own unnerved her. She presumed Maddie would feel likewise. It would be locked up anyway at this time of night unless the attendant had forgotten, which he had been known to.

Regardless, she stopped and looked through the railings. From what she could see it did look deserted but automatically she tried the gate. It swung open. Sarah shook her head. It was a wonder the attendant wasn't dismissed for his neglect.

She stepped tentatively inside, wishing George or one of her children was with her, and nearly turned back before a vision of Maddie lost and alone forced her on.

She had walked a short distance down a path skirting dense shrubbery when muffled sobs reached her ears. Sarah stopped and listened. Peering through the gloom, she could just make out a huddled figure on the bench beneath the oak and hurried over, praying that it was Maddie. It was. Sarah was so relieved to have found her she ran the final few steps and threw herself down beside her, placing a hand on her arm.

'There you are! You've had us all so worried.'

Lost in her own misery, Maddie had not heard Sarah's approach. She jumped up and shrieked in fright.

'It's all right, my dear,' Sarah reassured her. 'I didn't mean to frighten you. I'm just so glad to find you. Well, not knowing the area, you could have landed up anywhere, couldn't you now?'

Maddie stared at her. She hadn't expected anyone to bother to come looking for her and the relieved expression on the kindly woman's face surprised her. But Sarah's finding her in such a state horrified her and Maddie hurriedly turned her head, pretending she was removing something from her eye. When she turned back her tears had been wiped away and there was a forced smile on her face.

None of Maddie's attempts at a cover up escaped Sarah's notice. That smile did not hide the devastation in her eyes. Sarah's heart went out to her. She wanted to throw her arms around Maddie for comfort, try to allay her fears. But she might not take kindly to such an action, Sarah reminded herself. After all, George's daughter hadn't known of Sarah's existence until a couple of hours ago. She must be careful how she handled this situation. It was imperative that she got Maddie to return home with her and hear the rest of her father's story. She decided it would be best to pretend nothing was amiss and hope her ruse worked.

'I expect the fresh air did you good,' she said breezily, rising to her feet. 'But we'd best get off. The others will have returned by now. Given up, I expect.'

Bewildered Maddie looked at her. 'Given up?'

'Looking for you. We've all been out. We were all worried about you, especially your father. Still you're found now and that's the main thing.'

'Oh!' Maddie exclaimed, mortified. 'I'm sorry to have caused you so much bother.'

'It was no bother,' Sarah replied. In a friendly fashion she took Maddie's arm. 'Let's get out of here. I like this park in the daytime but at night it gives me the creeps. Strange how places look so very different in the dark.' She attempted to steer Maddie back down the path. 'I expect you could do with a cuppa. I know I could. And a hot meal. I hope you like faggots?'

Maddie pulled her arm free. 'Mrs . . . er . . . Look, I'm grateful to you all for bothering to come looking for me, really I am. But . . . I can't come back with you.'

Sarah had half expected this reaction but still managed to appear taken aback. 'You can't? Whyever not?'

'Because . . .' Maddie's bottom lip trembled. 'Because I've caused enough trouble. Now I really must be going.' Where to she had no idea but she had to let Sarah think that she had.

She made to walk away but Sarah caught her arm. 'Just a minute, Maddie. I don't understand what you mean by causing trouble?'

Maddie swallowed hard. 'Well, I have. I . . . I interrupted your meal. Inconsiderate of me to do that. I'll . . . er . . . call again at a more convenient time.' She thrust out her hand, then jerked it back. 'It was very nice to have met you. Goodbye,' she said brightly, raising her head as if she hadn't a care in the world and marching off.

Sarah rushed after her. 'We've finished our meal now, Maddie,' she said, walking beside her, 'so you're causing no trouble. And your father will be so upset if I don't take you back with me. Now come on,' she coaxed, again taking Maddie's arm. 'I'll not take no for an answer. While I get you something hot, you can finish your talk with George.' Sarah looked her straight in the eye. 'He has so much more he needs to explain to you.'

'No,' she erupted, stopping and pulling her arm free. Suddenly the reserves of energy she had summoned to try and convince Sarah all was well were all gone. Her whole body slumped. With head bowed, she started to shake. 'Please leave me alone, Mrs . . . Mrs . . . I . . . can't take anymore. I've ruined so many lives – yours too. Please, please, just go away.'

Horror filled Sarah's being. 'Maddie! Oh, Maddie dear, what makes you think you're responsible for anything?'

'Well, aren't I?' she uttered. To her horror, before she could stop herself she started to cry. 'I was a mistake,' she choked out. 'I should never have been born. How can I face my father again knowing that it's my fault he's . . . that he's . . . a bigamist?'

'A bigamist?' Mortified, Sarah could not control her own emotions any longer. She threw her arms around the distraught young woman, pulling her close. Maddie, having nothing left within her, rested her head on Sarah's shoulder, gently sobbing. 'Oh, my dear, dear girl,' she whispered. 'You have it all wrong. Your father is no bigamist. Neither were you a mistake. Nothing of the sort. You were very much planned,' she said, an icy tone in her voice. 'Whatever went on, you were in no way to blame. Not in the least.'

Totally bewildered, Maddie drew back her head, looking her straight in the eye. 'I don't understand?'

Sarah sighed. 'No, I don't expect you do, my dear. This must all seem very confusing. You should return with me and let your father finish his story. You owe it to yourself to hear the truth.'

Maddie stared at her.

'You must,' Sarah reiterated.

Maddie nodded. 'All right.'

Relieved, Sarah guided her back.

Maddie and George were both seated once more in the parlour.

'All I can say, Maddie, is that I'm very, very sorry. I was trying to shield you. Spare your feelings. It didn't work, did it?' He rubbed one hand across the back of his neck. 'I'm finding this very difficult. To me you're still my little girl. I forget you're a grown woman of twenty-six now.'

'Yes, I am, Father. I do understand how hard this must be for you. It's hard for me too. But I'd appreciate your telling me everything exactly as it was.'

'You're right, then there'll be no more misunderstandings.' George took her hands and looked at her earnestly. 'I would just like to put your mind at rest about one thing and that is that your mother planned to have you. You were no accident, Maddie. I don't like showing her in such a bad light, but . . .'

'It's all right,' she interrupted. 'Things . . . certain things have happened of late that . . . well, let me just say I think I understand my mother now far better than I used to.'

He shot her a questioning glance. 'In what way, Maddie?'

'I really don't wish to say at the moment if you don't mind, Father.'

He nodded. 'As you wish. But if ever you do want to talk . . . Maddie, I've never been allowed to be a parent to you, but I am your father in every sense of the word. I want to do the best I can for you.'

She smiled wanly. 'Thank you.'

He settled back in his seat. 'Right, so where did I get to?'

'Mother summoned you to tell you she was expecting.'

'Yes.' His eyes glazed over. 'It was certainly a shock. The very last thing I was expecting to hear. Then came her ultimatum. I was too dumbfounded to answer her at first.'

'What was it?' Maddie asked in a whisper.

'That if I refused to do the honourable thing, she would go to my bosses and tell them how their employee had taken advantage of her. She would make sure I was sacked and left with no reputation. Finding other employment would be very difficult – impossible in the trade I was in.'

Maddie couldn't believe what she was hearing. It was like history repeating itself. Harriet had warned her father, but she had done the actual deed to poor, unsuspecting Gilbert Frisby just because he'd dared to ask her daughter out.

'I felt the fear of God on me then. I didn't love your mother, Maddie. I had no feelings in that way for her whatsoever. Well, I hadn't really got to know her well enough for feelings like that to come about. I wanted to run away, emigrate, anything to get out of marrying her. The thought of losing the job I enjoyed so much didn't matter much then. I'd dig ditches, wash dishes if I had to. But once I had time to think about it, I knew I had to do as she said or I'd suffer the guilt for the rest of my life. My uncle and aunt had always taught me to face up to my responsibilities. I had a responsibility to my unborn child. To you, Maddie. My conscience wouldn't let me walk away. Accident or no, you were part of me. So for that reason only, I married Harriet.'

This confession shocked Maddie greatly. 'You did it for me?' she gasped.

'Yes.' He patted her hand. 'And in that respect I have no regrets. At first it was a very difficult time for me. Having come from people who showed they cared for me deeply, living with a woman with a nature like Harriet's was hard. Despite the money I gave her, and not forgetting what she was making in the shop which was something she never discussed with me, she made it very clear the business was hers alone. The house was always cold, even in summer, and the food she gave me hardly enough to feed a boy. Trying to talk to her about it was a waste of time. Whatever I said fell on deaf ears, and for a while after I dared voice my opinion she would create an atmosphere.'

She did not say a word but Maddie knew exactly what he meant.

George cleared his throat in embarrassment, wondering how best to word to his daughter the fact that Harriet had shunned any kind of physical advances. 'It . . . er . . . didn't take me long to realise that Harriet didn't want a husband in the . . . er . . . physical sense. After a while of trying all I could to make the marriage work, I decided it was best just to go along with her way of things. Call me weak but it made for a much easier life. I suppose I resigned myself.

'When we were first married I made a great effort to get home as often as I could, sometimes not getting there until very late in the evening and starting out the next day before the crack of dawn. But very quickly I found I was planning my appointments so that it was impossible for me to journey back daily. Your mother didn't seem put out by this at all. In fact, she seemed quite pleased, encouraged me even.

'When an area became vacant on the north side of Leicester I jumped at it, Maddie. It wasn't a good area. Mostly rural. Collecting penny policies from some of the company's poorest customers, that kind of thing. A come down from what I had been doing. I was delighted when I got it, although my boss couldn't understand why I wanted it so badly. Me, a newly married man with a baby on the way. How could I explain truthfully and expect him to understand that covering this area meant I would only have to put up with my wife at the weekends? He was happily married himself. But at least life was more tolerable for me then.'

George paused and smiled as a memory surfaced. 'It all seemed worth it when you were born. I can remember that day so clearly. I can honestly say, Maddie, that was the only thing that happened in my marriage to bring me any happiness. I asked Harriet if we could call you Laura after my aunt, but she wouldn't hear of it. She insisted you be named Maude. Where she got the name from I've no idea. To me it seemed such a harsh name for a pretty little thing like you.' He smiled tenderly at her. 'Your mother addressed you as Maude but I called you Maddie.'

Her mouth dropped open in surprise. She had always thought that to be her own idea.

George's voice lowered sadly. 'I soon realised I was expected to have little to do with your upbringing. Try as I might, your mother blocked me at every turn, to the extent that I was hardly allowed to touch you. It broke my heart. You were such a lovely child. Such a delight. You would lie in your cot gurgling quite contentedly. Harriet showed little interest in you. She did what she had to and nothing more. She never talked to you or played with you. She would let you cry for hours without picking you up. If I attempted to . . .'

He shook his head savagely, Harriet's harsh tones ringing in his ears. 'How's she supposed to learn discipline if you keep mollycoddling her?' 'But she's a baby, Harriet. Babies need affection. Teaching them right and wrong comes later, surely?' 'She gets affection,' his wife had hissed. 'Remember, you're not here most of the time. Babies fit in with adults, not the other way around.'

Sighing deeply he looked his daughter straight in the eye. 'And that's how life went on, you and I both doing exactly what Harriet wanted. You seemed happy enough, I can only hope that you were.' He leaned closer to her. 'I was miserable. For me life was just an empty existence.' His voice trailed off and Maddie noticed a spark of tenderness in his eyes as he whispered, 'Until I met Sarah.' He paused and looking at her intently. 'Is this all too painful for you?' he asked, deeply concerned. 'If you want me to stop, please say so?'

It was, very much so, but something she had to endure.

Having heard this much she wanted, needed to know the rest.

'Please go on,' Maddie urged.

'All right, if you're sure. Sarah transformed my life. We met by accident. We were both crossing a busy road, neither of us looking where we were going, and we collided. She dropped her bag of shopping and I helped to pick it up. I offered to escort her home. Maybe with hindsight I shouldn't have done, but I did, and I'm glad of it. Her widowed mother had passed away and she lived on her own in a small flat. "Flat" is exaggerating. Two shabby rooms it was with a shared toilet. It was all she could afford, her job as a shop assistant didn't pay much, but she had made it so homely. She invited me in for a cup of tea.' His voice lowered. 'I fell in love with her over that cup of tea as I was to find out very much later she did with me.

'Please be assured, right from the start I made no secret of the fact I was a married man with a child. I took my vows seriously and had no intention of breaking them. Sarah and I could never be more than friends, I felt. And for well over a year that's all we were. If I was in the area I would call in for a cup of tea and a chat. That's all it was, nothing more. And that's the way it would have continued if it had not been for me buying you that doll.'

'A doll?' Maddie frowned. 'I don't remember ever having a new doll. I had a rag doll I think someone made me.'

'You called it Rolly.' He smiled. 'You couldn't quite say dolly. It was made by your Aunt Laura not long before she passed away.'

'Was it? I didn't know that.' Fancy her father remembering the doll's name.

'Unfortunately she never got to see you. She was too ill by then to travel and your mother wouldn't accompany me or let me take you myself. She insisted you were too young to travel. But the doll I bought really did bring matters to a head. I'd seen it in Arbuthnot's shop window in the High

128

Street. It was a marvellous doll. It had eyes that closed when you laid it down, a frilly pink dress and hair styled in ringlets. I wanted you to have it. Two shillings and sixpence it was. Too expensive for me in one go. So I saved for it. Weeks it took me. I was always worried they'd sell it and so relieved when at last I had the money. That weekend I took it home. Couldn't wait to see your face.

'Your mother always made sure you were in bed before I arrived back. When she was busy elsewhere I'd sneak in and kiss you goodnight. I woke you then and gave you the doll. Oh, Maddie, I can still see your little face. You were so excited.' His own clouded over. 'Then your mother came in and threw a fit. Accused me of wasting good money on useless toys. She snatched it from you. You were not to be spoiled, were her words. The doll went on the back of the fire.' Maddie gasped, horrified. 'I . . . cannot tell you how outraged I was. That she could do such a thing. You didn't understand what was going on and were heartbroken to lose your new toy. Your mother scolded you for acting such a baby.' He shook his head ruefully. 'You were just coming up to three years old, Maddie.

'I had to get out of the house then, couldn't look at Harriet for fear I'd do something I gravely regretted. The next thing I knew I found myself back in Leicester, wandering the streets. All I could see was your heartbroken little face. I had to see Sarah. Go somewhere where I felt I was wanted. She knew something was seriously amiss as soon as she opened the door and I couldn't help but tell her what had happened. She just listened. Then, before I could stop myself it all came out, the whole story of how I'd landed up in this awful situation. I was so miserable, I cried. A grown man of twenty-five, crying like a baby. I felt utterly humiliated.'

He paused momentarily. 'It was then that Sarah kissed me. She leaned over, took my face in her hands and kissed me. Then she put her arms around me and held me tight. Can you imagine how I felt Maddie? The woman I was married to didn't show one iota of affection towards me and I had forgotten what it was like to be held by someone. I found it hard to believe a woman could want me. There was I, George Ashman, being told by this lovely woman that she loved me. I was deliriously happy.

'We talked all night and come morning it was decided I would approach Harriet and ask her to release me from our marriage.' He stopped and ran a despairing hand over his balding pate. 'It took a lot of courage for me to face her. She's not the easiest person to approach. And she laughed. Your mother actually laughed at me. She said I was a fool. Who in their right mind would want to take on me, a useless cripple? She said I should take a cold bath and come to my senses. And then she refused to discuss it any further.

'I don't know what came over me – if it was just that she had ridiculed the fact that someone could care for me, or her refusal to discuss something so important. But I was incensed. I'm sorry to say this to you, Maddie, but I think it was then that I realised I hated her. She had trapped me into marriage, used me for her own ends, and for that one terrible mistake I was going to have to pay dearly by being saddled with her for the rest of my life. If I hadn't met Sarah then that's more than likely what would have happened. But I had met her and things had changed and I couldn't carry on. I told Harriet that I was leaving anyway, divorce or not, and I was going to take you with me. And I meant it. I didn't want to leave you with her, knowing my daughter would be raised by such a cold-hearted woman.

'Stupid of me but I had thought, taking everything into consideration, that she would welcome the idea. At that time I was of the distinct impression she didn't want either of us. I was badly mistaken. She wasn't prepared to let either of us go.' His voice trailed off and he sighed, 'And that's when she told me, Maddie.' His eyes filled with pain. '"If you think," she said, "that I planned and carried out this whole charade for you to humiliate me with a divorce, then you're more stupid than I thought. I married you for life. I am Mrs George Ashman. My husband is a businessman. I have respectability in this town and that's the way it's going to stay."

'I couldn't believe what I was hearing. "You cold-bloodedly planned that night you fell pregnant with Maddie?" I asked her. She smiled. I can only describe her expression as evil. "Would you have married me otherwise?" she said. "You men are all the same. A pretty face, that's all you want. I was ostracised as a child because I was plain and it didn't change as I grew older. Marriage brings status, and I wanted a man to provide for me. I wasn't going to end up like my mother, scratting for every humiliating penny. People laughing behind her back because she made her living selling the rubbish they were glad enough to buy. Do you know how hard I worked to live that down after she died? Nobody knows what it was like for me. Nobody gave me a thought. I wasn't going to leave anything to chance. I wasn't going to go through life a spinster, and if you think I'm going to have the town sniggering behind my back again, people saying I couldn't keep my husband, then you can think again, George Ashman."

'Despite what she'd admitted to doing, Maddie, it wouldn't have been so bad if she'd made an effort to become some sort of wife to me. But she hadn't, and neither was she a proper caring mother towards you. It's no excuse and I don't feel proud but that's when I lost my temper and to this day I don't know how I held back from striking her. Thank goodness I didn't. I would never have lived with myself if I'd allowed myself to be reduced to that. But I told her in no uncertain terms that I was leaving and taking you with me and I would get a divorce and there was nothing she could do about it. Or so I thought. I should have guessed she had already planned what to do should such a situation come about.

'"Try to divorce me and I'll drag you and that floozy of

yours through the courts, and by the time I've finished neither of you will be able to hold your head up again. I shall tell them how you tricked your way into my home on the pretence of selling me insurance, forcing yourself on me to get me pregnant so I'd have to marry you and you could get your hands on my business. I shall say you've been carrying on with that woman all the time. As for Maude – take her and I'll have the police on you for kidnap. If you want your freedom it'll be on my terms or you won't get it."

"'And what are those?" I asked her. "Go and live with your whore," she said. "I don't want you here. The sight of you sickens me and I'll be glad to see the back of you. Making a good excuse for your absence will not be hard. You can write to Maude and send her a gift at Christmas, I'll see that she gets them. She can make her own mind up when she's older whether she chooses to see you or not. You'll continue to pay me my money every week, the amount to be reviewed annually, and the payments will not cease until Maude leaves home. We can make the necessary arrangements so we don't have to come into contact. I don't want you near Market Harborough ever again or to hear word that you have been. Break any of those rules and I will take the necessary action. I'll leave you to work out what revenge I will choose. Do you agree to those terms?"

'I had no choice but to agree and Harriet knew it. I had no idea she was going to play the part of a grieving widow, nor did I have any idea you never received my letters or presents. So many letters I wrote, Maddie, full of my love for you, begging you to reply to me and arrange for us to meet. I never gave up. I sent the last one only weeks ago.'

He sighed despairingly. 'Sarah couldn't believe what I told her. She couldn't believe anyone could be so callous and thought at first I was making it all up. I couldn't blame her. What sane woman would credit such a story? But I'm glad to say I finally managed to convince her. Both of us were devastated. We so wanted to be together as a married couple and that included having you with us.

'But the threat of Harriet's dragging us through court wasn't the reason we decided to go along with her wishes. You were, Maddie.'

'Me?' she uttered.

'Oh, yes. Your mother's no fool, Maddie. She knew how much I cared for you, knew I'd go to any lengths not to have you tainted in any way. I also knew Harriet meant every word she said. Everything was such a mess. It was all so awful. Sarah said she would stand by me whatever I decided. We both knew in the end that I had no choice but to agree to Harriet's terms. So that's what we did, living in the hope that as you grew older you'd decide for yourself to come and live with us and also that Harriet would tire of the situation and give me a divorce. Which never happened.'

Maddie's head bowed and she clasped her hands so tight her knuckles shone white. 'Oh, Father, you put up with this terrible situation all these years, just to protect me?'

George nodded. 'I love you, Maddie, it's as simple as that. I handed over the money to make sure you had a roof over your head and food on the table, and did not divorce Harriet so that you would not carry the stigma.'

Her eyes filled with tears, a lump formed in her throat. 'Oh, Father.'

'Sarah and I discussed what we would do. It was such a painful time, such far-reaching decisions to be made, and I can't say it's been easy for us, especially where Ruth and Roy are concerned. Due to Harriet's selfishness we have been denied the right to marry and forced to live a lie. Our children cannot bear my name. To all who know us in Leicester we are a married couple, and when the children were old enough to understand we explained to them.'

'They know?' said Maddie, aghast.

'Oh, yes. We've always been very honest, never kept anything back.'

'About me too?'

He nodded. 'Since the moment we told them, they have been desperate to meet their sister. Of course it wasn't possible. Sarah and I were very fortunate that they took it all so well. The fact that their parents are not married has never caused them problems. We knew there would come a time when it might. When they decided to marry and so forth, but we hoped that matters would have been settled by then.'

'I expect,' whispered Maddie, 'you were beginning to give up hope that I would ever leave home?'

'I suspect, Maddie,' he said, face clouding angrily, 'that your mother has made things very difficult for you there.'

He had touched a nerve and the tears already in her eyes flowed in answer.

George watched in increasing distress as his daughter wept. He did something he'd always wanted to do but which had been denied him. He threw his arms around her, pulling her close. 'Oh, Maddie, Maddie, I'm so sorry about all this. I hope you can forgive me?'

'It's not you who should be asking forgiveness,' she sobbed. Head bowed, she drew back from him. 'Father, please would you leave me for a while? I . . . would like to be on my own.'

He looked at her for several moments, unsure what to do. 'Yes, of course,' he said eventually, rising to his feet. 'I'll . . . er . . I'll just go and see about some more tea.'

Maddie heard the click of the door as it shut and her whole body sagged as all she had been told flashed through her mind. Now she saw it, and it was almost too awful to believe. But she had to believe it, she had no doubts whatsoever that her father had told her the truth.

She clenched her hands so tight her knuckles shone. So many lives Harriet had ruined! How could she have done it? How could she live with herself?

Maddie sat for an age, numb with shock, then unexpectedly a sudden feeling of intense relief flooded through her, an enormous weight lifting from her slim shoulders. Despite her uncertain future she was so glad she was away from her mother's clutches, that no longer could Harriet govern her life. She was free to make her own decisions and mistakes. But what was more important to Maddie was that her father could now seek his own freedom and marry the woman he loved. And their children, her half-brother and sister, would get their just entitlement.

And what of her own mother? Maddie pondered deeply and realised with shock that all she felt towards the woman who had given birth to her was a great sense of pity. Harriet would now have to live with the aftermath of her own callous actions. Maddie did not wish her ill, but felt if any punishment was due that would be enough. It was the one thing Harriet feared.

She heard the door open and raised her head to see Sarah poke hers around it, her face deeply concerned. She came in carrying a cup of tea. 'Your father is so upset, Maddie. He . . . we're both worried about how you are taking all this. Please forgive me for the intrusion but I just had to come and find out how you are.' Shutting the door she walked over, put the cup on the table and sat down beside Maddie.

She knew it wasn't just words, Sarah's whole persona radiated sincerity. Maddie warmed to her and managed a wan smile. 'With great difficulty. But I'll be fine once I've let it all sink in.'

Sarah hesitated at first then placed one hand gently on Maddie's. 'Your hearing it all was unavoidable, my dear. You could not have been expected to understand the situation between your father and me had you not been told the truth. Please don't think badly of him. He's a good man and loves you very much. You do know that, don't you?'

Head drooping, Maddie gulped hard to rid herself of the lump in her throat. 'I feel so cheated! I'm so angry that I've spent all these years thinking my father was dead just so my mother could hold on to what she saw as her respectability.'

Her shoulders sagged. 'All those lost years.'

'It's not too late, Maddie.'

She raised her head and looked at Sarah. 'Isn't it?'

'Of course it isn't.' She eyed Maddie hesitantly. 'I hope we can be friends too, although in fact I feel I know you already. Your father has always talked of you as though you were part of our family but didn't live with us, if you understand what I mean?'

Maddie stared in surprise. 'Did he? Really?'

'Oh, yes. So, you see, you're no stranger to us. I'm just happy finally to have met you in person. And he was right, you're very pretty. Ruth has a look of you.' Sarah paused and took a deep breath. 'This hasn't been nice for you or your father but I'm glad it's all finally come out. It's a relief.'

'Yes, it must be. And you must love him very much to have gone along with all this?'

'I do, Maddie. To watch him suffering in silence, year after year, with no end in sight hasn't been easy for me. There've been so many times I've wanted to confront your mother, make her tell you the truth about what was going on, let us get matters sorted once and for all. But I couldn't, it wouldn't have been fair to you. You were the innocent one in all this. Still, maybe we can now. But that's for George and you to decide.'

She paused for a moment. 'My dear, please forgive me for asking but George and I are both concerned over what brought you here. We are glad that you came,' she insisted, 'but we both can't help thinking that something . . . well, has something happened? To you? Or your mother?'

Maddie stared at her. She suddenly felt a great need to unburden herself to this kindly woman who until only hours ago she had not known existed. But she couldn't. She was still reeling, still trying to come to terms with her father's heart-rending story and she hadn't the energy. Besides, to explain fully she would be not only to add to Harriet's already hideous list of crimes but to reveal her own terrible secret. She wasn't ready for that.

Maddie clasped her hands. 'No, nothing's happened. After finding out my father was alive, I wanted to meet him and also felt it was time I left home. I hoped he would help me find somewhere to live and tell me where to start looking for a job, that's all.'

The forced lightness of her tone gave her away. But Sarah felt Maddie obviously had her reasons, and besides she had been through so much tonight that now wasn't the time to unburden herself further. Maddie would, she had no doubt, when she was good and ready. It still did not stop her from being dreadfully concerned about what the girl was hiding. Sarah gave a comforting smile. 'You've no need to look for anywhere to live. You have a home here with us.'

Maddie looked at her, startled. 'Oh, but I couldn't possibly impose.'

'Impose? My dear, you're George's daughter. This is your home too. I won't deny we'll be a bit squashed but we could make this room up for you, if you wouldn't mind sleeping on the sofa until we got you a bed? Between us we'll make it really cosy. We hardly use this room, and you'd be doing me a favour.'

'Would I? How?'

Sarah laughed. 'I've never liked this horsehair sofa. You'll give me an excuse to get rid of it.'

Maddie felt fresh tears stab the back of her eyes. The kindness of this woman!

Sarah sensed what was going through her mind and laid a reassuring hand on hers. 'We're your family, Maddie, and as such this is as much your home as it is Ruth's and Roy's. Now I know you have gone through a lot tonight and we'll all understand if you want to stay quietly in here. I'll bring a tray through and some bedding. But Ruth and Roy are desperate to meet you. Do you feel up to that first?'

Maddie gnawed her bottom lip anxiously. Ruth and Roy. They were her half-sister and brother, her own flesh and blood, the family she had always craved. Suddenly a sense of belonging overwhelmed her and her watery eyes brightened. 'Oh, yes, I'd like that very much.'

Sarah smiled in delight and took her hand. 'Come on then.'

Part Two

Part Zero

Chapter Ten

'I wish I knew what this meant.' Staring in confusion at the figures scrawled across the pages of the black leather-bound ledger, Agnes Clatteridge raised her head and looked at her younger sister in the hope she might receive some help. In her heart she knew she was wasting her time. Like Agnes, Alice Clatteridge hadn't a clue.

Closing the heavy ledger Agnes smoothed one hand absently over the fringed maroon chenille cloth covering the dark mahogany table. She sighed again as she glanced around the dimly lit room. Everything about it was dark – dark and dismal. Her sister and she matched the room. They were dressed as ever in dark colours. Always dark grey or black, occasionally brown so long as it was dark brown. Hairstyles severe, no jewellery, and absolutely no makeup whatsoever. In fact nothing frivolous about them at all. As per Father's instructions. And now they were in mourning for him they would have to wear black for at least six months longer as a sign of respect. Even in death he was still ruling their lives.

'Alice, you could show some interest. We have so much to learn. This funeral parlour will not run itself.'

Tutting, Alice let her embroidery drop in her lap.

'I know that. But if you haven't a clue how to interpret the books, then how do you expect me to?' She pursed her lips disdainfully. 'It's all Father's fault for leaving us so ill prepared.'

Agnes sighed sharply. 'I don't think he intended to die

just yet. I believe he had every intention of outliving us all.'
For an instant she felt guilty that neither of them was grieving
for the loss of their father. His sudden death had been a
shock but, if they were forced to be truthful, not entirely
unwelcome. An image of him came vividly to mind. His tall
thin frame looming before her, hawk-like, as if ready to
pounce on his prey; unblinking eyes glaring icily. She
shivered violently. As quickly as the guilt had materialised it
departed and her light grey eyes kindled. 'But I'm not sorry
he did, the old bugger! There was no love lost between us
and he made our lives a misery, one way or another. I'm
glad he's no longer around to do that. There, I've said it,'
she cried triumphantly.

Alice stared at her appalled. 'Oh, Agnes, he was very . . .
very . . .' She couldn't quite bring herself to speak as bluntly
as her sister, having a strong presentiment that, dead or
not, he would still somehow manage to show his disapproval.
A bolt of lightning directed straight at her, perhaps? Alice
shuddered. 'Well, I agree he was what you . . . er . . . said.
But actually to speak it aloud, Agnes, really! *And* you
blasphemed. You know Father couldn't abide bad language.'
Her eyes filled with fear. 'He'll come back and haunt
us.' Her face crumpled. 'You'll have to sleep in my room
tonight. Oh, Agnes!' she wailed.

'Stop it, Alice. Father's haunting us is the least of our
worries. Actually,' said Agnes flippantly, 'it might help if he
did, I've plenty of questions to ask him.' Her face grew grave.
'Our situation isn't what I expected it to be, and I can't
understand it. The business seemed to be doing all right,
and it's not as if Father was overly generous. In fact, you
know as well as I do we had to account for every penny he
grudgingly gave us, so why has he left us so badly off?'

Alice shrugged her shoulders. 'Do you think it could be
hidden somewhere? Father didn't have anything good to
say about banks. It could be under the floorboards or behind
a brick somewhere.'

Agnes sighed again. 'If Father has hidden anything it wouldn't be anywhere obvious. It could take forever to find it.'

'Mmmm, you're right. He was a . . .' Alice wanted to say 'devious old devil' but couldn't quite bring herself to. A sudden thought struck her. 'Perhaps Simpson might have an idea? He's worked for Father since a boy, knew his ways, might have seen him doing something suspicious. It could be worth asking.'

Agnes frowned thoughtfully, then shook her head. 'If Father was up to something like that, he wouldn't allow anyone to see him. He'd have had the curtains drawn tightly, the keyhole stuffed with paper and all the mantles turned low.'

Her sister nodded in agreement. 'But you could still ask.'

'I suppose I could. But how do I tackle a subject like that? Don't bother answering, it doesn't matter. He's an employee, Alice. You don't discuss family business with employees. But I suppose,' she added thoughtfully, 'the subject could be approached indirectly. I'm not quite sure how but that would be all right wouldn't it?' Her eyes suddenly flashed annoyance. 'Just a moment – what about *you* approaching him?'

'Oh, I couldn't,' Alice replied, aghast. 'You're the eldest, Agnes, you're in charge. Things like that are for you to do.'

'Alice, I'm not in charge, we're sisters. Whatever Father left is split between us, and whatever we do, we do as equals.'

'Huh! I expect if Father had realised he was going to die he'd have changed his will, left whatever he had to some good cause. He didn't like us, Agnes. Had no time for us at all. He made no bones about the fact he wanted sons.' Alice's voice lowered emotionally. 'How many times did he tell us we should have been sons for all the looks God had blessed us with?' Placing her embroidery on the arm of the worn leather armchair she rose, stepped across to the mantle over the fireplace and picked up a silver-framed photograph, looking with longing at the faded sepia image inside. 'Why couldn't we have taken after Mother, Agnes?' she asked wistfully. 'It's not fair we both took after him. Mother was so pretty, wasn't she? If she hadn't died having me . . . He never stopped blaming me for that.'

'Alice,' Agnes interrupted, 'let's not go over all this again. Not tonight, please. I have a headache.'

She eyed her sister. There was no missing the fact that they were related. Both were tall for women which only accentuated their slenderness. They had long faces, high foreheads, straight noses and spare lips. All inherited from their father along with wide hands and large feet – the very last features a woman would want to inherit. Had their father encouraged his daughters to dress fashionably or use a hint of colour on their lips, it still wouldn't have done much to disguise the fact that they were tall, thin and plain. There was absolutely no getting away from it.

At thirty-four years of age Agnes had resigned herself to spending her life as a spinster. Not so Alice. Despite reaching thirty-two years of age, with never a glimmer of romance, she permanently lived in hope that a man was out there somewhere who would want a wife for talents such as embroidery and cooking skills and not just as an adornment to his table. Agnes didn't blame her, and despite the fact that the terrible Great War had severely depleted the male population, thus greatly reducing her chances, wished with all her heart her sister's dream might one day come true. She loved Alice very much. But she was right: had their mother lived, their lives would have been so different.

Blanche Clatteridge had been a beautiful woman, small and petite, with a warm and humorous disposition. How she had come to marry dour, forbidding Cuthbert Clatteridge defied anyone's belief. They were so oddly matched. But according to those who knew them it was definitely a love match. Blanche had doted on her husband and he on her. The day before she died, it was said, was the last anyone saw Cuthbert Clatteridge summon a smile.

Agnes suddenly wondered what her father's face would have looked like smiling. His near white skin stretched taut over his bony face, the menacing arch of his great bushy eyebrows, his row of long tombstone-like teeth flashing . . . Despite the fact it was her father she was trying to picture, she shuddered at the horrifying vision she'd created.

Her thoughts were interrupted as she realised Alice was speaking. 'I'm sorry, Alice, what were you saying?'

'I asked just exactly what our financial situation was? You've told me it's not good, but you've not mentioned any figures.'

'Oh, er . . .' To divulge the exact sum was something she had been desperately trying to avoid. When she had very carefully broken the news to her sister of their precarious situation Agnes had been very generous with the truth. She had told Alice that their finances were not as good as she had hoped. The fact was they were extremely poor, bad enough to have rendered her speechless when the lawyer had told her. She hadn't expected to be told that they would only be able to keep both business and household going for four months at the most.

'You're trying to hide something,' Alice accused her. 'Just tell me, Agnes. I've a right to know.'

She scowled in annoyance. 'I did ask you several times to come with me to see the lawyer to hear Father's will. If you had, you wouldn't now be accusing me of doing something I'm not. If I'm guilty of anything it's not wanting to worry you.' Agnes paused for breath. 'If you really want to know the exact amount, Alice, after the estate has been settled we've four hundred and fifty-seven pounds ten shillings and fourpence three-farthing to our name. It's not a lot, I grant you, but . . .'

'Is that all?' Alice exclaimed, deeply shocked. 'I'll say it's not a lot! You were exaggerating when you said Father didn't leave us very well off. We've bills to pay, Agnes. He's left us not much better than paupers. What on earth are we going to do?'

'Hardly paupers, Alice. Paupers don't own property. The house and everything in it is ours plus the outbuildings, machinery and some stock.' She took a deep breath and forced a reassuring smile. 'Business will pick up, I'm sure. We only had our bereavement last week, people have probably kept away as a sign of respect, that's all. Father's by no means the first Clatteridge to die and the business didn't go under before.'

'I'm not so sure it will pick up. I think that now Father has gone, the business has gone too.'

Agnes gnawed her bottom lip worriedly. She wasn't certain whether to tell Alice but the lawyer had voiced a similar concern. Cuthbert Clatteridge had been the last male of the family and as such people might assume that the funeral business would end with him. At which Agnes had reminded the lawyer that he was forgetting there was herself and Alice, who were more than capable of keeping things running. The lawyer had rammed his pince-nez higher on his nose, picked up a sheaf of papers and shuffled them together, saying he hoped Agnes realised what she was taking on. Alice now voicing the same concerns was causing a niggle of doubt as to whether she actually did. Agnes forced the worry away and took a deep breath. 'Well, we'll just have to make sure people are in no doubt it's business as usual, won't we?'

Alice gasped in shock. 'You're not seriously thinking of trying to keep it going?'

'Why, of course. What else can we do? This business is our livelihood. It's been in the family for seventy years. We have an obligation to keep it going. And surely we have to consider our employees? I'm not so worried for Peabody.' She did not say she had never liked him, felt him to be sly and untrustworthy though she had never found anything to substantiate her suspicions. 'But Mr Simpson has worked for father for thirty years, since he was twelve years old. Surely we owe him . . .'

'So? He's not too old to get another job. And, besides, he was paid and received his living accommodation,' Alice cut in sharply. 'I don't see that we owe him anything more.'

'He doesn't get much according to the wages book. And as for his accommodation . . . A room over the stable is hardly a palace.'

'Even so, it's something other people wouldn't turn their noses up at.'

Agnes pressed her lips together, fighting her mounting annoyance at the way her sister was speaking so dismissively of Ivan Simpson. Alice may see him as just an employee but to Agnes he was much more than that. But her feelings were a secret, which she had shared with no one, not even her sister. 'I suppose not,' she conceded graciously.

'Anyway, haven't you forgotten something?'

'Like what?' Agnes looked at Alice frowning inquisitively.

'Like the fact that we're women. I don't know of any other funeral parlour that has women running it.'

The lawyer had mentioned that too and Agnes told him the same thing she was about to tell her sister. 'Personally I don't see what difference it makes. Before the war it was unheard of for women to deliver the post or drive ambulances or do numerous other things come to that. Women doing what are deemed to be men's jobs is becoming commonplace now. So why not run a funeral parlour? Besides, to my way of thinking clients are too preoccupied at the time to be much bothered whether the company they're using is run by males or females.'

'You sound like one of those suffragettes, Agnes,' Alice snapped haughtily. 'I don't agree. But anyway, what do you know about running a business like ours? Not enough . . .'

'That's not true,' she cut in, offended, 'and you know it. I know much more than Father would ever give me credit for. I learned over the years by listening and watching. I know just about everything there is to know. If you're truthful so do you. You just don't want to admit it. It's only the financial side I'm truly ignorant of because he never allowed anyone to see the books. But that I can learn too. It's just a case of working it all out. It'll take me time, that's all.' Agnes eyed her sister reproachfully. 'You keep talking about me. Can I remind you once again that there are two of us. It's we, isn't it, Alice?'

Her sister blatantly ignored this and just said, 'But if it all goes wrong we could end up worse off than we are now.' She took a deep breath. 'I think we should consider selling.'

Agnes gasped. 'What? No, Alice. Surely not without giving it a try first?'

'Then we might have nothing left to sell.' Alice paused and eyed her sister worriedly for a moment. She had news to break to Agnes that she probably wasn't going to like and wasn't sure how to go about it.

Agnes noticed her discomfiture and misconstrued it. 'We can do this,' she said, far more confidently than she actually felt. 'We have to, Alice, we need to make our living. I know it's not going to be easy but it's not as if we're starting from nothing. We'll show them all we can do it, you see if we don't.'

Before she could stop herself, Alice blurted out, 'But that's just it – I don't want to.' Her mouth snapped shut and she was acutely conscious that her sister was staring at her, astounded. A dreadful feeling of remorse filled her as she wished wholeheartedly she had picked a better time to tell Agnes of her decision, but then realised there would never be a good time to divulge what she was about to. She had opened her mouth now so had no choice but to get it over with and hope that Agnes would understand.

Sitting back down in her armchair, she clasped her hands tightly and looked her sister straight in the eye. 'I've made up my mind, Agnes. I'm going to take up Aunt Celia's offer. I don't want to live here anymore. I hate it. Hate everything about it. While Father was alive I thought I'd be stuck here forever. Well, now I don't have to be, I can make my own decisions. Going to live with Aunt Celia will begin a new life for me. Scarborough sounds a wonderful place.'

Her eyes filled with excitement. 'Aunt Celia can introduce me to so many people. I'll get to do things I've never been allowed to do before. Go to the music hall and to tea dances. Dress in nice clothes. All sorts of things that Father decided were unseemly.' Her voice lowered. 'I just want to be happy, Agnes. I'm not happy here and never will be if I stay. I know what people call us. You don't think I know but I do. The Sisters Grim.' Agnes's sharp intake of breath was audible. 'Yes, it hurts, doesn't it, Agnes? But we're not grim, are we? It was the way Father made us be. People don't understand that and make fun of us behind our backs. That won't change just because he's gone. Here we'll always be the Sisters Grim. I want to get away from that and the only way is to go and live with Aunt Celia. I might never get another chance like this. She's getting old. She's the only relative we've got. If I turn down her offer even just for a while she might never give it again.' She looked at Agnes pleadingly. 'It was extended to both of us. Why don't you come too? Please, Agnes, say you will?'

As she silently stared at her sister, Agnes's mind whirled frantically. Aunt Celia's letter of condolence had arrived two days ago, just after the funeral, and Agnes, with so much else on her mind, hadn't had time to give the contents much thought after hurriedly reading them. Obviously her sister had. Their aunt had been most insistent about their going to live with her, reiterating the invitation several times in her spidery scrawl. She would love their company, the change of scene and air would do them good, she had plenty of room and there was nothing now to put an obstacle in their way. The obstacle referred to, Agnes had deduced, being their domineering father.

She narrowed her eyes, feeling that in view of Alice's

decision she had better give the matter serious thought. To accept would be the simplest answer. All burdens of responsibility would instantly be lifted from her. All they would have to worry about was getting as much as they could for this property and the goodwill of the business to afford them some capital. Agnes's eyes glazed over. Oh, to start afresh somewhere where no one knew of them or their background! Yes, it did sound tempting.

Over the years they had not seen much of their mother's elder sister, two or three visits at the most. Cuthbert Clatteridge had not encouraged his sister-in-law to call and had not made her welcome when she had ignored his excuses and arrived on their doorstep, complete with enough luggage to last for several months. Inside a week she had departed, having had enough of Cuthbert's unsociable, blatantly rude attitude. Visits to Scarborough had never been suggested, everyone knowing in advance what the answer would be. Agnes felt angry to remember it now. Her selfish father had denied both sisters the right to get to know their only remaining relative. But though they barely knew Celia, Agnes had no doubt they would be made very welcome and life with her would be fun if nothing else. Small as their mother had been, despite her advancing years she still retained her youthful figure and her former beauty was very much in evidence. Celia was a loveable character and, Agnes imagined, very well thought of amongst her circle of friends and acquaintances.

As she pondered more deeply, Agnes absent-mindedly place her elbow on the table and rested her chin in her palm, unaware that her sister was watching her with bated breath.

Should the offer be accepted, she and Alice would have to get some kind of work. Aunt Celia wasn't rich by any means and they couldn't expect her to keep them after whatever capital they received had run out. But that shouldn't be hard. They were both adept with a needle and there were other lines of suitable work they could consider.

Another thought suddenly struck her. Depending on the amount of capital they received, she and Alice could maybe start their own small business. A gift shop on the sea front? She started to conjure up a picture of a shop and to visualise it filled to brimming with tasteful merchandise and a constant stream of well-to-do holidaymakers, she and Alice helping meet their requirements, falling easily into pleasant conversation. They could even offer tea and cakes. Or why not have a tea shop? Suddenly it all appeared most appealing.

If she was truthful with herself, keeping the family business afloat was going to take every conceivable effort, against cut-throat competition and with the odds stacked very heavily against her. Already business that would have been theirs had gone elsewhere. Could she stand up to all that continually, be one step ahead all the time, on permanent watch for not-so-scrupulous operators trying to steal their business in any devious way they could concoct?

She sighed. She had been fooling herself. She wasn't up to it. Her father, damn him, had seen to that. The competition would eat her alive, make her a laughing stock, and by the time they had finished the business would be worth next to nothing as her sister had predicted.

Alice was right. Now Father was dead, it was their one and only chance to start a new life, in a new town, well away from anyone who knew of them. Agnes would be stupid to refuse Aunt Celia's offer. And, just maybe, they might meet men who wanted their kind of women. She could hope, like Alice. Why not? Her mind was made up too.

Agnes raised her head and looked across at her nervously waiting sister. 'I wonder how long it will take to sell up? Not too long, I hope.'

The look she received back was a blank one until her words hit home and Alice's face split into a wide beam of delight. Jumping up, she rushed over and threw her arms joyously around Agnes's neck. 'Oh, Agnes, I knew you'd see sense!' she cried. 'Oh, I can't tell you how happy I am. I wouldn't have felt right, leaving you behind.'

Agnes stared up at her. 'If I'd decided to try and make a go of things here, you'd still have gone and left me to it?'

Alice's arms loosened and she straightened up. 'Yes,' she said without a moment's hesitation. 'If you'd stayed that would be your decision. Mine is to go.' She paused, eyeing her sister guiltily. 'Please don't be angry with me, Agnes, but I went to the Post Office in town today while you were at the lawyer's and telephoned Aunt Celia to tell her I was accepting but I wasn't sure about you. I just felt that if I waited, I'd never get out of here. I love you, Agnes, and I didn't want to leave you behind but . . .'

'It's all right, Alice,' she interrupted. 'I understand. As you said, now Father's gone we can make our own choices.' She smiled tenderly. 'I would have felt so guilty if you had stayed and I'd found out afterwards you did it for me. That wouldn't have been fair.' She took a deep breath. 'Anyway, it doesn't matter because we're both going. All we need to do is wait for a buyer then we can be off.' She ran her eyes disparagingly over the room. 'I can't say that I'm looking forward to packing up this house. I suppose we'll have to get rid of most of the furniture. We can't expect Aunt Celia to have room for any. But now our minds are made up we could make a start in the morning. The sooner the better. I'll make an appointment with the lawyer and he can give us advice as to how to go about matters.' She suddenly noticed the worried expression on her sister's face. 'What is it, Alice?'

She gulped and wrung her hands anxiously.

'Alice?'

'I won't be here. I'm . . . going tomorrow. On the early train. I have to change several times, shan't arrive until late-afternoon. Aunt Celia's expecting me.'

'Oh!'

'I'm sorry, Agnes,' she said ashamed. 'I could put it off, I suppose,' she said, implying otherwise. 'Go next week

152

instead. I'm sure Aunt Celia would understand, in the circumstances.'

'No, no,' said Agnes hurriedly. The last thing she wanted to do was to spoil Alice's enthusiasm at the thought of her new life. 'You mustn't do that. I'll . . . er . . . manage.' Though how without her sister she had no idea. It suddenly struck her that this would be the first time since Alice's birth that they would be parted. She didn't like the prospect, not because of what lay in store for her to deal with but simply because she would miss her sister greatly. She forced a smile. 'Aunt Celia will have your room aired and I expect will have rallied round her friends to come and meet you or arranged to take you to call on them.'

'Yes,' Alice replied excitedly. 'I expect she will. Anyway I'm not quite leaving you to do it on your own. You have Simpson and Peabody to help,' she said brightly. 'I'd only get in the way. Father was always saying I was a hindrance, wasn't he? Anyway if I go on ahead it'll make things easier for you when you follow, won't it? I can . . . well, I can get the lay of the land, can't I? Please say that's all right, Agnes? Please say you don't mind?'

Agnes wanted to tell her she did mind, that she couldn't cope with all that needed to be done by herself, the thought terrified her, but as she looked at her sister it suddenly struck her that Alice's keenness to leave stemmed from fear – fear that something would happen to prevent her.

She knew she had only to ask her sister not to go and out of loyalty Alice wouldn't. But Agnes wouldn't do that. She couldn't bring herself to blight her sister's newfound sense of freedom or the excitement she was experiencing at what she visualised ahead. For the first time in her life Alice was seeing a future for herself. She had had little to look forward to during thirty-two years here and Agnes felt she had no right to spoil things for her now. She would manage by herself.

She slapped Alice playfully on the arm. 'I don't mind,

really. As you said, if you stay you'll only get in the way. I'll get things done much quicker without you here to hinder me.' Tears pricked her eyes and she blinked to try and rid herself of them, not wanting Alice to see that she was getting upset. 'I'll miss you, though.'

'And me you, but it won't be for long, will it? Oh, thank you, Agnes.' Planting a kiss on her cheek, Alice spun round and headed for the door. 'I'd better start packing. I've not much but the sooner I start, the sooner it's done.' She suddenly stopped, spinning back round. 'Trunk! I haven't a trunk,' she blurted, panic-stricken.

'Oh, we've never had any need for them, have we?' Agnes rubbed her chin thoughtfully. 'Ah, yes, Mother's. If I remember rightly, they're in the attic. I'm sure Mr Simpson will get one down for you, if you ask him.'

'Oh, can you ask him, Agnes? I haven't the time,' said Alice, spinning round again and disappearing out of the door.

Agnes stood for several long moments staring after her sister. How would she feel when she waved her off in the morning? She gave a despairing sigh, wishing she could feel excited like Alice, but there was no room for such feelings with the worry of so much to organise. Her thoughts swam haphazardly. Just where did she start? She would make a list, that was the best thing, and work her way through it. But before she could do anything she had to see Mr Simpson about that trunk.

She suddenly realised that in fairness she ought to break the news of her decision to him, give him decent warning of her intentions. As she pondered on that task it struck her that, of all she had to do, telling Mr Simpson was the task she least relished.

Chapter Eleven

Agnes shuddered, wrapping her cardigan tighter round her as she made her way across the cobbled courtyard towards the stables. It had been an extremely warm day for the end of September but now the nights were drawing in and this one was beginning to turn chilly. Soon winter would be upon them. Agnes did not like the winter months one little bit. Winter to her had always meant a constant battle to keep warm.

Her father had had an aversion to any kind of heating and demanded fires be kept low regardless of how bitter the weather was or how cold his daughters. For at least three months of every year Alice and she had had to suffer the terrible agonies this lack of consideration brought. Chilblains; poor circulation; coughs and sore throats; solid blocks of butter; ice on water left standing overnight; the nightmare of Friday night stripping for baths of tepid water in a freezing cold room, to remember but a few. But, she thought, no longer. If she happened still to be here during this coming winter, whenever she wanted she could have a huge fire in every room without fear of retribution. With the warmth they brought all her other sufferings would be greatly alleviated.

Now that she had made her decision she hoped everything would be signed and sealed well before then but, regardless, the thought of not having to suffer the cold any longer cheered her greatly.

As she approached the stables, before making her way

up the rusting iron stairs to the side which led up to Mr Simpson's abode, she stopped for a moment before the half-open gabled door. 'Ned,' she called softly. 'Come, boy, see what I've brought you.' As she heard his snort of recognition and the sound of hooves she held out her hand, palm wide, and smiled as a brown head appeared. 'Hello, Ned,' she said tenderly as the old horse gobbled up the sugar cubes. Agnes patted his nose.

'Good boy. You like your sugar, don't you?' Suddenly her smile faded as she realised that the horse would have to go. But where? She would have to find a decent place for him, not just anywhere. She had a great deal of affection for Ned who had been with them for over ten years of loyal, unbroken service. She would not rest if she had any doubts he would be well looked after for his remaining days.

It had fallen to Mr Simpson to take care of Ned's well-being and he had done so more than adequately, in fact going so far as to treat him like a member of the family.

The sound of a footfall behind her made Agnes jump.

'Miss Clatteridge, I do beg yer pardon, I didn't mean ter alarm yer,' Ivan Simpson said worriedly. 'I was just on me way to swill me hands under the pump.' He respectfully whipped off his threadbare cap and grasped it between large work-worn hands. 'I'm sorry, really I am.'

'It's all right,' she reassured him. 'I didn't expect you still to be around at this time of night. I thought you'd be upstairs.'

'Oh, no, Miss Clatteridge, I was finishing off a batch of nails for the ironmonger down the road. I've one or two regular orders, as you know, to keep up with. And I've a small carpentry job to do tomorrow for Mr Cullins at number 'undred and two. So I want to get me bits together ready to go straight round in the morning. It's only fixing a window. It really wants a new 'un, it's near rotten, but, well . . . shouldn't tek me more than an hour. I like to keep on top of things for when our main work comes in. And especially if we get two or three in together. As yer know, miss, that can be a nightmare.'

She gave a half-hearted smile. There wouldn't be any more jobs. Although Simpson didn't know it, his nail-making had been a total waste of time. Well, maybe not a total waste. They could sell them with the rest of the stock. What she had to tell him burdened Agnes greatly.

'Is there 'ote wrong, Miss Clatteridge?' he asked her in concern. 'Only yer look . . . well . . . troubled, if yer don't mind me saying?'

'Do I! Oh.' She really ought not to delay. This man had been loyal to her father for many many years, though she would never understand why in God's name he had stuck it, having herself witnessed more times than she cared to remember how callously her father had treated him. So why had he stayed when other firms would gladly have taken him on? At least, she thought, one Clatteridge will treat him fairly. She took a deep breath. 'Mr Simpson, I would like to talk to you. If it's convenient, of course?'

A look of astonishment appeared momentarily on his face. Her father would never have addressed him so civilly, but then Miss Agnes was nothing like him in manner so he should not be so surprised. Whenever their paths had crossed she had always been politeness itself. That was one of the many things he had always liked about her. It was heartening to find she was not going to change now her father was gone and she was in charge. ''Course, Miss Clatteridge. About a funeral, is it?' he asked eagerly. 'Instructions like?'

She froze. 'No, it isn't.' She gazed around her uncomfortably. The yard was not the place to tell Mr Simpson he was about to lose his job and home. She felt he deserved better than this. But where? It wouldn't be deemed right to take him in to the house, she and Alice being two unchaperoned females, but there was nowhere else fitting.

Despite wondering what she could be wanting him for if

it wasn't about a job, he sensed her dilemma and, hoping she wouldn't think he was forgetting his place, spoke up. 'It's warm in the workshed, Miss Clatteridge, the furnace is still lit and I've the kettle on if you'd fancy a mash? We can talk there quite comfortably. And . . . er . . .' he added, choosing his words carefully '. . . we'll leave the door wide just in case yer sister should wonder where yer are. You'll hear her calling then.'

Warmth filled her. He had realised her problem and solved it very thoughtfully. It didn't make Agnes's task any easier.

'A cup of tea would be very welcome.'

He guided her through to the back of the shed by the cluttered workbench where two rickety stools stood. Grabbing up the cleanest rag he could find, he gave one a quick wipe before inviting her to sit down. The pitch black battered kettle was already singing on a little oil stove on the floor and deftly he set about mashing a pot of tea in a chipped brown teapot.

As he was busying himself, Agnes glanced around her. The workshed was very cramped. A small brick furnace was set at an angle against the far wall, its chimney disappearing through the roof. At the moment its iron door was ajar to let out some heat. In the middle of the stone floor stood a long sturdy wooden trestle where the coffins were made. At the moment it was empty except for a metal jig. Stacked down one wall were assorted planks of wood, from pine to mahogany, and down the other, three long lengths of higgledy-piggledy shelves housed containers of nails and screws and all manner of other things needed to complete their work.

For fifty years Clatteridges and their employees had worked inside these walls. She wondered whose turn it would be next.

'Seen some sights has this shed, Miss Clatteridge.'

'Pardon? Oh, yes, I expect it has.'

Ivan grinned. 'Could tell many a tale, I bet, if it could

talk.' He laughed. 'I could tell you a few meself but I expect now ain't the time.' He handed her an enamel mug. 'Excuse the crockery. I've given you the best one. I've more milk and sugar should you need it.'

Agnes accepted graciously and took a sip. 'Thank you, this is very good. You make a fine cup of tea, Mr Simpson.'

A warm glow settled in the pit of his stomach as he sat down facing her. She didn't need to say that. It wasn't good tea and he knew it. It had been made from the cheapest leaves, although he had been more liberal with the quantity in honour of her visit. But wasn't that just like Miss Clatteridge? Normally he would have felt uncomfortable to be facing a superior but he never felt that way with her. It was a pity her father hadn't been more like her, life would have been more tolerable if he had.

'You wanted ter speak to me?' he prompted.

'Oh, yes, I did.' Agnes nervously cradled her mug, studying the leaves floating on top before she took a deep breath and raised her eyes to his. 'Mr Simpson, I want to give you fair warning that my sister and I have decided we're going to sell the business. Once everything is settled up we're going to live with our aunt in Scarborough. I felt it only right you should know as soon as possible.' She took a hurried breath then added, 'I hope this hasn't come as too much of a shock?'

It had. It was devastating news. And not just because he would be losing his job and living accommodation. 'It's . . . er . . . appreciated, your tellin' me, Miss Clatteridge,' he mumbled.

His state of mind was not lost on her. 'I'm so sorry, Mr Simpson. If I thought I could possibly make a success of carrying everything on, believe me I would. But I'm not equipped to step into my father's shoes, I only wish I was. I know you're quite capable of finding yourself another place but should you need any help you have only to ask and I'll do everything I can to assist you.'

'That's very good of you, Miss Clatteridge,' he said gratefully.

'It's the least I can do after your service to Father. I maybe should not say this, but he wasn't the easiest of men to get along with and your loyalty was commendable. It will not be forgotten.' A thought suddenly struck her and she felt that in the circumstances it was the very least she could do. 'I'd like to be able to recompense you, to help with your future. I can't tell you by how much as yet until I have some idea of what we can expect to make from a sale, but I hope that whatever it is will be acceptable to you.'

Her thoughtfulness touched him deeply. She must know his wage had not left much to put by in savings. What bit he did have wouldn't go far now he had to find somewhere to live. His thoughts lingered on the woman seated before him. Plain, thin and tall, there was no other way to describe Miss Agnes Clatteridge, and he knew that was how others saw her. But not him. He saw beneath that plainness. Through the dark drab clothing. Past the thin, shapeless frame underneath. Agnes Clatteridge, to him, was the warmest, kindest woman he had ever had the privilege to meet. And he loved her. Had done since he had been twelve years old and frozen with cold, waiting nervously in the yard to begin his first day at work.

She had found him there as she had come out to pump water, and taken him into the austere kitchen to give him a cup of tea. Her father had descended then, dressed in his long black cloak and seeming like a demon from hell. When he'd spotted Ivan his long thin face had filled with rage and he had thrown him outside then slapped Agnes hard for being familiar with an employee. She had been barely five years old. Ivan had never forgotten that first show of kindness. Neither would he forget the numerous occasions since, when leftovers or anything she felt he could use had been thrust silently at him when no one else was around, without her seeming to care about the inevitable backlash should her actions be found out. There had been no need for words between them. She knew that what she gave him was desperately needed. He knew she did it for no other reason than natural generosity.

His deep love for her was his secret, she had no idea whatsoever and never would. He, a lowly carpenter cum jack-of-all-trades, could never expect the daughter of a businessman, especially Cuthbert Clatteridge, to be honoured by, accept or return his feelings. Even to give her an inkling would, he felt, be to offend her deeply. He would never risk that. He respected her far too much. His feelings for her would go with him to his grave.

Loyalty to Cuthbert Clatteridge? That was a joke. Ivan Simpson detested the very essence of the man. The only reason he had stayed for so many years, suffering his employer's harsh ways and downright rude manner, was Agnes. Leaving would have meant not seeing her again and he couldn't have borne that. But now he would have to as she was selling up and leaving for another town many miles away. The thought crucified him. The remaining years seemed suddenly to stretch ahead down a deep dark void. Without this lovely woman around to brighten his day, life for him would not hold a meaning.

Agnes herself was feeling terrible. She had tried to be businesslike in her approach, as she thought would be expected of an employer, but her outward poise had not in the least mirrored her inner turmoil. What she had just done was the worst thing she had ever had to attempt or would again. For Agnes loved Ivan Simpson; she had done since she was five years old and had first taken pity on him, a shabby, undersized twelve year old, clutching a battered blue billycan to hold his tea, frozen to the marrow in the yard on his first day of work.

Over the years her childish feelings for him had deepened to unrequited love. There was something about Ivan that drew feelings from her that would not die.

He was such a nice man, tender and kind, and so well-mannered considering his poor background. He had never been anything other than courteous to her. He wasn't tall, fat or thin, unduly handsome . . . just ordinary, in fact. But it was still surprising to Agnes that he had never taken a wife, or so far as she was aware courted at all. There must be many women around who would grab at the chance to become his wife. She had often worried about that happening, selfish though she knew it was of her, and been glad that nothing had ever transpired, knowing she would not have coped very well with the knowledge of Ivan's sharing his life with another.

Agnes raised her head to look at him and completely misconstrued his devastated expression. 'I do apologise if I've offended you,' she said hurriedly.

Ivan eyed her blankly. 'Offended me?'

'By my offer of recompense. I would prefer you to look upon it as a thank you.'

'I'm not offended, miss, not at all,' he insisted. No matter what she did, she could never offend him. 'I was just thinking what a kind gesture it was, that was all. And, to be honest, your selling up has come as a shock. I have ter say, it was the last thing I was expecting to hear.'

Face grave, she nodded her understanding. 'I've really no choice, Mr Simpson.' Sighing heavily, she placed the empty enamel mug on the workbench then clasped her hands tightly. 'My father didn't exactly equip my sister and me to carry on in the event of his death. If we don't sell now, we might not have anything left to sell soon. I suppose in the circumstances, your having worked for us for so long, I can tell you that he didn't leave us very well provided for so the business couldn't have been doing as well as I thought. Being inexperienced on the financial side, well, I can't risk devaluing it any further. If I had just myself to consider I would not hesitate to take the risk, but I have my sister to think of.'

'The business was doing well enough, Miss Clatteridge,' Ivan said. And added before he could stop himself, 'I expect yer'd 'ave bin plenty well off if yer father hadn't have bin . . .' He stopped abruptly, realising he was about to speak out of turn. The way his employer had carried on was really none of his business and as such he had no right to speak of it. 'Well, yer know,' he said uncomfortably.

Agnes frowned, confused. 'Know? Know what?'

He gulped, staring at her, a red tide of embarrassment creeping up his neck. He ran a hand through his thatch of iron grey hair, exhaling sharply.

'Mr Simpson?' she urged.

He eyed her, confused. 'Don't yer know, miss?'

'No, I don't, Mr Simpson, and I'd be obliged if you would tell me what my father was doing?' she said sharply.

He suddenly realised that she wouldn't know what her father's pastime had been. How could she? He groaned inwardly. Considering how he felt about her, why did it have to be him who told her? He took a deep breath, fixing his eyes on hers. 'Yer father was a gambler, Miss Clatteridge.'

Her mouth fell open. 'What! No. Never.' She shook her head vehemently. 'My father consigned everyone to hell who did anything of the sort. Gambling? No, I can't believe that.'

'He could damn as much as he liked, miss, but yer father must 'ave gone through a small fortune over the years. And it grieved me, so it did, to see the way he carried on but it wasn't my place to say anything about it. According to Seth Harrop, the chippy I took over from, it started after yer mother passed on. He reckoned it was yer father's way of coping with his grief. I could never understand it meself, but then folks do strange things at times like that. It was like a fever inside Mr Clatteridge. Woe betide anythin' should 'appen and his bets not placed. My God, we'd all suffer then. One of my daily jobs when I was the lad was to go between him and the bookie's runner. Bet on anything that moved he did. Only he wasn't often lucky. Oswald placed a bet for him the very day he died.'

Agnes was staring at him, astounded. 'Oswald Peabody, placing bets for my father? And you before him!'

'And those in between.'

'All of them?' she gasped, mortified. 'Every one of the young lads who have worked for us over the years?'

Ivan nodded, face filling with remorse. 'I thought you must at least have had an idea, Miss Clatteridge. Really I did. I feel so bad, being the one to tell yer.'

She stared at him, horrified. 'I had no idea. Neither has my sister.' She sat frozen in shock. Dear God, she thought, this revelation was dreadful. Had Ivan Simpson any idea of the hours she and Alice had been forced to read the Bible, learning parables and verses off by heart, and woe betide them should they recite anything wrongly. How could her father have been such a hypocrite? she thought savagely.

A sudden anger filled her like none she'd known before. Her father had ruled over her and Alice rigidly, never allowing them to do anything he deemed unacceptable, which had covered just about everything social. Oh, not quite. He had allowed them to go to church. His rules had even extended to their not mixing with the employees anymore than was necessary. To be caught in idle chatter had been a punishable offence. When all the time . . . She clenched her fists in fury. 'And what else was my father doing that you know of, Mr Simpson?' A thought suddenly struck her. 'Women! Are you going to tell me he visited women of ill repute too?'

'Oh, no, Miss Clatteridge.' Ivan vigorously shook his head. 'Not to my knowledge. It was just the gamblin'.'

'Considering the state of our finances, I'm glad to hear it,' she exclaimed. Then her face filled with shame. 'I'm so sorry, I'm not angry with you.' She felt a rush of tears prick her eyes and abruptly rose. She must not break down in front of Mr Simpson. She felt stupid enough for being

164

oblivious to all that had been going on under her nose. 'Please excuse me, I have things to do. Thank you for the tea,' she said, rushing out.

Ivan stared after her. For years he had stood by helplessly, watching in suffering silence Cuthbert Clatteridge's mistreatment of his daughters, especially of his beloved Agnes. And there was nothing he could do about it. To say one word to his employer would have resulted in his own dismissal, without references. The man himself, thought Ivan, had much to answer for. To Ivan's way of thinking, to rot in hell was no more than Clatteridge deserved. Ivan hoped he was, for all the pain he had caused and was still causing now.

Alice found her sister huddled in a chair by the fire, head buried in the crook of her arm, gently sobbing. She was so wrapped up in her own private thoughts that Agnes's misery did not register at first.

'Don't bother about the trunk,' she blurted out as she bounded through the door. 'I've got everything in those two old carpet bags of Father's. Agnes? Oh, Agnes,' she cried, rushing over and kneeling down before her. 'You're crying. Whatever's the matter? Look, I won't go,' she said, placing one hand tenderly on her sister's arm. 'I can call Aunt Celia tomorrow. She'll understand when I explain. We'll both go together when everything's been sorted out. Agnes, please don't cry.'

'I wasn't crying,' she lied, hurriedly wiping away tears with the back of her hand. 'Well, yes, I was but it's just because I'm going to miss you, that's all. I'm being silly. Please allow me to be silly, Alice. You're my sister and I love you.' She couldn't tell her the real reason for her tears. Alice was bitter enough against their father and it seemed had every right to be. There was no need to fuel her hatred further. The man was dead. Alice had a future to get on with. Maybe one day Agnes would divulge what she had learned, but not today. With a great effort she forced a smile to her face. 'You're not going to disappoint Aunt Celia and all the cronies she'll have summoned to meet you? I'm sorry it slipped my mind about the trunk, but anyway you don't need one so that's all right. Now give me a hug, then go and make us both a cup of tea. Then, my girl,' she said, wagging a finger, 'it's bed for you. You've a long day tomorrow and so have I, getting started on things here. Go on now,' she ordered. 'I'm desperate for a drink.'

Alice eyed her warily. 'Are you sure, Agnes, about my going? Really?'

'I said so, didn't I? Now, for goodness' sake, go and make that tea.'

A broad smile transformed Alice's plain face. 'I'm so lucky to have you as my sister,' she said earnestly and left Agnes to her own reflections.

Chapter Twelve

'Thank you, Mr Simpson,' Agnes said as he helped her down from the small cart they called the box, which had been commandeered to transport Alice and her bags to the station.

The pleasure was mine, he wanted to tell her. 'What would yer like me to do now we're back Miss Clatteridge,' he said instead.

Still straightening her attire, she raised her eyes quizzically to his. 'Do?'

'After I've put the cart away and seen to Ned. There's a lot, I expect. Where would yer like me and Oswald to start?'

'Oh, I don't know.' Agnes stood thoughtfully for a moment. 'I really need to see the lawyer and take advice. That's what I ought to do first, I suppose.'

'If yer don't mind my suggesting it, Miss Clatteridge, now that yer sister's gone, don't yer need to get someone in to give you a hand? Of course, it goes without saying I'll do all I can. Oswald and meself can tek care of things out here, but surely you'll need a woman to help in the house?'

Agnes frowned thoughtfully. She supposed she would. She would be stupid to think she could tackle it all by herself. And it wouldn't be right to ask either Mr Simpson or Peabody into the house to help go through all the family's personal things, deciding what to keep and what to do with the stuff they'd have no room for. But she couldn't deal with that now. All her thoughts this morning had been concentrated on seeing Alice safely on her journey. It had been traumatic for Agnes as she had fought to keep her own spiralling emotions in check so as not to spoil Alice's eagerness.

Standing alone on the wind-whipped platform, watching the train heave and choke on its way without bursting into tears, had taken all her restraint. So distressed was Agnes, she had sat in silence all the way back in the cart. Even the fact that the man she adored was sitting by her side had been of no comfort. But now Alice was gone and she had to get on with the sale of the business and all it entailed. Then it would be her turn to abandon her memories of the sorrow and harshness of these surroundings and begin her own new life.

She gazed around the cobbled yard. Apart from the house which fronted on to the main Uppingham Road – a two-storey, four-bedroomed, early Victorian dwelling which could have been made very comfortable had her father allowed – there were several outbuildings of varying sizes, all allotted their individual functions. An inventory would need to be made of their contents, that much she knew, as well as the contents of the house.

She sighed at this daunting prospect, suddenly feeling very tired. She had spent a fraught sleepless night trying to come to terms with her father's dreadful secret, which had left herself and Alice in such a precarious situation. All her bravado seemed to have drained away now and she felt she couldn't face giving orders or setting about making decisions on all that needed to be done. Tomorrow. She'd begin tomorrow. All she wanted to do right now was curl up in an armchair and just sit and think, hopefully find a part of her mind in which to lock it all away.

'Mr Simpson, take the rest of the day off. And Peabody too. And please rest assured, your pay will not be docked.'

It was the last thing Ivan had expected to hear and he stared in astonishment. 'I beg yer pardon, Miss Clatteridge?'

'You heard me, Mr Simpson. Do whatever you want to

do. We'll make a start tomorrow.'

He stood rooted to the spot, watching Agnes intently as she crossed the yard and disappeared inside the house. The rest of the day off? It was unheard of. Her father, he remembered, had expressed severe anger when the old Queen had died and the country had been given a day's mourning. A smile twitched the corners of his mouth. The old devil would be turning in his grave at his daughter's instructions. The thought amused Ivan.

He scratched his head. A day off? What was he going to do with himself? He'd never had a holiday. He was supposed to have half a day a week, but somehow that had never quite materialised. He himself always found something to do around the yard and Mr Clatteridge had never commented on the fact. Well, he wouldn't. Liked his pound of flesh, did that one. Taking the rest of the day off didn't feel right to Ivan, especially not when he knew Miss Clatteridge wasn't thinking straight with all she was contending with. He'd send Peabody home, though, and the lad wouldn't think twice about it. Be off before the words had left his mouth.

He was a wily one was Peabody. Ivan have never taken to him from the day he sauntered into the yard seeking work after hearing the last lad had left. No doubt his widowed mother had pushed him into it. But then, Ivan's opinion had never been sought. Mr Clatteridge hadn't been a man to ask others for advice, especially not a lowly employee.

The object of his thoughts popped his head out of the shed door. 'Thought I 'eard yer come back. Fancy a mash, Mr Simpson?'

'You can help me unharness the cart first. Then yer can make the tea, then you can go 'ome.'

'Eh?'

'You heard, lad. Miss Clatteridge's instructions. You could use the time to help yer mother. I expect there's plenty of jobs that need to be done around your house.' 'Hovel' would be a more apt description of the place where Oswald, his prematurely aged mother and several young brothers and sisters resided, but at least they had a home with a living parent to call their own. Ivan himself had come straight to Clatteridge's from an orphanage. 'Help me get the cart seen too. Then,' he said, suddenly feeling a desire to be rid of Oswald as soon as possible, 'yer can scarper. I'll mash up meself.'

Oswald didn't need another telling. In minutes the cart was housed. 'I'll be off then, Mr Simpson. See yer termorrow.'

Guiding Ned to the stables, he nodded. 'Don't be late,' he called to Oswald as he shot through the archway that led from the yard into the main street. Ivan sighed. He hadn't even had the thoughtfulness to close the large wooden doors after him, despite knowing they needed shutting. The lazy good-for-nothing.

The next afternoon, on her way back from making an appointment with the lawyer for later that week, Agnes walked into the local Post Office and handed over a card. She had given Ivan's advice much thought as she had sat in contemplation all the rest of the day and decided it should be taken. She would need help and hoped that someone suitable would apply. It would go some way towards getting her used to meeting and conversing with new people. She only hoped she had offered a reasonable rate for the job.

'Would you put that in your window, please?' she addressed the Post Mistress.

'That'll be twopence, Miss Clatteridge.'

Agnes handed over two pennies and left.

Tilly Potter studied the card. 'Domestic help required. Twenty-five shillings a week. Apply: Miss Agnes Clatteridge, 97 Uppingham Road'.

Tilly pursed her lips. 'She's offering twenty-five bob a week. That's well above the going rate.'

'Eh?' queried her husband Cedric as he emerged through

the door from the back, carrying several parcels which he stacked under the counter. 'What yer rattling on about, woman?'

'The elder Sister Grim's just been in. Wants me to put this card in the window. She needs help and she's offering twenty-five bob a week. Might suit our Violet's Flossie. She's desperate for work.'

He glanced over her shoulder at the card. 'She ain't that desperate, surely? Mind you, that's good money.'

'That's because Miss Clatteridge knows she's gonna have trouble getting someone. No, I won't bother mentioning it to Violet. I know she wouldn't set foot in the place with all them dead bodies. I'd take bets no one else around here will either. Miss Clatteridge has just wasted her twopence, if yer ask me.'

'Well, she didn't ask you, Tilly Potter. Now put the card in the window and have done with it. If folks want to pay for the service then it's not for us to question it.'

His wife sniffed. 'But I'm particular about my cards. And Mrs Connor might not take kindly to me putting it next to hers for dressmaking. All these twopences add up, you know. Make a nice little nest egg they do over a year. I can't risk our customers taking offence and going elsewhere, now can I?'

'I suppose not. Well, stick it right at the bottom in the corner, away from all the others,' he suggested.

'That's a good thought, Cedric. That way I'll cause no ill feeling, will I?'

She took several minutes to place the card strategically, not taking the trouble she usually did to check it could be viewed adequately from outside, and went back behind the counter.

'I've never seen her smile. Not once I haven't,' she mused as she gave the counter a wipe.

'Your letter should arrive the day after tomorrow, Mrs Rooney. Well give or take,' Cedric added. He gave his customer her change then turned his full attention to his wife. 'Who haven't yer seen smile?'

''Er. The elder Miss Grim. And those clothes she dresses in! They wouldn't look out of place on my old mother, should she still be alive, God rest her.'

'Well, I don't expect she's ever had much to smile about. Would you have, living her life?' He ignored his wife's comment about Miss Clatteridge's clothes. Women to his mind spent far too much time and effort worrying about what they wore. Tilly was always moaning about her wardrobe, yet she always looked all right to him.

'I 'spose not,' she answered, breathing hard on the counter then giving a stubborn spot a vigorous rub. 'Yes, I suppose if anything I feel sorry for her. I expect it's a huge burden lifted now he's gone. Wouldn't have wished him on anyone as a father. He used to scare the kids something rotten when he launched himself off down the street, that black cloak thing he always wore making him look like the devil himself. There's one thing for sure, I doubt many'll miss him.' She gave a dry laugh. 'His business certainly suited him, didn't it?'

Her husband laughed along with her. 'Most definitely. I wonder who'll take it on?'

'Take what on?' she mused.

'The business.'

'According to gossip they're selling up. And I'll tell yer another thing. The younger Sister Grim has gone. Molly Micklewaite saw 'em this morning in the cart. She had bags with 'er.'

'Can't say as I blame 'er. Who in their right mind 'ud want ter stay in that mausoleum of a place? Oh,' he mused. 'Well, if they're selling, why d'yer reckon Miss Clatteridge needs 'elp?'

'Well, I know I would,' said his wife grimacing. 'I wouldn't fancy having to clear that place out by meself. Anyway,' she said tartly, 'how would I know why she's decided she wants

172

help? We ain't exactly bosom pals, now are we?'

'I thought you'd have known – yer seem to know everything else around 'ere, Tilly Potter. Anyway, selling up meks sense. Can't keep it going, can they, them being women?'

'And what difference does that mek?' Tilly demanded. She folded her arms under her ample bosom. 'Let me tell you, Cedric Potter, women are just as capable as men. I managed fine wi'out you when you were away at war. I ran the Post Office just as good as you, and I raised three children at the same time. Let me see *you* doing that.'

'You've changed your tune just a bit. A minute ago you were saying no one would work for her.'

'And I doubt anyone will, considering. But that don't mean to say she ain't got the brains to handle it all.' Tilly snorted. 'You men think we women 'ud fall to pieces without yer, don't you?'

He shook his head. He was on the losing side of this battle and he knew it. 'I was just trying to make the point that there's some things men do best, that's all, and their kind of business is best done by a man in my opinion.'

'Mmmm,' she mused. 'I expect yer right. And lifting parcels is what you're best at. You forgot to deliver that one this morning.' She pointed to a large brown paper-covered box on the floor behind the door. 'You'll have to take it around for Mr Samuels. It's the parts he ordered for his grinding machine. Needs them urgent. Got a man standing idle waiting for it to arrive.'

Good-naturedly, she leaned over and pecked her husband on his cheek. 'Yer right, Cedric. I couldn't manage without yer. I wouldn't want to. I'll have yer tea ready by the time you get back.' She flashed a glance towards the door as it opened and a customer walked through. 'Get a move on, Cedric, looks ter me like there's a fog coming down. Brrr!' she shivered. 'Winter's coming. Yes, Mrs Stanton. Usual? Paper, envelopes and ink. No ink, just paper and envelopes?

Right you are. What a lot of letters you write! How's that sister of yours in Chapel St Leonards? I noticed you had a postcard from her this morning. Got a cold, hasn't she? Well, I hope she recovers soon.'

Cedric shook his head as he bent to lift the parcel. His wife had no discretion. All the locals knew Tilly knew their business before they did. She read their cards; poked and prodded parcels to work out what was in them; knew who had sent the letters they received. On one occasion Cedric had actually caught her steaming open a letter from Mrs Coggin's wayward daughter, Tilly being desperate to find out what she was up to.

What Tilly herself had got up to while he was away fighting in France didn't bear thinking about.

Chapter Thirteen

Maddie bent lower, squinting hard to read the words on the card. She'd nearly missed it as she had scanned the others, stuck right down in one corner, part of it obscured by an official notice of postal delivery times. This one must have slipped down, she thought. None of the other cards had offered work, just services, and as such this was the only one of interest to her. She didn't mind taking on a domestic situation and the pay offered was very good. Better than anything else she had been offered today.

It was two weeks since she had fled from her mother. That night seemed a lifetime ago now. So welcome had her father and his family – her family – made her that even after so short a time she felt a part of their life, as if she had always belonged here.

Sarah had been kindness itself, in fact in every way been just the kind of mother Maddie had always longed for. It was such a pity, she had thought, that Harriet did not possess just one or two of Sarah's many good qualities. Had she done life would have been so different for everyone.

Sarah had been as good as her word. Despite Maddie's insisting she should find herself a room, not wanting to put them out, Sarah had won her over. The old horsehair sofa was proving very comfortable and would more than suffice until money could be found to buy her a bed. Her father had bought Maddie a secondhand tallboy from the local pawnshop, as well as a wash stand with one leg loose which Roy had fixed. Ruth had come home with a pretty bowl and jug for her. The three women had sat over five evenings and pegged together a large round clippy rug, using odds and ends of material from Sarah's bit box. It was certainly colourful and brightened the room.

As the three of them worked away on the rug, they had chatted and gradually Maddie learned more about their lives.

Financially the struggle had been hard, at times they had been almost poverty-stricken. Harriet still demanded a rightful spouse's share of her husband's wage. So long as he stuck by their agreement, his own financial situation was nothing to do with her. Consequently Sarah had always had to work, doing anything that would fit around her family – taking in washing, sewing, minding children, even trudging several miles daily to the countryside to pick seasonal fruit – whatever bit of money she earned helping to ease the burden for her beloved George.

Now thankfully the children were earning – Ruth as stockroom clerk for a small leather company specialising in importing handbags and shoes for the wealthy which they delivered mainly to outlets in London, and Roy as an apprentice grinder for a local tool-making factory – Sarah was back full-time behind the counter of the Uppingham Road Co-op, her shop assistant's wage still not much but better than before and regular at least. And she did enjoy her job. Their finances had improved but the pennies still had to be watched.

'When Ruth came along,' Sarah had told Maddie, 'your father approached Harriet and asked her again if she would consider releasing him. She just laughed, told him to go to hell, reminded him of their agreement and of what she would do should he not stick by it. When Roy was born he asked her if she would take less of his money, considering she had an income of her own. She said if George expected her to relinquish any of her rights in order for him to raise his . . . children, then he was a fool. Their agreement was that until you, my dear, left home, nothing would change. And nothing has.' She had stopped her work then and looked at Maddie, smiling kindly. 'But things are different now, aren't they?'

She had merely nodded, still far too shocked by her mother's actions to comment.

Maddie had told them she did not intend going back to Market Harborough. Leicester was her home now, her life was here. She kept to herself that too much had transpired between Harriet and her for her ever to return. Too much trust had been lost, too much pain had been caused. Although not voicing their suspicions, George and Sarah knew she was holding something back but decided it was best to leave Maddie to tell her story when she was ready. They didn't want to push her. It was obvious to both of them that whatever had happened between her mother and herself, it was something momentous.

Satisfied his daughter knew her own mind, George was not going to put the deed off any longer. So far as he was concerned he had honoured his commitment for far longer than he had ever envisaged. Now he wanted a divorce, to be free finally to marry the woman he adored. He planned to confront Harriet this coming weekend. All of them knew he was not looking forward to the ordeal but awaited the outcome eagerly.

Sarah had managed to persuade Maddie to give herself time to settle in, get used to her new family and surroundings before she started looking for a job. The girl had insisted on paying her keep, regardless of the fact Sarah and George said they'd wait until she was earning. But Ruth and Roy contributed, and it was only right she should. She had pressed a pound upon Sarah, hoping it was enough.

Her initial savings of nearly five pounds were now down to one pound, six shillings, a portion of what she had spent going on toiletries and stockings but the larger amount on new clothes. Not brand new, but new to Maddie.

What fun she had had the Saturday afternoon she had bought them. Sarah and Ruth had insisted they come along to help her decide what suited her best. And what good advice they had given her. They had taken her to the best secondhand clothes shop in Leicester. Good quality and all from wealthy owners, so the proprietor had informed them. Whether that was entirely true or not was of no consequence; the clothes were far superior in quality and fashion to anything Maddie had ever been allowed by her mother.

She was thrilled with the results, her transformation startling. Pretentious though she thought it of herself, she couldn't stop trying the new clothes on and parading before the mirror, checking over and over that it was really her reflected back.

One dress was of crêpe-de-chine, pale blue, drop-waisted, sleeveless with a v-neckline and contrasting bow trim. Maddie had felt it was far too extravagant for her but Sarah and Ruth had insisted she should take it. The dress was perfect for an evening out. The other was a pretty leaf green belted day dress which perfectly fitted her slim, shapely curves, previously disguised under her dowdy clothes. Three good wool skirts, three fashionable blouses, a warm cardigan and several pieces of underwear completed Maddie's wardrobe. Her long hair was next. They told her a chin-length bob would suit her. She thought so too and couldn't wait to get it done.

For the first time she could ever remember, Maddie actually looked forward to rising in the morning and not just because she had such nice clothes to wear. She was wanted here, felt at ease, was experiencing family love and unity.

But forgetting all the bad things that had happened was proving a great struggle. The days were filled with so much going on around her she had no time to dwell on the past, but nights were another matter. Lying on the sofa, the night sounds filtering in hazily, her thoughts would wander and excruciating memories return. She knew that forgetting her past was too much to expect. Far too much had happened for her ever to hope for that. What she did hope for was for her pain to ease; that she should be allowed to live the rest of her life in peace. If she was ever to do that she knew she could not have come to a better place. Fate had been kind to her the night she had arrived, a devastated dejected woman with her life in ruins, at her father's door.

Two weeks after her arrival, Maddie felt she should start looking for work. Armed with a list of places to try that Sarah had written out for her, Maddie set off. It was a miserable early-October morning, damp and misty. She had never been job hunting before, wasn't quite sure what to do or say, but dressed in her new clothes was feeling confident and her hopes were high.

She got lost several times, only finding two of the five factories she had set out in search of, and she had had to wait to be seen for an age at both. At each factory interviews had been hurried, taking place in a dim corridor where she had been glanced up and down, and asked what sewing experience she had. The owner of the second factory she had visited had made her feel she should be honoured he was offering her a job sewing garments. The sewing room she would be working in was dark and dingy, the air thick with dust. The hundred or so other workers sat in long cramped rows, heads bent over their machines, the high-pitched drone of which she could still hear ringing in her ears. The pay wasn't bad if you worked hard. Sewing for a living, though, was a reminder of her previous life and for the time being Maddie felt she would prefer to do something different if that were possible. Regardless, it was a job she did not intend to refuse if nothing else came along by her proposed start day the following Monday morning, at six-thirty sharp.

The afternoon was closing in when she decided to start on the trek home. Tomorrow, she decided, she would arm herself with precise directions before setting off. As she walked briskly down the length of the Uppingham Road she realised that a fog was beginning to fall, rapidly thickening. Maddie shuddered and forced her pace. She had trouble enough with her bearings, without being hampered by fog. The thought of getting lost and wandering aimlessly did not appeal. Maddie looked forward to arriving home for the evening meal, listening to events in her new family's daily life and knowing they were eager to hear hers. If she hurried she could give Sarah a hand with the preparations.

Intent on going home, the cards in the Post Office window only caught her eye by chance. Automatically she stopped for a moment to view them. The one right down in the corner . . . Maddie bent closer to read it.

Swirling fog hit Cedric Potter full force as he emerged from the Post Office and he shuddered as the damp air closed in on him. Vision blocked by the bulky parcel he was carrying as well as the fog, he just managed to avoid colliding with the figure bent double to peer through his shop window.

'I'm sorry, me duck,' he apologised profusely. 'Didn't see you there.'

Maddie shot upright and moved aside to let him pass her on the narrow cobbled path. 'Oh, excuse me,' she said. 'Could you tell me in which direction number ninety-seven Uppingham Road is, please?'

He stopped and looked at her keenly. 'The card, is it?'

'I beg your pardon?'

'The job on the card. You interested, are yer?'

'Well, yes, I could be.'

'Mmmm,' he said thoughtfully. She won't take it, he thought, but won't Tilly be interested to know that someone's made enquiries. He wouldn't divulge that he had thought the woman rather pretty. 'It's that way,' he indicated with a nod of his head. 'Not far. Can't miss it even in this fog.'

Maddie expressed her thanks and proceeded on her way.

The fog was swirling more thickly. In places it was only possible to see a few feet ahead. Maddie kept close to the walls, counting off the number on the doors as she passed. She had to cross over several streets, hoping no traffic appeared suddenly out of nowhere. It did cross her mind that maybe she should leave it until tomorrow, it being rather late in the afternoon to be applying for work, but then she thought someone could beat her to it and the job would be gone.

Finally she arrived. From what she could see the house was reasonably large and there were clean nets at the downstairs windows. She glanced to her left and as she did so the fog momentarily lifted and she was afforded a view of the next-door building. It was obviously business premises. A window appeared to show a display. Further over an archway had doors painted with lettering she presumed gave the company's name. The fog closed in before she could view either. What the premises next door were used for was no concern of hers. What lay behind this door was. Without further ado Maddie reached for the knocker.

Chapter Fourteen

Agnes rubbed her eyes which hurt from straining to decipher her father's scrawl and method of bookkeeping in the large black ledger. She wasn't about to give up, though.

The night was unusually dark due to the fog and she had had to light an oil lamp. As it was old, the light it gave off was not very good. Another legacy of her father's penny-pinching ways. She decided to buy herself a new one. She was tired, having spent another sleepless night and rising early to journey into town to make an appointment with the lawyer, then a visit to the shops to buy provisions she had needed, finally alighting from the tram well before her normal stop to place her card in the Post Office window. She had trudged the rest of the way home on foot laden down with bags. On arriving home she had wanted to do nothing more than curl up in the armchair by a blazing fire, enjoying the feeling of decadently wasting time and money which would set her father spinning in his grave. But she couldn't quite bring herself to do that after a lifetime of being careful. She had stacked the fire higher than normal, though, and the heat it was giving off was very comforting, the dancing flames helping to alleviate the austerity of the room.

When she first opened the ledger an hour or so ago, the columns of figures jumped haphazardly out at her, making no sense. Now, though, she felt a certain amount of satisfaction. The figures were beginning to seem less daunting and their meaning was becoming clear. One of the columns obviously showed the cost of raw materials they had purchased. Another the purchase tax they had to pay the government – only by her calculation that did not appear to be as much as it should be, the figures were inconsistent. Despite her pride at beginning to make some sort of sense of it all, it was still very confusing. The thing she was totally sure of was that the columns were totalled up on a weekly basis. She had only ten more to work through until it all came together. Though she wondered if the effort was worth it since the business was going to be sold, but decided if she and Alice did open a shop or something else, they would need to keep books so her time would not be entirely wasted.

She heard the knocker, the sound seeming to echo down the passage. Closing the ledger, Agnes rose to answer the door, wondering who could be calling.

As she opened it a pretty young woman stared back at her. She seemed a mite nervous.

'Can I help you?' Agnes asked, thinking she had probably knocked on the wrong door.

Momentarily Maddie stared in amazement at the tall, thin, extremely plain woman standing before her. Entirely dressed in unfashionable black and peering at her through the dense fog, she appeared formidable, frightening even. Maddie gulped, her instincts screaming at her to run. But it wouldn't be right to do that. She cleared her throat. 'I've come to make enquiries about the job.'

'The job?' Agnes frowned. 'Oh, the job. I hadn't expected anyone to apply so soon. Please, do come in,' she invited, stepping aside.

An extremely apprehensive Maddie followed her down a long dark passage towards a room near the back. As they entered, she glanced around hurriedly. Despite the fire burning in the grate, the drab, dismal surroundings hit her full force, the forbidding atmosphere cloaking her like thick spider's webs. She shuddered, for an instant transported back to her home in Market Harborough, only this room was worse if that were possible. One thing registered: they were obviously God-fearing people judging by the huge Bible open on a lectern by the far wall.

'Please sit down.' Agnes indicated a fireside chair.

Maddie perched tentatively on the edge.

'Would you like some tea?'

She shook her head.

Agnes sat down opposite and looked at her prospective employee. She was well presented, had an intelligent forehead and direct gaze, her severe hairstyle not disguising a very pretty face. For a moment she was reminded of what God had failed to give her but pushed these thoughts aside. She could not hold against the woman the fact that she had been blessed with pleasing features. Whether she could do the job, whether she indeed wanted it, was the most important thing. It suddenly occurred to Agnes that she hadn't the first notion how to conduct an interview.

There was nothing for it, she felt, but to be honest. She looked at Maddie helplessly, shrugging her shoulders. 'To be honest, I don't know where to begin. I haven't done this before. You don't happen to know, do you?'

Her tone of voice was warm, her helplessness genuine, and Maddie suddenly felt this woman was not frightening at all. The apprehension she was feeling vanished. She liked this woman, there was something vulnerable about her. She didn't know why but Maddie felt an affinity to her somehow, knew instinctively that she was kind. Maddie relaxed back in her chair. 'Actually, if you want the truth, I have no idea. I've never attended a proper interview before.'

Agnes stared at her in surprise then burst out laughing, a high merry chortle. 'What a pair we make, don't we? Are you sure you wouldn't like a cup of tea? I know I would and I'd like you to join me.'

Maddie smiled. 'Then I will, thank you.'

Ten minutes or so later Agnes passed Maddie a china

185

cup filled with strong sweet tea, just the way she preferred it. 'Now, where will I start?'

Maddie thought for a moment. 'You could ask me my name.'

'Why, how silly of me, of course.' Agnes put down her cup and saucer and held out her hand. 'Agnes Clatteridge. I'm very pleased to meet you. Very pleased indeed. And you are?'

Maddie leaned forward to accept her hand and shook it firmly. 'Maude Ashman. But I prefer to be called Maddie. I'm pleased to meet you too.'

They settled back in their respective chairs.

'Maddie. What a pretty name,' mused Agnes. 'Well, Miss Ashman, I'd better explain the job I had in mind, which to be honest will be difficult. I don't exactly want . . .' She paused. 'Well, I suppose I do.' She sighed in exasperation, annoyed with herself. 'Let me start again. I should explain that my father died recently, last week in fact, and we, that's myself and my sister who's not here by the way – she's gone ahead to an aunt of ours in Scarborough. I'm on my own and I have to go about selling the family business and seeing to this house and, oh, there's all sorts of things that have to be done and seen to and I don't know where to start. I . . .' She stopped abruptly, knowing she was babbling, not at all the conduct of an employer. What must Miss Ashman think of her? 'I'm not making sense, am I?' she said apologetically.

'Not exactly, but I gather you're looking for someone to help you sort everything out?'

Agnes eyed her, impressed. 'Yes, that's exactly what I want. I just want someone I can rely on to work alongside me. And it would be nice if we got on well too.' She clasped her hands and frowned. 'There is one problem, though. I can't say for how long the job will last. It all depends how long it takes me to find a buyer. I suppose I should have put that on the card. How remiss of me.'

'So the job's just temporary?'

Agnes eyes Maddie tentatively. 'Yes, it is.' She leaned forward. 'You seem just the kind of person I'm looking for. Would you . . . is there any chance you might consider taking it?' Agnes knew she wouldn't, of course, she was hoping for too much. Maude Ashman was far too pretty, too intelligent, to want to accept a lowly position like this, even temporarily. She prepared herself for rejection.

Maddie, though, had no hesitation. It was just what she was looking for. It would be the breathing space she needed, and paid too, while she decided the direction in which she wanted to go. 'Yes, I'll take it.'

Agnes tried not to appear too disappointed. 'I understand, my dear.' Then Maddie's response registered. Her eyes widened, her mouth dropped open, her delight readily apparent. 'Oh! You will? Why, that's splendid. Oh, please have some more tea,' she urged her new employee. 'The wage I'm offering – is it enough?' she asked, replenishing Maddie's cup and passing it back.

'It's very generous, I'd say.'

'Is it? Oh, good. So when can you start?'

'When would you like me to?'

'Tomorrow?'

'Six-thirty?'

Agnes's face fell in dismay. 'That early? Do we have to?'

Maddie's mouth dropped open. 'I'm sorry?'

Agnes laughed at the look on her face. 'I've had a lifetime of rising at five-thirty. Such an ungodly hour. Especially in the winter. So shall we say eight? And we'll finish . . .' She shrugged her shoulders. 'Whenever. But never after six-thirty. Will that suit you? Those are my only rules.'

Would that suit her? Maddie had been made to rise early too as per her mother's orders, never allowed the luxury of a lie in. To begin her working day at that time suited her very well indeed. And finishing before six-thirty was perfect timing for her to get home in time to help with preparations for the evening meal. A warm glow filled her. Fate had played

187

its part by bringing her here. She could so easily have missed that card. She was going to enjoy working here. It was a pity it was only for a short space of time.

'Eight it is,' she happily replied.

'Now,' said Agnes, 'is there anything else you need to know?'

'I don't think so.'

'Well, if you think of anything, just ask. It's terribly foggy but I'll show you out the back way so you can get a feel for the place, and I'll introduce you to Mr Simpson. He's our carpenter. I'm sure you'll like him. And there's Oswald Peabody. He's our lad.' She failed to comment further on Peabody. Maddie looked astute enough to make up her own mind about him. Agnes glanced at the clock. It was six-forty-five. 'I expect Peabody's gone home by now. You'll meet him tomorrow.' Time enough, she thought. 'Oh, and, of course, I mustn't forget Ned.'

'And what does he do?'

'Ned is our horse.'

Ah, thought Maddie. A horse usually pulled a cart. The family business must have something to do with deliveries of some sort.

'I'll have to find a new home for him,' Agnes was saying, more to herself than to Maddie. 'That's just one of the things I have to do.' Her face filled with sadness. 'I shall miss him when he goes.' Still, she thought, when decisions were made, there were prices to be paid. 'If you've finished your tea, I'll show you around.'

Agnes rose. Putting down her cup, Maddie did likewise and followed her through the kitchen and out into the cobbled yard.

The fog was still swirling thickly. It was very dark now and visibility was bad. Through the fog a dull light shone from somewhere to the right of them. 'Ah,' said Agnes. 'Mr Simpson is still in the workshed. I might have known. Follow me and be careful – there are things lying around. I wouldn't wish you to harm yourself. Mind that barrel of pitch, it's just by the workshed door. Get some of that on you and you'll never get it off.'

'What's the pitch used for?' Maddie asked curiously. Must be something to do with the upkeep of the delivery wagons, she guessed.

'Oh, we use it to line the coffins.'

Maddie stopped abruptly, frozen rigid. 'Coffins?'

Agnes turned to face her. 'Yes. Apart from the odd occasion when we've been desperate, we make all our own,' she said proudly. The horrified expression on Maddie's face registered then and she frowned. 'You did know this was an undertaker's?'

Maddie gulped. 'No,' she uttered. 'Actually, I didn't.'

Chapter Fifteen

'The Sisters Grim? Maddie, you're not? You're never going to work for them? You must be mad.'

'Ruth, stop it,' Sarah scolded. 'Maddie's quite capable of deciding where she wants to work.' Privately she shared her daughter's views, though should she have voiced them she wouldn't have spoken quite so bluntly. 'Just eat your dinner up before it gets cold.'

'Your mother's right, Ruth,' George piped up, though he too thought Maddie should reconsider her decision.

Ruth forked a piece of sausage. 'But, Mam, I'm only trying to warn her. I mean, who in their right mind would want to work in a funeral parlour of all places? I wish I had working hours like that, though,' she muttered to herself. 'Fancy not having to start work until eight.' Though even considering the late start, nothing would entice her to work in that place. She put the food in her mouth and, still chewing, said, 'People reckon they're witches. Have you seen the way they dress and how ugly . . .'

'That's enough, Ruth. Stop being so unkind,' her mother retorted. 'You can't blame anyone for what God blessed them with in the looks department. As for witches, they don't exist. And stop speaking with your mouth full, it's rude.'

'I think Miss Clatteridge is rather nice,' said Maddie. 'I must admit, though, when I first saw her she appeared rather frightening. But that was before I talked to her. She's very kind, really. I know I shall enjoy working there. And she's assured me she doesn't expect me to get involved in anything other than helping to sort out the house. I won't have to go anywhere near where they deal with . . . well, you know.'

'If you change your mind, you can always look for something else,' suggested Sarah.

'Did you see any dead bodies?' asked Roy keenly.

Shuddering at the thought, Maddie shook her head. 'No. And I hope I never will while I'm there.' The very thought terrified her. Her first reaction on finding out just exactly what the family concern was shook her witless. A great urge to retract her acceptance of the job and run away had overtaken her. But she couldn't. She had made a commitment. Besides, she couldn't bring herself to upset Miss Clatteridge.

Death, her new employer had reminded her, happened to everyone. It was a part of life that was unavoidable. And someone had to take care of burials. It was just a job, if not one to most people's liking. Some people, due to ignorance, feared the dead. But there was nothing to fear. The dead couldn't hurt anyone. It had always been Miss Clatteridge's fixed opinion that those one should fear were the living. Maddie had found a great deal of sense and comfort in her words and with an effort had forced her fears away. Now she was looking forward to starting this job and wanted nothing to mar that.

Sarah thought it time the subject was changed. 'How was your day, dear?' she asked her husband.

'Oh, fine,' he replied absently.

Normally he had much to say, entertaining his family with incidents that had happened on his travels and tales of his customers' antics, especially those who tried anything to avoid their payments, but Sarah knew that as the time drew nearer he was becoming increasingly concerned about his imminent confrontation with Harriet. Not only was he going to tell her that Maddie was now living with them, which was not going to please her one little bit, but he had the daunting task of demanding a release from their marriage. Harriet had no hold over them now but nevertheless facing her wasn't going to be easy. Sarah wished she could accompany him, be a prop, give him her support, but this was something George had to handle by himself.

She noticed her son's glum expression. 'What's the matter, Roy?' she asked in concern.

'Can I still go to the football on Saturday? Leicester's playing Sheffield. Should be a good match. All me mates are going.'

George's head jerked up. 'Why do you think you can't go, Roy?'

'Well . . . I didn't think it'd be right, me going off enjoying meself when you have ter . . . well, yer know.'

George put down his knife and fork, and glanced at each of his family in turn. 'Now listen to me, all of you. What I have to do is for me alone. I want none of you to change your plans. Is that clear?' They all nodded. 'We've never kept secrets from each other and I'll admit I'm not looking forward to it, but it's got to be faced. Now Maddie is away from Market Harborough and I have no fear of her being caught up in any of this, my mind's at rest. Harriet can no longer hold out. I hope to catch the early train back. Enough time to sort matters out, I think. While I'm gone I expect you all to carry on as you normally do. All right? I'll tell you what's happened when I return and we'll face it together like we always do.' He picked up his plate and smiled at Sarah. 'Any more gravy, love?'

Ruth scraped back her chair. 'It's your turn for the pots tonight, Roy. Maddie, are you coming upstairs with me? I'd like your opinion on what to wear.'

'Another date. Who's it with this time?' asked her mother.

'Desmond. He's calling for me, Mam, so don't worry, you can give him the once over. He works in our despatch. I know you'll like him,' she said, heading for the door. 'I've fancied him for ages. Nearly gave up hoping he'd ask me out. He did this morning. Weren't that brave of him?' she said laughing. 'Come on, Maddie.'

This was the first time Ruth had invited her up to her private sanctuary and Maddie felt honoured.

'What d'yer think then?' asked her half-sister, holding a dress up against herself.

'It's very pretty,' Maddie said admiringly, delighted to have been asked. 'Where's he taking you?'

'To the pictures, I expect.'

Though Maddie had never herself had the pleasure of going to the pictures, had no idea what people wore to such a venue, she felt the dress would not look out of place. 'Then I think that dress is ideal.'

Ruth flung it over the back of a wicker chair and looked at Maddie fondly as she sat on the bed. 'I can't tell you how pleased I am we've finally met. All these years I've wondered what you looked like and what kind of person you were. Now I know.'

'I hope you're not disappointed?'

'What? Not at all. I think you're lovely. I couldn't have wished for a better sister. This is the first time we've really been on our own since you came and I want to tell you that since I knew I had a sister, I've been desperate to see you. Dad's always said we have a look of each other. Do you think we do?'

Maddie looked at her searchingly. Ruth, she thought, was so pretty, while her own mother had instilled in her for so long that she was plain she still had trouble thinking otherwise. 'We have the same colour eyes,' she said. 'And the same nose.'

Ruth scrutinised herself in her hand mirror. 'Yes, we do, don't we? And our chins, I think. I wish I was as pretty as you, though.' She clapped her hands. 'It's great having a sister, isn't it?'

Maddie smiled. 'Yes, it is.' And she sincerely thought so too.

'Having a brother's all right, but it ain't the same. You can't talk about women's things with boys, can you? Or go shopping?'

'No, you can't,' Maddie agreed.

Ruth perched beside her on the edge of the bed. 'Was it a shock?'

'A shock?' she queried.

'Finding out about all this? I mean, you knew nothing, did you? About us.'

Maddie took a deep breath. 'It was, yes. I had trouble taking it all in at first. But now . . .'

'Now?' Ruth asked, tentatively.

'I'm so happy.'

'And I'm glad. We all want you to be.' A frown crossed her pretty face. 'She sounds awful, your mother. Was she? Was it terrible living with her?'

Maddie bowed her head and clasped her hands. 'I knew no different,' she said softly.

'No, I expect you didn't. But you do now, don't you?' Ruth's face filled with concern. 'You won't ever leave us and go back to her will you, Maddie? I couldn't bear that to happen.'

She raised her head. 'No, I won't. I'm here for good.' She smiled. 'Shouldn't you be getting ready?'

Ruth jumped up. 'Yes, I should.'

Maddie watched with interest as Ruth's dress was hurriedly pulled on and she sat before her dressing-table mirror to brush her bobbed light brown hair and apply a trace of makeup. Although Maddie didn't think she needed any at all to enhance her features.

Ruth suddenly swivelled around in her chair and unexpectedly asked, 'Have you ever been in love?'

Maddie froze for a moment before answering, 'Yes, I have.'

'You have? Really? True love, was it?'

She nodded.

'It was? Oh!' Ruth exclaimed in awe. 'Did he love you?'

Maddie's eyes became distant as a great sadness enveloped her. A vision of Josh rose before her. He was smiling at her, arms outstretched invitingly. She forced it away. 'I thought so,' she murmured. 'But it wasn't meant to be.'

Ruth eyed her sadly. 'Oh, I see. But you'll fall in love again, Maddie. You will, you'll see.'

I doubt it, she thought. What she might feel for another man, should she be fortunate enough to meet one, would be deep fondness, but love like she had felt for Josh? Never. It wasn't possible.

She pushed the sadness away and smiled brightly. 'I've too much to be getting on with to be worried about falling in love.'

'But when you do,' Ruth urged, 'you must promise I'll be your bridesmaid?'

'If ever I get married, that goes without saying. Now you should really get a move on,' said Maddie, rising from the bed. 'I must go and see if Sarah needs a hand with anything.'

Ruth jumped up from her chair. 'Just a minute, Maddie.'

She stopped and turned towards Ruth who threw her arms around her and kissed her affectionately on the cheek.

Maddie was taken aback for a moment by such a show of affection, something she was not used to. 'What was that for?' she asked.

'Does there have to be a reason to show someone you love them?'

Maddie shook her head. 'No, there doesn't, does there?'

And she kissed her back.

Chapter Sixteen

'Maude living with you! With your whore and bastards? I won't stand for that! You'll send her back or I'll come and fetch her. You had no right enticing her to go. How did you do it, George? What did you bribe her with?' Harriet's face darkened thunderously.

'I didn't bribe her, Harriet, how could I? Maddie was under the impression I was dead. How could you do that? It's despicable, that's what it is. What happened to all the letters I sent her? And the presents? I expect they went on the back of the fire the same as that doll I bought her.'

'You're right, they did. I had every right to tell her you were dead, and everyone else for that matter, because the moment you walked out on us you were dead to me.'

'If you'd tried to be a wife to me, Harriet, that might never have come about.'

She sneered. 'Well, now Maddie knows your sordid secret! Now she knows what kind of father you are. How do you feel about that, George? Proud, are you?'

'Stop it, Harriet. Maddie came to us voluntarily.' His eyes narrowed questioningly. 'And I'm of the opinion that something happened to bring her to us. What was it, Harriet? What did you do to her to make her do that?'

She stared at him, her immediate worry that Maddie had talked thankfully lifted. If she hadn't said anything by now, chances were she wouldn't. What Maude had discovered would remain a secret. Satisfied of that, she felt better able to respond. 'How dare you question me like that?

I've been a good mother to her.'

'No, you haven't, Harriet. You ruled her life so strictly she hardly dared breathe without your permission. You never showed her any affection.'

'What would you know? You weren't here. You've only got her word, and let me tell you, your daughter is a liar.'

'That's not true. One thing Maddie is not is a liar. But you are, aren't you, Harriet? Anyway, you were glad I left. It's what you really wanted. You didn't want a husband. You just wanted my name and the money I gave you, and I suspect to keep Maddie by your side to look after you in your old age. What did you do with the money I gave you, Harriet? Nothing went Maddie's way, did it? Or on making this place homely. You haven't a clue how to make a home, have you? Or more likely you didn't want to. You like living like this, don't you? No warmth, no comforts. That's the kind of person you are.'

She was staring at him. He had never dared speak to her in such a way before. Suddenly she knew he was no longer afraid of her and that thought was a worrying one.

George exhaled sharply. 'Whether you like it or not, Maddie is with us of her own free will and she's staying.'

'I don't believe that! You had something to do with it. And she's selfish, thoughtless. I had no warning, nothing. You don't know your own daughter, George. She's devious, let me tell you. She's . . .'

'Stop it, Harriet,' he ordered firmly, his tone icy. 'Maddie is nothing of the kind.'

'Huh! You can think what you like but I've raised her for twenty-six years, I know exactly what she's capable of.'

'Oh, and what's that, Harriet?'

She ignored his question. She could tell him about the baby. That would shock him. Oh, wouldn't it just! Show him his daughter in her true light. And of course her deceitful relationship with that low-life from across the canal. But to do so would mean he'd probe and ask questions Harriet wasn't prepared to answer. 'You'll send her back,' she demanded.

'She's old enough to make up her own mind, Harriet. Are you forgetting she's a grown woman? She's made up her mind to live with us and there's nothing you can do about it. You know that.'

Harriet did. She had lost control of her daughter. Her life's plan, the one she had made twenty-seven years ago, lay in ruins and there was nothing she could do about it. Soon people would know what she'd been striving to avoid all these years. That she had made a sham marriage. They would talk and gossip would spread and her life would become hell. The thought of being the butt of everyone's joke, just as she and her mother had been years ago, crucified her.

George's shocking announcement that Maude was living with him had struck her rigid. Until that moment she had been absolutely confident that her daughter was licking her wounds somewhere and would soon return, begging forgiveness, and life would return to normal. But that wasn't about to happen. Harriet's mind whirled frantically. She hadn't schemed and carried out her plans just for her daughter to do as she pleased. Who did she think she was? Where was her loyalty?

'I'll come and fetch her myself.'

'You can try, Harriet. Maddie won't come with you. And don't forget, she won't be facing you on her own. She has all of us behind her.'

'You bastard!' she hissed, and clenched her fists in fury. She knew what was coming next.

And she was right.

George took a deep breath and steeled himself. 'I have honoured our agreement, Harriet, for more years than I thought to, you can't deny that. Now I want a divorce.'

'Well, you can't have one.'

'You can't stop me!'

'Oh, I can. I won't agree.'

'You won't honour our agreement after I've kept my side of it?'

'Did you expect me to? If so you're a fool. I'll still drag you through the court. My story will still hold good. People will think me a martyr for putting up with your deceit all these years. They won't blame me for making out I'm a widow, they'll understand totally by the time I've finished. And understand this, George. It's not just Maude's good name you should be trying to protect but your two bastards' as well, because I'll make sure they get dragged into it, rest assured.'

He stared at her for several long moments, knowing that to challenge her or argue further was a total waste of time and effort. He sighed in resignation. 'Have it your own way, Harriet. But I'll hand over no more money. If you want to challenge that then go ahead, you have my blessing.'

With that he walked out of the house.

She stood rigid for several long moments before her eyes glinted unpleasantly. All was not quite lost. Her 'widowhood' was still intact. And the story she had concocted to cover Maude's absence could be elaborated on to include the fact that she had left home for good. She harboured little feeling for her daughter, in that respect wouldn't miss her. The work she had done could be tackled by someone else should Harriet choose to employ them. And what of George's money? What of it? She smirked wickedly. He had no idea that she had never used what he had given her. Every penny was hidden inside a cash box, along with the unexpected windfall she had received last year. It had built into a nice little nest egg, just as she had intended. But he'd never get his divorce. She'd have to be dead before he was free of her.

Face stony now, she walked through to the kitchen where she set about cooking a solitary piece of offal for her solitary dinner.

* * *

Sarah shot out of her chair and into the passage as soon as she heard the sound of the front door. She threw her arms around George, crushing him against her. 'How did it go?' she asked eagerly.

'She won't divorce me,' he whispered.

Secretly Sarah had been expecting as much. 'Well, we've lived like this for twenty-five years, my dear, we can live through this setback too.'

He pulled away from her and scanned her face. 'Are you sure, Sarah? Really?'

'A piece of paper makes no difference to the way I feel about you, George. I've got everything of you, my darling, but your name. If keeping your name is what keeps her happy, then let her have it, that's what I say.'

'And the children?'

'What do you think.'

He nodded. His children, all three of them, would say the same as Sarah. 'But what about when Ruth or Roy want to wed? It'll have to come out then. The fact that we're not married.'

'If their chosen spouses don't understand then they've made the wrong choice, ain't they?'

He hugged her fiercely. 'Oh, Sarah, I do love you. What a lucky man I am.'

'And I agree,' she said, chuckling.

'There's one good thing come out of my visit.'

'Oh, yes, and what's that?' she asked keenly.

'My money to Harriet stops, so we haven't the burden of that anymore.'

She sighed in relief. 'Then that's more than I bargained for.' She eyed him worriedly. 'About Maddie, George. What was her reaction to that?'

'She . . . let's just say Harriet wasn't pleased. But I think she's accepted Maddie is with us now.'

Sarah knew much more had passed between George and his wife, the poor man had probably been to hell and back, but decided to let it drop. He'd tell her the fine detail when he was good and ready. Right now he needed food and rest surrounded by the love of his family.

'Come on,' she said. 'I've had the kettle boiling ready for you and I've your dinner keeping hot.'

Hands clasped, they walked down the passage to where the rest of the family were waiting.

Chapter Seventeen

'There's a Mr Snood to see you, Miss Clatteridge.'

Agnes raised her head and looked across at Maddie, standing in the bedroom doorway. Frowning, she placed the linen she was sorting down on the bed. 'I've never known Mr Snood call here before. I wonder what he could be wanting? Most odd. It's a bit late for him to be paying his respects. I can't see his doing that anyway. He and my father were more rivals than friends. Oh, there's only one way to find out what he wants and that's to go and see him,' she said, untying her apron. She smoothed her skirt, pulled down the sleeves of her blouse and ran a hand over her head. Tendrils of hair were escaping from the bun at the nape of her neck. 'Do I look tidy enough to receive a visitor?'

'You look very nice,' Maddie assured her.

'Well, I'd better see him then. Would you be kind enough to make some tea?'

'Of course. It would be my pleasure.'

'Thank you,' said Agnes.

Down in the kitchen, busying herself making the tea, all Maddie's thoughts centred on her job. She had been right to take it. Working for Miss Agnes Clatteridge was proving highly enjoyable, apart from the fact that the house was quite eerie, its dark wood and paintwork hiding odd nooks and crannies in endless dim passageways. Several times she had wrenched open doors in walls, expecting to find a cupboard, and been shocked to discover a dust-filled room which had not seen life, except for the collection of creepy crawlies it was home to, for numerous years. But she didn't let that deter her. It was only a house after all and since the curtains had been drawn wide and daylight allowed in, it wasn't quite so bad.

Miss Clatteridge and she had worked hard, side by side, and the closeness between them was building gradually. The more of an insight she gained into her employer, the more she found she liked her. Little by little she was seeing beyond the severe outward appearance to the warm, kind human being who lay underneath. A good man, Maddie thought, would not go far wrong should he take the time and trouble to do the same. Agnes Clatteridge had so much love to give the right person. It was a pity about her severe style of dress which did nothing to endear her to people. A softer, more colourful style and her hair done differently would do wonders for her. If only Maddie could somehow find a way to broach the matter, help her just as Ruth and Sarah had helped Maddie herself.

She had been at Clatteridge's a month now, in Leicester just on six weeks, and it seemed a lifetime. Her previous existence far removed from what she was living now. She did think of her mother, wondering how she was faring now she was alone, but her feelings were pitying not loving.

The tea mashed, Maddie took the carefully set tray through and returned to the kitchen, thinking she would take a cup across to Mr Simpson and Oswald. Mr Simpson was a nice man, very pleasant and most courteous. Oswald she hadn't taken much of a liking to. He was lazy, she knew that much, but she had been too busy to notice much more than that.

Over the last four weeks she and Miss Clatteridge had cleared the attic, an arduous task. Years of dust had had to be disturbed to uncover the secrets that lay beneath.

It had saddened Maddie greatly to stand aside and watch silently while Agnes had dusted off two large trunks, prised them open and carefully removed the contents. They were her mother's clothes, some badly moth-eaten. Maddie knew it had broken her heart to part with them all, except for an elaborately embroidered silk shawl which the moths had missed. She would keep that as a memento of the mother she'd hardly known. The good clothes, albeit dreadfully old-fashioned, had been aired outside, then bagged up to take to the Salvation Army. Hopefully they would find a use for them. The others had been thrown away.

'Your father must have loved her very much to have kept her clothes for all these years,' were the only words of comfort Maddie thought it fitting to express.

Agnes had nodded. 'Yes, I'd like to think that.'

They had found an old rocking horse, its saddle rotting, mane non-existent. 'I remember this,' Agnes proclaimed delightedly. 'I spent many happy hours riding on old Dobbin. That was, of course, until Father decided I was too old for him. Alice never got to use him. We weren't allowed toys then. I know we would have been had Mother not died.'

'Do you remember her?' Maddie had asked.

'Strangely, no, I don't. Funny that I should have memories of Dobbin but none of Mother while she was alive. But I was only two when she died having Alice and we weren't allowed to talk about her afterwards. We do have a photograph, though.'

'I've seen it.' Maddie stopped herself from saying she had thought her mother very pretty, sparing Miss Clatteridge's feelings. 'She looked kind.'

'Yes, she was,' Agnes had replied dismissively, making it obvious to Maddie that she was finding this conversation difficult. 'Now what were we doing? Oh, yes, Dobbin. Seems a shame to throw him out. Oswald has a young sister, I believe. I'll give him the horse for her. Mr Simpson can maybe do something with the saddle.'

The attic finally cleared of all its old clutter – just a few bits that could be worth selling, the rest burned in the furnace by Mr Simpson – and dusted and swept, they were now starting on the bedrooms. Maddie had been helping Agnes sort through the linen cupboard when the knock on the door had come and she had been sent to answer it.

She had taken an instant dislike to the man she found facing her. He was portly, stomach extending well in front of him. The chain of his fob watch, stretched very taut across it, looked to be in danger of snapping. He was well-dressed, but most obviously of all he oozed self-importance.

'Miss Clatteridge at home?' he had demanded in a bellow. 'Tell her Mr Snood wants to see her.'

'I'll go and enquire,' Maddie politely replied.

'If you're going to enquire from her then she's in. Don't fool with me, girl. Tell her I want to see her and that I haven't all day.'

He had pushed past Maddie then and made his own way into the parlour.

Now she was wondering how Agnes was getting on with that oaf of a man. After her remark that he'd never called before, Maddie could not help but wonder what he wanted. In the four weeks she had been here, the callers had all been tradesmen.

'Any tea going, Maddie?'

Her head jerked towards the door to see Ivan Simpson look around it.

She smiled a greeting. 'You smell it, don't you?'

He grinned. 'Well, it's better than what I can afford to mash for meself.'

'I was just about to bring you a mug across.'

'I thought as much so I came to save yer the walk.'

'Come in,' said Maddie. 'You can drink it in here.'

Ivan did not need another invitation. Leaning against the huge pot sink, he supped his tea appreciatively. 'This'd never have 'appened during Cuthbert's day.'

'Cuthbert? Oh, Mr Clatteridge. From what I gather he wasn't a very congenial sort of person.'

'If that word you used means he was awful, then he was.

And that's putting it mildly! Best day's work he ever did for his daughters was having that heart attack. I'm not being unkind – far from it, Maddie – but he wasn't a good man at all. Dreadful to work for.'

She eyed him searchingly. 'But you stayed?'

'Yes, I did,' said Ivan cagily and took another sup of his tea. 'Dropped stone dead without any warning, did Cuthbert Clatteridge, out in that yard.'

'Really?'

'Just by the water pump,' he said, turning slightly to point out of the window. 'Only six apart from family turned up for the funeral and I reckon that were out of morbid curiosity to check he'd really gone. Thank God he has, I say. Is . . . er . . . Miss Clatteridge not around?'

'She's entertaining in the parlour. A Mr Snood.'

'Snood?' Ivan frowned, obviously perturbed. 'I wonder what he could be wantin'?'

'Who is he?'

'Snood? He owns Snood's Funeral Parlour on Wharf Street.' Ivan bit his bottom lip thoughtfully. 'He's one to watch out for, is Mr Snood. I don't know him personally but I know his chippy well. Not got much of a liking for his boss, that much I *do* know. I hope Miss Clatteridge realises to be on her guard.'

Their conversation ceased abruptly as they both heard the click of the front door and moments later Agnes appeared. She looked pleased. Ivan looked somewhat uncomfortable to be caught drinking tea in the kitchen.

'It's all right, Mr Simpson, finish your drink,' she said. 'Anyway you might as well hear my news – I've nothing to hide from you. Mr Snood has made me an offer. It's . . . er . . . not what I was led to expect I might get, but at least it's an offer. He wants to expand, and having heard our business was for sale thought it an ideal opportunity for him. He did say he wasn't willing to pay for any goodwill. Well, I can understand that. We haven't been approached for our services at all since Father died, so I can't expect him to consider paying for something that doesn't in truth still exist. Anyway, I shall be giving his offer my utmost consideration.

'Oh!' she suddenly exclaimed. 'I forgot to return Mr Snood's gloves. I picked them up intending to as I showed him the door but it must have slipped my mind. Be a dear, Maddie. If you go through the yard entrance you should just catch him if you hurry.'

She took the gloves and ran.

As she stopped to open one of the tall arched doors she paused as voices reached her ears. She recognised Mr Snood's. Who on earth was he talking to? Politeness made her wait for a moment before she slipped through the gap in the doors and announced her presence.

'I thought you weren't coming, Pargitt?'

'You said two, Mr Snood. It's not quite that yet. I had that coffin ter finish off.'

Mr Snood, thought Maddie, had arranged to meet a man called Pargitt and from the mention of coffins she assumed it must be business they were about to discuss. Though, she thought, outside the entry to Clatteridge's yard was a strange place in which to have arranged their meeting. Nevertheless she felt she had better make her presence known and hand over the gloves before they got any further. She made to open the door wider when what Mr Snood said next made her hesitate.

'And were yer followed?' he asked.

'No, I don't think so.'

'You'd better not have been. Wouldn't do for us to be seen together, now would it?'

Maddie's ears pricked. Worried about being following and not being seen together? This was not a business meeting as she had first thought. Her suspicions mounted as she remembered Ivan's comments about the man and strained harder to hear.

'Did Mrs Snood ask where you were off to?'

'She did. I told 'er what yer told me to. I wa' just popping out on an errand you'd asked me to do. She told me to 'urry up.'

'Well, we'd better then, hadn't we? Wouldn't do for Mrs Snood to get wind of what I'm up to. God-fearing woman she is – and fair puts the fear of God up me all right! The less she knows about this the better until it's all done and dusted. Just you and me, that's the way I want it kept. You listening?' he snarled.

'Yes, Mr Snood. Yer know you can trust me.' Pargitt's voice grew louder and more insistent.

'Hush, you idiot,' his employer snapped angrily. 'There's ears everywhere, remember.'

Pargitt sniffed. 'So what's the score then, Mr Snood?'

Maddie heard the other man rub his hands together with a dry rasping sound.

'Well, the rumours we got going worked a treat. I was clever to think of that. She's not had a sniff of a job since the old sod passed over.'

'You owe me five bob fer my part in that,' mumbled Pargitt.

'What?'

'Nothin', Mr Snood.'

'Huh! And me letting it be known to the Undertakers' Association that the place is as good as mine has stopped anyone else from getting ideas. And as we know, don't we, Pargitt, word spreads. I know for a fact no one else has bothered even to make enquiries about the place. Don't fancy fighting against me.' He gave a gleeful chuckle. 'That plain-faced creature fell for my patter. I knew she would. Left her to mull over my offer. She'll accept, she's got no choice. But just in case she dithers, we'll do what we planned. You know what to do now. Just like I told yer. Eh, and no more than a shilling. I'm not made of money.'

'What about my half crown for arranging it?'

'You'll have yer money when I sign the papers. Now get to it.'

The conversation ceased and Maddie knew they had both departed. She stood for a moment going over what she had heard. Mr Snood was up to something crooked, she felt sure he was, but just what she'd do about it she wasn't sure.

She assumed Ivan had returned to the shed when she returned as he wasn't in the kitchen. Agnes was washing up.

'Did you catch up with Mr Snood?'

Maddie realised she was still holding the gloves. 'Oh, no, I didn't.'

'Oh, no matter. Leave them on the hall stand. I'll return them when he comes on Saturday.' She stopped her task and eyed Maddie in concern. 'Is anything the matter? You look rather preoccupied?'

'Pardon? Oh, no. Just . . . er . . .' She wondered whether to tell Miss Clatteridge what she had overheard, but decided to mull it over a bit longer first. Maddie didn't want to cause her needless worry over something she could just have misinterpreted. She forced a smile. 'I'm pleased you have an offer at long last, although I know it means my time here is nearly over. I've enjoyed working for you, Miss Clatteridge.'

Agnes smiled broadly. 'And I've enjoyed having you. I shall miss you, my dear. I hope what I say is not one-sided, but I feel we're becoming friends.'

'Yes, me too.'

'Then we must not lose touch. You must write to me, keep me informed of what's happening to you.' Agnes inhaled deeply. 'I have to say, though, that Mr Snood's offer has cheered me somewhat. I was beginning to think no one wanted this place.'

Maddie pressed her lips together. Something Mr Snood had said came back to mind. Rumours. He had said the rumours had worked. What had that meant?

'To be honest,' Agnes was continuing, 'financially things are getting worrying. If it wasn't for the little we make on the nails and bits of carpentry we'd have nothing coming in. I suppose I really ought to consider letting Peabody go – there's hardly enough to keep him occupied – but I don't really want to do that just in case we get a funeral in. We'd need him for that, you see. I couldn't expect Mr Simpson to manage on his own. Oh, dear, it's all such a dilemma. Still, I'll just about get through if this sale goes ahead. I don't see why it shouldn't, Mr Snood seemed keen enough.'

Maddie eyed her anxiously. 'Miss Clatteridge, what you pay me is generous considering. I would accept less if it would help you?'

'Oh, my dear, what a kind gesture! And it's much appreciated. But I'm quite happy with the way things are. You more than earn what I give you. Until the time comes when I cannot afford to keep you on anymore, I'm happy to pay you fairly. I hope to keep you here until the day I move.'

'You talk as if you've already made up your mind, Miss Clatteridge?'

Agnes looked thoughtful. 'Not quite my dear. I have until Saturday, but to be honest with you, I don't think I have any real choice. No one else has come forward, have they? I shall write a letter to Alice tonight, keep her informed of what is going on. I know she'll be pleased if the sale goes ahead. The letter I received from her this morning was so full of how much she's enjoying herself. It's good to know she's happy and I don't have to worry about her. She's been to several tea parties with acquaintances of my aunt's and to a theatre on the sea front. Oh, it all sounds so very nice.' She sighed distantly, then shook herself. 'Right, come on then, Maddie dear, back to the linen. It won't sort itself.'

As she always did at leaving time Maddie popped her head around the shed door to announce her departure. 'Goodnight, Ivan. See you in the morning,' she called loudly.

'No need to shout, gel, I ain't deaf,' he said, appearing to one side of her.

211

Maddie jumped. 'I didn't see you there. Thought you'd be at the back of the shed.'

'Well, I ain't,' he said, laughing. Then looked at her, frowning. 'What's up, gel?'

'Pardon? Nothing. Why?'

He shrugged his shoulders. 'Just looks to me like you've summat on yer mind. My mistake. Goodnight.'

'Goodnight,' she said again and made to walk away, then stopped, turning around. 'Ivan, can I talk to you, please?'

''Course.' His eyes narrowed in concern. 'I was right, there is summat wrong.'

'I don't quite know if wrong's the word. I would like your opinion, though, as you're the only other person I can discuss this with, really. I wasn't going to say anything. Well, not just yet until I gave it more thought.' She took a breath. 'But I need to tell someone, just in case there's something not right . . .'

'You ain't mekin' sense, gel. Come through,' he said. 'Oswald's gone 'ome so we won't be disturbed.'

He wiped a stool for Maddie before she sat down, Ivan opposite her, their knees not quite touching. 'Now,' he said, hands clasped, leaning towards her. 'Tell me what's ailing yer?'

'There's nothing ailing me, Ivan I'm just bothered, that's all, about something I happened to overhear. It was when I went to catch up with Mr Snood. I overheard him talking to someone. Pargitt was his name, I think. I'm sure I heard that correctly. Anyway . . .' Maddie related what she had overheard. When she had finished she eyed Ivan worriedly. 'What do you make of it?'

Face grave, he leaned back, folding his arms. 'I don't know. But I can tell yer this – I don't like it. As I said before, that Mr Snood is a slippery customer by all accounts. You sure that's what you 'eard?'

'As sure as I can be. Of course, he might not have been

212

talking about his business with Miss Clatteridge. But I'd guess he was.'

Ivan sat in silence for a moment, Maddie looking on. 'I think so too. He's up ter summat,' he finally declared. 'I can feel it in me water. But how we'll go about finding out is another matter.' He felt a surge of protective sympathy towards the woman he loved and before he could stop himself, blurted out, 'If he's planning 'ote to cause Miss Clatteridge grief then he'd better watch out.' Maddie jumped, startled at the savagery of his tone, which Ivan noticed. 'Well, what I mean is,' he continued, 'Miss Clatteridge is me boss. I can't stand by and let him do wrong against her, now can I?'

'No, you can't,' agreed Maddie. 'Neither can I.'

'Right,' he said, relieved, hoping he had given reason enough for his outburst. It wouldn't do for Maddie to get suspicions of his true feelings towards Agnes; they must remain his secret. He wouldn't want Maddie knowing what a fool he was. He liked her. Thought Agnes had made a good choice in taking her on. Maddie, in her own way, was doing a lot for Agnes. Since her arrival a new woman was emerging. One who did not carry herself quite so stiffly and was certainly more talkative. He loved Agnes regardless, but the changes taking place were making her more endearing if that were possible. Ivan sighed forlornly. Despite knowing it was selfish of him, he hoped no other man took notice.

'Anything wrong, Ivan?'

'Eh? No,' he answered more abruptly than he'd meant to. 'Listen, I don't think we should say anything to Miss Clatteridge just yet.'

'You don't?'

He shook his head. 'I want time to think on this. Mull it over, like. No point in worrying her unnecessarily. She's enough on her plate. Need to be sure before we say 'ote.' He paused for a moment. 'I might just pop over Wharf Street way tonight, see if I can find Bert Knapp. He's Snood's

213

chief chippy. I'll tek him for a pint. See if I can find out anything.'

'Such as?'

He shrugged his shoulders. 'You never know, do yer. Might be summat and nothin'. Better than doing n'ote.'

A thought struck Maddie. 'I could ask my father if he knows anything about Mr Snood. He comes into contact with all sorts in his line. Actually Mr Snood might even be a customer of his firm.'

'That's worth a try an' all. You get off home then and we'll talk in the morning. Try not to worry, Maddie.'

'I won't, but I like Miss Clatteridge.'

So do I, thought Ivan, and more than like. And woe betide anyone who thinks they can ride roughshod over her and hope to get away with it!

Chapter Eighteen

They were all sitting around the table talking, the only difference being that Sarah was unusually quiet.

'Mam? Mam!' Roy repeated. 'Can I have that last piece of pie or what?'

'Eh? Oh, sorry, Roy, 'course you can. Custard?' she said, reaching for the jug. 'Do you want any more rhubarb pie, dear?' she asked George.

'No, I'm full, thanks. That was grand, as usual,' he said appreciatively, rubbing his stomach. When he received no reply he eyed her in concern. 'You all right, love?'

'Mmmm? Oh, yes, I'm fine, just tired. We were very busy at work today. I never got time for a proper sit down. We had two assistants off sick. If you don't mind,' she said, scraping back her chair, 'I'll make a start on the pots and then I'm going up.'

'I'll see to the dishes,' offered Maddie. 'It's my turn anyway.'

'And Ruth's ter dry,' piped up Roy.

'I hadn't forgotten,' his sister snapped.

'You get off upstairs, love,' said George. 'I'll bring you a cuppa up, shall I?'

'Yes, I'd like that. Ta.'

She went round the table kissing each in turn on the cheek, including Maddie. 'Goodnight, everyone,' she said as she left the room.

'Is Mam all right, Dad?' asked Ruth. 'That's the second time she's gone ter bed early this week.'

'Yes, it is, isn't it?' he mused thoughtfully. 'But I'm sure

215

she's just tired like she says, so stop worrying.' His instructions to his children didn't stop him feeling concerned, however. He'd make Sarah a cup of tea and go and talk to her, to be sure she wasn't hiding anything. Come to think of it, she did look a little peaky.

Ruth and Roy had finished their share of the chores and had departed, and Maddie had begun to stack the dirty plates when she remembered she had wanted to ask her father about Mr Snood. 'Father, can I talk to you for a moment?'

'Of course. If it's private we could shut the door in case Ruth or Roy come in.'

'No, it's not private. Not really.' Besides, nothing was private in this house. The family kept no secrets and so she felt quite at liberty to ask her father what she wanted to know. After years of not being able to talk freely on any matter, being able to now, and being listened to and offered advice, was quite a revelation and something she welcomed.

'Do you happen to know a Mr Snood at all?' she asked, sitting down. 'I don't know whether he's one of your customers or not?'

George shook his head. 'No, not a Mr Snood. Wait a minute – the Snood you're referring to – is he the one who has the funeral parlour?'

'Yes, that's him. Do you know him?'

'Not personally. Just of him. I'm not sure if he uses our company for his insurance needs. He might not even have any. Lots don't bother or can't afford it. Why are you asking about him, Maddie?'

She told him what had happened.

'Oh, I see.' Thoughtfully George took off his spectacles, wiped them, them put them back on. 'I could make discreet enquiries?'

'Would you, Father. I'd be most grateful. I'm worried for Miss Clatteridge, you see.'

He smiled. 'You like her, don't you?'

'I do. Very much.'

'I'll see what I can do. Now I'm off to make your mother – sorry, Sarah – that cup of tea.'

Thoughts of Harriet flashed immediately to mind and Maddie became worried. 'Father, do you think my mother will be all right now that she's on her own? I mean, if she took ill there'd be no one to care for her, would there?'

He rose from his chair and came around the table to join her. He put his arms around her and pulled her close. 'Listen, my dear, I'm not a God-fearing man but I do know that the good book says "What ye sow, so ye shall reap". Your mother made it impossible for people to live with her.' He looked down at her meaningfully. 'I am right, aren't I, Maddie? She didn't make your life very easy, did she? You found it impossible to live with her any longer so you came to us, right?' She nodded. It was the truth. 'Well, then, I'm afraid your mother is suffering the consequences of her own actions. She'll not change her ways. I gave up any hope of that years ago. You're happy here, aren't you?'

'Oh, Father, more than I can tell you.'

'Well then, let Harriet get on with her life, and you, my dear, get on with yours. If your mother was ever ill enough to warrant being taken care of, word would get to us. So stop worrying.'

Maddie smiled. 'Yes, I will.'

He eyed her searchingly. 'My dear, if you've had a change of heart and want to go back, I . . .'

'No, Father! No, I've not. This is my home now.'

He sighed in relief. 'I'm glad to hear that. Now, Maddie, I'd like to take Sarah that drink, see how she is.'

'Yes, of course. And, Dad, thanks.'

Fierce love for his daughter filled him. She had called him Dad for the very first time.

Minutes later he entered the bedroom he shared with Sarah. She appeared to be asleep. He tiptoed across the room and placed the cup on the table by the side of the bed in case she woke up.

'Thanks, love.'

'Oh, you're awake.'

'Just dozing. I heard you come in.' She eased herself up to a sitting position, pulling the pillows up behind her back, and picked up her cup.

He sat on the bed beside her and looked at her tenderly. 'Is it just tiredness, love?'

She cast down her eyes. She didn't want to worry him but had never lied to him and couldn't start now. 'I don't know, George dear. I'm very tired, yes, but I don't feel quite right either.'

'Oh! In . . . er . . . what way, Sarah?'

'Just a bit under the weather. A bit peculiar, that's all. Could be me age. I am forty-three, remember.'

'Just a spring chicken! You don't look a day older than the one I met you. You're still a beautiful woman, Sarah.'

She patted his hand. 'I'm glad you still see me that way.'

'And I always will. Will you go to the doctor? Let him take a look at you? Please, Sarah?'

'But that'll cost a shilling, George, just to visit.'

'Sarah, remember I don't have to hand Harriet any more money. Besides, you're worth more than a shilling, especially where your health is concerned. Now you'll go tomorrow, promise me?'

'All right, all right, but you're fussing for nothing. I'm just under the weather, that's all. Now skedaddle. Let me drink this tea and have a sleep.'

He rose, leaned over and kissed her lovingly on the mouth before he left.

Maddie did not manage to see Ivan until mid-morning, volunteering to take him and Oswald both a mug of tea.

'They make their own,' Agnes had replied when Maddie had made her offer.

'Yes, but Mr Simpson prefers what we have. Better quality

leaves. There's plenty in the pot. It's a shame to let it go to waste.'

'Yes, it is.' Agnes had no objection to anything of this nature where Ivan was concerned. 'Take him a piece of the fruit cake that I baked,' she said. Then a thought struck her and she hurriedly added, 'Peabody too, of course.'

Tilting her head, eyes narrowed, Maddie looked at her thoughtfully.

'Is there anything the matter?' Agnes asked. 'Only you're looking at me rather strangely?'

'Am I?' Maddie hadn't realised and mentally shook herself. 'I didn't mean to. I was . . .' What she had been thinking of was Agnes and Ivan. There was something about them both she couldn't quite fathom. It had to do with the way they acted towards each other. Just little things: a hurried glance, the way they stood when in each other's company. And like now, Agnes insisting that Ivan be taken a piece of cake, Oswald only as an afterthought. It wasn't the fact of the cake, though not many employers would give their employees cake, let alone tea, it was the way Agnes had spoken. There had been fondness in her voice, only slight but it had been there, Maddie was certain. And that went for Ivan too whenever he spoke of Miss Clatteridge. Maddie couldn't, though, divulge to Agnes what had been going through her mind. 'I'm thinking about Sarah,' she said. She didn't like telling a white lie, but it wasn't entirely untruthful. She had been thinking of Sarah, knowing she was going to see the doctor today and wondering what his diagnosis would be. 'She's been feeling under the weather just lately.'

Agnes patted her arm. 'She'll be fine, stop worrying.' Her ears suddenly pricked. 'Oh, did I hear the door? Be a dear, Maddie, go and see who it is, please.'

'Who was it?' she asked when Maddie returned, puzzled by the annoyed expression on her face.

'A man enquiring after your services. His mother's just died.'

'Oh, really?' Agnes exclaimed, beaming brightly. 'Thank goodness! We could do with the money even though Mr Snood is keen to buy the place Did you show him through to the room at the back of the Chapel of Rest, like I asked you when a customer called?'

'No, I didn't.'

'You didn't. Why not? Oh, never mind. Where is he? In the parlour? I'd better go and see to him,' Agnes said, untying her apron and heading for the door.

'Miss Clatteridge, stop!' called Maddie. 'I didn't manage to put him anywhere. When I explained I'd fetch you to speak to him, he said he wanted the undertaker. I told him that you *were* the undertaker and he said he wouldn't deal with a woman and would go elsewhere. He just left, Miss Clatteridge.'

Agnes's face fell. 'Oh, I see.' She sighed deeply. 'My sister was right. She said people expected to be dealt with by a man. I don't see what difference it makes, really I don't. Isn't it more important that the job is done properly and considerately, not whether it's by a male or a female?'

'It wouldn't matter to me, Miss Clatteridge. I expect I'd be too upset at the time to be bothered.'

'My sentiments exactly. Obviously, though, we are in a minority in thinking that way. I've made the right decision to sell, then, haven't I?'

Forlornly, Maddie nodded.

Agnes forced a smile to her face. 'Better take this tea over to Mr Simpson and Peabody before it gets any colder.'

Maddie picked up the tray and took it to the shed. Ivan motioned her outside, out of earshot of Oswald.

'Did you ask your father?'

'I did. He doesn't know Mr Snood personally but he's going to make enquiries. But I've something else to tell you.' She explained about the caller they had just received.

'What?' snapped Ivan. 'Bloody fool! Miss Clatteridge woulda done a good job for him.' He frowned thoughtfully.

Something Maddie had told him about Mr Snood's conversation flashed to mind. What was it again? But for the moment it had escaped him. 'Let's hope your father can find out summat.'

'What about you?' she asked.

'I managed to find Bert Knapp in the White Swan, his head in a pint. He was quite willing to talk about Snood. As yer already know, Knapp ain't got much of a liking for his boss. He couldn't tell me much, though. Just that it's known among the workers that Pargitt is the one stuck up his backside.'

Maddie thought she had misheard him. 'I beg your pardon?'

'Sorry, Maddie,' Ivan said in embarrassment. 'Er . . . close to him. They've bin seen huddled together on one or two occasions, whispering. Definitely suspicious, don't yer think?'

'If they were whispering it would be.' She eyed him keenly. 'So what are we going to do then? Do we tell Miss Clatteridge?'

'No, not yet. I had a good think last night when I got back. These rumours . . . If anyone likes to listen to rumours and spread 'em round 'ere, it's Tilly Potter.'

'Who's she?'

'She's the Post Master's wife. Let me see if I can find out from her just what's what. Then we'll decide whether to tell Miss Clatteridge. She can mek up her own mind. I'll go and see Tilly Potter tomorrow. Shouldn't tek me long. I'll think of some excuse should Miss Clatteridge notice me missing.'

Sighing loudly, he ran a hand over the top of his head, glancing round him. 'There ain't hardly 'ote left to do around 'ere. I have a job keeping Oswald at it. I've enough nails made to keep our regulars happy for weeks to come. The workshed's like a new pin. So are the rest of the buildings, ready for inspection by any possible buyer for the place. Yer could sleep on the stable floor.' He laughed. 'I got Oswald to give Ned's home a good going over. Weren't happy about it, wasn't Oswald. He grumbled like hell all the time he was doing it. I've done all the lists of stock too. So, yer see, me slipping out won't cause a problem. It's not like we're up to our eyes in work, more's the pity. Some business coming in while the sale went through woulda stopped Miss Clatteridge being so worried about money . . .'

He stopped abruptly and said quickly, 'I'm rattling on. Sorry, Maddie.' Red spots of embarrassment appeared on his cheeks. 'She's been decent enough to me, 'as Miss Clatteridge,' he said gruffly. 'I'm just bothered for 'er, that's all.'

I'm beginning to think it's a lot more than bothered you feel, thought Maddie, but said, 'I can understand how you feel, Ivan. I think she's nice too. So what do I do in the meantime?'

'Not much you can do. Just keep yer ears open. Maybe yer dad will come back with summat.'

'Yes, let's hope.'

Maddie arrived home as normal at a quarter to seven that evening and walked into an usually quiet house. In fact there were no sounds at all. None of the usual chatter or noises coming from the kitchen. Someone was home, though, there was flickering light from the gas mantles shining through the crack of the back room door.

She hurried down the passageway, stripping off her coat en route, and on into the back room to find Ruth and Roy sitting silently at the table, arms folded, heads bowed. By the look on their faces she knew something was wrong. She laid her coat over the back of a dining chair.

'What is it?' she asked, fear building inside her.

They both raised their heads to look at her.

'It's Mother,' said Ruth.

'Sarah? Has something happened to her?'

'We don't know,' uttered Roy.

'Where is she?'

'Upstairs with Dad.'

'She went straight to see the doctor from work, didn't she? Is . . . is she ill?'

'We don't know,' said Ruth. 'She came in and ran up the stairs without saying anything to us. But I know she was crying.'

'Crying?' Maddie's fear mounted. 'Oh!'

'I tried to talk to her but she'd locked the bedroom door,' said Ruth.

'Locked it?' Maddie frowned. This wasn't like Sarah at all. Dear God, she thought, the doctor must have given her some dreadful news for her to act like that. She felt tears prick her own eyes. Sarah had come to mean so much to her, and if she felt this way, how must Ruth and Roy be feeling? 'And, Dad's with her, you say?'

They both nodded.

'When he arrived home,' said Ruth, 'we told him what had happened and he said to stay here while he went up to see her. They've been up there ages.'

It was serious, Maddie thought. She took a deep breath, not quite knowing how to handle the situation, and not wanting to say or do anything to cause further anxiety. Her brother and sister were worried enough as it was. 'This might have nothing to do with her visit to the doctor. Could be something that happened at work.' She hoped she sounded more convinced than she felt. 'Let's make a start on the dinner. Come on, Ruth,' she said, heading for the kitchen. 'Roy, will you set the table, please?'

Upstairs, George and Sarah were sitting on the bed, wrapped in each other's arms. Sarah was quietly sobbing.

'This can't be happening, George. Why me? Why now? I'm forty-three.' She raised her head and looked at him through swollen tear-filled eyes. 'The children!' she exclaimed. 'What are they going to say? How will they cope with this?'

He held her tighter to him and tenderly said, 'Sarah, my

223

love, it's a baby you're having. It's such wonderful news, the children will be delighted, you'll see.'

Giving her eyes a wipe with her sodden handkerchief, she bit her bottom lip worriedly. 'Do you think so?'

'You know them as well as I do, Sarah. You know they will.'

'Are you sure they'll not be ashamed.'

'Ashamed?'

'Oh, George, I'm forty-three. Fancy me being nearly five months gone and not noticing. I thought I was getting thicker round the waist but presumed it was just middle-aged spread. I was worried me monthlies had stopped because I was changing. I never dreamed it was this.'

'You're not the first woman to have a baby at your age, Sarah.'

'I know that. But I was looking forward to our grandchildren, I never thought to have another child of my own. I've been so blessed already, I never gave this a thought. And we'd such plans now you don't have to hand over all that money to Harriet. All the things we were going to do to the house . . .' She looked tenderly into his eyes and ran one hand down the side of his face. 'But that's not important, George. What is, is you being able to take things easier. I wanted that so much. It isn't fair on you. I'm so sorry.'

'Sorry? Oh, Sarah, you didn't exactly do this all by yourself, did you? Has it really come as a surprise, considering the loving way we still are with each other?'

She coyly averted her gaze. 'I suppose not,' she said, embarrassed. George was right, she thought. The way they made love was just as fierce, passionate and frequent as in the early days when they had first got together. Considering that, her falling for this baby should not have come as so much of a shock.

'As for the money, Sarah, we'll still be better off than we were, even without your wage. I gave Harriet a good sum each week, don't forget. Anyway, I'm glad you're going to be giving up work. It's about time you took it easier.'

'George Ashman, how can you say that?' she retorted with a twinkle in her eyes. 'Looking after a family is damned hard work. And, don't forget, I've not the energy I had when Ruth and Roy were little.'

'I know kids are hard work, love. I did my fair share in raising our two. But the difference this time is that you won't be having to work right up to the last minute, and when the baby comes you'll be at home just looking after it and us. You'll be able to enjoy this one.'

She sighed, eyes misting over. 'Yes, I will, won't I?'

He smiled. 'Mind you, it's my guess you won't get much of a look in when it does come. Maddie and Ruth will be fighting each other to care for it.'

Sarah laughed as well. 'I can picture them now.'

'That's better.' He eyed her for a moment. 'You are happy about this baby, aren't you, my love?'

'At first I wasn't. I was too worried about how you and the children would react.' She looked deep into his eyes. 'But, yes, I do want it. I want it very much. It's obvious you do too. I don't care whether it's a girl or a boy so long as it's healthy.'

'Nether do I.' He looked at her in concern. 'You told me the doctor said you'd be all right, Sarah. You are being truthful with me aren't you?'

She nodded. 'I've never lied to you, not once in all the years we've been together, George, and I'm not about to start now. There's nothing wrong with my constitution. After he'd examined me, he pronounced me as strong as a horse. He only thinks it best I give up work because I stand on me feet all day and I could end up with really bad varicose veins.'

'Then that's what you'll do. Tomorrow you'll give in your notice. You will, Sarah, won't you?'

She patted her stomach. 'I wouldn't do anything to risk our child George.'

'And I wouldn't do anything to risk you. So from this

moment forward it's feet up. Are you listening?'

'I'm listening. George?'

He drew slightly away and gazed at her. 'Yes?'

'I do love you.'

'I love you, too.'

He leaned over and kissed her tenderly. 'You've made me a very happy man, Sarah,' he said, voice thick with emotion. 'Now don't you think we ought to go and tell the children? Because at the moment they think you're terminally ill or something.'

'Oh, goodness!' she said, jumping up. 'I can't have that. Oh, the poor dears. Whatever was I thinking of? Come on,' she said, grabbing his hand.

'A baby?' Ruth cried. 'Oh, Mother, that's . . . oh, it's such wonderful news!' She jumped up from her seat and rushed over, throwing her arms around Sarah and hugged her tightly.

'Aren't you too old?' blurted Roy.

'That's enough from you, young man,' scolded his father.

'I . . . I didn't mean it nasty, Dad. I . . . well . . .'

'You're not ashamed of me, are you, son?' Sarah asked worriedly.

'Ashamed? Don't be daft, Mam. I'm pleased, honest. I thought you were going to tell us you were dying or summat. But that's just it. Arthur's mam did when she had hers and she were your age. I'm just . . .'

Sarah took him in her arms, smoothing one hand over his head. 'She wasn't a well woman, Roy. She'd had thirteen children already. She was worn out. It was just one of those things.' She pulled away, fixing her eyes on his. 'Nothing's going to happen to me, you hear? The doctor's told me I'm as strong as an ox. All right?'

He nodded. 'It's just that I love yer.'

'I know, I know.' She kissed him on his cheek, then turned to look at Maddie. 'How about you?'

A great surge of emotion had exploded within her when Sarah and George had broken their news. It had brought painful memories flooding back of her own baby and of how much she was still missing her. Will this pain ever leave me? she thought. Will there ever be a day when I don't think of her, wonder about the people who have her now, if they love and protect her? The worst thing of all was that she could not tell anyone, nor share this incredible pain. It was something she had to shoulder all by herself. She wanted desperately to rush out of the room, throw herself on her sofa and weep bitter tears. But she couldn't, she wouldn't be able to explain herself. And, worse, to act so selfishly would only mar the joy of their announcement for Sarah and her father.

'Why, Maddie!' exclaimed Sarah. 'You're crying.'

'With happiness,' she said hurriedly, quickly wiping away the tears she hadn't realised were there. 'I am so happy for you both.' And she was. It was only her memories that were causing her distress.

The rest of the evening was spent sitting around the table discussing the forthcoming event. It wasn't until Maddie was about to excuse herself to retire to bed that she suddenly remembered Miss Clatteridge's plight and her father's promise to make some enquiries.

'Dad, did you manage to find out anything about Mr Snood?'

'Mr Snood? What about him? Who is he anyway?' asked Roy.

'Yes, spill the beans, Maddie,' urged Ruth.

'Be a change to talk about something else besides this baby,' piped up Sarah.

Maddie explained to them.

'Oh,' said Roy. 'It's like one of them penny mystery stories.'

'Which you read too many of,' declared his mother. 'But I must admit, it is all very intriguing. So did you find out anything, dear?' she asked her husband keenly.

George laughed. 'I feel I'm being interrogated! I'm afraid to say I didn't. He's no policies with our firm, so I drew a blank there. I discreetly asked a couple of my business customers whether they knew of him.'

'And did they?' Maddie asked hopefully.

'No.'

'Oh!'

'Yer not going to give up though, are yer, Dad?' asked Roy, folding his arms and leaning on the table.

'No, I'm not. I'll try again tomorrow.' George paused for a moment. 'I tell you what I will do. Snood's parlour's a bit off my patch but I'll go there tomorrow and see if I can talk to him. Don't worry, I won't mention a word about this. He'll think it's a business call. But I should be able to get a feel for him.'

'Oh, Dad, that's a marvellous idea! Thank you so much,' enthused Maddie. 'And Mr Simpson is going to call upon the Post Mistress and try to get to the bottom of the rumours.'

'That's a good idea too,' said her father. 'Whatever these rumours are that have been spread, then Tilly's the one who'll throw some light on them. Why don't you ask Mr Simpson to come around tomorrow night and we can all discuss our findings?'

'He won't mind us sticking our noses in, will he?' asked Sarah.

Maddie eyed her for a moment. 'I don't think so. He wants to get to the bottom of this as much as we do. No, I'm sure he won't mind, just be glad of any help.'

'Ask him to come to dinner,' Sarah offered. 'To my mind such things are best sorted on a full stomach.'

'Can I? Oh, I'm sure he'd be delighted.'

Ivan was honoured to be asked and greatly relieved to have Maddie's family's help in this matter, not offended by their intrusion in the least. After all, if they were correct in their assumptions, Miss Clatteridge's future was at great risk.

The next evening at seven they were all sitting around Sarah's table, ready to begin their discussion, appetites more than adequately appeased by large helpings of mutton stew.

Maddie was beside herself, wanting to know what news the day had brought, not having had a chance to ask Ivan as he hadn't found it possible to slip away to the Post Office until late-afternoon due to Agnes's decision to spend the day in the washhouse, laundering the linen and towels she was taking with her to Scarborough when the time came for her departure. It was an usually good drying day for the middle of November and she didn't want to waste a moment with such a large amount to do.

They had laboured hard. Fires had been lit under the huge brick boiler and they had both dollied, then mangled, pegged, unpegged, folded and packed away. Both women were exhausted by the time Agnes declared a halt and they retired to the sitting room over a tray of tea and the rest of the fruit cake.

Hence it wasn't until after four that Ivan had felt it safe to make his escape without Agnes around to ask where he was going. Maddie did not get an opportunity to catch him before she left for the night as Agnes insisted on her departing by the front door and had waved her off down the street, not giving Maddie an opportunity to slip back in unnoticed.

On Ivan's arrival at the house at six-thirty, as arranged, they were all immediately ushered to the table by Sarah to sit down to eat. The conversation had dwelt on everything bar the one topic Maddie was so desperate to discuss and she was bursting with impatience by the time her father pushed his empty plate from him.

Thank goodness, she thought, the time had finally come. She opened her mouth to ask Ivan how he had got on when to her dismay Sarah beat her to it.

'More tea, Mr Simpson?'

'Please,' he responded, picking up his cup and holding it towards her. 'That wa' a delicious meal, Mrs Ashman.' No one batted an eyelid at his obvious assumption. 'Not the circumstances I would have wished to be invited in, but all the same I'm much obliged.' He didn't tell them that this was the very first home-cooked meal he had eaten, sitting around a family table, apart from the Christmas dinners he had shared with the Clatteridges. But they could hardly have been classed as family occasions, far from it, not with Cuthbert presiding over proceedings, his beady eyes ever watchful, everyone else present frightened to make one wrong move. Usually Ivan's own attempts at cooking or whatever Agnes slipped him were taken in solitude in his room over the stable. He did hope they'd ask him again.

'You're more than welcome, Mr Simpson, and you must come again.'

'Thank you, Mrs Ashman, I'd be delighted.'

'Right,' said George, 'we all know what we're here for.' And with a twinkle in his eye added, 'I know Maddie's been desperate throughout dinner to start the proceedings. So let's get the dishes stacked and we can begin.'

In under three minutes the table was cleared, dishes piled in the kitchen, and they were all seated around the table again.

'So,' said George, taking charge. 'Let's make a start. I'll go first, shall I?'

They all nodded in agreement.

'Not much to tell you, I'm afraid. I did manage to get to see Mr Snood. He wasn't interested in insurance. Wasn't a believer in it but might change his mind in the future, he said. At the moment all his money was tied up in other things. I couldn't get anything else out of him. He came across as a man who thinks well of himself, that's all I can say. I wasn't with him above five minutes. What about you, Mr Simpson? I hope you fared better than me? Maddie said you were hoping to see the Post Mistress to check out these rumours.'

Ivan folded his arms and leaned on the table. 'I didn't think I wa' going to get to, I thought Miss Clatteridge and Maddie'd never finish the washing. I managed to slip away just after four. I didn't need to ask Tilly Potter anything. She asked me.'

She would, thought Sarah, knowing the woman well. But wouldn't voice her thoughts and interrupt with a flippant comment.

'I've only ever had the need to visit the Post Office twice in me life but Mrs Potter knew who I wa' and where I worked. She asked what was I going ter be doing with myself once Clatteridge's had been sold. I asked her how she knew Clatteridge's was for sale. She said she couldn't remember who'd told her. Then she said she thought Molly Micklewaite had, but couldn't be sure.'

'Tilly's a nice enough woman,' piped up Sarah, 'but to my mind the trouble with her is that she listens to that much gossip, and adds so much to it herself when she's telling others, she doesn't know if she's coming or going.'

'I 'appen to agree with yer, Mrs Ashman. Anyway, I was waiting for me change after paying for me stamp and racking me brains on how to ask her if she'd heard any talk about Clatteridge's and what it was about, when she said, "Shame, in't it, what happened about Minnie Tallon? You'd a' thought Miss Clatteridge would have made an exception, being's she lived so close." "I'm sorry, I don't follow you," I says. She looked at me as though I was stupid. "Well, did you not know that two days after her father passed on, Miss Clatteridge sent word to Jessie Victor and Cissie Gower . . ."' He paused and flashed a glance around the table. 'They're local women who do most of the laying out around these parts.' Then he continued, 'Apparently they were told that any dyings that they'd have normally sent to Clatteridge's were to be reported straight to Snood's in future. Now the

231

old man was dead, business was ceasing. A man gave 'em both two shilling for their trouble, apparently. "What man?" I asked. "The man Miss Clatteridge sent to tell 'em – what man d'yer think I was talking about," Tilly told me. "Anyway, I told Cissie I'd help out by telling everyone who came into the Post Office. I didn't ask no payment from her for me trouble neither, so don't you go thinking I did. Just doing my bit to help.'"

Ivan drew breath deeply. 'I left then, learned all I needed to. But not before I told her that the rumours were untrue. Clatteridge's was still operating as normal and whoever had started them rumours must be a thoroughly bad lot. "I trust you'll do your bit in putting people straight," I said to her. And she will. I left her feeling thoroughly ashamed of 'erself, I can tell yer.'

'Good for you,' piped up George. He ran a hand over his chin thoughtfully. 'Well, you certainly found out more than you bargained for, Mr Simpson. At least we know now just what the rumours were.' He looked across at Maddie. 'That caller you told me of, the one who refused to have his mother buried by a woman undertaker . . .'

'What about him?' she asked.

'Seems a bit odd to me.'

'Me too,' said Sarah. 'If anything should happen to any of you, God forbid, I'd be far too upset myself to be bothered whether the undertaker was a man or not.'

Ivan gasped, it suddenly occurred to him just what he had been trying to remember a few days ago. 'Why the . . . so and so,' he proclaimed, just managing to curb a profanity. 'That's what Snood was arranging with Pargitt! That man who called was paid to do it. It's my bet his mother is still very much alive.'

'I'd come to that conclusion myself, Mr Simpson,' said George. 'The fact is, Maddie, you misinterpreted nothing of what you overheard.'

'He's not a nice man this Mr Snood,' said Sarah.

232

Maddie agreed tight-lipped. 'If he's done all this, then no, he's not.'

'Snood must have plotted his nasty little plan as soon as he heard Mr Clatteridge had died.'

George nodded. 'Seems very much that way to me.'

The room lapsed into silence. Sarah rose. 'I'll make some tea,' she said. 'Ruth, please come and give me a hand.'

Without a word she followed her mother into the kitchen.

'Oh, Dad, this is awful,' Maddie groaned. 'How could Mr Snood be so sly.'

'People do all sorts when they want something bad enough, Maddie love. He saw his chance to buy Clatteridge's cheap and obviously wasn't bothered how he got it. In my line of business this is mild, believe me.'

'I can't imagine,' said Maddie. 'This is terrible enough.'

'I could tell you a few stories,' said Ivan. 'You wouldn't believe some of the things people get up to when a relative passes on.'

'He's right,' agreed her father. 'Like Mr Simpson, I meet all sorts. I knew a man once who murdered his own mother to get her burial money.'

'You did?' gasped Roy, enthralled. 'How come you've never told us before?'

'Not the sort of thing you tell to children. You were nothing but a baby at the time. Hardly the ideal bedtime story.'

'Well, we ain't kids anymore so you can now, can't yer?' Roy pleaded.

Maddie was enthralled too. 'Yes, please do, Dad?'

'All right.' George slid his spectacles higher on his nose and relaxed back in his chair. 'Mrs Collins was a kindly old duck. Wouldn't harm a hair on anyone's head. She'd saved all her life, many times going without to make sure she kept up her payments on her policy so she could have a real posh send off when her time came. It was all she lived for. "Damned sure," she used to say to me, "I'm gonna go out of this world a better way than I came in." She died real sudden. I'd seen her on the Friday night and she was as right as rain, no ailment to my knowledge. By Sunday morning she'd gone. The son got his hands on the insurance payout and arranged the cheapest funeral he could. He pocketed the rest.'

'He didn't?' gasped Maddie.

'Yes, he did. It was only because I attended out of respect for his mother that he was found out. Each week I'd had to listen to what she had planned and agreed with her son should be carried out. Brougham and single for the vicar; carriages and fours, all decked out in their finery, for the mourners; hearse and black-plumed pair for herself. A shroud made special from best linen and a walnut coffin with solid brass handles and name-plate. And a big spread: ham on the bone, trifle, best sherry for the women, whisky and ale for the men. None of that comes cheap, the plywood box her son ordered certainly did. The mourners walked, and got paste sandwiches and a cup of tea for their efforts. The old lady would have been so upset if she'd known that saving for all those years was a total waste of time.'

'But how did you know he'd killed her, Dad?' Roy asked, agog.

'He told me himself.'

'He did?' gasped Maddie.

'Didn't realise he had, of course. But when I went to hand over his dues he remarked it was a good job his mother had had that policy to bury herself with as he'd used his last threepenny bit for the gas the night she'd died.'

Roy frowned. 'I don't see . . .'

'That threepenny bit, son, wasn't used to light the gas mantles, it was used to gas her while she was asleep. Of course, I'd no proof. There's many that never carry out the deceased's instructions. Can't brand everyone a murderer just going by that. But I didn't like the way he grinned when he grabbed that money off me. I was suspicious enough to alert the police just in case. They got the truth from him, eventually.'

'Did they hang him, Dad?'

'Roy!' his father rebuffed him sharply. 'Yes, as a matter of fact, they did.'

'Oh,' he mouthed. 'Fancy you knowing a killer!'

'It was a long time ago.'

Sarah returned along with Ruth, carrying the tea things. 'You telling that story about poor Mrs Collins, are you, dear?'

'I was.'

'Oh, did I miss something?' asked Ruth.

'I'll tell you later,' offered her brother.

'Poor Mrs Collins,' said Sarah, putting a jug of milk down on the table. 'What we think Mr Snood is up to is nothing to what her son did to her.'

'It's bad enough,' erupted Ivan hotly. 'Snood's trying to fleece Miss Clatteridge of a fair price for her business. That's wrong whichever way you look at it, and in my opinion he should be strung up too!'

Mouths open at his furious outburst they all stared at him.

I wonder, thought Sarah, as she studied Ivan, if Agnes Clatteridge has any idea how much her employee cares for her? No, more than cares, loves her.

Shocked at his lack of restraint in front of this gathering, Ivan reddened. 'Well, er . . . 'tain't right, is it? It's not even as if Miss Clatteridge was left well off. She weren't, yer know. That father of hers left her in a right bad state, through . . . not taking care of his money when he was alive.'

George cleared his throat. 'You're quite right to be annoyed, Mr Simpson. After all, Miss Clatteridge is your employer and she's also been good to Maddie. I've not had the privilege of meeting her personally but from what Maddie tells us, she sounds a damn fine woman and doesn't deserve to be treated like this by anyone.'

'You're right, Dad,' Maddie agreed. 'No one deserves to be, 'specially not Miss Clatteridge. So what can we do about it?'

'I know what *I* can do,' said Ivan, scraping back his chair.

'Where are you going?' Maddie asked him, astonished.

He stood up. 'To see Snood, that's where.'

'Sit down, Mr Simpson,' ordered George. 'You're angry. It's best not to tackle something like this when your dander's up. See sense, man, and sit down. Let's discuss this, decide what best to do.'

'With all due respect, Mr Ashman, what is there ter discuss? All we have is rumours and hearsay. All of which I 'appen to believe are true.'

'And I agree with you, Mr Simpson,' said George, rising also. 'All my instincts tell me so. But we can't accuse him without . . .'

'We've no choice, Mr Ashman,' Ivan cut in. 'There ain't time, you see. Mr Snood is calling upon Miss Clatteridge for her answer on Saturday and it's Thursday today. That gives us a day. What can we do in a day that'll stop him? Not much that I can see. So I'm going to call on him, tell him what we know and that I'm going to tell Miss Clatteridge.'

'He'll laugh at you, Mr Simpson.'

Ivan's eyes narrowed. 'We'll see who's laughing when I've finished with him.'

'I'll come with you,' said George. 'I'll just get my coat.'

'Me too,' said Maddie, hurriedly rising.

'Can I come an' all?' urged Roy.

Sarah's face filled with horror. 'Roy, sit down,' she ordered. 'This is nothing to do with you. George, should you really be getting this involved? And you, Maddie . . .' She wrung her hands anxiously. 'Look, shouldn't we at least ask the authorities for their help?'

'There's nothing they can do,' said George. 'Mr Simpson and I will go and have a talk with Snood, see if we can make him see reason. Maybe once we've had a word he'll . . .'

Ivan raised his hand in dismissal. 'I'm grateful for your offers, all of you, but I feel it best I deal with this alone. You've your job to consider, Mr Ashman. Snood could take umbrage and cause trouble for you. Maddie, this is no business for a woman. I've nothing to lose but Miss Clatteridge has and that's all that concerns me. Thank you for the meal, Mrs Ashman. I'll see meself out.'

They all stared after him as he marched from the room and out of the house.

'What's the meaning of interrupting me at dinner?' snarled Snood. He glanced Ivan up and down scathingly, then fixed angry eyes on him. 'Well, man, what's so important that it couldn't wait 'til tomorrow? Miss Clatteridge that desperate, is she, to clinch our deal that she's sent you round? Well, you can tell her from me I don't do business with lackeys. So yer can scarper. I'll see her as arranged, Saturday afternoon at two.'

Ivan fought desperately to suppress his anger. 'Miss Clatteridge doesn't even know I'm here,' he said evenly.

Snood frowned quizzically. 'Well, why are you then?'

Ivan took a deep breath to steel himself. 'I want yer to drop yer offer.'

'What?'

'You 'eard me correct, Mr Snood, or I'll tell Miss Clatteridge what yer up to. I know, you see. I know all you've done just to get the place cheap from her. About the rumours. About paying that bloke to come calling and say what he did. And yer let it be known around the Undertakers' Association that Clatteridge's was all but yours before you'd even been to see Miss Clatteridge with yer offer. You were 'eard discussing it all outside our yard, just after yer left yer interview with her.' Ivan saw a flash of fear cross Mr Snood's face and, taking a deep breath, puffed out his chest. 'If you won't do as I ask then I'll tell Miss Clatteridge, so I will.'

Mr Snood grabbed his arm and dragged him outside, pulling the door to behind them. 'Now you listen here,' he snarled, wagging his finger, eyes glinting menacingly, 'you ain't got nothing on me. You can't prove nothing neither. Tell Miss Clatteridge, go on. I'm a businessman, you're just a twopenny ha'penny chippy.' A smirk crossed his lips. 'Let's see who she believes, eh? Let me tell you, it won't be you. You'd better start looking for somewhere else to work, 'cos you won't be working for me when I take over that place.'

'That don't bother me one bit, Mr Snood. What does is what you're trying to do to Miss Clatteridge. If yer don't drop yer offer, I'll take a leaf out of your book. I can spread rumours too. I'll let people know how you use cheap wood and charge over the odds for best. Dyed the right colour and polished up, most of the bereaved don't notice the difference, do they? And what about brass handles? I'll put it round how yer pass off brass-plated for solid. And shrouds – using old ones you've took off bodies before the lid is closed and charging for 'em as though they were new. I could go on, Mr Snood. I've bin in this business all me life, I know what other operators get up to.

'One thing I'll say for Mr Clatteridge: he might have been a hard man to work for, but he never did 'ote so diabolical. And whether you have or not won't mek no difference betime I've finished. People listen to rumours as you should know, Mr Snood.'

'Why you . . . How dare you threaten me?'

'I dare, Mr Snood. But yer wrong, I ain't threatening yer. *I will do it*. I'll ruin your business if you go ahead with this offer.'

Mr Snood's face turned purple with rage. He raised one fist ready to strike.

'Do that, Mr Snood, and I'll make such a noise it'll bring Mrs Snood running. I'll tell her it all then, let's see what she has to say.'

'You bastard!' Snood erupted, dropping his arm and unclenching his fist. 'Get out of me sight,' he hissed.

'Not 'til I have yer promise. Though whether that's worth much I'm not sure, considering.'

'I . . . I promise,' he muttered.

'What was that, Mr Snood? I didn't quite 'ear yer.'

'I promise,' he snarled, slightly louder.

'Thank you, Mr Snood. I'll expect yer to inform Miss Clatteridge of yer change of heart first thing in the morning. If not . . . well, yer know what'll happen. Nice doing business with yer. Goodnight.'

And Ivan marched off, leaving an infuriated Snood glaring after him.

Maddie arrived first thing in the morning to find Agnes very upset.

'Are you all right, Miss Clatteridge?' she asked, shutting the door behind her as she took off her coat. A thought suddenly struck her. 'Mr Simpson . . . nothing's happened to him, has it?' After his departure last night, she had lain awake worrying over what had transpired, mind conjuring up all sorts of fears. She hadn't caught sight of him as she had crossed the yard, only Oswald. He had been sweeping up. As soon as she had stepped through the archway, he had stopped what he was doing, leaned on his brush and leered at her. Maddie had lowered her head and hurried away, painfully aware his eyes had not left her until she disappeared inside the kitchen.

Agnes raised her head, frowning. 'Mr Simpson appeared well this morning when I saw him. Why do you ask?'

'Oh . . . er . . . no reason. Just the first thing that struck me. You're upset about something, aren't you, Miss Clatteridge?'

She sighed. 'Yes, I am. When I came down this morning I found this had been pushed through the letter box,' she said, flapping a piece of paper in her hand. 'Must have been delivered while I was still sleeping. I can't understand it, Maddie. It's from Mr Snood. He's withdrawn his offer.' She sank down on a kitchen chair, rubbing her hand worriedly over her chin. 'He doesn't give any explanation.'

How Maddie managed to prevent herself from shrieking in jubilation was a mystery to her. It did hurt her to see Miss Clatteridge so upset and bewildered but she would have been more so had she known exactly what Mr Snood had been trying to do. God bless you, Ivan, she thought. I don't know what you said or did but it obviously worked. She wanted to run over to him now, find out whether he knew about the letter, congratulate him on whatever it was he had done. Then she wanted to go and tell her family to put their minds at rest. But doing anything would alert Miss Clatteridge and then explanations would have to be given.

All Maddie could do was say, 'Oh, Miss Clatteridge, I'm so sorry.'

'I wonder if I should go and see Mr Snood?' mused Agnes. 'Maybe this is a ploy to get me to consider dropping the price even further. I'll have to explain I can't. If I go any lower . . .'

'Oh, no!' Maddie cried, then realised her mistake. 'I mean, you might embarrass him, Miss Clatteridge. Maybe even at the low price he was offering, when he worked it all out he couldn't afford to go ahead.'

Agnes looked at her thoughtfully for a moment. 'You could be right. I assumed he knew exactly what he could afford when he came to see me. Oh, dear, what am I going to do now?'

'Something will turn up, Miss Clatteridge,' she said, more confidently than she felt. Something had to, she prayed. It wasn't fair that this lovely lady had so much to worry about. 'Someone else will come forward. There's someone somewhere who wants to buy a place like this. It's just finding them, that's all. Maybe the right people haven't heard it's for sale. Why don't you ask the agent for his advice?'

'I could. Yes, I could indeed. I know he's been trying his best for a sale but I could talk to him about what else we could do to arouse interest. Yes, I will, Maddie. I won't let Mr Snood's withdrawal get me down. Something will turn up just like you said.'

Maddie hoped so for Miss Clatteridge's sake.

Chapter Nineteen

Maddie arrived for work the next morning to be greeted by Oswald. Usually he was somewhere around when she entered the gates and would stop what he was doing and watch her closely. As she slipped through the gap today he was immediately beside her.

'Mornin', Maddie,' he said, falling into step beside her. 'I'm off to the music hall ternight. Got tickets, I have.'

She slipped on an icy patch and he grabbed her arm to steady her which she hurriedly pulled free, feeling distaste at his touch.

'That's nice for you,' she replied evenly, quickening her pace. 'I hope you enjoy yourself.'

'I will. Fancy comin'?'

She stopped abruptly. 'With you?'

He frowned, puzzled. 'Yeah, why not?'

'Oswald, you're much younger than I am.'

'Not by that much. Anyway, don't bother me none.'

'Well, it does me.'

The thought of going to a music hall was appealing, but the idea of going anywhere with Oswald repelled her. Besides, to accept an invitation from any man was beyond her. She still held too many feelings for the man she had lost. Maddie knew it was stupid of her, Josh was gone from her life forever, but she felt that to look at any other man in a romantic way would make her somehow disloyal.

'Thank you for the offer but I'm busy tonight,' she told Oswald now. 'I'm sure someone else would be glad to accept.'

'Wadda about termorra then? We could go for a drink.'

'I'm busy then too, Oswald.'

He grabbed her arm and pulled her to a halt. 'What's up, Maddie? Ain't I good enough fer the likes of you or summat?'

'It's not that at all,' she said sharply, indignantly wrenching free her arm.

'Well, why won't yer come then?'

'I've already told you, you're too young and I'm busy.'

'I don't believe yer.'

He was right not to.

'Oswald, if you don't stop pestering me, I will mention it to Mr Simpson.'

Thankfully she arrived at the kitchen door and managed to disappear inside before he could proposition her further. She would have to avoid him as much as possible in future before she ran out of excuses and had no option but to tell him the truth. Despite her dislike of Oswald, she didn't relish the thought of hurting his feelings.

Later that morning Agnes and she both happened to be in the kitchen when there was a knock on the door and Ivan came in. He looked pleased.

'Miss Clatteridge, I've just had a visit from Wilson's chippy.'

'Wilson's?' queried Agnes. 'Oh, yes, Wilson's are the undertakers in Evington. What did he want?'

'Our 'elp. Mr Wilson personally sent him. Seems they've got four come at once.'

'Four? Really! How fortunate for them.' Agnes's tone held no sarcasm, just genuine pleasure for a fellow undertaker. 'What do they want with us?'

'One of the four is from a monied family. They want a top quality mahogany with solid brass trimmings. Engraved too. Want to know if we can muckle one up quick smart, 'cos with the others they ain't got the time but didn't want to turn the work away. They heard we weren't busy so come here first.'

From the corner of her eye Agnes suddenly spotted the bewildered expression on Maddie's face and laughed. 'They want us to make them a coffin, my dear. Their carpenter won't be able to manage four together. It's a pity it's just the coffin they want. The full burial would have brought in much-needed money. Never mind.' She turned her attention back to Ivan. 'I hope you told him we would, Mr Simpson?'

'I did. I checked out our materials and we've more than enough to do the job. If I start on it now and work through, I can have it done by the morning. They want it vanning to their premises before nine so they can tek it up to the house ter put the body in for viewing.'

'They want us to deliver it too?'

He nodded.

'Good. We'll charge for that as well. Thank you, Mr Simpson.'

When he had left Agnes turned to Maddie, rubbing her hands. 'Better than a kick in the teeth. Isn't that what people say when something small but good happens?'

She laughed. 'It certainly is.'

Maddie was in good spirits the next morning. Talk at home still centred mainly around the new arrival in three months' time. Last night names had been discussed. There were several possibilities but nothing definite had been decided. There was plenty of time for that, Sarah had laughingly told them all as she had begun her task of balling up a cone of white wool which she had purchased to begin knitting the baby's first matinee coat.

Ruth had again requested Maddie's presence while she got ready to go out for a night with her girlfriends to a tea dance held regularly in rooms in Churchgate. 'It's such fun,' Ruth had told her, 'and you don't have to dance if you don't want to as there's plenty of tables just to sit at and chat.' But Maddie wouldn't be left sitting long, she had been assured. The nice men who went there would be swarming around her, especially if she wore that posh frock that hadn't seen daylight since she had taken it home. And when she did get around to having her hair cut she'd be pestered mercilessly. Maddie thought her sister was exaggerating her chances but kept her thoughts to herself. Ruth was only trying to be sisterly. Maybe one night Maddie would join her, but not yet, she wasn't ready.

On arriving at the yard that morning she had popped her head inside first to check for Oswald's presence. Thankfully there was no sign of him and she rushed across cobbles before there was.

Agnes arrived moments after, dressed in her outdoor coat, announcing she was taking Maddie's advice and travelling into Leicester to visit the agent, wanting to arrive early to ensure an interview. She left straight away, telling Maddie to take the morning quietly, which Maddie thought rather nice of her.

She was just mashing herself a pot of tea, having decided that she would busy herself giving the kitchen a thorough clean while Agnes was out on business, when she heard the sound of galloping hooves on the cobbles in the yard and the screech of the box cart as it came to an abrupt halt.

Before she even had time to put down the kettle she was holding and investigate what was happening, she heard Ivan shouting urgently.

'Miss Clatteridge, Maddie, come quick! Oswald! Where are yer, Oswald?'

Almost dropping the kettle Maddie wrenched open the door, shot through it and out into the yard. The box cart was parked askew, Ned snorting breathlessly, streams of warm breath billowing from his flaring nostrils in the icy air.

'What on earth has happened?' she cried, arriving at the side of Ivan who was desperately trying to prise open the lid covering the back end of the box cart.

'Blast this, it's stuck. Oh, there yer are, Maddie,' he cried, relieved. 'There's been a terrible accident. Oh, just terrible.

Where's that lazy so and so . . . Oswald!' he shouted. 'Get out 'ere quick and bring a crowbar with yer.'

Oswald appeared, wiping sleep from his eyes. It was obvious what he had been doing while he thought his boss was away for a couple of hours. 'What's up?' he asked, stifling a yawn.

'Where's the crowbar?'

'What crowbar?'

'The one I asked yer . . . Oh, never mind, I'll be quicker gettin' it meself.' As Maddie and Oswald looked on bemused, Ivan darted into the workshed and moments later reappeared, a crowbar in his hand. Like a man possessed he rammed the end of the jemmy into the crack at the side of the lid and fought frantically to free it.

'Ivan, what is going on?' Maddie demanded.

'I told yer, a terrible accident. We might need the doctor.'

'Doctor?'

Just then the lid shot up. 'Thank God!' he proclaimed. 'Oswald, 'elp me slide this coffin out and tek it into the Chapel of Rest. Sharp, lad.'

Maddie's eyes flew to the coffin. Just the end of it was visible, but she still recognised it as the one Ivan had made especially for Wilson's. She had been reluctant to view it due to its morbid association but Ivan had been so proud of his swift handiwork she felt unable to hurt him by refusing. She felt he had been right to be pleased with his efforts. Considering the time in which he had produced it, the coffin was a beautiful piece of carpentry. He was indeed talented at his craft.

'I thought you were delivering that this morning?' she said. 'Why have you brought it back?'

Ivan had managed to slide the coffin partway out of the back of the box cart and was struggling under its weight. 'Not now, Maddie,' he said breathlessly. 'Oswald, get the end, quick! Now, lift. Watch out, you're dropping your end . . .'

His sallow, acne-marked face contorted, Oswald replied, annoyed, 'I know! It's bloody heavy, that's why.'

'Well, it's bound to be. There's a man inside. Now lift higher before he suffers any more damage when we drop him on the ground.' Ivan flashed him a warning. 'Oi! And curb yer language. There's a lady present.'

Maddie was staring, astounded. There was a man inside the coffin? 'He's not dead, is he?' she uttered.

'I 'ope not, Maddie. If he is then I'm the cause.'

Her mind raced frantically but they had reached the door to the Chapel of Rest and Maddie could ask no more questions.

The room was near pitch dark, the black curtains at the small windows tightly closed, and Maddie, never having been in this room before, shuddered as she felt its eeriness envelop her, acutely conscious of its use. She stood stiffly in the doorway as Ivan and Oswald, hampered by the dim light and the weight they were carrying, struggled over to the long black-covered trestle in the centre of the small room and heaved the coffin on top.

'Light the candles, Maddie,' Ivan ordered as he slid off the lid and laid it on the floor. 'Can't see a thing in here. There's matches in that little cupboard just by the side of yer. Oswald, pull back the curtains, we need more light. Maddie, will yer hurry?' he snapped.

'Oh!' she exclaimed. To light the candles would mean having to enter the room. Frozen to the spot, she shuddered violently.

'For goodness' sake, Maddie, what's the matter with yer?' Ivan scolded as he shot over to the cupboard and took out the matches. 'There's nothin' 'ere ter frighten yer.' He grabbed her arm, pulling her inside. 'It's just a room, Maddie, and even if there wa' a dead body in 'ere, the dead can't 'urt yer.' His voice dropped worriedly. ''Sides, I'm hopin' this one ain't dead.'

He let go of her arm. As Oswald drew the curtains, dim

light filtered through the small glass panes and from where Maddie stood she could see to the back of the room where there was a long cabinet draped in black cloth on top of which stood a large silver cross, to either side two huge brass candlesticks. Ivan struck a match and lit the thick white candles. Flames flickered and sprang into life, shadows dancing on the walls. Again Maddie shuddered. The light, although welcome, was still not enough to lift her feeling of absolute revulsion. She didn't want to be in here.

'Shall I . . . shall I go and make some tea?' she offered as a means of escape.

'No, Maddie,' Ivan erupted. 'For God's sake, will yer get over 'ere and tek a look at this man?'

Seeing she wasn't about to obey him, Ivan sprang over, grabbed her arm and dragged her across to the top end of the coffin. 'What d'yer think, Maddie?' he asked. 'Do we need a doctor or what?'

With a great effort she forced herself to look down. As her eyes fell on the face of the man in the coffin she gave a gasp then a piercing scream. Simultaneously the man's eyes flickered open to fix on the face peering down at him, flames from the candles lighting it grotesquely. Eyes wide, his head lifted slightly and his hands came into contact with the padded sides of the coffin. His mouth fell open, face contorting in terror as the knowledge of where he was lying struck him full force. 'I'm dead. Oh, God, I'm dead,' he moaned, and slumped back, eyes shut.

Maddie screamed again. 'Oh, no! NO! NO!' she cried, bursting into a torrent of hysterical sobs. Wrapping her arms around herself, she rocked backwards and forwards, Ivan and Oswald staring at her in shock.

'What is going on in here?' a voice demanded.

Ivan and Oswald both spun around to see Agnes framed in the doorway. 'What's wrong with Maddie?' she asked, face wreathed in worry as she advanced into the room.

'Dunno,' muttered Ivan, totally at a loss. He had known

247

Maddie had been extremely reluctant to take a look at the man but this reaction from her was utterly unexpected.

Agnes hurried across to the distraught young woman, putting an arm around her shoulders. 'It's all right, Maddie dear, I'll get you out of here,' she said. As Agnes prepared to guide the sobbing Maddie away she flashed a frosty glance at Ivan. 'My instructions were disobeyed,' she said crossly. 'I specifically requested that Maddie was to have nothing to do with this side of the business. So what is she doing in here? And, for that matter, what is that coffin here for?' She raised her free hand in warning. 'Let me see to Maddie first, then I'll be back. And I'll be expecting answers.'

Minutes later a shocked and trembling Maddie sat perched in the armchair by the parlour fire, staring down into the cup of tea she was cradling in her hands. Agnes was sitting opposite, eyeing her in concern. 'Are you feeling better, dear?' she asked kindly. 'It's a good job I returned. It was threatening rain and I came back for my umbrella to be on the safe side. I can't apologise enough to you, Maddie. I gave strict instructions you were never to be asked to do anything connected with the burial side of the business. I don't know what Mr Simpson was thinking of, really I don't.' She stepped over to Maddie and placed a hand on her shoulder. 'Will you be all right for a moment while I go and find out what is going on? I'm concerned about that coffin not being delivered. We made a firm commitment. I must go and see to things. I won't be long, I promise.'

Without lifting her head, Maddie nodded.

It was a good twenty minutes before Agnes returned. 'How are you feeling now? Better, I hope?' she said, sitting back down, her hands in her lap.

Sniffing, Maddie lifted her head. 'Yes, I am, thank you. I'm so sorry for causing a scene, Miss Clatteridge. I don't know what came over me.' She paused momentarily. 'Is he . . . is he dead?' she whispered.

'Dead? Who? Oh, the man in the coffin. No, far from it.

He's in the kitchen, having a cup of tea with Mr Simpson. He suffered no more than a bump on the head. He fainted, that was all, when he realised what he was lying in. And I suspect seeing you peering at him didn't help. Must have thought you were an angel or something. He was sure he had died.' She fought to control the mirth that was building. 'Oh dear, if the situation weren't so terrible it would be very amusing.'

'It seems Mr Simpson, in his rush to get the coffin delivered on time, was pushing Ned too hard. The wheels of the cart slipped on an icy puddle and it skidded sideways. The back end caught a ladder which unfortunately this man was climbing. He fell off, hit his head on the cobbles and passed out. Poor Mr Simpson thought he had killed him. That part of town is usually quite busy in the morning but for some reason today there was no one around. Mr Simpson did the only thing he could think of which was to put the man inside the coffin and bring him back here. Let me assure you, apart from a bump on his head, Mr Jenks is no worse for his experience, thank goodness . . .' Her voice trailed off at the look on Maddie's face. 'What is it, my dear?'

'You . . . you did say his name was Mr Jenks?' she uttered.

Agnes nodded. 'Joshua Jenks he introduced himself as. Why?' She frowned. 'Do you know him?'

Maddie froze. She hadn't been wrong then. It *was* Josh. Her Josh. The last person she had ever expected to see again. She nodded slowly. 'Yes, I do.'

Agnes stood up. 'Then you must come and greet him properly.'

'Oh, no,' cried Maddie, alarmed.

'Whyever not?'

'I . . . I just can't.'

'Can't? Are you on bad terms or something?'

'No . . . not exactly. Well, I don't know. But Jo— Mr Jenks might not be pleased to see me, that's all.'

Agnes sank down on her chair again, eyeing Maddie

closely. 'It's not for me to pry, Maddie, but from what I know of you I can't imagine anyone not being pleased to see you. Did something unpleasant happen between you, is that it?'

'Yes,' came the low response. Maddie locked eyes with Agnes. 'We were engaged to be married. Something happened which forced us to part.'

'Oh, I see.' Agnes observed her thoughtfully for a moment. 'And you still think a lot of Mr Jenks, don't you?'

She nodded.

'The fact is, you still love him?'

She nodded again.

Agnes sighed in distress, deeply aware of Maddie's pain, which was so apparent she could almost reach out and grab it. She realised how little, if anything, she knew of Maddie's past. As weeks had passed, with them working closely alongside, her fondness for Maddie had grown and she had come to regard her employee very highly. Agnes corrected herself. No, Maddie was now more than an employee to her, she had become a friend. Seeing her so obviously grieved was troubling.

The man Maddie thought so much of was in the kitchen recovering from his accident; very shortly he would leave and probably their paths might never cross again. What did Agnes do? Did she let them walk away from each other or did she bring them together? The burden of responsibility was heavy. What she did now could have a dramatic effect on Maddie's life. Was it her place to intervene or should she do nothing and leave Maddie's future for fate to sort out. Was it not fate, though, that had brought Mr Jenks to this house?

Agnes made a decision. Whether right or wrong, she just knew she could not sit back and do nothing.

She rose and headed for the door.

'Where are you going?' Maddie asked.

'I have something I must do,' was Agnes's matter-of-fact response.

Maddie heard the door click shut and her heart thudded painfully. Only feet away from her, on the other side of the wall, was the man she loved more than life itself. In moments he would be gone. She felt a great urge to run to him and beg his forgiveness for what her mother had done to them. It was taking all the courage she could muster to control it, but somehow she must. There was no point in her announcing her presence to Josh. What good would it do? He was a married man with a child, maybe two now for all she knew. Presenting herself to him was bound to rake up the past, bring back memories he had put behind him. It would be unforgivable of her to cause Josh further unnecessary suffering when enough had been dealt him already. His mother had said he was happy now and that was how she must leave him. He was getting on with his life, so must she.

She heard the door click as it opened, felt someone entering the room. 'Has he gone?' she faltered, fearing the answer.

When no reply came she lifted her head and turned towards the door. She gasped in shock, jumping up. 'Oh!' she exclaimed.

Slowly Josh strode towards her to stand just inches away. 'Maddie?' he said. 'Oh, Maddie. It really is you.' His deep blue eyes bored into hers, drinking her in. 'I couldn't believe it when Miss Clatteridge told me you were here. I thought I'd dreamed I'd seen yer. But it *was* you . . . I never imagined it could be. It was you looking down on me. Oh, Maddie, Maddie, me darlin', I never thought I'd see you again.' He took one more tentative step towards her. 'You don't know how long I've prayed this would happen, that somehow we'd meet up again. You . . . you are pleased to see me? Please tell me you are, Maddie?'

She was far too stunned to speak so she nodded.

He covered the final distance between them and threw his arms around her, crushing her to him. 'I've missed yer so much. Not a minute 'as gone by when I haven't been thinking of yer.'

Maddie's mind was whirling, not believing what she was hearing. She was having terrible difficulty convincing herself that these were really Josh's arms enveloping her. She eased herself slightly away from him and looked up into his face. 'You wanted to see me? But, Josh, how could you after what happened? My mother . . .' Her head drooped. 'How can you ever forgive me?'

'Forgive you! There's nothin' to forgive yer for. Look at me, Maddie. Look at me, I said.'

She lifted her head and gazed into his eyes.

'When my mother told me what yours had said to her, I was devastated, Maddie. My whole world caved in like my very soul had died. I knew you wouldn't just up and leave me, Maddie. I knew your mother had everything to do with it. She was lying when she told me mother you'd accused me of forcing meself on yer, that I got yer pregnant on purpose to get my hands on her business.

'I went round to see her, begged her to tell me where yer were. She laughed, Maddie. Told me that if I thought I'd allow her daughter to marry a low-life like me, then I was mad as well as stupid. I begged her then, Maddie, pleaded with her like a madman not to get the baby adopted. I was its father, I said, bring it to me. My family would help me raise it.' He stopped and Maddie felt him shudder. 'She said that what she decided to do with the baby was nothing to do with me. She would see me in hell before she lived in the same town as my bastard. She wasn't risking people ever finding out and pointing the finger at her.'

'Oh, God!' Maddie groaned.

'She slammed the door in me face then, Maddie, telling me that if I ever dared show up again she'd call the police.' He felt her body sag against his and tightened his grip on her. 'I was like a man possessed. I looked everywhere for yer. Everywhere I could think of. But there was no sign, nothing. I locked meself away for days afterwards. Wouldn't leave the house. My mother was beside herself and so were the rest of me family. They didn't know what to do for me. I couldn't eat or sleep. All I did was cry. I couldn't carry on like that. I knew I had to get away, start afresh. So I came here.

'But I never gave up hope, Maddie. Every night I've prayed to God he'd somehow send you to me.' He looked down at her, the immense feeling he still held for her plain to see. 'And He's answered me, ain't He?' He eyed her beseechingly. 'Maddie, tell me you still love me? Tell me you still want me as bad as I do you? Please, Maddie, please?'

'Oh, I do, Josh, I do. There's never been anyone else for me but you. I just can't believe you're here. I'm worried I'll wake up and it'll all have been a dream. Oh, Josh,' she said, trembling, fat tears rolling down her face. She buried her head in his shoulder and sobbed.

'Don't cry, Maddie. Please don't cry,' he whispered, distraught.

'I can't help it.'

After several long moments she pulled slightly back and looked up at him. 'I went to see your mother, Josh, just before I came to Leicester a couple of months ago. She told me what mine had done. That's why I left Market Harborough. I'm living with my father and his family now. That's another story.' She stopped abruptly, eyeing him, afraid to ask him a question, terrified of the answer. 'Your mother . . . she told me you were . . . that you were married with a baby on the way. Are . . . are you married, Josh?'

He shook his head vigorously. 'No, Maddie, I'm not. The only woman I would ever marry is the one I'm holding now. Me mother was angry, Maddie. She was hurt and wanted to hurt you for the pain you'd caused me. Don't think badly of her, she was only trying to protect me.'

'I don't think badly of her, Josh. I know she loves you. But when she told me what she did it was like someone had ripped my heart out. I tried so hard to forget you, get on with my life.'

His eyes narrowed in alarm. 'And did you?'

She shook her head. 'No, I couldn't. My feelings for you are just as strong as they've ever been.'

He leaned forward then and kissed her, long, deep and passionately. She responded willingly, savouring the feel and the smell of him, the sense of belonging inside his arms. Finally he gathered her to him again, crushing her so tightly she could hardly breathe

'You'll marry me, Maddie. Now, right now. I'll not wait, not risk losing you again. You will, won't yer?'

Great joy exploded within her. 'Yes!' she cried. 'Yes, Josh. Yes.'

They stood for a moment, locked in each other's arms.

'Maddie,' he said softly, voice thick with emotion, 'there's something I need to ask yer.'

Her heart thumped painfully. She knew what this was about.

'Our baby, Maddie? What was it?'

'A girl,' she whispered. 'She was beautiful, Josh. She was perfect in every way.'

'Oh, Maddie,' he sighed painfully. 'Your mother had no right to do what she did. No right at all.' His tone lowered savagely. 'How could she give her to strangers? Could we get her back, Maddie? Will your mother tell us where she is?'

'Oh, Josh, if only she would! If only it was possible to get her back.'

He stepped slightly away, hands gripping her arms, face filled with urgency. 'There must be a way. If your mother won't tell us, someone else must know what happened to her. Someone must, Maddie. After we're married, the two of us will go and see your mother. She'll have to tell us then. She's our child, *ours*, and your mother's no right to keep her away from us. Not when she must know where she is.'

Brightness filled Maddie's eyes as hope which she'd thought never to feel again flowered within her. She had Josh back. With their daughter too, her life would be complete.

Only one thing marred her joy. The thought of confronting her mother again, even with Josh beside her, was daunting. But if it meant there was a slim chance of getting her baby back she was prepared to face anything.

George shifted uncomfortably in his chair. He'd always known an occasion like this would come, but not out of the blue. He wasn't prepared. For any man to give permission for a beloved daughter to wed was hard. It was proving extremely difficult for George. He felt that he was just getting to know his eldest child, making up for so many lost years, and now it seemed he was about to lose her again.

He hadn't known of this man's existence until fifteen minutes or so ago when Maddie had bounded into the room, radiant as he'd never seen her before. She had been unable to control her excitement and had blurted out the fact that she had someone with her she wanted them to meet.

He had to admit, though, his first impression of Joshua Jenks was very favourable. Instinct told him the young man was honest and genuine and there was no doubting the depth of his feeling for Maddie. Neither was George in any doubt of Maddie's feeling for Joshua. They both loved each other deeply. In the light of that he knew he had no right to refuse or ask for a delay, and anyway Maddie was above the age of consent. Josh did not have to be here at all to ask for her father's permission. It told George much about the man.

When Josh had asked to talk to him privately, Sarah had immediately despatched a reluctant Roy off to a friend's house then ushered the girls into the kitchen to make some tea. They were in there now and it wouldn't surprise George if they had their ears to the door.

He took a deep breath. 'So, Mr Jenks, you want to marry my daughter, you say?'

'Yes, I do, sir.' A nervous Josh raked his fingers through his thatch of hair and inched to the edge of his chair. 'I know this might seem very sudden to you, Mr Ashman, but I've known Maddie for four years or more. We had an understanding. But . . . well, sir, her mother didn't take kindly to me and we were forced to part. Neither of us wanted that, but we had no choice. When I met up with Maddie again today it was like a miracle, for both of us, sir. Our feelings for each other hadn't changed a bit. Neither of us wants to wait. We can't see the point. That's, 'a course, if we have your permission?'

So, thought George, that was why Maddie had come to Leicester. Harriet had been up to her usual tricks. How come he wasn't surprised? He was hurt, though. Hurt for Maddie and what she must have suffered due to her own mother's boundless selfishness.

'Can you provide for Maddie well enough?' he asked.

'I can, sir. Until now I was quite happy to earn enough to keep me going and put a bit past. I'll work harder now I've Maddie. Well, I've good reason to.'

'And what is it you do?'

'Window cleaning, Mr Ashman. I'm a machine mechanic by trade, but when things happened between meself and Maddie I decided a change was what I needed. When I first came to Leicester I took anything I could, then I was lucky enough to be asked if I fancied cleaning a few windows to help a man out with his round and I liked it so I stayed. I've got me own round now. Cost me a fiver and it's bin worth every penny. You're yer own boss, see, Mr Ashman, you can set yer own pace. I intend to build it up. I can afford ter rent us a little house. Nothing grand, but that won't be for long, I can assure yer.'

George nodded, impressed.

In his nervousness, Josh inched further to the edge of the

chair and nearly fell off. He shuffled back, embarrassed, hoping his future father-in-law hadn't noticed. 'Mr Ashman,' he blurted, 'I love your daughter. I'm honest, reliable, and I'll be the best husband to her, I promise, 'til the day I die.'

'Seems fair enough to me. But let me assure you, Mr Jenks, should you not, you'll have me to contend with. Like you, I love my daughter.'

Josh stared. 'You're giving your permission, Mr Ashman?'

George rose, extending his hand. 'I'm giving my blessing. Welcome to the family. You can call me Dad.'

In the kitchen Maddie was pacing worriedly.

'Maddie, for goodness' sake, will you stop that? You're wearing a trench in the slabs. And, Ruth, get your ear off that door.'

'I can't hear anything anyway,' she grumbled, and looked at her sister in awe. 'He's so good-looking, Maddie. No wonder you weren't keen to come to the dance with him in the closet.'

'Ruth, stop being coarse,' her mother scolded. 'But I have to agree, Maddie, he certainly is a handsome man and very well-mannered. You had an understanding, you say, and drifted apart and met up again for the first time today in well over a year?'

Maddie stopped her pacing and nodded.

'Like one of them penny romances,' said Ruth, sighing longingly.

'Hardly romantic,' said Sarah. 'Maddie's just told us he landed up in a coffin, remember. That must have been terrible for him,' she said, fighting to control her mirth. 'And poor Mr Simpson, thinking he had killed him. Oh, dear.' She couldn't stop herself then. The laughter was so infectious they all joined in.

'What's so funny?' said George as he entered the kitchen. 'This is supposed to be a solemn occasion when a man asks a father for his daughter's hand in marriage. That tea mashed yet, Sarah?'

'Did you agree, Dad? Did you?' pleaded Maddie.

He purposely eyed her blankly, but there was a twinkle in his eyes. 'Pardon? Oh, I forgot about that. Well, you'd better come through and ask your young man yourself, hadn't you?' he said matter-of-factly as he turned and headed back out.

'George!' Sarah called. 'Oh, your father,' she erupted, annoyed. 'He's enjoying keeping us on tenterhooks. Quick,' she said to Ruth. 'Bring the tea tray through. Come on, Maddie,' she ordered, grabbing her arm and propelling her after her father.

258

Chapter Twenty

'What about this material, Maddie? It's such a rich cream and the fabric would look lovely made up just as you described.'

Maddie came over to join Agnes and fingered the material. 'Yes, I do like that. You've made my choice, Miss Clatteridge, thank you. I want six yards, please,' she said to the assistant behind the counter of Marshall and Snelgrove's drapery counter. 'It's not curtain material, is it?' Maddie whispered to Agnes.

She giggled. 'I don't think so. If it is, does it matter? It's just what you wanted.'

'Yes, it is. It's perfect.'

The material was measured out and parcelled up and another fifteen minutes was spent choosing cottons, hooks and eyes and braiding to adorn the dress Maddie was going to make. Her wedding dress.

'Sarah is helping me to cut it out tonight.' A thought suddenly struck her. 'Would you like to come around, Miss Clatteridge, and lend a hand? Your help would be much appreciated.'

Agnes stared at her astounded. 'Are you sure you want me to come? What about your family? Shouldn't you ask them first?'

'Why? They'll be delighted to meet you at last. They feel they know you already as I speak of you so often.' Maddie's eyes twinkled. 'All nice things let me assure you, Miss Clatteridge.'

259

'I'm glad to hear that,' she replied, smiling.

'So will you come? This is the ideal opportunity. It'll be nice for you to meet my family before the wedding day.' Her face suddenly grew worried. 'That's if you don't mind lending a hand, of course?'

'Maddie, I'd be honoured too. Thank you for asking me. I'm quite adept with a needle, you know.'

'Yes, I did know. I've seen samples of your handiwork, Miss Clatteridge, and if I say it myself, I thought I was a neat sewer but you're much better than me.'

'Oh, go on, there's no need for such flattery, Maddie dear. I'll still help sew your dress without such praise.'

She laughed. 'I was speaking the truth. Oh, look,' she said, stopping before a sign pointing to the shop's refreshment area. 'There are plenty of free tables. Have we time for a cup of tea? My treat. My father gave me some money towards my trousseau, I'm sure he won't mind my squandering a few pennies of it. I've spent all my savings on accessories. I do feel extravagant. Maybe I should have made do with second-hand.'

'Second-hand? Not on your wedding day surely, Maddie? If you hadn't had the money saved that would be different.'

She smiled brightly. 'Yes it would, wouldn't it? I do want to look nice for Josh.'

Nice? thought Agnes. Maddie would look stunning. She was such a pretty girl with a figure for which she herself would give anything. Why did Maddie always undervalue herself?

'Well, what about this tea?' she said, cutting into Agnes's thoughts.

'Pardon? Oh, er . . .'

Maddie eyed her anxiously. 'Have I suggested something I shouldn't have, Miss Clatteridge? I do appreciate your letting me shop during working hours. Have I overstepped my position? If I have, I'm very sorry.'

'Nothing of the sort,' Agnes said sharply. 'Anyway it was

at my insistence we came out. I was being selfish. I wanted to help you choose your wedding dress material and the other things you needed to buy.' She wondered if Maddie realised how exciting their excursion into town had been for her. 'It's just that . . . well, I've never actually taken tea out before.' She had never been shopping like this before either, but did not want to confess that, she felt embarrassed enough voicing her last declaration.

Maddie stared at her. 'What, never, Miss Clatteridge?'

She cleared her throat. 'No. Father didn't approve.'

'Well, if it's any consolation, I only have once or twice. My mother didn't approve either.' She saw the strange look Agnes was giving her. Of course, she had mentioned her mother for the first time. She knew Agnes assumed Sarah wasn't her real mother because she had always addressed her by her Christian name. Agnes must presume that Maddie's own mother was dead and that her father had remarried. Oh, how complicated life had become. She didn't feel it was her place to inform Agnes of her father's and Sarah's situation, nor did she feel she could cover up her slip by elaborate lies. All she decided to say was, 'Sarah is my father's second wife. My own mother lives in Market Harborough. Let's be daring and have tea.'

'This really is delicious, Maddie dear. I'm so glad you persuaded me to come in.'

'Have another scone?' offered Maddie, pushing the half-empty plate of cakes towards her.

'Oh, no, I couldn't really. I've had two already.' Agnes gazed around her. After they had given their order the seats around them had started to fill. Next to her sat a couple, obviously very much in love by the way they were acting with each other. 'I wonder,' she said wistfully, not realising she was voicing her thoughts out loud, 'if anyone will ever care for me enough to want to hold my hand over a table in public?'

Maddie looked at her. There is already someone who cares for you very deeply and would be only too willing to do that, she thought. But she couldn't say as much.

'Never give up hope, Miss Clatteridge,' she said. 'I never thought anyone would love me as much as Josh does.'

'Really? You surprise me, Maddie. I'd have thought you had many beaux chasing after you. I think I *will* have another scone. They really are very light.'

'What are you going to wear for my wedding, Miss Clatteridge?'

'Oh, my wool dress, I expect.' She picked up a scone, put it on her plate and began to butter it. 'I hadn't given it any thought, too engrossed in your plans.' Her thin face beamed. 'I can't tell you how happy I am for you, my dear.' She stopped her buttering, eyes glazing distantly. 'It's like a fairy story, isn't it? Your meeting up again so unexpectedly.' She resumed her buttering. 'Josh's bump on the head has gone down now, I trust, Maddie, and he's no worse for his ordeal?'

She laughed. 'None. He actually thinks the whole thing quite funny. He tells me he would have suffered any amount of damage to have found me again – although he did say he'd sooner Mr Simpson had slung him across his shoulder to get him back to the parlour instead of what he did do.'

Amusement sparked in Agnes's eyes. 'Yes, well, I don't blame him.'

'Thank you, Miss Clatteridge.'

'What for?'

'For what you did. I wouldn't be getting married if you hadn't intervened.'

'You've already thanked me, Maddie dear. Several times, in fact. Now please let that be the end of it. I did take a risk in telling Mr Jenks you were in the other room and I was concerned matters could have turned out very differently. I'm glad to say they didn't.'

'So am I.'

Agnes made to take a bite of her scone but changed her mind and asked, 'Will you be wanting to leave me after the wedding, Maddie?'

She frowned. 'Leave you? Oh, no, Miss Clatteridge. The day I leave you is the day you leave for Scarborough. That's providing of course, you are still happy to employ me? Josh and I have talked about this and he is quite all right about my working. He's happy to go along with whatever I want to do.'

Agnes sighed in relief. 'I was dreading the thought of losing you, my dear, although pleased by the circumstances.' She leaned over and patted Maddie's hand. 'From what I've seen of him, I approve very much.'

A warm glow filled Maddie. The opinions of those close to her mattered very much and that included Miss Clatteridge. Her glance caught the bag on the vacant seat to the side of her containing her wedding dress material. 'I can't wait to make a start on my dress,' she said excitedly. A thought suddenly struck and she looked at Agnes tentatively. 'Er . . . the dress you're wearing for my wedding,' she asked casually. 'Your best black are you referring to?'

'Pardon? Oh, yes. I have a brown but I'm still in mourning, my dear.'

Maddie reached for the teapot, busying herself refilling their cups. How could she tell Miss Clatteridge that her style of clothes made her look hideous? But an opportunity had arisen in the guise of her wedding to broach the subject of Miss Clatteridge's unbecoming style of dress, and Maddie felt obliged to seize it. She might not have the opportunity again. But she had to be very careful to act without upsetting her friend, the very last thing she wanted to do. 'Miss Clatteridge, could you not wear something a little brighter? I'm sure it wouldn't be seen as disrespectful, not considering the occasion.'

Agnes stared at her thoughtfully. 'Do you not think so? But I haven't anything in my wardrobe that's brighter.'

'You could make something?'

'I could, but there isn't time. Your wedding is in two weeks, and I haven't a sewing machine. Father wouldn't allow us to have one. He said were not our hands adequate enough? I don't mind hand sewing but it's so laborious.'

'We have a sewing machine. I'm sure Sarah wouldn't mind us using it to help you get started.'

'It's a very kind offer, Maddie, but I couldn't take such a liberty. Besides, you have enough to do as it is.'

'It wouldn't be a liberty and I have plenty of time to make my dress. Don't forget, Sarah and Ruth are helping too. But, all right, why don't you buy something to wear?'

'Buy something? Oh! I've never bought a dress. I've always made everything I've worn, Father insisted. No, I couldn't. I really cannot justify spending good money on such a frivolous item. I'll wear my black dress.'

But suddenly the idea of having something new to wear to Maddie's wedding held such appeal. If ever Agnes had felt there was a time she wanted to look nice it was for Maddie's special day. She always felt so self-conscious in everything she wore, it would be such an exciting prospect to have something of her own choosing. But she couldn't justify the expenditure, not when the serviceable clothes she possessed still had many years of life left in them.

Then she remembered how her father had squandered his money. Remembered his harsh ways; the rigid rules her sister and she had been governed by. Memories of them sitting silently round the table eating cold porridge washed down with icy water while their father had tucked into liver and onions, just because they had dared to run barefoot through the dewy grass, their skirts around their knees. 'Hussies and harlots!' he had screeched at them before giving them a whipping. She had been seven at the time, Alice barely five. And all the time he was gambling away good money, had wasted a fortune according to Mr Simpson.

Agnes's lips tightened. Father had been such a hypocrite.

Why shouldn't she have a new dress? Why shouldn't she indeed? She had no one now to justify herself to, be frightened of. She was in charge. In truth she was wearing her black clothes now not out of respect for her father but because it was expected by society. Wasn't that hypocritical of her? Her eyes sparked. 'You're right, Maddie dear. I do need a new outfit for your wedding and I shall have one. Nothing too frivolous and not too expensive and definitely not black.'

Maddie beamed. She was going to have such fun helping Miss Clatteridge choose an outfit to wear for her special day and it wasn't before time. A thought struck her. Dare she? Dare she push her luck any further? It was worth a try. She had just succeeded where she had feared she'd fail.

'I'm going to have my hair cut on Saturday afternoon. Sarah and Ruth suggested a style which I think will suit me. I had to think about it, though. I've had this style for years and sometimes change can be frightening. Anyway I've made up my mind. Why don't you come with me?'

'To watch?'

Maddie shook her head. 'No, to have yours done too. A Marcel wave would look a treat on you.' It would go a long way to soften Agnes's sharp features, Maddie knew.

'Oh, I couldn't,' she said aghast, patting the tightly wound bun at the back of her head. 'A new dress is one thing . . .' She paused, looking at Maddie keenly. 'Do you think I should?'

With a sparkle in her eye, Maddie nodded.

'Then I will. It's about time I struck out, Maddie, did things I want to do, dressed the way I want.' She scraped back her chair. 'Come along, my dear,' she ordered. 'Let's go shopping before I change my mind.'

Several hours later the two women made their way home, laden down with bags. In the end Agnes had purchased more than Maddie. She was still having trouble believing

265

her employer's behaviour. This was a Miss Clatteridge the likes of whom she had never envisaged.

The styles and colours they had chosen together were soft, not exactly the height of fashion but definitely much more becoming on Agnes's long straight frame than any she had previously worn. There really was no comparison. They made her appear slender instead of thin. The hemline of her four new skirts and three dresses had ridden up dramatically from ankle-length to just above her calves and Maddie had been surprised and delighted to discover Miss Clatteridge owned a pair of very shapely legs.

Maddie herself liked best the blue-grey, drop-waisted dress she had chosen for the wedding. The sleeves were elbow-length, the neckline scooped gently across the shoulders. Agnes looked lovely in it, a woman transformed. As she had sought the mirror to view herself, when on Maddie's insistence she had tried it on, she had actually passed by it, not realising the reflection that had caught her eye was actually herself, thinking it was another customer.

'Oh, Maddie!' Agnes had declared in disbelief when she had studied herself. 'Is that really me? It can't be.'

Maddie had joined her, smiling. 'You look beautiful, Miss Clatteridge.'

'That is an extreme exaggeration but I'll agree that I do look nice. What you wear really does make a difference, doesn't it?'

Maddie knew that only too well herself and had nodded.

On finally arriving home a thankful Agnes plonked her bags down on the table, sighing heavily. She stood back and looked at them. Suddenly her face crumpled worriedly as what she had just done struck home and all her new resolve began to disintegrate. 'Oh, I must have had a brainstorm. Maddie, what have I done? All that money I've just wasted. I didn't go out with the intention of spending any on myself and I must have spent at least thirty pounds. Oh, dear,' she groaned clasping her hand to her mouth.

'With due respect, Miss Clatteridge,' Maddie said, putting down her own bags, 'I think you did very well with all you have for that money.'

'Really?'

'Absolutely. Those skirts had been reduced in the sale and so was your new coat, which I must say looks a treat. The dresses ... Well, they weren't that expensive, considering their quality. The special one you chose for my wedding was maybe a bit extravagant, we could have made it for a fraction of the price. But ... to hell with it, Miss Clatteridge! You fell in love with that dress. Why shouldn't you have had it, or the rest for that matter?'

Agnes stared in surprise at this blasphemous outburst, then a smile lit her face. 'You're right. Why shouldn't I indeed? I shall look forward to wearing it so much.' She patted her hair. 'Complete with my new wave.'

'You're still coming with me to get it done?'

'I've gone this far, my dear, I can't stop now.' Agnes's smile grew wider. 'Won't Alice get a shock when she sees me?' Her smile faded. 'I forgot to mention, I had another letter from her this morning asking again how the sale was proceeding. Oh, I do hope those people the agent sent around yesterday decide to go ahead. Only I'm very much afraid they won't. As I told you, the first man wasn't very keen on the area. He wanted somewhere in a more affluent situation. Told me there wasn't that much profit in plain pine which was all he suspected the people around here could afford. Anyway I saw his face after he had looked over the books. He wasn't impressed, I could tell, and muttered something about the business not being as good as he had been led to believe by the agent. I was a bit embarrassed. It's weeks now since we had a funeral to deal with and the agent had told him we were flourishing.

'As for the other undertaker who came, he wasn't too concerned with the way matters had dropped off, said he'd soon get it going again once he was installed. His wife wasn't keen on the house, though. I heard her say something to her husband about there not being a water pump in the kitchen and having to go outside in all weathers. She wasn't pleased about that.' Agnes glanced around the drab room. 'It's not just the water pump, I know. This whole house is so dreary. Enough to put any woman off. I haven't the money to brighten it up to encourage people. It would cost me far too much. More than I spent today.'

'Stop feeling guilty, Miss Clatteridge. The house has great potential. Anyone wanting to buy the business and live here will see that, and the cost of paint and wallpaper won't be an issue. Someone will come along. The agent told you he was going to do his best to push it, didn't he, and he's proved his worth by sending those people who came yesterday. So he prettied up his descriptions a bit. That's what they do to get people to view, isn't it? At least something is happening now.'

Agnes smiled wanly. 'Yes, you're right as usual, my dear. I'm still cross though that he took it upon himself not to tell people about it after he heard of Mr Snood's interest. Still, that's all over. Let's hope the next people who arrive do go ahead. But after my hairdo, my spending will have to stop. If you don't mind, would you put the kettle on? I'll take my clothes upstairs then I must get the ledger out and try and work out what my situation is after this afternoon's expensive excursion.'

It's not going to be good, she thought. And neither would it take her long to work out. Her many hours of poring over the ledger, night after night, after Maddie had gone home and she had cleared away her solitary meal, had started to make sense of the columns. She filled in the ledger weekly now, although considering how little they were doing, it wasn't a large task. The bit coming in from the nail-making and odd carpentry jobs did help a little to ease their outgoings, as had the revenue from the coffin they had supplied for Wilson's, but she had still had to supplement her income from the money her father had left. Except for her madness of today, she had been extremely careful but regardless the balance was dropping.

She heard a knock on the kitchen door and her name being called.

'In here, Mr Simpson. Come through.'

The door opened and Ivan came in. Both women looked at him.

'What is it, Mr Simpson?'

'Oh, yer back,' he cried. 'In the family room.'

'What is?' she asked, frowning.

'The couple. Mam's passed on. They've been waiting an hour. I told 'em you were out on business. I did right, I 'ope?'

Agnes's mouth dropped in disbelief. Maddie's too.

'A funeral?' Agnes cried. 'They've come to me to arrange a funeral?'

'Really, Mr Simpson?' Maddie interrupted.

He nodded. 'Said Tilly Potter sent 'em. Want the best they can afford apparently. I told 'em they'd come to the right place. Miss Clatteridge'd do 'em proud.'

Agnes clapped her hands in utter joy. 'Oh, Mr Simpson, Maddie. Oh! I look a mess. I . . .'

Maddie grabbed her arm. 'Take a deep breath, Miss Agnes. Calm down. You look fine. That's better. Now go and deal with them. I'll bring some tea through, shall I?'

'How kind of you, Maddie. Yes, that's the least we can do for keeping the poor people waiting,' she said, heading for the door. She paused then and addressed Maddie. 'You called me Miss Agnes. I like that, dear. In future you will address me as such.'

With that she was gone, leaving Ivan and Maddie staring at each other. There was no need for words.

Chapter Twenty-One

'There you go, Sarah,' said Maddie, handing her a mug of steaming tea.

'Ah, thank you, my dear,' she replied gratefully accepting it. 'Ruth said for me to say her goodnights. She's gone up. So will I after I've finished this. I told your father I wouldn't be long over an hour ago. Still, I expect he'll be fast asleep and not notice what time I came to bed.' She relaxed back in her chair, eyeing Maddie who was sitting opposite her, feet resting on the fender. 'Isn't this cosy, just the two of us for a change?' She sighed contentedly. 'It was so nice meeting Miss Clatteridge properly at long last. Of course, I've seen her around but I didn't realise what a lovely woman she is. I know what you've told me of her, Maddie, but then I think you speak well of everyone. It was good to find out for meself. I know it's awful of me but I was itching to try and bring up the subject of her clothes. They do nothing for her, do they? It's such a shame.'

'I did though,' Maddie said with a twinkle in her eye.

'Did what?'

'Something about her clothes. When we went shopping today I managed to persuade her to buy a dress for my wedding.'

'Not black, I hope, dear?'

'No. It's a lovely soft bluey grey. She looks a different person in it. And that's not all. She bought skirts, day dresses, and a coat too. And . . .'

'There's more?'

Laughing, Maddie nodded. 'She's coming with me to the hairdresser's on Saturday to get her hair cut and waved. She looks a new person in her clothes, and with a new hairstyle as well, I know it's going to make such a difference to her.'

'So do I,' Sarah said sincerely. 'People round here are frightened of her because of the way that father of hers made her dress, and her sister too. He never let them mix. Shame on him, I say. But you can't blame them, Maddie. She did look . . .' Sarah shrugged her shoulders. 'Well, frightening. 'Course her occupation doesn't help her none, does it? But she's not frightening at all. You should congratulate yourself, Maddie, achieving what you did. When you've spent a lifetime doing things certain ways change doesn't come easy, so she's to be congratulated too. You, Maddie, are so thoughtful, taking the trouble. Not many women with as much on their minds as you have at the moment would bother.'

She sighed. 'It's all happening so quickly, isn't it?'

'Yes, but you can't wait to marry Josh, can you? And why should you? It was quite funny how you wouldn't let the poor lad across the doorstep tonight.'

'Well, I couldn't, could I? He'd have seen what we were doing. He understood anyway.' Maddie's face filled with excitement. 'I can't wait to see the little house he's found for us to rent. He's warned me it's not up to much but it'll do us 'til we can move to something better. I don't care what it's like, to be honest. So long as we have somewhere. I like the fact it's very close, handy for here and for work.'

'I'll say one thing,' Sarah said, impressed. 'He ain't letting the grass grow under his feet, is he? He does what he says he's going ter do. You want to keep well hold of him, Maddie, me duck. Not many men like that around.' She grinned. ''Cept for yer dad, 'course.' She took a sip of her drink while casting her eyes around the room then settled her gaze on the part-made dress hanging on a coathanger on the back of the door. 'It's going to look beautiful when it's finished.'

Maddie looked across at it too. 'Yes, it is. Thank you so much for all you're doing.'

Sarah smiled tiredly. 'It's my pleasure.' She laughed merrily. 'Your poor father couldn't believe his eyes when he arrived home after a late visit with a client and found this room in such a state. He was expecting to put his feet up after his dinner for a quiet read of his paper. I had warned him what to expect when he left this morning but he obviously forgot by the look on his face when he opened the door tonight.'

'It is a mess, isn't it? Maybe I should try and clear up a little,' offered Maddie, attempting to rise.

'Sit where you are. Tidying up will be a waste of time. I shall only get everything out as soon as you've all gone to work in the morning and it'll be back in the same state. So what's the point?'

'You're supposed to be resting, Sarah. You are expecting, remember.'

'I am resting. Helping you with your dress isn't work to me, Maddie, it's too pleasurable.'

'You are kind, Sarah. I do appreciate it.'

She stared, taken aback. 'Why should I treat you any differently from your sister?'

'Well . . . Ruth *is* your daughter.'

'And you're not, is that what you mean? No, I'm not your mother unfortunately. I only wish I was.' She looked fondly at the younger woman for a moment. 'We never have the chance to talk, just the two of us. There's always someone around. Please let me take this chance to tell you I'm not trying to ease my way into your affections and take your own mother's place, believe me. I just wanted . . . Oh, Maddie, you're such a lovely girl. Your arrival here has brought us such happiness. Your father's so proud of you, I can't tell you how much.'

Maddie's bottom lip began to tremble and tears pricked

her eyes as all of a sudden everything crowded in on her. It was all too much. The unexpected arrival of Josh, the rush to get things done for the wedding, but most of all Sarah's generous acceptance of her. 'I don't deserve your kindness,' she murmured.

'Don't be silly, of course you do.'

'But I don't. And you wouldn't think so much of me and neither would Father is he knew . . .' Maddie's head drooped. She suddenly felt a great need to unburden herself of her dreadful secret. She had to, she couldn't carry it around anymore and let her family believe so well of her, when the truth was she wasn't such a good person. 'I don't deserve it, Sarah. I've been dishonest with you. It's unforgivable of me, considering the way you've all been so open with me about everything that's happened.'

'Dishonest? What are you going on about, Maddie?' Sarah asked, confused.

A sob caught in the back of Maddie's throat as she uttered, 'I have a dreadful secret. I couldn't bring myself to tell you.'

'Maddie, you don't . . .'

'Please, let me finish, Sarah.' She raised her head and stared her straight in the eye. 'I know you've always suspected that something awful brought me to Leicester, not just deciding I wanted to start a new life. You were right to think that.' She wrung her hands. 'I had a baby,' she blurted out. 'A daughter. Mine and Josh's. She's nearly two years old now.'

'Oh, Maddie!' Sarah's shoulders sagged in distress. 'What happened?'

Maddie sniffed. 'My mother realised I was expecting before I had the courage to tell her. She took me to the house of a woman far away from us and left me there until after I'd given birth, with no means of leaving. She told Josh awful lies to cover up what she'd done. She wouldn't tell him where I was, nothing. When my baby was born she came to take us both home, or so I thought. While I was

274

getting ready she handed my baby over for adoption.' Her face crumpled in pain. 'What do you think of me now? My father will despise me, won't he? He, you and everyone else thinks I'm such a lovely person. Well, now you know I'm not.'

'Oh, Maddie,' Sarah whispered softly, the other woman's desperate pain filling her being. How could Harriet have done that to her, acted so callously? To her own grandchild too. Now Sarah knew the reason for the sadness of the dispirited woman who had first arrived on their doorstep so unexpectedly. And why Maddie had almost cried when she had announced the arrival of her own baby. Sarah suddenly felt dreadful. She patted the side of her chair. 'Come and sit here beside me. Come on.'

Obediently Maddie got to her feet and went over, dropping down to sit on the floor next to her. Sarah ran her hand gently over Maddie's hair.

'You poor child. Yes, you're right, I did think there was more to what you were telling us, as did your father. But we knew you'd tell us when you were good and ready. You think I'm shocked? That your father will disown you?' Sarah shook her head. 'You're with a woman who has lived in sin with a man for twenty-five years. We've two children, born out of wedlock, and another on the way.

'But, Maddie dear, even if none of that had happened, if your father had got his divorce and we were respectably married with the children bearing his name, we would never, ever think badly of you. I'll always be grateful for the way you've been with me. You could have hated me, Maddie, thinking I took your father away. And I wouldn't have blamed you if you had. Anyway, you're not the first it's happened to and you won't be the last. It's times like this when families are supposed to be understanding, my dear. And we are. Do you want me to tell your father or shall I leave it for you to do? Or it will go no further than me if that's what you want?'

Maddie eyed her beseechingly. 'Would you tell my father for me? He really ought to know. I can't tell him, I feel so ashamed still.'

'And I've told you, you shouldn't, so stop it. What's happened has happened, you can't carry the blame for the rest of your life. I know your father, Maddie. His anger will be all for Harriet. She took your baby away. She stopped you and Josh from being together. You could have been a family. That was unforgivable of her. If she hadn't made it impossible for you, forcing you to sneak around behind her back, none of this would have happened, would it? If anyone's to blame your mother is, Maddie.'

She pulled a handkerchief from her cardigan pocket and dabbed her wet eyes and blew her nose. 'Josh wants us to go and see my mother after we're married, ask her if she'll tell us now what she did with our child so we can try and get her back. I want her back, I desperately want my baby back,' sobbed Maddie. 'Josh feels the same too.'

Sarah sighed. 'It's worth a try, I suppose.'

'You don't think she will?'

'Do you, my dear?'

Maddie shook her head. 'I know it'll be a waste of time. I don't want to put Josh through it. He's suffered so much through my mother already. I know what our reception will be.' She wiped away fresh tears. 'It's stupid of me, I know, after all she's done, but I still can't help worrying about her now she's all alone.'

'She's your mother, Maddie, and being the sort of person I know you are, it doesn't surprise me to hear you feel like that. I wish I could go with you for support, but that's out of the question.' Sarah suddenly had a thought. 'Where you had your baby, would they know who adopted her?'

Maddie sighed. 'Mrs Baldicott. She was a lovely old lady, and treated me so well. I grew really fond of her. At the time I begged her to tell me but she said even if she knew she couldn't, it was more than her job was worth. I couldn't

276

expect her to risk everything for me. She's a widow, it's her only income.'

'No, I suppose not.'

They lapsed into silence, each with her own private thoughts.

Maddie suddenly sat bolt upright. 'I could go and see my mother by myself. Try and reason with her. She . . . she might be different now, mightn't she, Sarah? Now that she's been on her own and has had time to think, she could be sorry for what she's done. She could be a changed person, couldn't she? I'm stronger now too. She can't bully me like she used to. And I have to consider Josh. I really feel I couldn't put him through the ordeal of facing her again.' She took a deep breath. 'Yes, that's what I'm going to do. If I achieve nothing else, I can see she's all right, can't I? I'll go tomorrow. I'll explain to Miss Clatteridge I've important business to attend to, I know she'll understand.'

Sarah eyed her sharply. 'Are you sure about this, Maddie?'

No, she wasn't, not really, but what else could she do? I have to do this,' she said, and gave a wan smile. 'I do feel so much better now that I've told you about the baby.' She raised herself, leaned over and kissed Sarah affectionately on the cheek. 'Thank you so much for being so understanding. I love you, Sarah.'

She smiled tenderly. 'Oh, Maddie my dear, I love you too.' She reached over and put her arms around Maddie, giving her a hug. 'Go to bed,' she ordered. 'I'll be just behind you.'

As Maddie left the room Sarah's face creased in concern. Maddie was heading for trouble, and Sarah wanted desperately to try and stop her. People like Harriet did not change. They saw no wrong in what they had done. In Sarah's opinion, Harriet did not deserve her daughter's concern. But she knew Maddie had to do this to set her own mind at rest. Sarah suspected Maddie was wasting her time but sincerely hoped she herself was wrong.

Chapter Twenty-Two

Maddie paused as she turned the corner of the street and stared nervously down it. These familiar surroundings, an area she had grown up in and knew like the back of her hand, suddenly seemed so alien, offering no feeling of belonging whatsoever. Only yards away was the person responsible for her fleeing the town of her birth a few months before. Then she had been a woman whose very soul had been destroyed. So much had happened during the short intervening period. Maddie had discovered truths so shocking she had had to search to the very depths of her being to understand and accept that people could act so deviously to get their own way. With the help of her new family, with their love and support, she had managed to acknowledge it, then put it all aside. To forget was impossible, she knew, but no longer did the cruelty her mother had inflicted on her affect her daily life.

Yet here she was again, by her own choice, preparing to stare her tormentor in the face. Sarah had taken her aside that morning as she was getting ready to leave and asked her if, now she had slept on it, she was still determined to go today? Sarah was deeply concerned for her, that much had been apparent.

In fact, Maddie hadn't slept a wink. She had tossed and turned all night, going over and over what she was about to undertake. But she had no choice. She had to do it. Now that time had passed and she was herself about to embark on a new phase of her life, she had to try and put matters on

279

an even footing with her mother, at least be on speaking terms if nothing else and set her mind at rest that Harriet was faring all right on her own. And there were questions she had to ask that only her mother could answer. But now she had actually arrived, the determination that had steeled her throughout her journey on the slow train suddenly vanished. All she wanted to do was turn and run, back to the security of Josh and her family.

An image of Josh's face swam before her, his handsome features soft with love, and courage and strength flowed through her. She was doing this not only for herself but for him. For Maddie that was reason enough. Taking a very deep breath, she pushed all her fears aside. As she was about to enter the shop a booming voice just behind her made her jump and she spun around.

'Maddie Ashman. Well, well, well. How good it is to see you.'

'Mrs Green! Goodness, you startled me,' she said, exhaling sharply. 'It's nice to see you too.'

'I'm so glad you're back,' said the woman with obvious sincerity. 'Old lady recovered now, has she? Your mother's a saint to let you go off again. I have missed you, my dear. I've been getting what I needed done at Pringle's across town but the girl they have there doesn't hold a candle to you. I'll be in first thing in the morning. How's your mother by the way? To be honest, I haven't been into the shop since you went off so suddenly.'

Maddie gnawed her bottom lip uncomfortably. 'I'm just about to find out, Mrs Green. I'm just paying a visit myself.'

'A visit? Oh, you're not back for good then?'

Maddie shook her head.

The rotund face looked dismayed, monstrous jowls wobbling dangerously. 'Oh, that's a shame. That means I'll still have to patronise Pringle's. When will you be back?' she asked hopefully.

'I won't, Mrs Green.'

'Oh! Never?'

Maddie swallowed hard. 'I have a life in Leicester now.'

'Really? I'm sure your mother said the old lady lived in a village near . . . where was it . . . Coalville, I think.' She eyed Maddie quizzically. 'Is your mother going to be joining you?'

'I can't answer that, Mrs Green.'

'Oh, well, I expect she'll have no choice soon if her business continues to drop off as I know it is. She lost much of her custom when you went, my dear. It was a good little shop once but times change, don't they, and your mother doesn't stock the sort of thing I use now. Except for the basic white and black cotton. And, of course, spare suspenders.' Realising she was speaking of delicate articles of women's clothing, her loud voice was lowered dramatically. 'But I wear blue now as well as my pink and I can't get blue at Ashman's. Yes, you have to move with the times, don't you, dear?' Her voice rose again. 'Pringle's have and that's why most people who shopped at your mother's go there now. And they sell very nice lingerie, you know. And of course Woolworth's have such a good selection of cottons and the like at very reasonable prices. I have to watch my pennies. Well, must be off. I do wish you well. Good day.'

'Good day, Mrs Green.'

Maddie felt even more worried. According to Mrs Green her mother wasn't doing very well at all. Despite herself, Maddie couldn't help but feel sorry.

The bell on the door jangled dully as it was opened and Harriet glanced up. A look of utter astonishment fleetingly crossed her face when she recognised the person who was entering, to disappear just as quickly. Stony eyes glared at Maddie, thin lips twitched into a sarcastic grin.

She was horrified by the sight of her mother who didn't look well. Harriet had always been thin but she appeared gaunt now, lines criss-crossing her drawn face. Her fine hair was sparser, patches of scalp visible. Her clothes too looked in need of a clean and press. Her movements were slow, laboured.

'You took your time.' Her voice was cold and hard. 'Got fed up living with that whore and her bastards, did you? I bet that was a shock. Well, now you know what that father of yours is really all about and what I had to put up with all those years. I must say, I didn't think you'd last this long with them. Where are your bags?'

Maddie was staring at her, shocked by her savage tone and foul language. 'Bags? Oh, I haven't brought them,' she replied absently, still shocked by her mother's state.

'Ah, left them at the station, have you? Decided to test the water first. I see. Well, go and fetch them,' Harriet commanded. 'Your room's just as you left it.'

A great desire to turn and run overwhelmed Maddie. It took all her strength to control it. She stepped back, flattening herself against the glass in the door. 'I . . . I haven't come to stay, Mother. My home is in Leicester now.'

Harriet's lips pressed tightly together, eyes narrowing darkly and nostrils flaring. 'Well, why have you come then?'

'To see you. I was concerned about you.'

'Concerned!' she hissed. 'I don't want your concern. I want nothing from you. You walked out on me, remember, after all I did for you.'

'Mother, please.' Maddie took a tentative step forward. 'Don't be like this. How are you managing?'

'Perfectly well. I don't need you to survive. Is that it?'

'Pardon?'

'Have you got what you came for? If so, go.'

'Mother, please. You don't look well. Let me help you . . .'

'I've told you, I'm fine. Perfectly capable of looking after myself.'

Maddie sighed. 'All right, Mother.'

'So is that it?' she spat again.

'No, it's not. I . . . was hoping we could talk. I was hoping we could . . .'

282

'Could what, Maude?' she demanded icily.

'Be friends?'

'Friends!' spat Harriet. Then she laughed, a nasty spiteful cackle. 'You really amaze me. Friends indeed. Why, you're the most ungrateful, disloyal specimen of a human being a mother could ever be saddled with as a daughter. Mind you, what can I expect with who fathered you?'

A great anger surged through Maddie. Before she could stop herself, she cried, 'Don't speak like that about my father. He's a good man, kind, and I love him. As for his wife – yes, and she *is* his rightful wife, Mother – she's a good woman and neither of them deserves the way you've treated them.'

Harriet's face contorted furiously. 'I'll not have you speak of them in such terms in my house. Now get out. Go on,' she ordered.

Maddie faced her, eyes blazing. 'No, I won't. I came here with the best of intentions but I was wasting my time, wasn't I? I hoped you might have changed. How foolish of me. I'll go, Mother, and I'll not return now you've told me what you really think of me. But before I do I want to tell you that I'm getting married. To Josh. Remember him, Mother? He's the man you told such lies to. He's the man whose baby you gave away. I want you to tell me where our daughter is. I won't move from this spot until you do.'

'Well, you'll stand there forever then, won't you, because I'll tell you nothing.' Harriet moved around the counter and came to stand before Maddie, looking her up and down scathingly. 'Look at you, dressed in your trashy clothes. You've turned into a low-life like them. I'm ashamed of you.' She pushed Maddie aside and opened the door. 'Now get out. Get out, I said, and don't dare darken my door again, do you hear?' Eyes suddenly flashing wickedly, she pushed her face closer to Maddie's, lowering her voice maliciously. 'Oh, and something else to tell your father. That money he gave me – I've never spent a penny. Not one farthing in all these years. Tell him he's left me very well off. Tell him I said thank you. Now get out!'

With that she pushed Maddie out of the door and slammed it shut so hard the glass rattled and the dusty bell above fell off.

Harriet watched for a moment as Maddie, head bowed, walked off down the street, then walked through to the back. The fury that filled her was so intense she shook with its violence. How dare Maude come back, saying she wanted them to be friends? Friends! Harriet had never needed a friend in her life and certainly did not want one in the guise of a daughter. Or rather harlot, she thought. After all Maddie had done, to walk calmly into the shop as though nothing had happened! And the worst of it was the way she'd been sticking up so blatantly for that sorry excuse for a man and the hussy with whom he lived in sin.

Suddenly a vice-like grip tightened round her heart and her hand flew up to clutch her chest. Harriet opened her mouth to scream but all that came out was a gurgle as she breathed her last and her lifeless body crumpled to the floor.

As soon as he heard the key in the lock Josh ran down the passage to meet Maddie. 'Sarah told me where you'd gone. Oh, Maddie!' he cried, gathering her to him. 'You shouldn't have gone on yer own. I wanted to go with you.' He felt her slump against him and lowered his voice. 'It was bad, wasn't it, my darlin'?'

'Yes,' she sobbed. 'It was dreadful. I'd gone with so much hope . . .' Her voice trailed away. She couldn't tell anyone, not even Josh, what had happened. It was just too terrible.

He sensed her deep distress and said nothing, just held her tightly.

'She wouldn't tell me anything about our baby, Josh, I'm so sorry.'

'Don't worry about that, Maddie love. We'll find out some other way. You're home safe and sound and that's the main thing. Come on through, your father and Sarah have been worried sick. She's had the kettle permanently boiling its lid off ready to mash you a cuppa and she's kept your dinner hot in the oven.'

A warm feeling of belonging washed through her. Gripping his hand, Maddie walked with him down the dimly lit passage to where the rest of her family anxiously awaited her.

Chapter Twenty-Three

'Well, Mrs Jenks, I think it's all going off really well. What do you say?'

Maddie gazed around her happily. There wasn't one person in this room who wasn't delighted for Josh and her. And they had shown it in such a wonderful way. When it had become known that a reception was beyond their means, everyone chipped in. George and Sarah had insisted their house be used and had provided most of the food, the rest being kindly donated by neighbours. Roy and Ruth had rearranged the furniture to allow access to the food and drink, leaving plenty of space in the middle for dancing for those who wished, with seats against the walls for those who preferred to chat. Agnes had provided the drink and had organised a professional photographer to take a selection of photographs of their special day. Ivan had dipped into his savings and bought them a silver frame. The Jenks family had all pitched in together and bought the happy couple sheets and towels. Other friends and neighbours had arrived bearing gifts. Except Oswald Peabody. He just brought himself.

Maddie gazed up at her new husband, eyes shining. 'The day has been perfect, Josh. I couldn't have wished for better.'

He looked down at her fondly. 'Would you sooner have delayed things 'til we'd saved and been able to afford a posher do?'

'What? All that pomp and ceremony! No, thank you. And

besides, that would have meant having to wait and I wasn't going to.'

Josh increased the pressure of his arm around her waist, pulling her closer to him. He had several times caught her unawares looking wistful and had known she was thinking of their child, feeling that the day was not quite complete with her absent. He didn't want to spoil her enjoyment though by raising the subject. 'Happy?' he whispered.

She was ecstatic but for one solitary regret. She knew Josh was feeling it too. She had caught him several times with a faraway look in his eyes. One special person was missing from their special day: their daughter. But Maddie didn't want to spoil his happiness by mentioning it. 'Never been more so,' she whispered back. 'I'm so happy, Josh, I could walk across hot ashes and not feel the pain.'

'You look beautiful, Maddie. I couldn't tek me eyes off yer when you walked into the chapel. I can't believe you're really my wife at last.'

'If you've told me that once, you've said it a dozen times today.' she said, laughing.

'Well, let me say it again. You look beautiful, Maddie.'

'Thank you, kind sir,' she said, giving a mock curtsey.

She turned her attention to their guests. 'My family and yours are getting on so well, but then I never doubted they would.' She looked up at her husband. 'Your mother is happy about us marrying, isn't she, Josh?'

'Maddie, she's over the moon. Stop worrying.' He started to laugh. 'Look at me sister with your Roy. Eh, that's not sherry they're drinking, is it?'

'No, it's dandelion and burdock.'

'That's all right then.'

They both lapsed into silence, each savouring the atmosphere, storing memories to resurrect in the years to come.

Across the room Ivan Simpson was standing with his back against the wall nearest the door, sipping a glass of dark ale, eyes fixed on Agnes who was engrossed in conversation with Sarah.

Agnes looked lovely. He wanted to gather her into his arms and declare his undying love for her. He sighed. Her transformation was breathtaking, so much so that the first time he had seen her crossing the yard late the previous Saturday afternoon, sporting her new Marcel wave and dressed in a smart new coat, his mouth had opened wide enough to drive a tram through, eyes popping near out of his head. He had been unable to move, despite the fact that she was aware he was watching her.

She was so much softer-looking. Not that it mattered to Ivan. He had loved her the way she was before. But now he was a worried man. It wasn't the thought of her eventual departure for Scarborough that was causing his present unhappiness. It was the knowledge that someone of her own sort was definitely going to notice her now and snap her up and Ivan couldn't bear the thought.

Lounging beside him, Oswald Peabody was slyly ogling Maddie over the top of his glass. He was inwardly furious. He had set his cap at her. Then Jenks turned up out of the blue and in an instant, seemingly, had married her and all Oswald's hopes lay shattered. He wouldn't have minded so much if he hadn't lied to his friends about his conquest, telling them how this older woman at work was all over him. Now they knew the truth, he was suffering constant taunts and snide comments.

He suddenly realised that Ivan had spoken to him. 'What?' he responded, easing himself away from the wall.

'I said, I'm off.' Ivan could no longer bear to watch Agnes, his mood of depression worsening by the second. He wanted to return to his room, shut out the world and wallow in self-pity.

'Yeah, me too,' Oswald mumbled. 'N'ote round 'ere for us, is there?'

'You're not leaving so soon?' Maddie said as Ivan, Oswald

behind him, came to say goodbye.

'Yes, stay a little longer. Me father's going to play some tunes on his fiddle soon. We're going to have some dancin',' said Josh.

Ivan looked across at Albert Jenks, eyebrows raised. 'Plays the fiddle, eh?'

'Amongst many other talents. He's better at cobbling shoes, though, me mother reckons. She says his fiddle playing sounds like cats screeching.' Josh laughed. 'He's not that bad. Why don't you stay and judge fer yerself, Mr Simpson?'

'No, if yer don't mind, I'll pass. I, er, have a few things I want ter do back at the yard.' He leaned over and pecked Maddie on the cheek. 'Thanks fer asking me, Maddie love.' His eyes twinkled fondly. 'Yer do look beautiful. See yer Monday, eh? Tarra.'

'Thank you for coming, Ivan. Goodbye. Goodbye, Oswald.'

He grunted something inaudible as he followed Ivan out.

'I like Ivan Simpson. He seems a thoroughly decent sort. Can't say the same fer that young fellow, though,' Josh remarked.

'Off home then, lad?' Ivan asked Oswald as they stepped out into the street.

'Nah,' came the sullen response. 'Thought I'd go fer a pint down the local.'

Ivan looked unimpressed. 'Thought yer'd have had better things to do with yer money?'

'Money! Huh,' he growled. 'What bit I get paid you're referring ter, eh, Mr Simpson?'

'Oi, Oswald me lad, you should count yersel' lucky. You gets paid more than most in our business fer what you do. Miss Clatteridge put yer wage up the other week, I know she did.'

'Not by much, she din't.'

'Better than a slap in the gob, ain't it?'

'S'pose.'

Ivan thrust his hands deep into his trouser pockets and looked up and down the street. He sighed audibly. 'I'm off then. And if you've n'ote better to do than piss yer money up the wall, yer'd better get off too. See yer Monday first thing sharp.'

'Yeah, tarra, Mr Simpson.'

They each went their separate ways.

Oswald had slouched along for several yards before he realised someone was walking alongside him. He stopped abruptly and turned to face the man.

'A' you following me or summat?' he snarled at the youth alongside him.

'Hardly followin', am 'a, Oswald Peabody?'

Oswald's eyes narrowed questioningly. 'How d'yer know me name?' he demanded.

'I made it me business ter find out. I've bin watching yer, see.'

'Watchin' me! Wa' for?'

'Checkin' yer out. I reckon you look like a man who wouldn't turn up 'is nose at the chance of earning an extra bob or two.'

The boy's eyes sparkled keenly. 'How?'

'Are yer interested?'

'Might be.'

'Off ter the pub, weren't yer?'

'Mighta bin.'

'I'll join yer. We can find a quiet corner and discuss it, if yer like?'

Oswald looked at him, then nodded. 'Okay. N'ote ter lose, 'ave I?'

'Excuse me a minute, son,' said Sadie Jenks, squeezing her large round body between Josh and Maddie. 'I want a quiet word with this wife of yours. Women's talk. Go on, skedaddle.'

Maddie smiled. 'I wouldn't mind a glass of lemonade, please, Josh.'

'An' I'll 'ave a stout,' said his mother.

Sadie hooked her arm through Maddie's and pulled her aside. 'I just want ter get things straight between us, me dear, and don't look so worried. I've not 'ad a chance since we arrived. I must say, yer dad and Sarah 'ave made us most welcome. Very good of 'em to squash us all in like this and fer you to give up yer bed last night and share wi' yer sister. Good of yer all. Well, we couldn't afford lodgin's.'

'It's the least we could do, Mrs Jenks. And we were only too glad to. It meant everything to Josh and me that you all came here today.'

'There's no way I'd 'a missed our Josh's wedding. Not on your nelly. An' it's all bin quite exciting really. I ain't never bin ter Leicester before. 'Tain't such a bad place from what I've seen of it.' Her jolly face grew serious. 'Look, Maddie love, we didn't get off to a very good start, did we?'

'Mrs Jenks . . .'

'Let me finish, me duck. It's all my fault. I took yer ter be the same as yer mother. I was wrong ter do that. It was 'cos I wa' upset for our Josh. Anyway, I just want ter ask if we can start afresh like, 'cos I'd like us ter be friends?'

'Oh, Mrs Jenks, so would I. If ever you want to come and see us, you'll be more than welcome. And Josh and I will come and see you as often as we can.'

Sadie's face filled with joy and relief. 'Oh, yer a lovely gel all right. Our Josh 'as done 'imself proud.' She threw her powerful arms around Maddie and crushed her in a hug. 'Welcome ter the family, me duck.' She released her hold on Maddie and turned her attention to the spread on the table. 'Better get a sandwich afore it all disappears.'

'Where's me mother gone?' asked Josh, handing Maddie a glass filled with home-made lemonade.

'She's there, look, at the table.'

'Oh, ah.' He eyed Maddie searchingly. 'Everything all right between you and her?'

She smiled broadly. 'Everything's fine. She was just welcoming me to the family. She's a lovely woman, Josh. All your family are so friendly.'

He leaned over and kissed her. 'Thanks. I'd better take this to her before she starts complaining. Did I tell you that new hairstyle looks great?'

'Only a dozen times! For goodness' sake, give your mother that drink before you spill it,' she said, laughing.

'Enjoying yourself, Maddie?'

'Hello, Miss Agnes, Yes, thank you. Are you?'

'Oh, I'm having a wonderful time. This is the first wedding I've been to.' Absently she patted her week-old hairstyle. 'I hope I get asked to another. I shall have so much to write to Alice about.' She paused, casting her eyes hurriedly around the room. 'Er . . . have you seen Mr Simpson at all?' she asked casually.

'He's gone home, Miss Agnes.'

'Home? Oh.'

'Said he had things to attend to.'

The fleeting look of disappointment that crossed her face was unmistakable. 'Oh, I was just wanting to see if he was all right. As his employer I felt it my duty.'

Maddie did not believe a word of what she said, but declined to comment. 'He was his usual self, Miss Agnes. I think he was just ready to go.'

'Yes, well,' she murmured, feigning disinterest. 'Oh, Mr Jenks is getting out his fiddle. Your father has promised me a dance.'

'*Can* he dance?' asked Maddie.

'He doesn't know himself, dear, and I don't know if I can. We're going to see if we can together. Oh, isn't it exciting?' said Agnes, hurrying off.

Josh came back to join Maddie. 'Well, Mrs Jenks, everyone seems to be enjoying themselves. Everyone's occupied. Sarah is talking to my mother. Me dad is providing the entertainment. Me sister and Roy are squashed together on the settee, staring adoringly into each other's eyes. Budding romance in the meking there, if I ain't mistaken. Your dad and Miss Agnes are about to dance once me father gets into tune. And all the rest of the neighbours and friends are eating, drinking and making merry. Who else is there? Where's your Ruth?'

'She's around somewhere. I saw her a while ago chatting to Bill Wiggins from next door.'

'That good-looking lad that came in with his mam and dad an hour or so ago?'

'That's him.'

'Probably kissing and cuddling up the entry by now then.'

Maddie nudged him. 'Josh, really,' she laughed. 'Good luck to her if she is. She can look after herself, can our Ruth.'

He turned and looked at her. 'So?' he said, cocking an eyebrow.

'So?' she repeated, frowning.

He smiled wickedly. 'So is it safe for us to slip off?'

A pink tinge flushed her cheeks. 'Won't anyone miss us?'

He shook his head and grabbed her hand. 'Too bad if they do. Come on, Mrs Jenks. We've a house of our own to go to.'

Chapter Twenty-Four

'Oswald, are you listening? The strip of black board needs putting up against the window, advising everyone who passes to be respectful as there's been a death in the house. Please secure it as quietly as possible. And don't forget to take the bale of straw with you to spread on the cobbles outside and dull the noise of the horses and carts passing by.' Agnes paused thoughtfully. 'Now have I forgotten anything? Oh, the wreath to hang on the door. It's outside by the doorstep.'

'I do know all this,' he muttered sulkily. 'I 'ave done it before.'

'I'm quite aware of that,' said Agnes, putting on her coat. 'I just want everything to be right. Remember, it's our task to guide the poor bereaved family through these dark days. Our job does not finish until the family are safely back home after the funeral service. Now, so far as the Dunns' funeral is concerned, there's no need to polish the hearse, it's just the dray we'll be using. I must check with Maddie to make sure the black cloth we drape it with has been washed after the last time it was used . . . Oh, yes, and organise the pall-bearers. There's only the father and an uncle so we'll need another four. Jones, Biggins, Fellows and Bogs, I think. They're all about the same height and I know they could all do with the bit of money they get for doing it. Although I must have a quiet word with Mr Bogs. His black suit is really threadbare, not up to the standard I like to see my pall-bearers keep.' She frowned thoughtfully. 'I expect another suit is well beyond the poor man's means.

I'll speak to him, see if I can help.'

Oswald's unattractive features twisted in a scowl. Old man Clatteridge never made all this fuss, he thought, just barked out orders and let his workers get on with it. Now here *she* was treating him like an imbecile and acting as if she was personally responsible for guiding the souls of the dead. Most folk round here, he thought wickedly, were bound straight for hell from what they got up to while they were alive.

Still, his daily work wasn't such a bind now that his mind was occupied with the deal he had struck. Could be very lucrative, he'd been told. And after he'd thought about it, he was in no doubt that it could indeed. It was risky, 'course it was. Making money on the side didn't come without its dangers. But the money in his pocket and what he could do with it far outweighed thoughts of what would happen if he was discovered.

'Oh, the flowers . . .'

'Flowers!' he exclaimed. 'What, them ones, Miss Clatteridge?' he queried, staring at the bunch on the table. 'You ain't expecting me to walk through the streets wi' a bunch of flowers, are yer?' Oswald looked at her aghast. 'I mean, I'll 'ave me hands full wi' everything else I've ter carry.'

'Yes, of course. I'll take them myself,' Agnes said, pulling on her gloves. 'Well, off you go then. I'll be directly behind you. And please remember, Oswald, act courteously at all times. You're a representative of Clatteridge's.'

'Yes, Miss Clatteridge,' he muttered, turning away from her and heading out of the door. It was not until he was out of sight that he pulled a disgruntled face and stuck two fingers up.

'Oh, what lovely flowers for this time of year, Miss Agnes,' Maddie declared, arriving in the kitchen laden down with a full basket of dirty washing.

Agnes eyed her blankly. 'Pardon, dear? I was miles away. Going over in my mind everything for the Dunn family.'

'I was admiring the flowers. For you, are they?'

Agnes smiled. 'No, dear. Who do I know would buy me flowers? No, I bought them to place in the room where the body is to lie.' She lowered her voice. 'You see, Maddie dear, after a few days . . . I thought the flowers would be a nice touch and help scent the place. The family aren't very well off. In fact, I've had to cut our price to the bone so they can afford to bury their daughter. Oh, such a terrible state of affairs! Only fourteen and struck down by the influenza. She was well one day, a week later gone. She's to be all in white, of course, because she was virginal.' Agnes pulled a face and added, 'Well, I hope so at her age. I did suggest we brought her body here to lie in the Chapel of Rest but the poor mother can't bear to part from her daughter until she really has to.'

Maddie tried not to shudder. 'Oh, I see. I thought I'd set to with the washing while you were out,' she said to change the subject.

'Thank you, dear. I hope to be back before twelve-thirty so you can get off to see to your husband's dinner. Although I might have a problem because the bereaved do like to talk about their loved ones and I don't like to rush away. I feel it's very much part of our job to listen to them. It all helps ease their grief, doesn't it?'

'You're so kind, Miss Agnes. I don't suppose many undertakers would do the extra things you do.'

'I like to think that Clatteridge's is a bit special. Oh, that reminds me. I had a letter of introduction from the agent today for a Mr and Mrs Moss. They're in a village situation at the moment but want to move to town and are looking for a suitable place. Let's hope they like this one enough to make an offer.'

Six potential buyers had been shown around now and not one had taken matters further, which was most discouraging. Agnes did not say as much but Maddie knew the situation was deeply worrying for her. At least once a week a letter arrived from her sister wanting to know what was going on. Agnes was running out of excuses. Still, with business coming in steadily now, her main worry over money had been greatly relieved and she was being kept fully occupied and seemed to be thriving on it all.

Maddie smiled as she watched her bustling about readying herself to see her clients. Despite being dressed in black, which for work purposes was only fitting, she looked very efficient and smart in her flattering blouse and skirt and a good wool wrapover coat, its single large button fastening at the hip. A cloche-style hat was pulled down over her Marcel wave.

'Right, I'd better be off then,' Agnes announced, picking up her handbag.

'I hope it all goes well,' said Maddie. 'Don't worry if you're late back. If Josh arrives home and I'm not there, he'll help himself out of the larder. He never makes a fuss.'

'He's so good your husband, dear. A real treasure. But in this weather, with what he does for a living, he needs a hot meal inside him in the daytime. And of course you're still newly-weds . . .'

'Miss Agnes!' Maddie cut in, laughing. 'We've been married nearly two months. We had our first disagreement last night.'

'Oh, you didn't, dear?' Agnes gasped in concern.

'Don't look so worried, Miss Agnes, it was only over where we'd put the table and chairs we bought last week from that couple who were selling them. I thought they would look best by the window, Josh said by the wall under the mantles so he could see what I was trying to poison him with.'

'Who won, dear?'

'Neither of us. We both decided on the middle. The room looks really nice.' Well, as nice as they could make it, she thought, with what little they had by way of furniture. The house, if she was honest, was not in a good state of repair, the rooms small and narrow, the amenities outside shared between several other families. But at least it was not damp or riddled with bugs, as were many of the surrounding near-slum properties. Josh had been lucky to find it, the landlord being a very pleasant old gentleman who wasn't charging an extortionate rate for what he was offering, and until the day came that they could afford to move to something better, Maddie was perfectly content to live there with her husband. If truth be told, she'd live in a shack to be with Josh. 'You'll have to come round for tea,' she invited.

'I'll look forward to it.'

'And we've had our first Christmas together . . .'

'Oh yes, Maddie dear, wasn't that wonderful? I thought you were so brave, considering you'd only just got married, inviting all your family round for the day and including me and Mr Simpson.' Her voice lowered. 'Pity he didn't manage to come,' she said, more to herself than Maddie. 'I think he would have enjoyed himself. I didn't like the thought of him being in his room all by himself. On previous Christmases, give Father his due, Mr Simpson was always invited to our table for dinner.' She took a deep breath. 'Still, it was such a lovely afternoon. All that food you managed to cook, and helping gave me such pleasure. Then we had carols and opening our presents. I have to say again, Maddie, I really am delighted with that brooch you bought me. It's so pretty.'

'It wasn't expensive, Miss Agnes. We just hoped you'd like it.'

'What it cost is not important, dear. It's the thought that counts. You had enough to buy for as it was. Anyway, apart from deeply missing my sister, it was the best Christmas I've ever spent.'

Agnes had told her this several times already.

'Josh and I wanted to do it by way of thanking everyone for helping make our wedding so special. And, of course, I didn't want Sarah to have the burden, what with the baby on the way. She would have insisted we all went around and

I know we'd all have helped but I didn't want her to have the fuss and worry of it all, so I got in first. Anyway, I really enjoyed it too. It seems like only yesterday, doesn't it?'

'It does, dear, and what is it now – the middle of February? I can't wait to see the back of this dreadfully bitter weather myself. Burying people isn't the happiest of jobs at the best of times, but believe me it can be utter misery, standing blue with cold, trying hard not to shiver by a graveside. Still, I shouldn't be complaining, I'm far too gratified that people are coming to us now instead of going elsewhere. At least we have the goodwill back as an incentive to buyers. Now I've got my bag . . . my hat's on my head . . . What else? Oh, the flowers,' she said, picking them up. 'Mr Simpson is on hand should you run into difficulties, Maddie, though I don't envisage you will. And I'll do my best to be back.'

'Stop worrying, Miss Agnes. You might think of me and Josh as newly-weds but I feel like we're old hands at it. Now go on.' And Maddie laughingly shooed her off.

Humming a merry tune to herself, weighed down by the laundry basket, she made her way across the yard, hoping the fire underneath the boiler had heated the water sufficiently to boil the sheets. She raised her eyes. Dark clouds were gathering and rain, or more likely snow, was threatening. Miss Agnes was lucky she didn't have to have wet washing dripping in her kitchen, or suffer the terrible condensation it caused, like most people around these streets did. There was a small room just off the main laundry building that had cradles hung from its rafters and in bad weather washing hung in there, dried rapidly by the warmth of the fire under the boiler.

Maddie was feeling so happy in herself. Settling into marriage with Josh had been practically effortless, their both falling into living together easily, and she saw the years stretching ahead filled with joy. Her family, particularly Ruth and Roy, ever eager to escape their parents' watchful eyes, were frequent visitors as they themselves were to George and Sarah's. A trip to the Jenks family had not yet been attempted, Josh not pushing as he felt it was too soon for Maddie to return to the town after her last painful experience with her mother.

Now that their wedding was out of the way Maddie and Josh talked often about what, if anything, they could do to find their child. They had explored all sorts of possibilities, even to scouring surrounding areas on the lookout for a child who appeared familiar. That, they both knew, was a silly idea. Their child could take after either or neither of them, with features inherited from forbears, and the adoptive parents could live anywhere.

A visit to Mrs Baldicott had been suggested and was, they knew, the only option left open to them. They were going to journey to see her as soon as the weather improved a little and work on both sides allowed them a free Saturday, Maddie knowing it would not be right to call on Mrs Baldicott on the Sabbath as the old lady liked to attend two church services and spent the rest of the day resting her aged legs, sitting by the fire with her current charge, either knitting or sewing garments for the new arrival. Well, that was what she had done with Maddie at any rate. From what she knew of older people, they did not like change.

Maddie prayed Mrs Baldicott would somehow be able to find it in herself to furnish them with the information they sought. She knew that the old lady was under her own moral code not to divulge information but maybe the change in their circumstances would sway matters in their favour.

Maddie smiled to herself as she thought of her work. All the rooms in the house had been sifted through and what Agnes was taking with her crated up ready for the eventual move. Now Agnes was fully occupied elsewhere, Maddie's job had become that of housekeeper. She cleaned and washed and shopped for Agnes, always making a point, no matter how busy she was, of making sure a hot meal was cooking in the oven for Agnes by the time she left. She purposely prepared too much, knowing that what Agnes did not eat went straight across to Ivan. She had never mentioned this so neither did Maddie. She was also more than willing to lend a hand where required so long as it did not bring her into direct contact with the bodies, her revulsion at the very idea still as strong as ever. Despite Maddie's receiving a more than adequate wage for her work, Agnes was always very grateful for all she did and was forever thanking her, much to Maddie's amusement.

As she made to enter the laundry Ivan came out of the workshed. 'Hello, Maddie me duck. Busy, I see? Oh, and the stew last night was very tasty, but I like me gravy a bit thicker.'

'Cheeky devil!' she giggled.

'Miss Clatteridge out, is she?'

She nodded. 'Just left to see the Dunns.'

'Ah, right. I was just hoping to catch her to tek a look at the coffin for the gel. She likes to give her approval, does Miss Clatteridge. I ain't disappointed her yet, though, so I'm sure she'll be 'appy wi' what I've done. Mind you, you can't fancy up plain box wood however much yer try.'

'Where's the undertaker?' a deep voice demanded. 'I've been hammering on the front door but I got no reply.'

They both looked over to a man standing just inside the yard, having slipped through the arch unnoticed. He was tall, very good-looking and extremely harassed, judging by the look on his face. Maddie knew straight away he was a doctor by the black Gladstone bag he was carrying.

'Miss Clatteridge is out, Doctor,' she replied, putting down her full basket and making her way across to him. 'Can I give her a message?'

'*Miss* Clatteridge? Oh, of course, I had heard the daughter had taken over when the old man passed on. I've had good reports too. My patients tell me they're very impressed by the service they get from her.' The man scratched his head, thoughtfully. 'Message? No, I need her now. Terrible case.

302

I've just returned home after my rounds and my wife met me at the door. Have to go now, I'm afraid, this can't wait. The police are anxious for me to get there.'

Maddie looked perplexed, not quite sure what to do.

Ivan saw her dilemma and stepped over to take charge. 'What sort of case is it, Doctor? Nasty disease? 'Cos if it is the Infirmary mortuary is the best place. . .'

'I know that, man,' he snapped agitatedly. 'I'm a doctor, remember, and the police would hardly be present if that were the case. According to the message my wife received it appears the cause of death was a car accident. I've no other details until I get there. I don't know what I'm going to find either.'

Car, thought Ivan. Must have money. In his mind's eye a huge funeral procession loomed. The black glass-sided hearse would be gleaming; a well-groomed Ned decked out in plumed headdress. He saw a mahogany, no, walnut casket with solid brass trimmings. Oh, how he enjoyed working with such lovely wood. He couldn't wait to get started. But more important to Ivan was the revenue it would bring in for Miss Clatteridge. Damn and blast! he inwardly fumed. Of all the times for her to be out on business.

'Er . . . look, if Miss Clatteridge isn't available I'll nip over to Snood's,' said the doctor. 'They're the nearest undertakers to here, I think.'

At the mention of Snood's Ivan bristled. 'I'm sure we can handle this, Doctor. I can collect the . . . er . . . unfortunate deceased and Miss Clatteridge can visit the relatives as soon as she gets back, to find out their wishes and arrange matters.'

'Two.'

'Eh?'

'Bodies. There's two.'

'Really? Oh, dear,' Ivan said gravely. 'I'll get the box cart and follow yer in yer trap, Doctor.'

'Yes, all right. I wonder if I should send for an ambulance?'

303

he mused, then said, 'No, there's no point in wasting resources when those still alive are in need. My wife is very precise with her messages and these people are past hospital treatment. Bring the box cart then, and be quick about it, man.'

'Be with yer in two ticks, Doctor. Where is it we're going?'

He consulted his notebook. 'Number two Grange Lane, Thurnby Hill.'

'Them's decent houses,' Ivan whispered to Maddie, taking her aside. 'Explain to Miss Clatteridge as soon as she returns, won't yer?'

'Yes, of course,' she replied as he disappeared into the stable.

The doctor acknowledged Maddie with a hurried glance and a nod of his head before making to rush away, then stopped and turned back. 'You, miss,' he called, 'you'd better come too.'

'Me?'

'I'll need someone to help deal with whoever's in the house until Miss Clatteridge can take over. Get your coat,' he ordered. 'You can travel with me in the trap.'

His decisive manner told Maddie there was no point in refusing.

In other circumstances she would have found the journey exhilarating and exciting, never having ventured this far along the road she worked and lived off or realised it extended so far. There were many questions she would have liked to ask the doctor but she kept silent, not wanting him to realise the extent of her ignorance.

A half mile or so along, terraced houses, new semis and shops had been left behind, giving way to open countryside, the cobbled road to rutted mud. Intermittently the red gabled roofs of several imposing houses were visible over high laurel hedges. Presently they came to a scattering of smaller gabled properties on the edge of Thurnby village and the doctor expertly began to guide his trap through a brick-pillared gateway. One of the pillars was practically demolished, the remains of the cause of the damage embedded at the base of it.

At the sight of the crushed vehicle Maddie froze and turned her head away. The doctor immediately pulled the trap to a halt. A policeman appeared.

'Dr Giddons,' he said, introducing himself as he alighted.

'Ah, bin waiting for yer, sir.' The policeman eyed Maddie questioningly.

'Oh, this is Miss . . .' the doctor began.

'Mrs Jenks,' Maddie answered for him.

'She's from the undertakers,' said Dr Giddons.

Ivan pulled up behind them and jumped out. 'D'yer want me to make a start, Doctor?'

'No. I don't want anything touching until I say so. I have to determine the cause of death first.'

'I think that's obvious, don't you?' the policeman remarked.

'Oh, so you trained as a doctor before you joined the police, did you?'

The constable shuffled his feet uncomfortably. 'D'yer want me to stay or go up to the house to find the Inspector, tell him you're here?'

'No, Mrs Jenks can do that. I'll need your help.' The doctor held up his hand to help Maddie down. 'Tell the Inspector I'm here, Mrs Jenks, then see what needs doing.'

She gulped. She hadn't a clue what he meant but all she said was, 'Yes, Doctor.'

She walked up the short drive which led to a pretty red brick house, the bare stems of a climbing rose scrambling up the front wall and over the top of the door. The gardens she passed were bare of flowers but green with shrubbery and very well-kept. Before she reached the door it opened and a large man in a macintosh strode out. 'That dratted doctor turned up yet?' he wondered aloud. He spotted Maddie. 'Who are you?'

'Mrs Jenks. I'm from the undertakers, Inspector.' She assumed this was he. 'The doctor's dealing with matters at the end of the drive.'

'About bloody time!'

'What do you want me to do, Inspector?'

He looked at her blankly. 'I dunno. What you normally do, I expect.'

With that he slapped his trilby on his head and strode purposefully off, macintosh billowing, leaving her staring after him.

Maddie took a breath and looked at the house. What would Miss Agnes do now? she thought. Go and speak to the relatives, was her answer. But what did she say? Maddie shrugged her shoulders. She would have to use her instincts.

Tentatively she walked through the door into a very tastefully decorated hallway. To the left of her, halfway down the wide hallway leading towards the back, was an occasional table on top of which stood an ornate vase filled with wax flowers. The stairs leading to the first floor were in front of her. Several landscape prints hung on the walls.

'Hello,' she called.

There was no response.

As she stood and listened she could hear the soft sounds of someone crying. They appeared to be coming from somewhere down the hallway. Listening intently, Maddie followed the sounds.

She eventually found the woman sitting at the kitchen table, her head bent, face buried in a large piece of towelling. She was obviously a maid judging by the black dress, white cap and apron she wore.

'Excuse me,' Maddie said softly, 'could you tell me where I can find the relatives, please?'

The maid's head shot up, face blotchy, swollen eyes red-ringed. She sniffed. 'Ain't none. I've already told that Inspector. Anyway, who are yer?'

'I'm Mrs Jenks, from the undertakers.'

'Oh, God,' the maid wailed, again burying her head in the towelling. 'I can't believe it. I can't. Lovely people, 'specially the Missus. Best job I've ever had.'

Maddie sat down on the chair nearest her, leaned over and placed a hand gently on the maid's arm. She was only young, eighteen or nineteen at the most Maddie guessed. 'Would you like me to make you a cup of tea?' she asked.

The girl shook her head. 'If I see anymore tea I'll scream. That's all I did for that blasted Inspector, mek tea and get asked questions I don't know the bloody answers to. I'm only the maid. I ain't bin 'ere all that long. They'd just bought the car. Mr Bingham were tekin' the Missus fer a quick spin. Said they wouldn't be long. Missus were ever so excited. Foreign she wa'. When she got excited 'er arms went everywhere, talking 'er own lingo which yer can't understand a word of.' She shuddered, sniffing back the tears. 'I saw it 'appen. I wa' standing at the door waving 'em off.'

'You did?' Maddie asked, shocked.

The maid nodded. 'A dog shot out the 'edge and Mr Bingham swerved to avoid it and 'it the stone pillar. It collapsed on top of them. Ohhh!' she wailed. 'I can still hear the Missus screamin'.'

'There, there,' Maddie soothed. 'Look . . . er . . . I don't mean to upset you by asking more questions but I'm really here to talk to the relatives. I need to know where they are?'

The maid's face became even blotchier if that were possible. 'And I've already told yer, there ain't none.'

'Oh, dear,' said Maddie. 'There must be someone, surely?'

'There's no one I know of.'

This is dreadful, thought Maddie.

'Inspector sez lawyer'll have ter deal wi' it all. Got the papers he did out the bureau.' She wiped her face, blew her nose noisily, scraped back her chair and stood up. 'He sez I can go 'ome.'

'Are you sure you're feeling all right to?'

'Yeah, he sez it's best place fer me. Me mam'll look after me. What about 'er?'

'Sorry?' Maddie said, eyeing her blankly.

''Er,' she repeated, inclining her head over Maddie's shoulder.

Frowning in bewilderment Maddie turned her head to look behind her and then gasped. 'Oh, my goodness!'

Huddled right inside a narrow gap between the back wall and the side of the pantry Maddie could see a little girl of about two. She had her thumb planted firmly in her mouth, large blue eyes staring unblinkingly.

'Oh, but she's beautiful. The poor little mite!' said Maddie emotionally. 'What's her name?'

'Penelope. They called her Penny. Loved 'er they did. Treated that kid like bloody royalty. Me mam reckoned it weren't 'ealthy the way they pampered 'er.'

'Oh, but I can see why they did,' Maddie declared wistfully, gazing at the child and momentarily forgetting the gravity of the situation.

'Yeah, I s'pose she ain't a bad kid,' the maid sniffed begrudgingly. 'Can't stand 'em meself though.'

'What did the Inspector tell you to do with her?' Maddie asked the maid who was by now pulling on her coat.

She shrugged her shoulders.

Maddie swivelled around in her seat, giving the maid her full attention. 'Well, he must have said something?'

'He didn't ask about 'er.'

'Didn't ask? You mean, he doesn't know?'

The maid shook her head. 'I wa' so upset meself, I forgot to mention 'er.'

'What?' Maddie cried, fighting anger. 'Were you just going to go off and leave her here?'

'Well, no, but you're 'ere now, ain't yer?'

'Yes, but I'm from the undertakers. I've come to assist with the funeral arrangements.'

'Well, ain't she part of 'em? I can't tek 'er wi' me. Me

mother'd go mad. I'm worrying I won't get me wage this week now. Look, I godda go. I'm too upset, really.'

Bursting into a fresh torrent of tears, she ran from the room.

Maddie's shoulders sagged. She looked at the little girl helplessly, her heart going out to her. At this moment it appeared that the child had no one. Maddie wondered if she sensed the tragedy going on around her. Easing herself off her chair, mindful any abrupt movement could upset the child, she slid on to her knees on the cold red tiles. 'Hello, sweetheart,' she said, holding out her hand and smiling warmly. 'Would you like a drink? Milk? Do you like milk? Take my hand and show me where the milk is. All right, Penny dear?'

The child stared at her for several long moments, Maddie waiting patiently, then taking her thumb out of her mouth she struggled to her feet. Maddie gently put her arms around her and picked her up. 'My, you're a lump,' she said, smiling. 'Now can you point to where the milk is kept?'

The child looked at her then pointed her tiny finger towards the larder to one side of Maddie. 'Good girl,' she said. 'My, you are clever, aren't you?'

Maddie found the milk and a clean cup amongst the several the Inspector and the maid had used between them. She filled it with milk and gave it to the child, who grabbed it and drank greedily.

'My, you were thirsty,' Maddie said. 'Would you like some more?'

The child nodded.

The process was repeated.

'Now,' said Maddie, 'why don't we go and find that nice policeman and find out what we're to do with you, eh? All right, so that's what we'll do then.'

After finding the child's coat, she put it on. She took hold of her hand, Penny toddling alongside her, and went in search of the Inspector.

The activity that greeted her at the end of the drive shook Maddie rigid. Realising it was no place for a child, she hurriedly turned and retraced her steps. 'I tell you what, Penny, why don't we go and see what toys you have and we'll play a game while we wait for that nice policeman to come back,' she said as they re-entered the house.

Upstairs Maddie found a room that was filled with all sorts of toys, and taking out a box of wooden bricks she settled herself on the rug in the middle of the spacious room, the little girl to the side of her, and began to pile bricks on top of one another. They collapsed and the child giggled. Then she joined in with her own clumsy attempts. Maddie watched her, fascinated. Time passed as they played. At length Maddie raised her head and realised it was growing dark.

'My goodness,' she exclaimed, scrambling up. 'I think it's time we put all the toys away and went back downstairs. What do you think, Penny?'

Thumb in her mouth, the child just looked up at her with big blue eyes. 'My, you'll break a few hearts when you're older,' Maddie said tenderly. Though you're breaking mine now, she thought.

Hurriedly she packed the toys away, gathered the child up and went downstairs. The house was empty. They were taking a long time to deal with matters at the end of the drive. She ought to go and see what the situation was. She needed to tell them about the child. The poor little mite must be hungry and Maddie could tell she was getting tired. She also wondered why Miss Clatteridge hadn't arrived, then it struck her. In the doctor's urgency for them to depart, she hadn't left Miss Clatteridge a note informing her of the situation.

Placing the child on the floor, Maddie rummaged around in the larder, finding a biscuit in a tin. Squatting down before her, she gave it Penny. 'Now you stay here just for a moment while I go and find someone. I won't be long, sweetheart.'

She didn't like the thought of leaving the child unattended and as swiftly as she could ran from the house and down the drive. As the gates came into view she stopped abruptly.

There was no sign of anyone. The area was deserted, the only evidence of the terrible accident hidden under a large tarpaulin.

Maddie stared around her in dismay. Were they coming back or had they all forgotten about her?

Frowning worriedly, she retraced her steps and entered the kitchen, thankful to find Penny just where she had left her. She knelt before her, mind racing frantically. What on earth was she to do? It was getting late. There was only one thing for it. The child would have to spend the night with her and Josh and matters would be dealt with in the morning.

After gathering together items of the little girl's clothing and having the foresight also to include a couple of soft toys and the box of bricks, she dressed the child warmly, pulled the front door securely behind her and set off.

The journey was slow. Maddie weighed down by the child in her arms and the bag containing her belongings. The long road that had fascinated her several hours ago now seemed endless. And to make matters worse the evening had turned bitterly cold and it was beginning to snow. She was tired herself, frozen to the marrow, but all her concern lay with the child in her arms and she hurried along the slippery road as fast as she could.

Exhausted and bedraggled, she arrived home much later, Penny's sleeping head on her shoulder. It was just approaching seven o'clock and the snow was falling thickly. As soon as Maddie managed the struggle to insert her key in the lock it was opened by an extremely worried Josh. He looked at her, the child, then back at Maddie questioningly.

'I'll explain in a minute,' she said, stamping her numb feet on the straw mat just inside the door.

He took the bag from her and followed her down the dark hallway to the room at the back. The fire was blazing, the table set for dinner, and an appetising aroma greeted Maddie. She laid the child down gently in the old armchair they had picked up from the pawnbroker's for next to nothing, and quickly grabbed Josh's jacket from the back of the door to cover her with. He meantime watched silently.

Satisfied the child was comfortable, Maddie turned and looked at her husband.

'It can wait a minute longer,' he ordered, putting the bag down. 'You're soaking wet. Get yourself dry and then sit by the fire while I mek you a cuppa. Then you can tell me. I'm just glad to see you home, I've bin worried sick.'

Too tired to argue she did as he said and ten minutes later, Josh sitting in his armchair, Maddie by his feet, cradling a mug of tea, she told him what had happened.

When she had finished he sighed. 'Sad state of affairs. Well, yer did the right thing, me darlin', bringing the kiddy back here. There was n'ote else yer could do.'

'You don't mind?'

'Why should I? You know me better than to ask that, surely?'

'Yes,' she said, smiling tenderly. 'I do.' She glanced sadly at the sleeping child. 'I really ought to go round and tell Miss Agnes about the little girl.'

He put his hand on her shoulder. 'You'll stay put. The mornin'll be soon enough. N'ote else can be done tonight, it's too late. That kiddy needs a good night's sleep after what she's bin through, and so, me darlin', do you. When we've had dinner I'll sort something out for her to sleep on. Now you sit there while I go and dish up. It's just sausage and potatoes. You know I can't mek gravy for love nor money.'

'I don't care what it is, Josh, I could eat a horse.'

'Well, let's hope it don't taste like one!' he laughed as he rose and made his way into the kitchen.

Maddie raised herself to look more closely at the child and check she was all right before settling herself again, feet resting on the fender, to thaw out before the fire. Not many women, she thought, would have returned home to a husband who'd welcome in a little stranger as Josh had. Nor would a blazing fire and a meal be waiting them. She was certainly a lucky woman.

She heard an urgent knock on the front door.

'Stay there, I'll get it,' ordered Josh.

She heard voices and moments later he returned, followed by Agnes.

'Oh, Maddie dear, I was so worried about you!'

'You won't mind me, will yer, Miss Agnes? I'm just seeing to the dinner.'

'No, of course not, Josh, please carry on.'

'Won't you sit down?' Maddie offered, moving aside to allow Agnes to sit in Josh's armchair.

'Thank you, dear. I'm sorry to intrude at this time of night, but I had to see you were home safely. When I returned from seeing the Dunns, it was after one o'clock. I didn't know what to think when I found the place deserted. I thought you'd gone home to see to Josh's dinner. Then, when you didn't return and there was no sign of Mr Simpson, I became worried. Of course, Peabody hadn't any idea as he'd been at the Dunns' most of the morning.' Tightening her lips, she shook her head. 'That young man takes such a long time to do things, doesn't he? But that's another matter.

'Then those people turned up – you know, the Mosses to have a look round. I heard Mr Simpson return about three but couldn't just abandon the visitors. It was well after five before they left. They seemed very keen, I have to say. Anyway, as soon as I had said my goodbyes to them, I went straight to see Mr Simpson. He explained what had happened. Such a terrible thing, wasn't it, dear? He told me he'd left you up at the house with the doctor and we both thought, as time wore on, that the good doctor had driven you straight home. Well, that was until I had a courtesy visit from him just now.

'When he was leaving I thanked him for taking you home and he said he hadn't. When he went to look for you at the house after Mr Simpson had left, he found it empty.'

'I was upstairs,' explained Maddie.

'Oh, I see. Well, he presumed you'd made your own way home. The police had left by then too with all they needed. I suppose with all that was going on there was bound to be a little confusion. I know you're very capable, Maddie, but I had to come and see you were safe. You are all right?' Agnes frowned then as a thought struck her. 'Why were you upstairs when the doctor came to look for you?'

Maddie's eyes filled with sadness. 'I was looking after a precious penny.'

'I beg your pardon?' she said, bewildered.

Maddie nodded and turned, looking back at the armchair behind her. Agnes followed her gaze, mouth dropping open at the sight of the little bundle nestled in its depths. She rose to her feet and peered down. 'I thought I was mistaken but it's a child!' she exclaimed. 'Whose . . . Oh, my goodness, is this the child of the deceased couple?' she said, shocked, hand before her mouth.

'The maid forgot to inform anyone.'

'She *what*? How on earth could a thing like that have slipped her mind?'

'Well, she was very upset, she witnessed the accident, but I still feel it was inexcusable of her.'

'It certainly was.' Agnes stared down at the child, eyes filling with tenderness. 'Isn't she a lovely little thing?' She smiled at Maddie warmly. 'It was good of you to bring her home with you, my dear.'

'I couldn't do anything else, Miss Agnes, could I? From what the maid said the couple doted on her. You should have seen her bedroom. It was filled with toys and clothes enough to stock a shop.' Maddie gave a deep sigh. 'I wonder what will happen to her now?'

'Relatives will take her, I expect. That's what usually happens in cases like this.'

'The maid said she didn't know of any.'

'What? None at all? Oh, she must have that wrong. They can't both have been without relatives. We'll know more when the solicitor makes contact. The doctor told me the police were going to inform him of the tragedy as soon as possible. I can't do anything with the remains until I receive instructions. The solicitor will pay a call on me in the morning, I expect. In my experience solicitors are full of their own importance so I do hope it's at a convenient time as I've a hundred and one things to do. We've two funerals, one in the morning, the other later in the afternoon. Timing's very tight as it is.'

'I'm sure you'll manage,' Maddie said, smiling.

'I'll have to, dear. But I couldn't without you and Mr Simpson, that's for certain.'

They both looked down again at the child.

'Josh is going to make her up a little bed on the floor in our room,' said Maddie. 'We'll make sure she's comfortable.'

'That's good of you, my dear. What about bedding?' asked Agnes, mindful that Maddie had precious little, her married life just starting. 'I've some things you can have to help. A couple of blankets I didn't part with just in case. I'm glad I didn't now. I'll send Mr Simpson around with them shortly. I know he'll still be working in the shed and he won't mind. Now I'd better go and leave you to eat your meal and sort the little one out. I suggest you bring her with you in the morning, ready to hand over to whoever's going to take her.' She patted Maddie's arm affectionately. 'Goodnight, my dear. Goodnight, Josh,' she called.

He popped his head around the kitchen door. 'You off, then, Miss Agnes? Thanks fer calling.

'You ready to eat your leg of the horse?' he asked after Maddie had shown Agnes out.

She nodded. 'Yes I'm ready to risk it. Penny must be

315

hungry but I don't think we should wake her.'

Arms around each other, they both looked down at the sleeping child.

Chapter Twenty-Five

'What do you say, Josh? Can she stop with us?'

Sighing, he shook his head. 'I'm not sure if it's best, Maddie. It's you I'm worried for. Worried you'll get too attached to her.'

'And you won't? I saw your face this morning when you thought the authorities were about to fetch her. You had tears in your eyes, I know you did.'

'Well, maybe I had, she's a lovely little kiddy. I know she's only bin with us a week but . . .'

'I know, Josh,' Maddie said softly. 'We've both fallen in love with her, haven't we?'

He nodded. 'Hard not to. You told me that maid said her folks spoiled her, but she don't act spoiled, do she? Where is she anyway?'

'Miss Agnes is playing with her. Offered to watch her so I could speak to you without interruptions. She adores her too. It's so good of her to let me take Penny to work with me while we wait for news. It's a wonder we get any work done. You should see the way Miss Agnes runs around the house playing hide and seek with her, it's so funny. She has Penny in fits of giggles. And as for Ivan – he has her sitting on the stool for hours, watching him work away. It's amazing to see a child just sit like that. It's funny, though, the only person Penny won't go near for some reason is Oswald.'

'Children sense things,' said Josh matter-of-factly.

'Anyway, if you agree we can keep her, Sarah is going to watch her while I go to work.'

'And she's all right about that?'

'Josh, she's delighted. Says it'll get her in practice for when the baby arrives. She offered, honestly. Said a funeral parlour is no place for a kiddy, even though Miss Agnes was quite happy about me taking her there. She said if you agree we can keep her until the family come forward, she'll start this afternoon.'

He sighed again. 'Apart from Peabody it seems Little Miss Twopenny has us all wrapped around her little finger. So tell me again what the solicitor said?'

'Tell me if she can stay with us first?'

'Maddie . . .'

'All right. As you already know the lawyer has no information about any relatives and has decided to put advertisements in newspapers to see what happens. In the meantime there's not much else he can do. Mrs Bingham was German but from whereabouts in Germany he hasn't a clue. So it's a case of finding Mr Bingham's family.'

'Strange state of affairs, if you ask me.'

'What do you mean?'

'The solicitor not having any details of his family.'

'Maybe they're all dead.'

'What, all of them?' Josh shook his head. 'Summat don't feel right somehow. Anyway, what happens to any money they left? Who get's it?'

'Mr Grantham didn't divulge that information, Josh.'

'No, I don't suppose he did.'

'He's placing advertisements in local papers to start with and if that turns up nothing he'll widen the search. It could take a while. In the meantime we just have to wait.' Maddie eyed him expectantly. 'So can we keep her until then?'

'Mr Grantham did say it was all right?'

She nodded. 'He was surprised how well she's adapted to being with us, considering. I think he was only too glad we offered. Saves him the trouble of finding people to look after her in the meantime. And the authorities are only too

318

glad not to have the bother either. The children's homes are bulging as it is.' She shuddered at the thought of Penny's being incarcerated in one of those dreadful places. 'So can we, Josh?'

She saw him hesitate and wrung her hands. 'Josh, I know you and Sarah think I'm using this child to fill the space left by my own baby. Neither of you has said as much but I know you're thinking it. I'm right, aren't I?'

He eyed her gravely and nodded.

Maddie's face fell in dismay. 'Oh, Josh, I'm not, please believe me. How could you think the child I gave birth to could ever be replaced?' She sighed, long and deep. 'I admit, I watch Penny, I hold her, and especially when she's sleeping there's something in me that . . . I can't explain it, it's like this child *belongs* to me. But I know she doesn't. It's just that she's lost her own parents and she's so little and vulnerable and I want to do anything I can to protect her until her own people turn up. That's not wrong of me, is it? I can't replace her own mother but I can try while she's with us can't I? Then it's for her own family to take over.'

He sighed. 'So long as you understand that she'll have to go sooner or later, Maddie. I just can't bear the thought of you getting hurt again when you've already suffered so much.'

'I know you're trying to protect me, my love, but there're some things you can't shield me from. Let's just enjoy little Penny while we can. I can't promise not to be hurt when the time comes for her to leave, and I know you'll be as upset as me, but that's something we'll face together.'

He eyed her searchingly. 'All right, Maddie.'

Her eyes lit up. 'So she can stay?'

'I don't know why you're asking me. You know I can't refuse yer nothin'.'

'Yes, but I'd still go with whatever you decided, you know that, Josh.'

'Yes, I do.' But there was no real decision for him to make. Maddie was right. He could no more bear the thought of

319

Penny going to strangers than Maddie could, and he too would miss the child deeply when it was time for her to leave. 'We'd better clear out the little room then, make it a proper bedroom for her, if she's stopping longer than we thought.'

'Oh, thanks, Josh,' Maddie cried, joyfully throwing her arms around him.

'Hang on a minute, I ain't finished.'

'Oh?' she said, stepping back and eyeing him worriedly.

'I want you to write to Mrs Baldicott and ask her the first Saturday it'd be convenient for us to call on her. We need to make a start finding our own child, Maddie. If Mrs Baldicott can't for whatever reason tell us anything then we'll rack our brains as to what else we can do to find her. Now Sarah and George know our secret, we could even rope them into helping us.'

'I'll write to Mrs Baldicott tonight.'

'Good. Now I'm off back to work,' he said, kissing her on her cheek. 'And you'd better get back too. I'll finish sharp so I can read madam a story before her bedtime. Oh, and there's summat I want ter discuss with yer. It's just about work, it'll keep.'

Later that afternoon Agnes walked into the kitchen. 'Maddie, you can finish now if you want to.'

She put down the potato she was peeling and turned around to her employer. 'I've not finished preparing the meal yet.'

'I can do that. With no funerals today I've caught up with all I need to do. Tomorrow's burial is well in hand. Don't you want an early finish?'

'Yes, that would be nice. I could have a cup of tea with Sarah when I pick up Penny. It's not often we have time on our own.' She eyed Agnes thoughtfully. 'Please excuse me, Miss Agnes, but you've something on your mind, that's obvious. Do you want to talk about it or do you want me to mind my own business?'

'You're very observant, Maddie dear. I didn't think it showed.' Agnes took a deep breath. 'It's just a little bit confusing for me. I don't really know what to make of it.'

Maddie flattened her back against the pot sink, folded her arms and looked at her. 'Make of what, Miss Agnes?'

'Well, you remember me telling you about the Mosses coming to view? Seemed really keen and the price was just about right for them. Mrs Moss wasn't at all bothered about there not being a water pump in the kitchen. She said she was used to going outside. They went away saying they'd be straight around to the agent's to sort out the details. Well, I never heard anything until this morning when I received a letter from Mr Moss. He wrote asking if I thought it fair to quote one price then, when someone is interested, put that price up. His tone was very angry. I went out this morning, didn't I? Said I was going into town. That was true, Maddie, but my sole intention was to see the agent. He was quite furious that Mr Moss had written to me. Said all dealings should go through him. He said he didn't know what Mr Moss was going on about. The price was the price, and besides he hadn't heard from them again after they left his office to come and view this place.'

'Very strange,' mused Maddie. 'Did the Mosses seem all right to you?'

'Perfectly, dear. They were a charming couple. Most odd, isn't it? Still, nothing I can do. I really was hopeful about them too. Anyway enough of this.' Agnes forced a smile. 'Now off you go. Give Mrs Ashman my best and I'll see you in the morning.'

'You look tired,' Maddie said as Sarah opened the door. 'Penny hasn't been too much for you, has she?' she asked in concern.

'Too much? Maddie, the child's keeping me occupied. I'm not used to having so much time on me hands. She's been a little darlin', as usual. It's a shame she doesn't talk much. Our Ruth was chattering away at her age, even though I couldn't work out what she was saying. I suppose little Penny's gone through so much, it's understandable. She must be so confused and I reckon she's a bit on the shy side. She'll talk when she's good and ready. Anyway, we went for a walk in the park and she had a nap this afternoon. I'm not tired, Maddie love.' She wasn't, it was worry that Maddie could see on Sarah's face. 'I just wish everyone would stop fussing.'

'We're not fussing, Sarah,' Maddie said as she followed her down the passage. 'We just care about you. You are keeping well, aren't you?'

She sighed. 'You asked me that yesterday and I'll tell you the same today. I ain't ill, I'm having a baby. Sit yerself down, I'll mash a cuppa.' She addressed the child playing on the rug with a toy train Ivan had bought for her from a man he knew who whittled toys from old bits of wood to supplement his living. 'Penny want a crust to gnaw on? Oh, good girl. She nodded, Maddie,' Sarah exclaimed in delight. 'Did you see her? She understands everything you say.' She held out her hand. 'Come with Auntie Sarah then into the kitchen and let's see what we can find, eh?'

'I'll make the tea,' offered Maddie, swinging the kettle over the fire.

They all trooped through to the kitchen.

Maddie began to gather cups together and fill the jug with milk. 'Ruth and Roy all right?'

'Fine,' Sarah said, her back to Maddie, spreading a crust of bread with butter for Penny. 'Ruth's off out tonight. Eh, and I think our Roy's got himself a girlfriend.'

'Really?' Maddie smiled, scooping a spoon of tea out of the caddy to put in the pot. 'What's she like?'

'Dunno. I haven't seen her. I don't know what her name is either. In truth I'm only guessing. But our Roy's washed his neck three times this week without me telling him, that's how I know.'

Maddie laughed. 'Oh, Sarah, you are funny.' She watched Penny take the crust. 'How's Dad?'

Sarah sat bolt upright and flashed her a strange glance. 'Fine. He's fine. Why d'yer ask?'

Maddie frowned. 'I always ask how Dad is, don't I?'

'Yes, 'course yer do. Sorry, Maddie, I'm still fuddled from me sleep.'

'Is there anything the matter, Sarah?'

'Matter? No, why should there be? Did you warm the pot before you put in the leaves?'

'Yes, I did. I might stay a bit longer tonight and wait for Dad to come in. Is that all right?'

'Why?'

Maddie shrugged her shoulders, bemused. 'Because he's my dad and I haven't seen him all week. Isn't that reason enough?'

'Oh, Maddie love, forgive me. Yer dad's had to go away for a few days . . . on business. I'm just missing him that's all.'

'Why didn't you say so, Sarah? I was beginning to think something was wrong. When will he be back?'

'I dunno,' she said, a bit too hurriedly for Maddie's liking. 'He didn't say. He should be back before the weekend, I think.' There was something wrong, Maddie knew Sarah well enough by now to see that. But whatever it was, Sarah was obviously not going to tell her.

'Shall we go through?' she suggested.

'Er . . . yes,' Maddie agreed reluctantly.

'Come on then, Penny,' Sarah said, taking the child's tiny hand.

Later that evening, Penny had been settled down for the night and Maddie was curled up in the armchair, an open book in her lap, staring thoughtfully into the dancing flames of the fire.

Josh lowered his newspaper and looked across at her. 'Good book, is it?'

'Pardon?'

'Your book. It's that good you haven't read a word of it for the last hour. What's bothering yer, Maddie?'

She smiled wanly. 'Nothing. Well, that's not entirely true. Just a couple of things. Maybe something and nothing.'

'Oh? It obviously has you bothered. Come on then,' he said, folding up his paper. 'Tell me.'

She smiled at him tiredly and closed her book. 'Sarah acted really strangely with me today when I asked how my father was.'

'Strange? In what way?'

Maddie shrugged her shoulders. 'That's it, Josh, I don't know. It was just the way she acted . . . But then, I was tired myself and worried that Penny was too much for her. Sarah's nearly seven months pregnant after all. But she insisted that having little Penny around was doing her a world of good. Anyway it was nothing to do with the child. It was how Sarah reacted when I asked about my father.'

'They've maybe had a row or something.'

'I've never known them to, Josh. Oh, maybe it was just me. I'll be seeing her again tomorrow so I'll see how she is then. She said Father was away on business.'

'Ah, that's it. She's missing him, that's all.'

'That's what Sarah said. You're right, I'm being silly.'

'I wouldn't call it silly, Maddie. You care for her very much, don't you?'

'Yes, I do.'

'So what was the other thing that was bothering you?'

'Oh, again, something and nothing.' She related to Josh what Agnes had told her. 'I wouldn't have thought anything of it but after what Mr Snood tried to do . . . Of course, we kept that from her. Miss Agnes knows nothing about that.'

'Yeah, best thing too.'

'But you can see why I took notice?'

'Mmmm, I can.'

'Do you think there's something to it, Josh?'

324

'Can't see what.' He paused thoughtfully. 'I'll mention it to yer dad when I next see him, though. See what he thinks just to be on the safe side.'

'So you think there . . .'

'I don't think anything, Maddie,' he cut in. 'But I like Miss Agnes and I wouldn't want to see anything bad happen to her. I'll just mention it to your dad when he returns from his business trip ter put our minds at rest. Now you just forget about it. You've got enough on yer plate with that little mite upstairs.'

Maddie smiled. 'All right.'

'So, d'yer feel better now?'

She nodded. 'Yes, thank you.'

'And I can get back to reading me paper in peace now, can I?'

'Oh, but didn't you say this morning you had something to discuss with me?'

'What? Oh, yeah, how could I have forgotten about that?' Josh clasped his hands and leaned forward, eyeing her intently. 'I've bin offered a round. Not a bad one either. Wally Cribbins passed on last week and his widow's put it up for sale. She's given me first offer. It's in town, mostly businesses, some houses. It's worth considering, Maddie.'

'What about your own round? Can you do them both?' she asked. 'You work very hard as it is, Josh. And how much is she asking?'

'Ten pounds. And, no, I can't do them both. Before you say anything, let me tell yer what I thought then yer can give me your opinion. I've five pounds saved, Maddie.'

She gasped. 'Five pounds? How on earth have you managed to do that?'

'By being careful. Walked when I could have taken a tram, them sorta things. And I don't booze money away at the pub, do I? And with your wage coming in, Maddie, well, that helps us too. It soon mounts up. But that money was intended for another house for us. I was wanting to surprise you. But, well, what I was thinking was to offer Mrs Cribbins the five and pay the rest off. I think she might agree 'cos she knows I'm genuine and she needs the money. Me and her Wally got on well enough. Then, for my own round, I was thinking of getting another bloke in, and paying him.'

Maddie frowned. 'I don't understand.'

'I'd employ him, Maddie. Pay him a decent wage for the job and keep the rest. I know a number of blokes I can trust who'd be willing.'

'Oh, I see. Well, then, you must do it, Josh.'

His eyes shone. 'Really? Yer don't object?'

'Absolutely not.'

He flung his arms around her, hugging her tightly. 'Thanks, Maddie.'

'What are you thanking me for?' she said, laughing.

''Cos there's no way I'd have gone ahead if you hadn't been happy about it. You know that.'

'Yes, I do, but I am happy, so get on with it.'

'You don't mind staying here a while longer? Or having ter keep working 'til I get things off the ground?'

'I love my job, you know that, Josh. And as for this house, there's many in a lot worse than this, so stop worrying. I'm quite happy to stay here forever if necessary.'

'You won't have to if my plans work out. I want a few rounds, Maddie. That's me intention. Oh, I do love you,' he said tenderly. 'Do yer fancy an early night?' he asked meaningfully.

'Mmmm,' she agreed thoughtfully, eyes humorous. 'That's a good idea. I am tired.'

'Not that tired, are yer, Maddie?' he asked huskily, kissing her lips.

She giggled. 'You lock up and I'll see you upstairs,' she said, pushing him playfully away. 'And be quiet when you come up so you don't wake Penny or you'll be disappointed.'

Chapter Twenty-Six

Ivan sat upright and peered around him in the darkness – something had woken him. He sighed miserably, lying back down, wriggling to get comfortable on the lumpy straw mattress. He hadn't been fully asleep anyway, restlessly tossing and turning, the same as he did every night now. Agnes Clatteridge was the cause, damn the woman. Why did she have to go and make herself so attractive? Agnes had always been beautiful to him. Now he felt all male eyes were on her and it could only be a matter of time before one of them took matters further.

Ivan wasn't selfish, he wanted Agnes to be happy, but he wanted her to be happy with him.

He sighed again, pulled the worn blankets aside, swung his legs over the side of the narrow iron bedstead and got up, plodding across to the window overlooking the yard. Moving the bit of old curtaining aside, he peered out, looking skyward. The weather was definitely improving. Low cloud meant a frost was unlikely and the warmer weather had removed the threat of more snow. He was glad spring was beginning to put in an appearance, knowing Agnes didn't like the cold.

He was just about to step away and return to bed when something across the yard caught his eye. He strained harder, pressing his face right up to the glass. That was strange, he thought. It looked to him like the Chapel of Rest door was slightly open and he was positive he could see a flicker of light through the crack.

Ivan groaned. Oswald obviously hadn't done his duty for the night by blowing out the candles and securing the door properly. The casket containing the deceased whose funeral was arranged for the morning had been placed there earlier in the day and Agnes had insisted that candles be lit in case any last-minute visitors called to pay their respects.

He would have to go and do the chore himself, despite the fact there was no threat from any outside intruder, the gates to the yard having been secured by him personally before he retired for the night. But candles left burning in a breeze could cause a fire. He'd speak to Oswald severely in the morning. The trouble with that lad, fumed Ivan, as he pulled on his old coat over his long johns, was that he was too lazy by far, over eager to race away come leaving time.

He lit his oil lamp and made his way out.

He had reached the bottom of the iron staircase by the time he'd realised he'd forgotten to put on his hob-nailed boots and the soles of his feet were sopping wet. Oh, he'd suffer that, he thought, he wasn't going back now. He had arrived at the Chapel of Rest's door and was about to pull it open and enter when he stopped abruptly, hearing a low voice. His heart raced. Someone was inside! But who on earth could be in there at this time of night? Certainly not Miss Clatteridge. So far as he knew she hadn't taken to talking to herself, or the dead for that matter.

Heart hammering, he put down the lamp and inched the door open wide enough to peep through. The sight that met his eyes froze him rigid.

Two men stood bent over the open casket. One, a man he did not recognize, held a scalpel in his hand, raised ready to do his business. There was a large black Gladstone bag by his feet, containing what looked like glass jars holding some sort of liquid which gleamed eerily in the flickering candlelight. Ivan's eyes went to the other figure. It was Oswald.

Ivan knew immediately what they were up to.

328

A great fury filled him and without a second thought he snatched up the lamp, raised it high and pushed open the door.

'And who d'yer think you two are?' he hissed. 'Burke and Hare?'

Shocked, the two of them spun around, faces paling.

'Who's he?' the stranger asked Oswald. 'You said we'd not be disturbed.'

'Then you're a fool to 'ave listened to 'im,' snarled Ivan, stepping forward.

'Now look here, my good man,' the stranger addressed him. 'It's not what you think . . .'

'Oh? Tek me for an idiot, d'yer?' he erupted. 'Get yer stuff and get out.'

'Now look . . .'

'I'd leave while yer still can,' Ivan warned him.

The stranger flashed an angry glance at Oswald before grabbing his belongings and leaving hurriedly.

'Not you, Oswald. You stay where yer are.'

'Look, Mr Simpson,' he blurted, stepping nervously away from the black-draped trestle holding the casket to flatten his back against the side wall. 'I can explain . . .'

'There's n'ote to explain, lad,' Ivan said gravely, shaking his head. 'I had you down as some things, but stooping so low as to desecrate bodies . . . Doctor, was he?'

Oswald hung his head. 'Learning ter be.' He looked up, eyes pleading. 'It's medical science, Mr Simpson. They can't get enough innards to practise on. This is the only way they can do it.'

'Who told yer that?'

'The bloke what first approached me.' Oswald's eyes narrowed. 'Look, Mr Simpson, there's money ter be made. The doctor gave me half a crown for letting 'im in.'

'And how'd you do it? I secured the gates meself tonight.'

'I din't go 'ome. I 'id in the stable 'til I 'eard the doc knock, then I let 'im in.'

329

'How did he know to call tonight?'

Oswald sniffed. 'I tells the bloke when we have summat in the Chapel of Rest. He let's me know then if they're interested . . .'

'Oh, they pick and choose, d'they?'

Oswald nodded. 'Depends what they need at the time and which bits they want.'

'Bits?' spat Ivan. 'Them's people's bits yer referring to,' he exclaimed, horrified.

'But they're dead so what's the difference? They don't know.'

'But *you* do. And so do I now. D'yer fancy someone cutting you up without yer permission when yer time comes, eh?'

Oswald shuffled uncomfortably. 'I dunno what yer problem is, Mr Simpson. They're dead, where's the harm taking a few bits for the doctors to practise on? It ain't like they're gonna need 'em anymore, is it?' His eyes glared defiantly. ''Sides we ain't the only place that lets the hospital folk 'elp 'emselves.'

Oswald shrank back at the look of utter disgust on Ivan's face.

'I don't give a toss what other parlours get up to. This is a decent place. Decent and honourable. Did you give a thought ter what would happen if you'd 'ave bin caught? No, I bet yer didn't. All you could think of was the money yer were getting. Did yer think of Miss Clatteridge? What this woulda done to her? This carry-on could 'a bin the ruin of her. She could 'a landed in jail as well as yerself.' Oswald opened his mouth to speak but slapped it shut as Ivan's hand came up in warning. 'Don't dare. Don't dare suggest I go along wi' any of this. You make me sick,' he spat. 'How many times have yer done this, eh? How many?'

'Once or twice.'

'What?' Ivan eyed him, horrified. 'You're lucky I don't take me fist ter yer. But yer ain't worth it, Peabody. Yer ain't worth the effort.'

Oswald eyed him fearfully 'What yer gonna do, Mr Simpson?'

'I ain't gonna do nothin' and yer can wipe that smirk off yer face. The only reason I ain't gonna get the authorities involved is 'cos I don't want Miss Clatteridge dragging into none of this. Now you get out of 'ere before I change me mind.' As Oswald shot past him Ivan grabbed his shoulder and jerked him to a halt, looking him straight in the eye. 'Just be warned, Peabody. If I ever so much as catch a glimpse of your ugly mug anywhere near this place again, I'll 'ave yer. A' yer listening?'

Terrified, the boy nodded.

Ivan pushed him forcibly away. 'I'm glad we understand each other. Now get out.'

After he had gone Ivan stood rooted to the spot, calming himself. He was sill having trouble believing what he had just, by sheer accident, discovered. Thank God, he thought, he'd decided to look out of the window or there was no telling what might have happened had Oswald's betrayal gone on. Miss Clatteridge must never find out about this. It would mortify her. Taking a deep breath, he blew out the candles, locked the chapel securely the back gates too, and returned to his room. He did not sleep.

The next morning he approached Agnes. 'Peabody ain't turned up, Miss Clatteridge.'

'Oh, do you think he's ill or something?'

Ivan thrust his hands deep into his pockets. 'He . . . er . . . was all right yesterday. To be honest, Miss Clatteridge, the lad's a waste of your good money. Neither use nor ornament. There's plenty of good lads around that'd jump at the job 'e has and do far better.'

'Are you suggesting we get rid of him, Mr Simpson?'

'I am, yes.'

She looked at him for a moment. 'Then I trust your judgement. Can I leave you to do it?'

'You can, Miss Clatteridge.'

'I'll make up his dues. Can I leave you to take on a replacement too?'

Ivan was surprised. 'Me? You want me to hire a lad?'

'Of course, Mr Simpson. You're better qualified than I am. You'll be in charge of him, know what you'll be expecting him to do, and you'll need to be sure you'll get on with him. So can I leave you to see to it then?'

Ivan puffed out his chest. 'Yer certainly can, Miss Clatteridge. Yes indeed yer can.'

Chapter Twenty-Seven

'A letter? For me?'

'Got your name on it, Mrs Baldicott. Mrs Baldicott it sez. Look, there,' the postman said, pointing. 'It's all the way from Leicester.'

Nancy Baldicott's eyes narrowed quizzically. 'But I can't recall knowing anyone in Leicester. No one that'd be wanting to write ter me, at any rate.'

'Well, yer must know someone else I wouldn't be delivering this to yer, now would I, eh?'

She frowned. 'No, I expect not.' Then, tongue in cheek, said, 'Who's it from?'

The postman's eyes narrowed indignantly. 'How should I know, less you're accusing me of tampering with His Majesty's mail?'

She laughed. 'I wouldn't put n'ote past you, Sidney Box. I remember when you used ter run round with no arse in yer britches, yer mam 'ollering 'er 'ead off callin' yer name 'cos yer'd scarpered wi'out doin' yer chores. Nine times outta ten yer were up ter no good. I lost count of 'ow many times I caught you in my garden scrumping me Granny Smiths.'

He reddened. 'All right, all right, no need to rake up me mis-spent youth.' Sid thrust the letter at her. 'D'yer want it or not?'

''Course I do. It's addressed ter me, ain't it?' Taking the letter from him, she eyed him for a moment. 'Can yer do summat for me?'

'Want me ter read it for yer, is that it, Mrs Baldicott?'

Her eyes narrowed haughtily. 'I'll have you know, Sidney Box, I can read it meself, thank you.'

He looked surprised. 'Yer can?'

''Course,' she said briskly. 'That's shocked yer, ain't it? A few years ago we had a particularly bad winter. I had a young gel stopping with me. She used ter read ter me ter pass the time in the evening. She asked me if I wanted her to teach me to read. I thought she'd be wasting 'er time meself, but she insisted. I took to it like a duck to water. Soon learned enough to get me by.' Nancy flapped the letter and cackled. 'Any more than six letters gets me a bit flummoxed, though. So just in case, yer can hang on a minute, see if I need yer.'

'I will, on one condition.'

She folded her arms under her ample bosom, eyeing the young postman warily. 'Oh?'

'I get a cuppa and a slice of your famous slab cake.'

Nancy sniffed. 'Deal. Come on in, yer young scallywag.'

Ten minutes later she clapped her hands in delight. 'Well, well, well. Once my gels 'ave left me I rarely 'ear from 'em again, so I never expected to 'ear from young Maddie. Or Mrs Jenks as she is now. You did say that word was Jenks?'

'That's right.'

'Well, I never, Mrs Jenks.' Her eyes narrowed thoughtfully. 'I could swear that young man that left 'er in the lurch was named Jenks,' she muttered. 'I could be wrong, though. Age gets yer like that.'

'What was that, Mrs Baldicott?'

'Eh? Oh, just talkin' ter meself. Mmmm,' she mouthed thoughtfully. 'I 'ave a terrible suspicion I knows exactly what she wants to come and see me about too.' She sighed forlornly. 'Oh, Maddie me duck, you know I can't tell yer 'ote even if I wanted to. Coming all this way will be a waste of your time and good money.' It was a shame, she thought. Of all the girls she had seen through their troubles over the years, Maddie was the only one she could truly say she would have enjoyed seeing again. Nancy took a deep breath. 'Will yer do me another good deed?'

Sid leaned towards her, grinning mischievously. 'Depends what it is, Mrs Baldicott.'

She slapped his hand. 'I ain't in the mood fer games, young Sidney. Will yer do me a favour or not?' she snapped.

'Yeah, 'course,' he replied sulkily. 'I was only gonna ask fer another cuppa and slice of cake.'

She tutted disdainfully. 'Help yerself while I go and hunt for the implements. I want you to post me a letter. And don't worry,' she added, 'I'll give yer the pennies for the stamp.'

Chapter Twenty-Eight

'There's still no word from Mrs Baldicott,' Maddie remarked as she dished up the dinner. 'Is that enough potatoes? I've done plenty if you want more. Put Penny's on the window to cool, would you, Josh, please?'

He did as she bade, then eyed his plate. 'I'll have another couple, love, I'm famished. Oh, pie,' he said appreciatively as she opened the oven door. 'What's in it?'

She laughed, eyeing him teasingly. 'It's called Surprise Pie because you get a surprise when you eat it. Sarah made it for us. I'll be getting a surprise too because she wouldn't tell me either. It was nice of her to make extra for us, wasn't it?'

'She's a good woman is Sarah. Anyway, to answer yer, yer only sent it on Tuesday.'

'Sent what?'

'The letter to Mrs Baldicott. By the time it's delivered and her reply gets back yer looking at next week, I reckon.'

She sighed. 'I expect you're right.' She looked at him in concern. 'I hope she'll agree to see us, Josh.'

'Maddie, just sit down and eat yer dinner and try to put it out of yer mind for a bit. Come on, Twopenny-ha'penny,' he said, picking Penny up and making her comfortable on a chair at the table. The child protested loudly. 'Now, now,' said Josh patiently. 'Yer can play with yer toys after you've eaten else yer won't grow big and strong. Maddie, where's that strap we use to secure Twopenny to the chair so she don't fall off?'

'Er . . . it's there, look, on the back of the door.'

Fifteen minutes later Josh put down his knife and fork and sighed loudly in satisfaction. 'That Surprise Pie was grand. Corned beef and potato and there was summat else in it. What was it, Maddie?'

'Turnip, I think. Whatever it was it was very tasty. There's some left.'

'I'm full, thanks, love. If there's enough for two we'll have it tomorrow, save you cooking.' He eyed her expectantly. 'Any pudding?'

'I thought you said you were full?' she replied, pretending to be annoyed.

'Oh, Maddie love, I can always manage a pudding. I meant, I was full up with dinner.'

'Good job I did plums and custard then, isn't it?'

He jumped up from his chair. 'I'll get it.' As he passed by he kissed her on her cheek. 'I only married yer fer yer cooking.'

As he was tucking into his pudding, she eyed him questioningly. 'Aren't you ever going to tell me then?'

He lifted his head, frowning. 'Tell yer what?'

'Stop playing games, Josh,' she said, feigning annoyance. 'Did Mrs Cribbins accept your offer or not?'

He grinned sheepishly. 'I was saving that 'til later,' he said, teasingly.

'I can't wait until later, I think I've been patient enough. So?'

He beamed jubilantly. 'As a matter of fact, she did.'

Maddie's own face lit up with delight and she clapped her hands. 'Josh, that's wonderful news. All you need do now is set on a man to help you.'

'Already have. Danny Long. Good lad he is and trustworthy. He's happy with the pay I'm offering and I've told him if he gets any new customers I'll give him a bonus.'

Maddie folded her arms and leaned on the table, eyeing him proudly. 'I'm really happy for you, Josh, I know how

338

much you wanted this round. Oh, who's that at the door?'

'Sit there,' he said, rising. 'I'll get it. I hope it ain't visitors. I was looking forward to a quiet night with just the three of us.'

As he left to answer the door, Maddie turned her full attention to the little girl and her face lit up merrily. 'You've more on your face than in your belly.'

Penny, heaped spoon raised precariously, looked at her innocently through large blue eyes. She giggled, showing several milk teeth and bare gums. The spoon tilted further, spilling its contents.

Maddie laughed and got to her feet. 'Oh, I see, feeding the table now, are we? Come on,' she said, easing the spoon from Penny's tiny hand. 'Let's get you cleaned up then you can play for a bit longer before bedtime.' She wiped the remains of the meal from face and hands, unstrapped Penny and picked her up, kissing the child affectionately on the cheek. 'Uncle Josh is going to read you a story. What would you like tonight? Three Little Pigs?'

Voices approaching down the passage reached her ears and she looked up.

'It's yer dad, love,' Josh announced as he entered, followed by George.

She was so delighted to see her father that the flatness of Josh's voice and the grim look on both faces went unnoticed.

'Dad!' she exclaimed, putting Penny carefully down on the floor. She was about to rush over to him when his expression registered and she froze. 'What's wrong, Dad?' she demanded.

Josh scooped up Penny. 'Come on, Twopenny. Let's get you ready fer bed.'

Instinctively Maddie knew that it was something very serious. 'Just a moment, Josh,' she cried, eyes darting from him to her father. 'What's going on?'

Josh flashed a glance at George before answering. 'Yer dad needs ter talk to yer, Maddie.'

339

'Be as quick as you can, Josh. Maddie's going to need you,' George whispered to him.

Face sombre, he nodded and hurried away.

George sat down on the lumpy settee, patting the space to the side of him, simultaneously putting on the floor a tin box which he was carrying. 'Sit down, Maddie.'

Heart thumping erratically, face grave, she sat down next to him, eyes fixed on his. 'It's not Sarah, is it, Dad?' she blurted. 'The baby? Nothing's happened, has it?'

He shook his head. 'Sarah's fine, love. Look . . . er . . . it's your mother, Maddie.'

Her heart pounded harder. 'My mother. What's happened to her? Is she ill?'

He took a deep breath. 'There's no easy way to tell you this, love. Your mother, well . . . she's dead. I'm so sorry.'

'Dead!' gasped Maddie, stunned. 'I can't believe it.' She wrung her hands. 'How? How did she die, Dad? Was it an accident? What?'

George averted his gaze uncomfortably. He could never tell Maddie the truth about Harriet's death, it was just too terrible, something he himself was still finding it hard to deal with. He had been told her body had been discovered by a neighbour who was curious about the strange smell she had caught a whiff of when she had walked past the shop. She had entered out of curiosity and was still recovering from shock at what she had found in the back room: Harriet's decomposing body.

An autopsy revealed she had been dead for at least a month, so far as they could tell from a massive heart attack, not helped by the fact that she was dreadfully undernourished. From what the doctors had told him George knew that Harriet's death must have happened soon after Maddie's visit to her, but had decided not to mention a word of this.

The death had been ascribed to natural causes. Informing the authorities of Maddie's visit could have resulted in their deciding to question her, that no doubt leading to Maddie's discovering the terrible circumstances of her mother's death. He could not risk that. Maddie had already shouldered more than enough hurt and pain at her hands. He knew she would feel needlessly guilty and torture herself for the rest of her life, wondering if there was anything she could have done to avoid this situation.

He took Maddie's hand gently in his. 'It was heart failure, my dear.' He gave her hand a tender squeeze. 'I was assured she didn't suffer.'

A grim-faced Josh returned and perched on the arm of the settee, sliding his arm protectively around Maddie's shoulders. She turned her head and looked at him. 'Dad told you at the door, didn't he?' she whispered.

He nodded. 'I'm so sorry, Maddie.'

She lowered her gaze to her hands. 'It's terrible of me, I know,' she said softly, 'but I can't feel much at all. I should be dreadfully upset, devastated even, should be crying my heart out. But all I feel is sorry that she died without any of her family around her. But she didn't want her family, did she? It's just sadness I feel for the closeness we could have had but didn't.' She wrung her hands, voice barely a whisper. 'Is it wrong of me to feel like this?'

'No, it isn't, Maddie,' her father said earnestly. 'My dear, how can you expect to feel love for a person who never showed you any? In fact, spent her life causing you nothing but pain.'

'But she was my mother, I should feel more than merely sorry that she's dead.'

Josh's arm tightened around her shoulder. 'She mighta given birth ter yer, Maddie love, but mother ter yer she wasn't.'

She took a deep breath. They were both right, she knew, but it didn't make her feel any better. She looked at her father. 'When's the funeral?' She looked at Josh, putting a hand on his arm. 'I wouldn't expect you to come.' She turned back to her father. 'It will be just me and you, won't it?' Her face filled with sadness. 'There's no one else, is there? No friends. Maybe Mrs Green and one or two of her old customers will attend. I'll contact them anyway, leave it to them.'

George raked one hand over the top of his head, body sagging tiredly. 'Maddie your mother was buried this morning. I was the only one there.'

'Buried today?' Her face creased in bewilderment. 'I don't understand? I should have been told. I should have been there to pay my last respects. She was my mother.'

'Maddie, listen to me,' George said firmly. 'By the time the authorities summoned me with the news and I'd travelled to Harborough, your mother had been dead for two days already,' he lied. 'You know the formalities better than me, considering where you work. She had to be buried the next day. Even if I'd got word to you, you'd never have arrived in time. You've got to remember I was very upset myself. Your mother and I might not have got on but I never wished her ill.'

A lump formed in Maddie's throat. She was being selfish, hadn't considered her father's feelings, only her own. She took his hand. 'I'm sorry, Dad, I wasn't thinking straight. You did what you had to, I understand that.' She sighed forlornly. 'I didn't mean to get angry with you, I'm just . . . just . . .'

'I know, my dear, this has all come as a terrible shock.'

She nodded and sat in silence for a moment. 'Will you take me to her grave?' she asked finally. 'I can pay my last respects there.'

He patted her hand. 'Of course I will, my dear.'

'What about the house?' she asked. 'You'll need a hand clearing it out.'

'I'll help too, if you want me,' offered Josh.

George flashed a grateful smile at him, then brought his gaze back to his daughter. 'It's done, Maddie,' he said softly.

She stared at him. 'That too?'

The house and its contents had been cleared on the orders of the sanitary department. They ordered its fumigation and fresh whitewashing to eliminate any risk of disease. The furniture and Harriet's personal belongings were burned for the same reason. But he could not divulge this to Maddie either.

'I just thought it best,' he told her. 'The landlord insisted,' he added to placate her.

'Oh, I see,' Maddie said tonelessly. 'Next tenant lined up already, I expect, as soon as he heard about my mother.'

'Your mother wasn't much for bits and pieces, you know that, Maddie, so there wasn't a lot for me to clear. I decided to give it all to the Salvation Army to divide amongst the needy. As you know, she had no jewellery. Except, of course, for this,' he said, fishing in his pocket and pulling out Harriet's wedding ring which he held out towards her.

Maddie took it, placed it in the palm of her hand and studied it intently. She raised her eyes to his. 'This had no meaning, did it, Dad? She didn't wear it for the reason it should have been worn. In the light of that, I can't wear it either.' She handed it back to him. 'You do what you want with it.'

He laid a hand on her arm. 'You don't want it as a keepsake, Maddie?'

'No,' she said firmly. 'I know she wouldn't want me to have it so I wouldn't feel comfortable about keeping it.'

'As you wish,' he said, putting it back in his pocket. 'Oh, there was this,' he said, picking up the tin box the authorities had given him. 'This was found . . . I found it in the back of her wardrobe.' He put his hand in his inside pocket and pulled out a key. 'This was on a chain around her neck.'

Maddie looked at the tin then at him. 'Why are you giving it to me?'

He eyed her closely. 'There's money inside, Maddie. A lot, judging by the weight, and I feel in the circumstances

343

whatever your mother left should go to you.'

She frowned. 'But I don't understand how Mother could have left any money. Mrs Green told me the business had been doing very badly and the shop certainly didn't look well stocked to me. Oh!' she suddenly exclaimed as memory returned. 'I know what's in here. I have no right to this money, Dad. It really belongs to you and Sarah.'

'Us?' he asked, puzzled.

'Open the tin and I'll explain,' said Maddie, handing the key back to him.

George put the key in the lock and turned it, then lifted the lid. On seeing the contents his jaw dropped in amazement. He stepped across to the table and tipped out the contents in a jangling heap. He stared agog at the mound of coins. 'There . . . why, there must be a small fortune here. I don't understand . . .'

Maddie rose to join him. 'It's all the money you paid her, Dad. She told me the day I visited her that she never spent a penny of it.'

George's face darkened angrily. 'How could she? Harriet insisted on having half my wage off me every week. She knew how I struggled. That Sarah and the children suffered because of it.' He shook his head disbelievingly. 'I don't understand how her mind worked, really I don't.'

'I'm sorry if this hurts yer, Maddie, George, but I have ter say that to my mind it probably gave her pleasure to know how much hardship she caused,' said Josh.

Maddie sighed. 'Knowing what I do of my mother, I have to agree with Josh, Dad.' She laid a hand on his arm. 'It's yours and Sarah's, though, all of it, there's no doubt of that.'

George exhaled sharply. 'I can't deny we could find good use for this but it gives me no pleasure having it this way,' he said gravely. 'It won't Sarah, either.'

Josh joined them at the table. Thoughtfully he picked up the tin box. 'Yer wouldn't think such a small box could hold so much.' Something wedged inside the lid caught his attention and he prised it out. 'It's an envelope,' he said, handing it to George. 'Got something inside it.'

It was folded in half and George flattened it out. 'It's not addressed to anyone,' he said, frowning.

'Open it, Dad,' Maddie urged.

He ripped open the sealed flap and pulled out the contents. As he did so their jaws dropped.

George counted off the crisp white five-pound notes. 'There's a hundred pounds here,' he gasped. 'I wonder where it came from?'

'Profits from the shop?' offered Josh.

'Could be, I suppose. Wait a minute, what's this?' he said, peeling off a piece of paper stuck to the back of the last note in his hand. 'Why, it's a carbon copy of a receipt!' he exclaimed. As he scanned it, his face paled alarmingly.

'What is it, Dad?' Maddie asked him, frowning.

'Er . . . nothing,' he stuttered, stuffing it in his pocket.

His whole manner alerted her suspicions. 'It has to be for something. You did say it was a receipt?'

'I was mistaken. It's just a blank piece of paper, that's all,' he answered too hurriedly for Maddie's liking.

Her face creased knowingly. 'It wasn't blank, was it, Dad?' she accused. 'Whatever that receipt was for has something to do with me and I want to see it,' she challenged, holding out her hand.

'Maddie, what's got into you?' Josh asked, grabbing her arm.

'Dad?' she demanded, ignoring her husband.

George's whole body froze. He stared at her for several long moments then, resigned, delved into his pocket, pulled out the piece of paper and handed it to her.

Maddie smoothed it out and stared down at it.

'What does it say?' Josh asked.

'It's for . . .' She froze, face stricken, the receipt falling out of her hand to flutter to the floor. With an agonised wail she doubled over, clutching her stomach and sobbing wildly.

Completely shocked and bewildered by his wife's unexpected reaction Josh stared at her then grabbed her, holding her protectively. 'Maddie, what's wrong? Please tell me?' His attention returned to George. 'What was that receipt for?'

'Tell him, Dad,' wailed Maddie.

George's whole body sagged. 'It's a receipt for a baby girl. Josh, I'm so sorry.'

He stared, stupefied. 'What? But I don't understand . . .'

Maddie pulled away from him, her tear-blinded eyes staring straight into his. 'It's dated the tenth of April 1926. The date my mother handed our baby over, Josh. She *sold* our baby. Took money for her.' Her voice rose hysterically. 'It wasn't enough just to give her to some deserving couple, not for *her* it wasn't.'

As Maddie's words slowly sunk home Josh let out a deep groan and tears spilled down his face.

Maddie ran one hand tenderly down the side of his face. 'Oh, Josh,' she whispered. 'I thought she could do no more to hurt me . . . us. I was wrong, wasn't I? Oh, so very, very wrong.'

Her eyes suddenly blazed with anger. She jumped up, went to her father and grabbed the notes out of his hand. 'I know where these are going,' she cried, crushing them tightly. She swung back her arm and flung the bundle into the fire. They all watched as the paper caught light to burn brightly, flames licking upwards then giving way to blackened ashes which withered and died.

Tears streaming down her face, Maddie fled from the room and up the stairs.

Stricken, Josh stared after her. Then he rose awkwardly, looking at George. 'She'd no heart, had she? She was evil. There's no other word for her. I'm glad she's dead,' he spat savagely. Bending down, he picked up the receipt Maddie had let drop and stared at it, sighing painfully. 'There's a signature on this but I can't read it.' He shuddered, a wave of great sadness washing through him. 'This is all we've got to show for our child. That we ever had her.' His face contorted bitterly. 'I wonder if *she* took this out and looked at it often. I wonder if this was why she had kept a copy, so she could . . .'

'Stop it, Josh,' George ordered. 'Stop torturing yourself. Throw it away.'

Josh shuddered. 'I can't . . . I can't do that. I feel if I did I'd be wiping out all memory of our baby.'

George laid a hand on his arm. 'Then don't just yet, until you feel able. But hide it, Josh, so Maddie doesn't find it.'

Sniffing, he nodded and folded the receipt neatly. He put it in his pocket, to hide it later in a place where Maddie would never look.

George could find nothing to say to bring even a morsel of comfort to the man who had married his daughter, a man George had come to respect very much. He eyed him sadly. 'You'd better go and see to Maddie. You'll be needing each other at this moment more than ever. Me and Sarah will be round in the morning. I'll see myself out, son.'

After Josh had left George stood for a moment staring blindly into space, then he lifted his eyes. 'I hope wherever you are now, Harriet, you're truly satisfied that you've finally punished your daughter.'

Grim-faced, he walked across to the table, scooped up the coins and put them back in the box. He closed the lid, and quietly let himself out, the sounds of two people's grief ringing in his ears.

Much later that night, in a deserted, dimly lit church, George turned to Sarah. 'You're sure about this, my love?'

She nodded. 'We agreed, didn't we? Neither of us wants any part of it. Let's just hope it brings happiness to people who'll benefit.'

Standing side by side, together they painstakingly slotted every coin into the poor box.

When their task was complete George put the tin box aside to discard later and said emotionally, 'It's finally over, isn't it, love?'

She sighed. 'For us it is, George. I'm not so sure if it is for Maddie and Josh. The damage Harriet caused them I doubt will ever heal.' She looked at the man she loved, smiling wanly. 'But they say time heals all. Let's hope so, eh? In the meantime we can only support 'em as best we can.'

He sought her hand and gripped it tight. 'Come on,' he said. 'Let's go home.'

Chapter Twenty-Nine

'Let's talk about something else,' said Agnes diplomatically, picking up the teapot. 'More tea, Maddie dear?'

She leaned over, holding out her cup. 'Yes, please.' She watched silently as Agnes refilled her cup, then her own, and settled back in her chair, sighing deeply. 'Miss Agnes, I've already stressed I don't want people pussyfooting around me. I appreciate you're trying to spare my feelings but I'm all right, really. Besides, it's not as if we can avoid talking of death, all things considered, can we?' she said lightly. 'I want to hear all about you leading the funeral. I want to hear every detail. I was so disappointed you didn't get back before I finished for the weekend. That's why I'm here, so please go on.'

Agnes eyed her in concern. She had to agree that on the surface Maddie appeared to have coped with her mother's death remarkably well, but Agnes wasn't convinced Maddie was being entirely honest about her mental state. There was something she could see in the younger woman's eyes. Maddie had such lovely eyes that sparkled with life, or had done until a week or so ago. There was a dullness, a haunted look, in them now. It was understandable considering her loss, but Agnes felt it went deeper than that. The sadness wasn't just in Maddie, it was in her husband too. There was something different about the pair of them that she couldn't quite put her finger on. But, she had reasoned with herself, people tackled grief in such different ways and she herself was probably just overreacting since she felt such affection for Maddie and her husband.

Agnes was, though, delighted to go along with Maddie's wishes. She really did want to talk of her morning. 'I was so honoured, my dear. I didn't suggest it, you know. People have taken to dealing with me, a woman, better than I ever expected but I still feel they assume a man will lead the funeral party. To be asked to by Mrs Dunn was such a privilege.'

Maddie smiled warmly. 'I was thinking about you when you left this morning. I knew you were nervous, and I know I'm repeating myself now, but I thought you looked just lovely in your outfit. So smart. The milliner certainly did a first-class job of altering your father's top hat to fit you and making it more feminine by adding the black feathers. So much better, I think, than the severe black ribbons undertakers usually have around their hats. Anyway, it all went well then, did it?'

'Yes, very. Well . . . almost.' Agnes paused for a moment to check on Penny who was playing happily on the rug, her childish chatter a delight to hear.

'Not that I know much about children, but I can't get over how contented she seems. You and Josh are doing a splendid job with her.'

'Thank you.' Maddie smiled, directing her gaze towards the child. 'She's very good but occasionally has her moments. She can lift our roof with one of her tantrums. Usually that's because she's tired but fights sleep. And meals! She gets more down herself and on the floor than in her mouth, but she refuses to let either me or Josh feed her. Sarah told me Ruth and Roy were just the same. And she's started to say a few words, so she's overcoming her shyness.'

'Mmmm,' Agnes said distractedly as all her own maternal instincts came to the fore. She had always managed to quash these feelings whenever they had surfaced previously, in fact had managed to persuade herself that mother she would